I0788153

The
Lagniappe
Saga

Book 1
The Bayou Boy

T L Stark

ABOUT THE AUTHOR

T. L. Stark is an 82-year-old retired army officer. He obtained a double major at Northwestern State University of Louisiana. During his undergraduate studies, he participated on the college gymnastics team. From there, he went on to join the military with a career comprised of almost 11 years of command time and 3 years as an inspector general. He also had over two years of formal military-related class work and training. He spent the rest of his service time as a staff officer. While in the military, Stark obtained a master's degree from the University of Southern California and eventually retired from the army after 20 years of service. Stark also holds a diploma from the Gemological Institute of America.

Following military life, Stark owned a small business before retiring for health reasons. Nowadays, he regularly nurses his keen interest in sports and military history, which often manifests in his historical fiction writing.

He has been married to Elizabeth Stark for over 60 years. Together, they have two children, a son and daughter, and two grandsons.

ACKNOWLEDGMENTS

Thank you to my family for their thoughtful feedback and contributions to the LANGNAPPI SAGA.

My wife, a former schoolteacher, keeps me on the straight and narrow day by day.

My son, at three months, was diagnosed with neuroblastoma. At the time, he was the youngest human ever diagnosed with a fast-growing cancer. Now, at age 58, he is thought to be the longest-living human to have survived this type of cancer. His story offered inspiration for this series.

My daughter is a Duke graduate with experience in military and law enforcement. She gives me excellent feedback for my writing.

Lastly, thank you to Aaron D'Anthony Brown for helping me get my books together and ready for publishing and fulfilling a dream of mine.

DEDICATION

This book is dedicated to those whose names appear on the EOD Memorial Wall at Eglin Air Force Base in Florida. These brave warriors paid the ultimate price for freedom.

ABOUT LANGNAPPI SAGA

The LANGNAPPI SAGA is a fictitious story about a BAYOU BOY, Joe Hébert, who lives in poverty on the bayous of Louisiana during his formative years. Out of high school, he joins the Navy to be a hard-hat diver, before attempting to become a SEAL. After a cold intolerance condition causes him to fail out of the program, Joe finishes his stint with the Navy and then enlists in the Army. For the next decade, the BAYOU BOY finds love and adventure in FRIENDS AND FAMILY, CASH, and becomes FILTHY RICH. Then, the FIRST SHOT is fired.

This rags-to-riches, action-packed love story begins in the turbulent late 1960 era. For continuity, the author recommends reading the saga in sequence.

PROLOGUE

On September 20, 2010, at 10:00 A.M., the Chairperson of the Chairman, Crime, Terrorism, Homeland Security, and Investigation Subcommittee slammed his hammer down hard and loudly proclaimed, "This Committee is now in session. We are here today to consider an investigation into Hébert Enterprises, a well-known and established conglomerate, and it is political connection, which allegedly has allowed the company to skirt federal and state laws since the company's inception. We have a witness Mister Joseph A. Hébert, founder and majority stockholder in Hébert International Enterprises."

From his perch at the center of the curved platform where seven Congresspeople, members of the subcommittee, were sitting overlooking the witness's table, the cold-eyed Chairman continued.

"Mister Hébert, through your company's foreign country connections, you are accused of skating our tax laws. By a man's dying testimony, he implicates you in numerous other high crimes to include, but not limited to murder, drug trafficking, smuggling, income tax evasion, security and are treasonous in nature and related to organize crime here in the States.

"As a personal note, based on your outstanding military record, I am astonished anyone with your background would be setting in front of this subcommittee, facing such allegations. To satisfy my own curiosity, sir, how many people have you killed?"

Hébert leaned forward, adjusted his Mic., looked up, and took time to made eye contact with each of the members. All of them, dressed in black suits with dark ties and white shirts, looked like undertakers. A couple of them wrung their hands like morticians.

Hébert finally said, "Mister Chairman, my attorney, sitting to my left, has advised me to take the Fifth and not answer any of your questions. However, on my right is my grandson who will soon become the CEO of Hébert Enterprises. I have asked him to sit with me today where he can learn what he faces in the business world and life in general."

Joe paused before continuing. "I consider your outrageous subpoena and allegations as an affront to a lifetime of achievement by, not only myself, but my family and every employee in our organization. They are simply preposterous.

"You delivered quite a litany of charges against me and my company. You may have missed the event where I, or someone working for me, molested an old lady leaving church. I want to emphatically state. Every one of the employees of Hébert Enterprise is innocent of all these false allegations.

"Because of my past and present open support to the Republican Party and its nominees, I feel your investigation is a political witch hunt." Hébert spoke with a slight Cajon accent. He looked around the room at his lawyer, his grandson, and then at the half-dozen members of the press sitting behind him.

"Mister Chairman, you know what? Contrary to my lawyer's advice, I will answer all your questions. However, because we will discuss potential classified and embarrassing personal information, I highly recommend you dismiss the press.

"We should take this discussion behind closed doors. I realize this may not sit well with your personal agenda of burning a supporter of the minority party, while hoping to learn something which is useful against the Republican Party. The party, which, in my opinion, will shortly be in the majority.

"Now, sir, to answer your question about how many men I've killed, I'll remind you, I was a soldier in war. If I knew the number of people I have killed, then, there would not be too many. I can assure you, Mister Chairperson, I have never killed anyone who did not deserve it, and their departure from this world makes it a better place to live! I do remember an occasion where I killed at least five men in the Delta of Vietnam where your nephew served. I may have saved his life. Since your son was still on a long pleasureful vacation to Canada, I could not save him." Hébert words were defiant.

The stoutly faced Chairperson declared, "What an interesting comment, Mister Hébert. But let us not get personal. I'll recognize the Senior Member of the Minority Party for his comment."

The elderly and balding man, sitting to the right of the Chairperson and directly in front of the American flag, began.

"Thank you, Mister Chairman. I would like to echo your astonishment about why we are here this morning. This witch hunt is nothing more than the Chairman's party trying to deflect attention away from the serious issues of today, for which you have no answers.

"I have seen no legitimate evidence against Mister Hébert which would stand up in a court of law. There is nothing supporting the allegations against Mister Hébert and his business. You proclaimed your evidence came from a death bed deposition. But you did not mention and consider the fact the gentleman providing your so-called evidence had been diagnosed with Alzheimer's disease years before you interviewed him."

"Mister Hébert, I want to apologize to you and your grandson for the convenience and embarrassment this Committee has caused you."

"Thank you, sir. I look forward to addressing any questions which will putting clarity on this issue. However, as I said before, we should go behind closed doors for this." Mister Hébert continued his plea.

"Mister Hébert, as the Chairman of the Subcommittee, that's my decision to make. I think it's only right the public hears your testimony. The press stays!"

"So be it, Mister Chairman, but for the record, I would like to state, I believe the only reason we are here today is because the President has assured you that he would support you for the Speaker's position, should you uncover any significant information with this fishing expedition."

Hébert threw his first punch.

"How dare you question the integrity of this Committee! I demand you withdraw the statement!" The red-faced Chairperson sounded like a hothead.

"No, sir, Mister Chairman, I will not. I have said nothing about the integrity of this Committee, only you, sir. I'll stand by my words. However, it should be noted, you didn't deny my statement." Hébert's argument showed finality and defiance.

"Since there is no way, you could ever prove your statement, and because of time restraints, we'll pass and recognize the Gentleman from Michigan." The Chairperson brushed Hébert off.

The gentleman on the far left of the Chairperson adjusted his microphone. He looked as if he could be Alfalfa's, from the Little Rascals, grandfather, thin faced with hair standing up. He said, "Thank you,. Mister Chairman. Mister Hébert, I would like to address the allegations about the evasion of taxes. Will you explain to this Subcommittee why, you need a bank account in George Town, Caman Islands, a place which is world renowned for hiding untaxed, taxable money? After all, you do own several other banks around the world."

"Sir, Hébert Enterprises is an international company. We often have a need to move funds from one country to another without delay. The bank we are affiliated with, in Kingston, also has a fine reputation of providing this service. I know the bank very well. The answer to your question is, I own a large percent of the bank. However, your question prompts one from me. Why would, let us say, the wife of a certain member of this subcommittee makes large cash deposits, three times this year, in the same bank you referenced?"

"Mister Hébert, I'm sure you're not referring to my wife with your comment!" The Gentleman from Michigan demeanor changed. He stared hard at Hébert.

Mister Hébert smiled and said, "Sir, I'm sure you and some of the other members of this subcommittee have forgotten, or neglected the fact, I'm half owners of a mighty fine international investigation business. Let the record reflect you did not answer my question."

"The Chairman will recognize the minority, the Gentleman from Alabama."

In his Alabama accent, a southern drawl, the skinny Alabamian said, "Thank you, Mister Chairman. Gentleman, I would like to remind you, we are no longer the House, Un-American Activities Committee, and have not been for years. We are not the Committee on International Security. As those committees were certainly our forerunners, we do not need a reputation for political biases like they did. I think we should rethink the subcommittee's goal for dealing with this matter. As a minimum we should go behind closed doors, as the witness suggested."

"Like I've said, as the Chairman, the decision is mine. I recognize the Majority Representative from New York."

Hébert broke in. "Mister Chairman, may I ask the Gentleman from New York a question before he speaks?"

The intractable Chairperson looked at the youthful, first term, New York Representative who said, "I yield to the witness."

"Sir, I was wondering if you were competent enough today to execute your duties on this committee…After all, last night you were at the Marriott until after midnight, with one of your young staff members. Since you told your wife you were working late at the office, I must presume, your young staff member was taking dictation."

The New York Representative yelled, "Objections, Mister Chairman! This is outrageous! Mister Hébert is implicating me without any evidence. I'll get you for this, Hébert. You are out of line."

"Mister Chairman, the Representative's comment was a blatant, open-ended threat. I am no more out of line than this subcommittee, whose actions against me and my company are also outrageous and without credible evidence. I assure you; I can prove any allegations I make! Now, Mister Chairperson, can we do something about this situation?" Hébert did not withdraw.

"Gentlemen, Gentlemen, I believe this situation is getting out of control. I would like to adjourn this meeting for today. If the members agree, we can set another date to continue."

Hébert knew the Chairperson was finally conceding.

The Senior Minority member quickly made a motion to adjourn the meeting, and as promptly seconded by two other members simultaneously.

When walking, down the hall toward the rotunda, Hébert addressed his grandson who wore a brown suit and stood an inch shorter than Joe. "Joseph, what did your best take away from this meeting?"

"Grandfather, call me, Joe. Everybody else does."

"No, Son. Joe is a good name for an uneducated guy like me. You are well educated, an MBA from Duke, and a lot better person than I have been or ever will be. Joseph is a better name for a young CEO. It demands more respect.

"Now, Joseph, what about the meeting?"

"You kicked their ass, sir!" Joseph beamed. A twinkle appeared in his slightly Asian eyes which came from his grandmother on his father's side.

"Yes, son, but what did you learn?" They continued to walk.

"Other than to not mess with you, maybe to stand tall in the face of adversity." The young man, who was dark-haired proudly said.

Mister Hébert scoffed, "Any idiot can stand tall in the face of adversity. It's what allows him to face hardship that matters. It's certainly not sufficient to rely on ego or stubbornness. Your other grandmother, Ava, taught me that gathering information about people is especially important. My knowledge of everybody sitting on the Subcommittee allowed me to, as you say, stand tall and kick ass.

"Your first lesson, for today, is to never, never, go into an important meeting without being extremely prepared.

"Now, we need to get to Reagan Airport. We have a helicopter waiting on us to carry us to Fayetteville, North Carolina."

Once reaching Fayetteville, a limousine waited for Mister Hébert and his grandson, Joseph, to carry them to an old cinder block building on Bragg Boulevard, a short distance from the main gate of Fort Bragg. The equipment parked outside the building revealed a demolition project being prepared. A man wearing an orange jumpsuit, and a white hard hat opened the limousine's door and said, "Good afternoon, Mister Hébert."

"I hope we haven't delayed your work very long. For sentimental reasons, I wanted to take a final look at her." Mister Hébert stood on the sidewalk gazing at the old two-story building.

He turned to Joseph and said, "I'm sure you do not remember this place very well. You only visited it a couple of times as a young child. Of course, your mother and her sibling grew up here.

"The important thing about this place is, it's the birthplace of dreams. Your grandmother, Ava, and I raised our family here. With the aid of our dearest friends, we started our business here. This is where she and I dreamed of building a dynasty. You're a product of those dreams. Being the oldest grandchild, you'll soon be tasked with a great portion of continuing the dynasty that we built from a humble start.

"Your second lesson for the day is to look at this rustic building which your grandmother and I purchased for thirty-five thousand dollars. The site is now valued at nearly a half-million dollars and is the site of our next bank with an adjacent jewelry store.

"Understandable, you can accomplish your objectives and dreams in life, but to do so, you'll need to rely heavily on your immediate family members and trusted friends. You can trust your Aunt Rachel. She knows more about the entire business than anyone. She will help you make important decisions.

"Since you are single, perhaps the most important decision you'll make in your life is choosing the right partner. I understand, with your looks and money, you're fortunate enough to have any woman you want, or almost any woman.

"Sooner or later, you'll meet someone who affects every cell in your body, captivating you. If she truly loves you, she's the one you want to lock down as a partner for the rest of your life."

"Oh, Grandfather, I know about girls. I went to college!" The young man smiled.

The man wearing the hard hat interrupted, "Gentlemen, I hate to break in, but would you like to walk through the building?"

"No, you can start the Caterpillars anytime. I'm sure there is nothing to be seen but bare walls. I have a million fond memories of love and laughter in there, as well as a couple of horrific events. I'll simply remember this place the way it was.

"Joseph, I could tell you a long story which begins at this place. Well, the love story began two years before we bought this home." The aging man slightly smiled.

When the first Caterpillar crashed into the side of the old cinder block building, Joseph saw tears sliding down his esteemed grandfather's cheeks. For the first time in his life, his grandfather looked old.

After a minute and the sound of a wall of the building crumbling to the ground, Joseph said, "Grandfather, why don't you and I find a place to drink a beer. I'd like for you to tell me your story of love, adventure, and how you, an impoverished bayou boy from Louisiana, made your millions."

Hébert threw an arm around his grandsons' shoulder and said, "Son, I'd like to tell you, but it's a long story and may take several trips to the bar, at least five, and more than a few beers. It's a fantastic saga about true love, war, friends and family, money, and building a dynasty. Of course, the adventurous story also has its angelical and dark sides. It may take time. I prefer to tell you about the brighter side of my life and omit the really dark or bad part. I have spent the latter part of my life asking for God's forgiveness.

The story, or saga, begins in Germany in 1967, when I first met your grandmother, Ava, a couple of years before she and I purchased the old building which is now being demolished."

BOOK ONE

BAYOU BOY

CHAPTER 1

Winter had been cold in Kaiserslautern, Germany in 1967. At times, four feet of snow covered the countryside, and temperatures fell below zero degrees Fahrenheit. However, the fifty-five-degree spring weather had melted the snow, except for the eight feet huge piles of ice near the edge of the parking lots. They were now turning brown. The ice had accumulated there as the results of scraping the parking area after snowing.

Staff Sergeant Joseph Hébert hurried through the parking lot to the three-story building in front of him which housed a lunchroom. The building lay next to the Headquarters of the 21st Theater Support Command, commonly referred to as the 21st SEPCCM, the hub of the Army's logistical operations in Europe.

The lunchroom always attracted a crowd for lunch. Officers, Non-Commissioned Officers, enlisted, and civilian personnel sat together at tables and mingled in homogeneous groups.

Dress greens, fatigues, civilian suits and slacks with sweaters or light jackets were the attire for men. The civilian ladies wore stylish skirts and slacks with heels. The military women were in their duty green uniforms.

Except for a Major paying homage to two Colonels, commonly referred as brow-nosing or ass-kissing, rank looked to have little tradition here.

The longer and warm days of spring seem to have everybody moving a little faster and light-footed, and in a better and cheerful mood.

Being the end of March and only three days to payday, Staff Sergeant Joseph Hébert considered himself broke, as usual. He still had to visit the barbershop to keep his deep brown hair high and tight as military regulations mandated. He knew, he could get a good bowl of beef goulash here on the cheap.

He had intended to meet Specialist Fourth Class Pamela Marsh for lunch. But she had backed out at the last moment because of unexpected work. Pam, a clerk typist in the Staff Judge Advocate

General office, better known as the JAG office, and Staff Sergeant Hébert had been dating for almost two years.

Standing in line alone, waiting to pay for his bowl of hot goulash, he scanned the lunchroom with his sharp brown eyes, and realized he did not know a single soul. Suddenly, a sharp pain caused Joe to instantly arch his back and jerk forward. "Wae-weh," he cried brassily. *Obviously, a clumsy oaf has spilled hot coffee on me.* He wheeled around expecting a halfhearted apology from someone in uniform. As he turned, his senses told him tea, not coffee.

He saw the silky blonde head of a woman, inches away from him, looking down, trying to wipe her, amply full, white blouse and sky-blue skirt which ended about four inches above her knees.

She looked up with blinking, sultry-blue eyes, and with her mouth half ajar. "Oh, oh, I beg your pardon."

She was horrified.

As a German, she spoke perfect English, British-English, not American English. The Queen would be proud.

Joe thought no more of his aching back but only of the beauty of this young German woman. His first thought was, she must be a decedent of the historical Nazi Selective Breeding Program which was initially intending to create a superior Aryan master race. If so, Hitler was surely a damn genius.

She was the most beautiful creature, with a flawless, soft creamy complexion, he had ever seen. He guested, she stood about five-four, weighed less than one-twenty, and had more than an ample bosom. At least he managed to keep his mouth closed. He stood admirably looked at her for a couple of seconds, as she collected herself.

She finally spoke again, "I am truly sorry. I should not be so clumsy."

Trying to soothe the situation and to assure her, Hébert said, "I yi yiee, Jamais de la vie, lordy mercy, dat hurt, blee dat. If you wanna meet me so badly, all you hadda do was dap me on da shoder."

His six-feet and nearly two-hundred-pound frame towered over her. After a long ten seconds, she looked deeply into his eyes, this time with a bewildered expression. She finally cracked a slight smile and repeated herself, "I am so sorry. I hope it did not hurt badly."

Hébert smiled for the first time and replied with an achy expression, "Nothing a little first aid won't help. I'm sure you'll apply it, won't you?" His expression changed to cockiness.

Her perplexed look continued for a moment. She finally managed to ask, "What kind of accent do you have? You are obviously not French. I have never heard an American speaking this way, with such an accent."

Ah, a personal interest, he thought, and said, "I'm a Cajun, a Bayou Boy."

"Cajun? I do not understand this word."

"Long story! Get another cup of tea. I'll pay and meet you at the vacant table over in the corner." He nodded in the direction. Without giving her a chance to reply, he at once turned and paid for his goulash and her cup of tea.

He arrived at the table in enough time to watch and appreciate her walking toward him.

When she arrived, she set her tea on the table with her left hand and placed her wallet down with her right hand. He noticed a wedding ring with a large diamond. A sudden feeling of despair washed over him. *Oh crap, no chance. She's married to an American.* He knew, if she wore the rig on her right hand, she would have been married to a European.

"Now, Sergeant He Bert, what is a Cajun?" She looked at his name tag and pronounced it incorrectly.

"First, my name is pronounced A Bear, not He Bert. But, please, call me Joe."

"Of course, French, and yes, I will call you, Joe. I am Ava. Now, what is a Cajun?"

"A Cajun is a Creole, a Bayou Boy, and we are sometimes called a Coonass." He paused for a response.

When nothing came from her except for a blank stare, he continued. "The word Creole comes from the Spanish word Criollo, which translates to locals or natives. In my case, a native or local is from Louisiana, specifically South Louisiana. Do you know anything about my home state?"

"Yes, of course, New Orleans," she replied and paused. "But I do not know Coonass."

"Coonass is supposed to be a defamatory word."

She nodded her head and said, "Yes, I understand. It is like a derogative word for Negros, colored, or Black people."

"As I'm sure you know, it is not cool for a white person to call a Black person disparaging words. But it is quite common and perfectly acceptable for a Black person to call another Black person anything. You understand what I'm saying?" Joe cocked his head.

"Not cool. Does it mean not politely?"

"Well, yes. I guess that's a good way to say it."

"I am sorry, Joe. I do not understand American slang words. But I am learning a few words and phrases."

"Now, back to Coonass. At one time, it was meant to be a demeaning term and was used as such. It's not like this today. In the past it referred to someone who ate raccoons, and was lower class than coons, another derogatory or slang word for Black people."

"You eat raccoons!" Ava sounded horrified at the thought.

"Look!" Joe raised his voice. "I grew up in a very poor family who lived on a bayou in a large swamp. We eat raccoons, opossums, muskrats, squirrels, rabbits, ducks, and alligators. You name it, we ate it, or we went hungry. We had no local grocery stores on the Bayou. We ate almost everything living in the swamp, both animal and plant." He leaned forward and stared hard into her wide-open, blue eyes to stress his message.

"I must apologize. I, I did not know people still lived like you described," she paused. "You say Coonass is not a derogatory term today?"

"No, I'm sorry Ava. I'm a Coonass. A lot of times, I'm simply an ass. I can get sensitive about my heredity and background. You see, most Cajuns are industrious people who simply try to get along and provide for their families.

"Ava, my ancestors, left Canada in the middle-to-late 1700s when basically the English threw the French out. As we often say, they left Canada when the King of England demanded they swear allegiance to him. Since they could only swear at the King, they migrated out of Canada. The smart ones went all the way to south Louisiana, which was scarcely populated at the time.

"We're like any other minority ethnic group in the world. Cajuns were looked down upon and were thought to be ignorant and uninformed. But like most ethnic groups, over time they assimilated into the masses. My grandparents couldn't speak English, only Cajun French. Obviously, it's a dialect of French.

"Fifteen years ago, many radio stations in South Louisiana were still broadcasting in Cajun French. Today, fewer, and fewer of the young people speak any Cajun French. I know only a few words and phrases and now have a slight accent, as compared to someone who's never left the Bayou. English is the primary language of my generation. I only use my heavy Cajun French dialect when I'm trying to impress a beautiful young lady.

"Now, as far as Coonass goes. To us, it is a feeling, a sense of pride, or a state of mind.

I feel, absolutely, no shame or inferiority associated with Cajun, Creole, or Coonass. Cajuns are happy people, known mostly for their festive music, spicy food, and most of all for being the best lovers in the world." Joe paused for with a broad smile. He thought the comment should bring a response, but it did not. He continued, "Still thinking about me eating turtles and alligators?"

They said nothing for a couple seconds. Joe took a bite of his goulash, thinking he had said something wrong and had completely turned her off.

Ava sipped her tea, trying to understand this Staff Sergeant, Joe Hébert. "Staff Sergeant Hébert, Joe, I do not know what to say. You are an interesting man."

"You can tell me something about yourself. I've done all the talking. The only thing I know about you is your first name is Ava, you meet men by pouring hot tea on them, you are very inquisitive, you don't understand American slang, you're married to an American, and you are lagniappe." Joe presented a creasy grin.

"This must wait until another day. I am a working girl and must go." She gathered her wallet and stood.

"When might another day be?" Joe asked, hopefully.

"I am here, almost every day, between 11:45 and 12:30, and I do apologize again for the tea incident.

"One more thing, what is lagniappe?"

Joe stood and replied, "As you say, this will have to wait until another day." She smiled and walked away.

Joe watched as Ava walked out. Lagniappe! Yes, incredibly special.

CHAPTER 2

On Monday, the third day of April, Joe returned to the lunchroom at the 12th SUBCOM Headquarters. Having a little more money in his pocket made him feel better than he felt his last visit here. He had been paid three hundred and thirty-five-dollars base pay and fifty-five dollars for Explosive Ordnance Disposal (EOD), or hazardous duty pay. Of course, nearly all of the money had already been used. Paying bills is necessary for a young and upcoming NCO. He came to have lunch with Pam but hoped to get a glimpse of Ava.

He and Pam had crossed the border at Zweibrucken and spent the weekend in Bitche, France, not necessarily to see the huge fortress there, but simply to be together. She would be returning to the States and getting out of the Army in two weeks. It was likely the last chance for them to spend any amount of time together.

When he arrived in the lunchroom, he saw Pam, already seated at the same corner table he and Ava had occupied the earlier time he was here. They waved, and he headed directly to the meal counter. He ordered his usual, a bowl of beef goulash. After paying, he went to the corner table and sat directly across the table from Pam. Because regulations forbid showing affection to another soldier, while in uniform, he could not hug or kiss her, not even on the cheek.

"Hi, Honey, how was your morning?" Joe reached across the table and squeezed her hand but quickly released it.

"It was fine. And I enjoyed the weekend." Pam presented a million-dollar smile.

"I did too. We should've done that type of thing more often." Joe sounded wistfully or maybe ruefully.

"We still have two weeks. However, the time will be used clearing my desk, processing out and getting my stuff straight. I should know my departure date and flight time by Wednesday. One way or the other, I'll be a civilian on the twenty-second of the month. I don't think the Army wants me to be in Germany at that time." Pam took a bite of her lunch.

"You could be out of here as early as the fifteenth or sixteenth. I'm sure you'll be flying to Fort Dix, in New Jersey, and discharged from there. I'd bet good money everything is driven by the turnover there.

"You know I'm going to miss you. I do dearly care for you. I'll have to make a couple of extra jumps every few weeks to help pass the time." Joe tasted his goulash.

"Ha, jumping is all you do now. You jump out of an airplane every Saturday and jump out of an airplane two times every Sunday. Why is it so much fun? What's wrong with staying inside a perfectly good airplane?"

"If you had taken some lessons, you'd understand why. I love skydiving. It's great!"

Pam shook her head negatively, and replied, "I never wanted any part of it. I like all my body parts intact. However, I did enjoy the plane rides when you'd take me up. I got to see a lot of Germany from a different perspective."

Being optimistic, Joe said, "Maybe when I get back to the States, I can talk you into it. Well, forget it. When you get back to the States, you'll trade the uniform in for a miniskirt.

"There'll be so many of those college boys chasing after you. It won't take you more than a month to forget me. You'll probably turn into a completely crazy hippie."

Joe noticed a striking long-haired blond coming through the door.

"Joe, I'll never forget you and the time we have shared together. Females never forget their first lover. I'll write often. You'll write seldom. When you get back to the States, come see me. I'll put my shortest miniskirt on for you and tell all those college guys that they'll have to wait until you leave." She smiled broadly.

"Sure." Joe said, wondering if Ava had seen him. He could not help himself. He had to take another look, Pam or no Pam, even though her striking beauty could not be overlooked. Sure enough, he caught Ava's eyes as she stood in line. They both smiled and he broke contact. This might get interesting, he thought and returned his eyes to Pam. "Speaking of college, I forgot to ask you if you've heard from Georgetown?"

"No, but I should hear something any day, as I plan to start taking classes in June. One month at home will be enough. If I don't get in, I'll take some basic classes at Townsend State, or the University of Maryland this summer. They are only a short distance from home for either of them. I can, then, keep trying for Georgetown or some other school which offers foreign studies as a major."

"Hello, Sergeant Hébert." Joe heard Ava's voice over his shoulder.

Joe looked up. "You're not going to pour hot tea on me, are you?" He raised his eyebrows and grimaced in mock fear.

"No. I only pour hot tea on people I do not know." She replied laconically.

"Well stated. Sit down with us." Joe rose and gestured for her to take his seat. "Do you two know each other?" Without waiting for a response, he made the introduction. "Ava this is Pam Marsh. Pam, this is Ava, and I don't know Ava's last name."

Pam thought she recognized Ava as the wife of one of the Inspector Generals, or IG's. "McCoy, Ava Braun McCoy." Pam quickly said, "Your husband is in the Inspector General office, isn't he?"

"Yes." Ava nodded.

"Is Braun your middle or maiden name? How do you two know each other?" Joe asked her, as he set down beside Pam.

"Braun is my maiden's name--"

Pam cut in. "We don't actually know each other, but I've been in the German Liaison office where Ava works. She's also been to my office several times."

"Yes." Ava replied. "And I remember you from the Christmas party. The guy from the Safety Office was, how you say, occupying all your time?"

Joe expectantly asserted, "Tell me more. I don't know about the party."

"You don't have to be worried, Joe. If you remember, I'm out of here in two weeks. Your only concerns should be those college guys." Pam tauntingly smirked.

"Am I to take it, you two are romantically involved?" Ava shockingly asked bluntly.

"Only for two more weeks, then I'm getting out of the Army and going to college." Pam appeared ecstatic.

"What part of the States are you from. Where are you going to college?"

Pam answered Ava. "Bowie, Maryland, and I hope to attend college in D.C."

"I cannot wait to get to America. I want to see all the States. I hope my husband is assigned to a wonderful place. D.C. would be excellent." Ava sighed.

Joe asked, "May I ask, what gave you the impression, we're involved?"

"It was the way you talk, and the expression on your face. It was more than simply veneration."

"Well, if you say so. You better hope your husband doesn't get assigned to Fort Polk."

Joe thought, *I'll bet all these officers are wondering, who the hell I am, a lowly Sergeant, sitting here with the two most beautiful women in the house, if not the whole of Kaiserslautern. Ava is gorgeous, a long, blonde haired China doll look alike with everything neat and manicured. Pam's beauty is more like one would expect to find in a Playboy magazine centerfold. Her smile exposed small cheek dimpled. She has hazel sleepy eyes and amber hair, rolled into a ball on the back of her head to meet Army standards. At five-six, close to one-twenty, and well-endowed bosoms, her wrinkled Army fatigues can't camouflage her striking figure.*

"Fort Polk. Where is Fort Polk?" Ava questioned Joe.

"Louisiana. Fort Polk is the worst assignment a single soldier can have. There's nothing there. There's not a bar within forty miles." Joe sounded disgusted.

"But you are from Louisiana. You do not like it?" Ava looked puzzled.

"I love parts of Louisiana, but not all. One should always have fond memories of their home. I'll bet there are parts of Germany you don't like." Joe stressed his point of view.

"Joe, let us change the subject. What is the badge under your jump wings?" Ava pointed to each badge above his left chest pocket on his fatigues. "I know what the jump wings are. My husband wears the same badge."

"It's my rocket pilot badge." Joe managed to keep a straight face.

"Rocket pilot. Rocket pilot. I do not understand." Ava looked perplexed at Pam for help.

Pam giggled and said, "I can tell he likes you. He's teasing. It's an EOD badge. He calls it his crab or bomb because, there is a bomb on it, and it looks like a crab. Do you know what EOD is?"

"His EOD badge?" Avi shook her head. "No, I do not."

"EOD means Explosive Ordinance Disposal. I'm a technician who works on hazardous bombs or hazardous devices.

"In laypeople term, I'm a member of a bomb squad. I work on explosive items to make them safe and dispose of them."

"Are you still teasing me?" Ava asked in a condescending manner.

"No," Pam answered for Joe. "He does."

"You take bombs apart, and you jump out of airplanes, eat alligators and turtles, and weird things. What kind of a man are you? You are going to drive me crazy, thinking about this." Ava sounded somewhat bewildered.

"I'll let you two sort this out. I have to get back to work." Pam gestured to Joe to let her out.

Joe stood and said to Pam, "I'll walk with you." He turned to Ava, "Seeing you again was a pleasure, and thanks for sitting and talking with us. I certainly hope you and I can do this again. I know so little about Germany. Maybe you can answer some questions for me?"

"I am here every day for tea. And yes, I would love to discuss my homeland with you." She flashed a pleasing smile which exposed her pearl like teeth.

As Joe and Pam walked slowly to her office, Joe said, "She's very nice, isn't she?"

Pam stopped abruptly and turned to look up into his eyes, "Yes, I can tell, you like her, but--

"But!" Joe hung his head, "She's married, married to a Lieutenant Colonel."

"You're right, Joe, so be careful. I might be leaving, but I don't want to see you hurt. I want you to remember something. No matter where our paths take us, I will always love you. And that's not simply because, you were my first love. Tho', as I said earlier, every woman remembers her first lover until her dying day."

CHAPTER 3

Pam left. Joe understood, his life would change. Pam was his lover, but what is more important, she assumed the role of his best friend. Sure, he had male friends, but none he could communicate with as well as Pam. He could probably tell her he robbed a bank, and she would support him. She proved to be as loyal and dedicated to him as his old hound dog. He certainly felt comfortable, even warm, and fuzzy, with her. He realized this sounds like love, but he knew true love should be different. He would write and see her in eleven months when his three-year tour in Germany ended. From then, when he reenlists, the Army would dictate his future, likely Vietnam.

To occupy his time, he would simply skydive as often as the weather allowed. He would also help teach beginners who joined the skydiving club. He would contact Ava and see where it takes him. Being honest with himself, he did not think it would go far. Her marriage complicated things. He had spoken with her for maybe twenty minutes total, but she had mesmerized him. At the same time, because of her husband, she scared him to death, even to talk with her.

Joe hated the thought of meeting Ava at the lunchroom again. It created an impersonal air, one not conducive to a real conversation, as he defined it. He thought about it and finally built up enough nerve to call her office. He would ask her to have a beer with him after work. Hell, if it works, it works. If not, he could crawl back to the lunchroom and try again. He reached for the phone, and then, put it down.

Joe mumbled to himself, "Am I being too forward? Am I reading this correctly? She may not even recognize my name. She's friendly, but she may be this way with everybody. Crap, man, get it together! You work with explosives daily. She's simply a woman. You have been told no before. Maybe not by a woman like this, but, yet rejected. Nevertheless, get a pair and do it!"

He reached for the phone again. This time he dialed the number. "German Liaison Office, this is Ava. May I help you?"

"Oh, uh, Ava. This is Joe. Joe Hébert."

"Yes, Joe, I recognize your voice" Ava's voice seemed very formal.

"I'm flattered. I didn't know if you'd remember me. After all, it's been almost a month." Joe managed to get the words out. Not only did he have trouble talking, his palms where sweating.

"Of course, I do. How could I forget you? I have looked for you every day at lunch. I thought you must be spending all the time you could with Pam, before she leaves, or maybe, you had forgotten me." Her voice softened.

"No, no, I've certainly not forgotten you. However, Pam has been gone for a while now."

"So, why haven't you come to see me?" Now her voice sounded perky.

"I've been busy." He lied. *This is going well.*

"So, Joe, when are you coming to see me?" She sounded eager.

"I'm calling to see. But I'm not comfortable talking with you in the lunchroom."

"Not comfortable! What do you mean?" She sounded puzzled.

"Well, Ava, I'm a junior NCO. You're married to a Lieutenant Colonel. Everybody there knows you and your husband. It makes me nervous. Officers and enlisted personnel do not socialize or fraternize together." He laid it out.

"I am not an Officer, and I do not know what you mean by fraternizing. I doubt there is a problem. I will have lunch with you any day." She sounded assertive.

"I would be more comfortable if we could meet somewhere after work. I'll buy you a beer or whatever you drink." After a short pause, Ava sounded emphatically, "No!"

"Oh crap!" He hoped she did not hear him.

After another short pause, Ava said, "Joe, I said, I would have lunch with you. Do you know where Harry's is?"

"Harry's? Do you mean the gift shop downtown?"

"Yes, I will meet you there at twelve noon, Saturday. We will have lunch together and talk. I do not have the opportunity to speak

English with anyone except my husband. It will be nice talking with you."

Joe took a deep breath. "Women, how can they say no and yes at the same time?"

He showed confusion, but he got what he wanted from the beginning.

He tried to apologize, "How stupid I am for not coming up with something better than buying you a beer?"

"It is fine." She reassured him.

"Ava, at our first meeting, I said you were lagniappe. You asked me what it was." Joe reminded her.

"Yes, I remember. What does it mean?"

"You are lagniappe."

"I do not understand."

"It's something uniquely surprising or something extra special. Think, the thirteenth doughnut in a box. I'll let you go back to work. I'll see you Saturday at Harry's at twelve noon. We'll meet and decide where we go from there."

Yes. There is a restaurant a short distance away. We can go there if it pleases you."

Seeing you will please me. He hesitated to say, "It will."

"Joe! Thanks for calling." She hung up.

CHAPTER 4

Harrys had a reputation as the best-known gift shop in Kaiserslautern. Here, one can select from an excellent inventory of Hummels, cuckoo clocks, and a vast number of other collectibles to buy.

Numbers of Americans, mostly military personnel, and their families, visited here daily for their vast selection and best prices in town.

Joe did not look out of place as he stood close to the front door waiting for Ava. Like a good soldier, he arrived ten minutes early. Ten minutes should give him ample time to assure his need to arrive first. Upon arrival, he checked the crowd inside, and as expected, did not see Ava. He turned his attention to an extremely beautiful Llardro figurine of Cinderella and her chariot in the window. The four-thousand-dollars price tag shocked him.

*One can afford a fine car for that price. Yes, it is truly magnificent, but...*He almost lost himself in its splendor. Suddenly he heard a voice saying, "Joe, Joe?" He turned to face Ava. She wore a light-blue blouse, which matched her eyes, and a dark-blue spring jacket which matched her slacks.

Her long blond hair was in a pony-tale. Her makeup was thinly applied, almost nonexistent.

"Hi, I was not sure it was you. In your civilian clothes, I almost did not recognize you." He wore a zipped, black jacket, brown slacks, and oxblood sandals.

"I would recognize you wearing anything. You look nice as usual." *She is gorgeous, simply gorgeous.*

"Her name is Cinderella's Arrival, or something similar. Are you thinking about buying her?" Ava nodded toward the Llardro figuring.

"I wish I could. It's almost a year's pay for me. However, I do enjoy beautiful things." *She's not naive enough for this comment to go over her head.*

Joe's statement did not seem to faze her. She simply smiled and said, "Shall we take a walk?"

"Of course, you lead the way."

"You look different out of uniform." She looked him up and down.

"And you are gorgeous as usual." He smiled broadly.

Again, Ava ignored Joe's complement. "What do you know about Kaiserslautern, or K-Town as locals say?"

"Well, I know how to get a bus or taxi from any of Kaiserslautern's bars to the next, and how to get over to Ramstein Air Base." He smiled while still admiring her.

"Exactly what I thought. Our history dates to before Christ. Somewhere around three hundred, we were well established. Being on the West side of the Rhine, it was occupied and settled, for a time, by the Romans. If you do not know, Rome never conquered, and held on to, the land East of the Rhine. You, of course, could probably care less about our ancient history." She sighed and cast her eyes downward.

"You know a lot about the area. Were you born and raised here?"

"No, neither." She replied. "I have been here for a little more than two years. I was born and raised in Landau. Do you know where Landau is?"

"Somewhat. I've never been there but it's about sixty miles southeast of here. isn't it? Joe was not sure.

"You are close enough." She turned on Ludwis Strasse. "Down here is Fammkucken, one of my favorite places to eat pizza."

"I'll follow your lead." Joe looked at her intensely and smiled.

They entered the incredibly old building with stone flooring and rustic tables. A couple of Old Master paintings hung on the walls. As soon as they were seated, Joe noticed two tables with dogs sitting under them. This was a common sight, as the locals take their hands everywhere. It showed; the local people eat here. Americans had picked up the custom of taking their dogs with them to eat.

They both ordered a small pizza. Joe ordered a BBK, a local beer. Ava ordered a bottle of Egon Braun Spatelese wine.

Surely, she's going to drink a whole bottle of wine with pizza! "So, did your job bring you here from Landau?"

"I came here for the job, but I came here from Frankfurt. I went to school there, Frankfurt University for one year."

"What did you study?"

"I was in a business curriculum but did not finish. I left after two semesters." She hung her head.

"Am I too presumptive to ask if there is a story there?" Joe leaned forward.

"Yes, it would be intrusive, but I will give you the cliff notes. There is nothing to shame me. It was not bad grades. They were fine. The bottom line for me leaving school was because of my boyfriend. I caught him with another girl, a teammate of mine. I played field hockey for the school club team. So did the other girl. I decided to get away from the situation and found a job here."

"Wow! How--?"

"No questions." She interrupted. "Let us change the subject. I want to know more about living in the swamps of Louisiana."

"I was only going to say, how could anybody be so stupid to cheat on you?" Joe paused.

She did not respond and looked away in deep thought.

Quickly changing the subject, Joe continued with his story. "As a boy, the swamps weren't bad. It was all I knew. We didn't have anything in the form of luxury or material things, mostly only what the swap provided.

"My father was gone most of the time. He worked on pipeline construction throughout Louisiana and Texas and only came home for three or four days at a time. Then, one day he did not come home. He died in an accident.

"I had an older brother, who was killed in hurricane Audrey. When the water rose, all of God's creatures tried to occupy the high grounds. We were on the top of our house. That is when my brother was bitten by a Cottonmouth moccasin. There was no way to get medical assistance."

"I am sorry, Joe. I have a younger brother, and it would be devastating to lose him."

Joe hung his head and continued. "It was a long time ago. I missed him.

No, I still miss him.

"Mama, a good Catholic, never remarried. She was never the same, and I fear, she never will be. She always said; the Good Lord didn't intend for parents to outlive their children. I don't think she misses my father like she does my brother."

"You are Catholic? So am I." Ava turned the discussion to a more positive subject.

"Yes. My parents raised in the Church. After all, my name is, Joseph. In my neighborhood, they named everybody after a disciple or a president. In my case, I got both. My middle name is Abraham." He smiled and continued, "I don't attend church as regular as I should."

"Nor do I. What did you do while growing up?"

"Normal boys' stuff for a Cajun. We lived on Bayou L'Eau Blou. I went to school in a very small town called Lockport, which is southwest of New Orleans."

"Did you say south of New Orleans?" She looked amazed.

"Yes, southwest. And I hunted, fished, played football, and chased girls. I was better at the former two than the latter two. I was fortunate. After my fathers' death, I had his 1955 Ford pickup truck to drive. I caught bullfrogs and crawfish and sold them to pay for gas and shotgun shells. I could sell frogs for thirty-five cents a pound if they hopped.

I had a Winchester, model twelve, pump shotgun to hunt with. I could keep meat on the table with it. Mama, grew a large garden and canned a lot."

"I am sure you did fine with the girls." Ava teased.

"I dated some, mostly a majorette. But I was always in love with our head cheerleader. I certainly did not have a Casanova reputation down on the Bayou. Do you know what cheerleaders and majorettes are?

"I was an offensive and defensive lineman on our football team. They aren't glorious positions for the girls. The cheerleader was in love with our running back, an amazingly fast running back, who ended up playing college football for LSU, Louisiana State University. I never dated her. Do you know anything about American football?"

"I probably know as much about American football as you know about field hockey." She had a large smile on her face.

"Anyway, I am sure you were a good lineman. Was your team good?"

"I admit, I don't even know what field hockey is, so you have me there. Yes, we were good. During my senior year, we were exceptionally good, undefeated. Undefeated up to our last game. Then we played a team from up north for the State Championship."

"Up north, as in Ohio or New York? " Ava interrupted.

"No. I'm talking about up north as in North Louisiana. Anything fifty miles north of the Gulf of Mexico is up north to a real Cajun.

"Remember, I said I lived southwest of New Orleans? Anyway, in our last football game, we scored on our first two possessions, the first two times we had the ball. Afterwards, they kicked our butts all over the field if you know what I mean."

"Yes. Unfortunately, I know exactly what you mean. As most athletes, I have been there too many times. I was supposed to be incredibly good in high school. In college, competition got harder, but I kept up. I played goalie and dreamed of playing on our national team." She sipped her wine.

"I dreamed of playing college football but was apparently not good enough. So, I joined the Navy when I got out of high school." Joe sipped his beer.

"Why are you in the Army now and not the Navy?" Ava showed puzzlement.

"I was in the Navy for four years before joining the Army. I joined the Navy to learn how to do underwater salvage. I knew the oil companies were drilling increasingly offshore in the Gulf, and I thought they would need Hard Hat qualified divers for such things such as underwater maintenance such as welding. I also knew, they paid extremely well. From there, I went to SEAL training, but didn't make it."

"Joe, I know about your strange diet. I know you disarm bombs. I know you jump out of airplanes, and now you tell me you dive underwater. Is there anything else you do which is so dangerous and crazy?" Ava leaned forward and looked into his eyes.

Joe sat for a moment marshaling his thoughts and finally said, "I'm not sure it's in the same category or not, but there is one more extremely dangerous thing."

"You said extremely dangerous. What, on earth, is more dangerous? Do they shoot you from a cannon in the circus? Do you fly on a trapeze or walk a tightrope? You are not a James Bond type, a spy, are you?" Ava looked perplexed.

"No, no, I'm not a spy. Walking a tight rope may describe it best. But that would be easier."

"What is it? What is so dangerous?" She now leaned as far forward as she could.

"How do I say this tactfully? I'll simply say it. Well, I'm beginning to have...I do have certain fond feelings for a very beautiful Lieutenant Colonel's wife." Joe stared into Ava's blue eyes.

"Oh, Joe, be serious! You had me scared. I was thinking you were wrestling alligators, a member of the Mafioso, or something similar." She leaned back and flipped her hand at him in a dismissing manner.

"Ava, I have wrestled alligators before, and it did not scare me nearly as badly as you do." Joe displayed a deadly serious face.

"No, you have not! Have you for sure wrestled alligators?" Ava's mouth went ajar.

Joe nodded and smiled. "Once, as a boy trying to impress a cheerleader."

"Joe, you do not have to be afraid of me."

"I know, it's your husband who scares the crap out of me. I don't know him, nor do I want to know him. Speaking of him, where is he?" Joe quickly changed the subject.

"He is playing golf. It is what he does with his free time, play golf. He goes and stays at the nineteenth hole. At home he sits and reads about golf." She looked away.

Joe noticed a lonesome look in her expression. Not knowing what to say they remained silent for a moment or two.

Ava broke the silence. "Now, you have finished your beer. I want you to try a glass of this wine. You do like wine, do you not?"

"Yes, I love German wine." Joe perked up.

"Do you know enough about German wine to understand what you are drinking?"

"I know there's a difference in quality: Cabernet, Spatelese, and Auslese wine. I know I like wine from the Rhinehessen region."

"You know enough to get by. I want you to try this and tell me what you think." She passed him a glass and the bottle.

He read the label on the bottle, "Egon Braun, Spatelese, Rhinegau. "Oh, the Rhinegau region is my second favorite. The area is south of the Rhinehessen region. This must be a good wine."

He poured himself a glass.

"It is my favorite. Have you ever seen this label before now?" She glanced at him as she took the bottle and poured herself another glass.

"Not that I can remember." He shook his head. "Once I get past the quality and the region, I'm more concerned about drinking it. Why do you ask?"

"Did you notice the name on the label?"

Joe picked up the bottle again. "Egon Braun, Braun, it's your maiden's name. Is that you?"

"My father. He has been making wine for years, even before I was born. Have you heard the Braun name?"

"Braun? No. I did look up Ava to see what it means in German. It means a bird." Joe proudly displayed his knowledge.

"Wow! I am impressed. Does the name Eva Braun mean anything to you?"

"No, not off the top of my head. Is it supposed to?" Joe shook his head.

"You said off the top of the head. This is obviously slang, meaning your first thought?"

"Yeah, something like that. I'm sorry."

"Well," Ava said. "My father named me Ava, Ava with Eva in mind. He knew Eva. It should tell you something about my father. You may have a problem with my parents. Your homework is to find out who Eva was. Do it before our next meeting. Now, shall we go elsewhere?" She finished her wine and stood.

"Yes, Mrs. Colonel. As I said, I'll follow you anywhere. I like the scenery." Joe quickly finished his wine while thinking about her comment about the next meeting.

She smiled and led the way. "Do you know where the Volks Park is?"

"Does it matter? If you're going there, so am I." He followed her out of the restaurant. "It is not far, but I will drive. My car is down the street."

After a short walk and a short drive in Ava's Fiat, Joe and Ava arrived at a small parking lot Filled with cars. Joe asked, "Where's the park?"

"Be patient, follow me." Ava insisted.

"Follow me, follow me. Sounds as if we're in the infantry," Joe quipped.

Ava looked at him in a questionable manner but said nothing.

"Well, at least we're establishing a pattern in our relationship. You lead; I follow." He did not mind in the least. He realized he would follow her anywhere.

She smiled, and led the way to a small, tree-lined walking trail. River rocks covered the walkway. After a couple hundred meters, they came to a well-maintained and manicured park, filled with people. Joe could see why families came here. There were more children playing than parents seeing them. Joe and Ava continued walking around the park, before finding a bench for them to sit.

Ava asked, "Do you want children, Joe?"

Joe appeared stunned by the question but answered. "Yes. In fact, I would like to have three boys. And you?"

"Wow! Three boys. It sounds as if you want to set up a child labor situation. I would like to have three girls but will have none. Ava lowered her gaze.

"Why?"

"My husband does not like children and does not want them."

"I'm sorry. Maybe he'll change his mind."

The two sat on the bench, walked around the park a half dozen times, watched the children play, and talked until the sun began to lie down.

"It's getting chilly." Joe folded his arms around his chest trying to keep warm.

"It's not cold!" Ava chided him.

"To me it is. I have a condition called Raynaud's Phenomena, which means, I'm cold intolerant. It causes my hands and feet to have spasms. I sometimes start an uncontrollable shivering of the whole body. When it happens, I almost get as stiff as a board. This condition doesn't affect most people nearly as badly as it does me."

She smiled and said, "So, you are not Superman after all. I guess, we had better leave. I will drop you off wherever you want to go. I live in Vogelweh."

"Now, you know I'm not Superman, you're ready to get rid of me? I'm hurt! But since you're going my way, if it's not a lot of trouble, you can drop me off at Pulaski Barracks." Joe realized he did not want his day with Ava to end.

Ava drove, and they sang along with the music on the radio. Before dropping Joe off, Ava asked, "Joe, have you ever been on a *volksmarch,* a peoples march?"

"Yes, Pam and I went once. We drove somewhere on the other side of Pirmasens. I didn't necessarily like it, too early in the morning and too cold for me."

"I understand. I usually go to bed late. So, I do not like getting up before the sun rises either. By the time I get there, part of the people has gone home. There is one close to Zweibrucken next Saturday. Would you like to go and walk with me?"

"Yes, of course. What time?" Joe answered excitingly.

"If the weather is nice, my husband leaves for the golf course about 9:20 in the morning. If the weather is bad, he will stay home and read and watch TV. Either way, I will pick you up at 10:00 o'clock. Okay?"

Joe leaned over and tried to kiss her. She initially pulled back, then offered a cheek. She took his hand, squeezed, and said, "I enjoyed the afternoon. I will see you next week. You can call me at the office anytime. I always answer the phone."

"I will." Joe got out of the car and closed the door behind himself.

CHAPTER 5

For a week, Joe thought only about Ava. Her voice, her smile, and her smell were imprinted into his brain. He called her as promised. More precise, he called her every day. One time, telling her to pick him up at the American elementary school in Vogelweh. Public transportation would carry him within a short walking distance of the school. This is where Joe found himself waiting for Ava.

He arrived early. He had begun worrying whether she would come or not. This concern eased when he saw the familiar blue Fiat approaching the parking area and coming directly toward him.

"Sorry I am late." Ava apologized.

"Don't worry about it, I've spent half my life waiting on a beautiful woman." He threw his backpack into the back seat and settled in the front seat.

"I am almost always prompt, but this time, I had some last-minute things to do. Ten minutes will not matter. We have all day."

"Good." Joe was extremely pleased to hear her, all day, comment.

Ava asks, "What did you bring to eat?"

"I brought *brochen* (bread), cold cuts, cheese, and a bottle of your father's wine, Oh, also an army blanket."

Ava laughed as she drove off.

Joe asked, "Where are we going?"

"We are going to Kashoken," she replied. "It is about twenty-five kilometers. I hope we get there before the march officials leave. I have a rather large collection of volksmarch medals which I've collected for several years, and I would like to add this one to my collection."

"I have one medal. You can have it."

"No, Joe I want only what I earn. My parents taught me that early in life." She turned the radio on.

They both began singing along with Fats Domino music. It did not take long for Joe to reach over and placed his left hand on her thigh and gently patted with the beat off the music. She placed her right hand on his and tapped with her finger.

Ava wore a gray running suite, trimmed in red, and a tight, white pullover blouse. Her Adidas running shoes matched her running suit. Joe wore his army issued running gear and a white T-shirt. Stained-white, Converse tennis shoes and white socks covered his feet.

After arriving at the designated area, they were able to buy a medal for Ava. Afterwards, they headed down a trail through the woods. They walked about four kilometers, all the way holding hands, laughing, skipping, and playing like kids. Only a dozen or so people were still walking the trail. As most yolks marchers start at the break of dawn, the early birds had already returned home.

The privacy of the springtime woods allowed them to see the wildlife to include a beautiful stag galloping and stopping to pose which, by itself, made the day worthwhile.

When they arrived back at the Fiat, Ava asked, "Are you hungry?"

"I could eat a little. Where do we go?" Joe pulled his backpack from the rear seat.

Ava opened the trunk of her Fiat, pulled out a basket, and said, "Follow me. I saw a place on the trail which is perfect for a picnic."

"Okay. What did you bring?" Joe through his pack over his shoulder.

"I brought the same thing as you." She answered with a smile. "It's why I was late. I had to get it together this morning."

"Let me carry it." Joe reached for her basket.

"No, I will. You try to keep up. You look tired." She displayed a cocky swagger.

"Go on. I'll keep up with you." He followed her down the trail for about four hundred meters to where it paralleled a small stream. There, they turned off the trail and went upstream for a couple minutes, until they found a secluded and beautiful place for their picnic. They selected a dry place, under an extremely rare and large hardwood close to the babbling stream, to spread their blanket.

"What else do you have in your basket? I know you brought extra stuff," Joe said and sit down.

She handed him his favorite beer, a BBK. "I thought you might like this." She then placed the rest of her food and drink beside his.

"I'll wait on the BBK. It looks as if we have enough for lunch and dinner." Joe smiled.

"You know I cannot stay for dinner," she said, and began placing cold cuts and cheese into the selected bread, *brochen*.

"I see you forgot wine glasses. We can use these." She handed him a paper cup.

"Oh, crap. But don't get snooty, I was hopefully thinking of getting you on a blanket."

"You are for such a man! Men think of only one thing, while letting women do all the work."

After finishing his *brochen* and BBK, Joe lay down on his back and stretched out listening to the flowing stream.

Ava finishing her meal and began packing her basket. She said, "You see what I mean? The man lays down and leaves the dishes to the woman."

Joe grabbed her and wrestled her over him to the other side of the army blanket beside him.

"You, see? You, see? The woman does the dishes and then gets roughly managed!" Ava grinned and giggled.

"I wish I could manhandle you." He stared deeply into her eyes knowing she got the message.

"I know! I understand. Joe, you must remember, I am married." She lay on her side facing him.

Joe turned toward her and placed his arm over her shoulders. "I wish you weren't."

They looked at each other for a fleeting moment. Finally, Ava turned her head away from him, and said, "Joe, you are a very dear friend." She then rolled over on her back and looked upward.

Joe's heart sank. Friend is the most dreaded word in the English language for a man, when it comes from a woman. No man wants to hear a woman say, 'We're friends'. Disheartened, he hardly noticed, as she turned away from him, his hand cupped her breasts.

"Joe, I, I enjoy talking with you more than anybody since my first love, Ian. When I lost him, it nearly destroyed me. I have always loved him. I guess since I was a child. We grew up together, and we became lovers our senior year in high school. I followed him to Frankfurt. I, I do not know why I am telling you this. But I feel comfortable with you, and I trust you.

Joe interrupted. "I'm sorry you were hurt. You're obviously still suffering, and you still have fond feelings for him." Joe softly caressed her breast.

"To be honest, I may always be in love with Ian. I do not know. There is a difference in the way I felt about him, and the way I feel about my husband. They are the only two lovers I have had."

"You don't truly love your husband?" Joe gently caressing her breast.

"Yes, I think I do, but I do not feel the same. I love him. I love my parents. I love neither of them in the same way as I loved Ian."

"I think I know how you feel. If you were not sure, why did you marry him?"

"I was sure at the time. He took me places. He treated me well, like a Queen. Marrying him also gave me the opportunity to move to the States." She looked around, but not at Joe.

"Marrying your husband got you as far away from Ian as possible?" Joe softly and politely suggested.

"Maybe, I do not know. Maybe it was an age difference. I was barely twenty-one. He was forty. He was very mature and cared for me. At the time, I needed him."

"You were his trophy wife. I assume he was married before and divorced." Joe surmised.

"Yes, he was divorced. His wife did not come to Germany with him, and he got the divorce while here."

"Do you truly love him?" Joe finally got to the important aspect of the matter.

"Yes. Sometimes, no. I get lonely. I know he loves me and would do anything for me. Right now, it may not be right, but I would rather be here with you than at home with him. I do realize he is not there." She finally looked into Joe's eyes.

"Ava, have you even noticed, I have been fondling your breast?" Joe squeezed harder on her breast.

"Of course, I have." She placed her hand over his hand. "It is not a problem. You are touching only my clothes. It is okay. It is nothing."

"Do you feel anything?"

"Yes, of course. You surely noticed my hard nipples." She smiled.

Joe moved his hand and rubbed her lower belly and then lowered his hand to her crotch. "And this?"

"It is nothing, only my jeans."

Joe tried to put his hands inside her jeans.

"No, no! That is private," she said. "You cannot touch me there. Do not have a libido attack."

Joe moved his hand back to her breast and tried to kiss her. As on the earlier occasion, Ava offered her cheek and said, "I am sorry. I cannot. Remember, I am Catholic. I would have to go to confession."

Joe knew he could compete with the husband, but competing with the Father, Son, and the Holy Ghost could only be considered impossible. He lay on his back. "I guess, I'll have to go to sleep. But surely you know I'm enamored with you. Right now, I feel like I'm standing in a stampede of elephants."

Ava turned toward Joe, laid her arm on his chest, and placed her hand on his cheek. "I understand." They lay there silently. After a moment she crossed her legs over him and relaxed.

When Joe suddenly awoke, face-to-face staring into Ava's blue eye, only inches from her face he asked, "How long was I out?"

"Not long. I also dozed." She whispered.

"Well, this is a great way to wake up. I can't think of anything better" He pulled her closer.

"We do not have time." She pushed him away and raised up. "We need to go. I presume; I will drop you off at your barracks."

"It's a little out of the way."

"No problem. As long as I get home before dark."

They gathered their possessions and walked slowly back to the car. Spring had brought the best out of the countryside, which made the stroll back to the parking lot pleasant. During the walk, they did little talking but communicated very well using other senses. Joe thought about the upcoming week. He feared, he would not see Ava again unless he had lunch with her at the 12th Support Command lunchroom.

When Ava drove into his barracks parking lot, Joe said, "Next Saturday, why don't you meet me at Ramstein? I'll show you what skydiving is all about, and you get to ride in the airplane with us. This way I can get a couple of jumps in."

"No." She emphatically said.

"You don't like flying?"

"I have flown before. I like it. I was thinking; you could meet me back at Vogelweh at the same time. We can go jogging. We can go up to the castle. Have you been up there before?"

"No, but I've heard about it. If climbing a mountain is what you want to do, I'm all in."

"Come prepared. If you cannot keep up, I will run off and leave you." She smiled broadly.

"I'll keep up. Remember. I like following you, anywhere, anytime. I can't think of anything I'd rather do than watch you run up a hill. Well maybe one thing." He smiled, knowing she had known exactly what he meant.

"Men!" She pulled to a stop to let him out. "Joe, I had a nice time. Be sure to call me."

"I always like being with you," Joe squeezed her hand. "And yes, I'll call you. What are you doing tomorrow? I'm going over to Ramstein. You're more than welcome to come."

"I need to go to Mass, but I will probably stay home and do wifely duties." She sounded disgusted.

"Cool, but if you do anything I'd enjoy, think about me. And to let you know, I'm sure, when I hear the rest of the story about Eva, I'll have no problem with your family."

"What do you mean?"

"You forgot! You gave me homework last week. I went to the library and read about Eva Braun. I can't wait to hear your story, and how your family is involved." He grabbed his pack, closed the door, and walked away smiling to himself.

CHAPTER 6

The next week's meeting did not happen. She and Lieutenant Colonel McCoy had to attend a formal function.

After two weeks without seeing each other, they met at the school to go jogging.

The trail up to the castle began behind one of the military housing units at Voleghew. The first half mile, they jogged through woods of the pine family. The trail seemed flat and easy to walk. They made suitable time and crossed over a two-lane, paved road and then entered more woods.

After another mile, they had barely started sweating. Then, they cane to a long severe slope. It was almost a half mile up to the castle. The jogging became more demanding.

With Ava leading the way, Joe followed closely. She had jogged this trail regularly since moving to the housing area.

As a once collegiate level athlete, she showed excellent physical fitness. She was surprised Joe could still be with her so easily. She had no idea what kind of physical conditioning he had endured throughout his time in the Navy, and he too jogged regularly.

Joe, constantly stayed three or four yards behind her as she pushed hard up the first half of the steep incline, trying to leave him behind.

She wore nylon jogging shorts, with a long sleeve tight top.

He wore the standard military issued, gray-cotton warm-ups, with gray shorts and T-shirt underneath. A hundred yards before they reached the top, Joe turned it on and passed Ava with ease. At the summit, both were breathing dreadfully hard, trying to catch their breath.

"Not many people can stay with me, coming up the hill, and pass me with ease. Maybe, you are Superman, after all. Or perhaps, you are some sort of alien with mysterious powers." Ava gave excuses while panting deeply.

"Due to my ego, I couldn't allow you to outrun me. I could've easily passed you at any time. But the view from behind was marvelous and motivating enough to keep me there." Joe managed a sheepish grin.

"Joe, you think about nothing else!"

"Well, yes. To be honest, you're right. You are a beautiful woman. What's wrong with thinking about you and lusting for you?"

Ava punched him on the shoulder and walked toward the castle ruins. "There is nothing here except for the boulder from the old walls. However, the view over the valley is very appealing. What do you know about this place, Joe?"

Joe proudly recited, "This is Nanstein Castle, built around 1162 by Frederick Barossa, to guard the western approach to Kaiserslautern. It was destroyed in 1668 by French troops."

Ava bent over laughing, cutting him off. "You did your homework, but you fail. You have the wrong castle. You have the castle at Landstuhl. I am impressed. You tried."

Joe ran his hands through his short hair and frowned. "I thought this was going to be easy and I would get some brownie points. I'm embarrassed. I knew you'd ask me that question. So, while I was thinking of you last week, I went to the library and looked it up. My research must have been faulty. I'll try to do better the next time and not to make the same mistake, three or four times."

"It is okay and not important. You tried and that impresses me more than getting it correct.

"Anyway, it has been proved. I cannot outrun you. So, what shall we do with our time?"

"If you are asking me, I think you know my answer." He wore a grin on his face, as his eyes roamed her body.

"Joe, I keep telling you, you have a one-track mind!" She smiled and shook her head. "Come this way. We will walk around the ruins."

The ancient walls were constructed with large stones and were about four feet thick. The remains were only about five feet tall in most places. Part of the old stones were strewn around the area. The castle was obviously plundered for many years.

"Ava, now I have a question about your history. Why do you think all the castles throughout Europe were destroyed about the same time?" Joe factually asked a stimulating question of relevance.

"I have never given any thought to the subject. I assume, since you ask, you know the answer to the question? So, you tell me."

"One word, gunpowder. The walls couldn't stand up to the constant bombardment from cannons, as they could survive the catapults of its time." Joe believed he had taught Ava something.

"Thank you! The day is young, yet, and I have learned something from a man who eats turtles and frogs, no less!

"Here, we can rest for a while." She looked at him and climbed upon the old ruins' wall. "You can see forever from here. Rolling hills and spring, green meadows are as far as you can see."

Joe obliged and followed her up the boulders. He saw how lighthearted Ava could be. Joe also enjoyed how the sun had warmed the smooth weathered boulders, not to mention how the sun played off Ava's blonde hair. He removed his sweatshirt and used it as a pillow as he stretched out to bask in the sun.

Ava joined him. She snuggled close and rested her head over his chest.

"Ava, I think, it's time you tell me something about yourself that I don't know. You know everything about me and are always asking more questions. I want to know about you."

"I doubt I know everything about you, but I would like to. I enjoy gathering information about people. You never know when it might become useful. When I was a little girl, my father taught me to be quizzical. He also taught me not to have loose lips. I learned the lesson early, in life.

"Now, with this in mind, what would you like to know about me?"

"Let's start with Ava versus Eva. I think you mentioned this in the past." Joe looked into her soft blue eyes.

"You picked a good place to start." She paused, raising up and looked directly into Joe's eyes. My father was a Nazi, Joe. He knew Adolf Hitler and Eva Braun."

Joe gaped at her and raised up. "Wow! I wasn't expecting such a response!" He stared at her, searching for more.

"I said he knew them. They were not friends or anything like sociable. During the war, Father was a truck driver and assigned, only occasions, to be the personal driver for the Fuhrer. There was only a dozen or so people allowed this so-called honor. "When I was a child, my father sometimes told me stories about what he had done during the war. As I remember, he only drove people and supplies to various places. On one occasion, he was given the honor of driving Eva Braun from Berlin to Berchtesgaden and function as her personal driver while she was at Berghof, Hitler's house."

"I don't know whether to be impressed or disgusted. However, I do know, as a soldier, you do what you are commanded." Joe reassured her.

"I do not think it was a matter of him being commanded. He liked them and was incredibly supportive of the Fuhrer, even after the war ended. He hated the Soviets with a passion and disliked all the Allied Forces. You can imagine what he said when I told him; I was marrying an American Army Officer."

"Is he like some of the old men you sometimes see around here, the ones who shake their walking stick at American and yell something as we are passing by in cars sporting green license plates?"

"Yes, yes, exactly! You described him." Ava pumped her arms to emphasize the point.

"Even after more than twenty years since the war ended, I don't understand." Joe sounded bewildered.

"You cannot understand why they feel the way they do. After World War One, and the Treaty of Versailles, the worldwide depression of the 1930s was particularly severe if not savagely in Germany. Like other places in the world, there were no jobs. Germany had one of the highest unemployment rates in the world. Paper money was inflated daily to the point a loaf of bread cost several million Reisch Marks. The currency was printed in denominations of billions.

"The economic chaos paved the way for Hitler to convince the people of a better manner. Of course, they wanted to believe in him, as there was little choice. He gained control of the government and greatly improved the standard of living for the German people, at least until he went crazy.

"After May 8, 1945, the official ending date of World War II, the war was not over for most of the German people, by any stretch of the imagination."

"As usual, I don't understand. I'm sorry." Joe looked at Ava in a concerned manner.

"After the war ended, and after the Potsdam Conference, in August 1945, the Allies divided Germany into the occupational zones of Soviet, US, British, and French. Millions of Germans died.

There was essentially no international aid for a war-torn Germany. There were forced labor camps, or in other words, slave labor camps, food rationing, and many innocent children died of starvation.

"On top of this, the Red Army raped virtually every woman they could get their hands on, often as many as sixty to seventy times. People estimate the number of raped women was two million. It was as if the Soviets wanted to exact extraordinary revenge for the Wehrmacht by inflicting massive trauma on the hapless population. So, I guess some of the old people have a right to remain angry."

"I've never heard anything about any of that." Joe shook his head in disbelief.

"Did not Churchill say something to the effect, 'The victors of war write the history of war'?

"Did you know, for a time after the war, American troops could not even speak to a German civilian? This was the so-called Non-Fraternization Policy. It was as if Germans were nonexistence and were nonhuman."

"No, I had no idea." Joe hung his head.

"Why should you? You are a bayou boy who learned American history." Ava punched Joe on the shoulder.

"So, after all this, am Ito conclude you were named after Eva Braun? If so, why name you Ava, rather than Eva?"

"I accuse my parents of not knowing how to spell, but my mother said, because I was her little bird, she insisted on the spelling."

"You were born in 1946, right? When did your parents get married?" Joe asked.

"I was told nine months before I was born." She smiled.

"Was your father put in a POW camp or used as slave labor?"

"No, I do not think so. He seldom talked about what he did after the fall of Berlin. All I know is he left Berlin to go north toward the coast shortly before the Russians entered the city. From there, he hid his uniform and started home to Landau. I should tell you, both his and mother's families goes way back in that area."

"It must have been hard for him to get home without being captured." Joe gave thought to this achievement.

"I understand he used his Jewish heritage to manage the trip." Ava knew what Joe's reaction would be.

"He has a Jewish ancestry!" Joe barked. "And he was essentially a Nazi!"

"If you remember, a couple weeks ago, while on the phone, I asked if you knew who Anne Frank was."

"Yes, I remember. I told you everybody who went to high school in the States after nineteen fifty-nine, when her diary was published, knows the story about her. What does it have to do with your family?" Joe looked puzzled.

"My father and Anne share the same great-grandfather, Zacharias Frank, who lived in Landau back before the turn-of-the-century. Since Landau was a large Jewish community before the war, I think; he used the connection to return home and escape capture. I am sure he had connections and information about people who helped him. Anyway, when he returned home, he married my mother. They started a vineyard. nine months later I was born. And this is the end of the story."

"Oooh! I'm sure there's more to the story. For instance, how did you become a Catholic? Never mind, it had to be your mother who converted your dad."

"Actually, my grandparents did it. My grandmother was born with the Frank name, and my grandfather was the Catholic. He converted her. Now you know my secret, how mixed up I am."

"Speaking of mixing it up," Joe smiled. He grabbed her and rolled her on top of him. She straddled him and leaned back, placing her hands on his chest. It took only a couple seconds for mother nature to take its course. Joe had to reach down to adjust himself. At the same time, he managed to get a good feel of her.

"You are bad." She smiled and began making gentle pelvic movements.

"Only an emblematic biological reaction!" Joe pulled her toward him.

She resisted and stayed upright and continued her gentle pelvic movement for a moment.

"Joe, do you want to make love?" Her eyes twinkling.

"With you? Oh, hell, yes!"

She stopped her movement and lost her smile. "I do too, but I cannot.

You must understand. I do not want to hurt you. I cannot do it. I do care about you, and you must surely know it."

Joe was crestfallen. He exhaled in a defeated manner and asked, "When? What can I do? I'm in agony. My libido just spiked like a phoenix flying out of an erupting volcano and you shot it down."

"It is nothing you can do. It is a problem for me, one which I must resolve." She looked away.

"Holey Mary, mother of Jesus! You know this is killing me. I'm not into self-flagellation, but this must be similar." Joe pleaded.

"You are incorrigible. But you know this is also killing me!" She replied. "As for when, I will tell you. When I wrap my arms and legs around you and hold you as hard and as tight as I can, you will know."

"I guess it's better than nothing, but I'm completely whipped." He sighed from frustration.

"I was going to say, until such a time comes, I will have to go to Mass every Sunday and ask for forgiveness for my fanatical feelings about you or better stated with you." Ava looked down, obviously in bereavement and deep turmoil.

Joe hated it when she looked at him in this matter.

"I don't think you're going to Hell because of your thoughts." Joe tried to reassure her.

Ava moved to a sitting position next to Joe. "I believe your thoughts are sometimes as sinful as your actions. Let us not talk about this. It is too philosophical. I cannot continue to sit here, this close to you. It is too dangerous. My willpower is not strong now. I desperately want you, but I am trying to be good. It is time to go." Ava struggled with her feelings.

When they stood up, they embraced closely with her arms around his neck. Joe placed his hands on her buttocks and held her close. He gently patted and caressed her.

After a long embrace, Ava smacked him on his shoulder. "I said, arms and legs."

"As you know, I'm a good soldier. I'll follow your wishes, but there's no way I can stop dreaming about you." He tried to be cheerful.

"I truly understand. We will take a different trail back. It is further and we can cool down. "

CHAPTER 7

When Joe called on Wednesday, Ava told him she had to visit her parents the following weekend on an important matter. She told him, he could ride with her, but he could not go to her parent's house. Of course, he accepted the invitation, with the understanding he would walk around town and act like an American tourist while she visited her family.

Few words were spoken on their way to Landau. They held hands and sang along with the music on the radio. After the quiet drive there, Joe did as she directed, about touring the city. When he arrived at the designated rendezvous place, he did not have to wait too long for her.

Ava displayed an unusual quietness on the drive back. The radio's volume remained low, and no small talk occurred. She drove straight to Kaiserslautern, directly to Joe's barracks without stopping.

When asked about the important matters which took her home, she simply replied, "It was estate related," and said nothing more.

At the barracks, Ava said without a smile, "Thank you for going with me. I will see you next week."

Noticing the coolness in her tone and expression, Joe squeezed her hand, kissed her on the cheek and said, "I'm looking forward to next Saturday. I'll call you every day."

Except for the third Saturday in June, when Ava called in sick, they drove places outside of Kaiserslautern like Heidelberg and Zweibrucken. They never went to a place which provided them any privacy. Joe knew, or at least thought he knew, why Ava did not want to be alone with him, except to be in a moving automobile. He did not confront her on this issue, as she had already explained. She had a problem and needed to find its resolution.

On the second Saturday of July, after a walk in the botanical garden in Zweibrucken and driving home, Joe told Ava, "There's a parachute contest next Saturday. I would like to compete in it."

"How do you compete in jumping out of an airplane?" She looked at him in a perplexed manner.

"Obviously we don't attempt to see who can jump out of the plane the fastest." He did not break a smile.

Ava looked at him trying to figure out his seriousness but said nothing.

Joe explained. "You simply put a target on the ground, one which can be seen from a relative altitude. You go up in a plane or helicopter, jump out, find the target, and try to land as close to the target as possible.

"It sounds simple enough, but does not your parachute go straight down or where the wind takes you?"

"Far from it. In the old days you could barely steer your parachute. You must remember, parachuting is primarily a military activity, and the military isn't going to allow the paratrooper a lot of flexibility as to where he lands.

"Let me back up a little. Parachuting is believed to have started in the tenth century when Chinese jumped off mountain cliffs using a parachute. I don't know how it worked for them, but they probably used a sky device similar to the one featured in Leonardo da Vinci famous drawing of a triangular shaped gimmick. I'm sure you've seen the drawing. And you've probably seen the standard round military parachute used worldwide. Sports jumpers wanted more control, so they started to modify the military chute." He paused making sure she understood.

"Go on." She nudged him.

"A couple years ago things changed significantly. The Golden Knights, the Army's elite parachute team, showed a proven modern design. Their parachute is very steerable and is now used by most of us.

"Steerable! You mean you steer it like a car?" Ava could not believe her hearing.

"Not exactly, but we can turn left or right, and make it go forward."

"Is this supposed to be a lot of fun? Parachuting sounds dangerous to me." She still did not understand Joe's fascination with jumping out of an airplane.

"It can be dangerous. However, safety is our primary concern. And we call ourselves skydivers, not parachutists. They are two very different activities." Skydiving infers a free fall, falling for a while, before the parachute opens. Parachuting is usually associated with the chute opening at once after jumping.

"Flies through the air, faster than a speeding bullet, are you sure you are not Superman?" She teased him.

"No, Baby, but you haven't seen all my skills, yet." Joe said lasciviously, while emphasizing the word yet.

"And do I dare ask what those skills are?" She flashed a huge smile.

"I would prefer to personally demonstrate them." He looked at Ava, with a twinkle in his eye.

"Okay, get your mind back on next weekend. Your competition is a public event. It may not be wise for me to show up there with you. You do remember; I am married."

"Oh yes, every minute of the day." Joe linked his fingers, placed his hands over his head. and slightly bowed his head. "How can I, a lowly Sergeant, forget the woman of my obsession is married to a Lieutenant Colonel? And to answer your first question, yes, it's a public event and I would dearly love for you to be there."

Ava shook her head "I will think about it and let you know when you call me next week. I'm sure we can come to some kind of arrangement as to where we meet."

"I would like to give you some lessons and get you to skydive with me sometime."

Ava pointed her finger at him for emphasis. "Wait a minute! That is a big leap, literally, from going to watch you skydive, to me jumping out of an airplane."

"I know. I was dreaming. But I swear, you would love skydiving! You are, obviously physically fit enough, and you have a competitive ego. Don't be intimidated by the thought of it. The idea of jumping out of planes seems idiotic to many people, but to others it's simply a leap of faith. I'll teach you everything you need to know." Joe tried to encourage Ava.

"What kind of equipment would I need?"

"Only a harness, a reserve parachute, helmet, gloves, goggles, coveralls, and shoes. Something like running shoed is fine. Boots will help prevent ankle injury, but they are not fashionable."

"What are coveralls?" Ava looked puzzled.

"In relations to skydiving, think of a tightfitting outer suit. Something like ski suits, but not as thick."

"I have a ski suit. But we are getting ahead of ourselves. I will think about it."

"Great!" Thinking he may have a chance to get her in a plane, Joe seemed thrilled.

"It will take some planning. I cannot imagine what my husband would say, when I tell him, I am going," she paused, searching for the word, "skydiving."

"I'm sure it would go over well." Joe mocked.

"When you skydiver, how do you control yourself?" Ava seemed seriously interested.

"Basically, it's done by manipulating the shape of your body. Once you're in a belly-to-earth position, which is simply like lying in bed on your belly, with your arms and legs extended outwardly, you can virtually go in any direction other than up. If you want to turn right, you look right and lower your right elbow. It is the same going left. By closing your extended legs and bringing your arms to your sides, you will increase speed and go forward."

He paused, waiting for it to sink in. "With those positions and others, you can do anything a bird can do, other than to go up. In the belly down position, you are going about one-hundred, twenty miles per hour. If you want to go faster roll forward into a head-to-earth position. This will increase your descent to approximately two hundred miles per hour. This is a rudimentary explanation, but I hope it gives you some idea."

"You are going fast! The wind must be terrible." She interjected.

"Not necessarily. You don't feel how fast you are going because, you don't feel the sensation of falling."

"What!" She almost shouted.

"Remember Sir Isaac Newton. Things fall at thirty-two feet per second. After you reach a certain speed of miles per hour, you begin to feel resistance, or wind as you called it. from the air. The resistance gives you weight. With weight, you no longer feel as if you are falling."

"I do not know if I understand that, but if you say so, I believe you." Ava slowly spoke and shook her head.

Joe grinned. "I wish you were so easily convinced about other subjects. But back to jumping out of an airplane. Once your parachute is open, you have a new ball game. You become a parachutist.

"Between you and the chute are lines, call steering lines or risers. You use these lines to change directions. You simply pull down on the lines of the parachute in the direction you want to go. For example, if you want to turn left, you pull down on your left risers.

Landing is the most dangerous part. Simply because this is when most injuries occur. They are very few and are normally caused by improper landings techniques. I promise you, not all landings are perfect. So, you don't have to make a perfect landing. Any landing you walk away from is a good landing. Safety in all aspects is paramount when parachuting."

"Joe, is this a gender thing?"

"No, not at all. I read somewhere about a woman, who was parachuting and doing free fall shortly after the turn of the century. Free fall was the term generally used before skydiving, which became vogue about ten years ago.

"Joe, I am not going to jump out of a perfectly good airplane! So, let's change the subject."

"Come on. You would love it! You would need only five or six hours of training."

Ava put both hands up in front of her, in the well-known signal across the world, which means to stop. "Joe, stop it."

"Okay, okay, but you could go up in the plane with me. I never could get Pam to jump either, but she went up with us a bunch of times and enjoyed it immensely." Joe tilted his head and raised his eyebrow, silently issuing a challenge.

"Maybe I would, but as of right now I will only consider watching from the ground. As for next week we will see."

"Think long and hard on it." He pleaded.

"Think long and hard! Are we still talking about parachuting?" She flashed a grin.

"Well, when you say it like you did, maybe it has a significantly different connotation than I was thinking." Joe moved his left hand up her thigh. "I like the way you think."

"Okay, I started it, but I could not resist. I am sorry. The devil made me say that." She moved his hand away.

"I'll call you next week. And by the way, if you're wondering, I enjoyed the walk and the day."

"I also enjoyed the day." Ava assured him.

As he closed the door of Ava's car, Joe turned looking her in the eyes and while smiling said, "Do me a favor. Keep thinking about the long and hard thing."

CHAPTER 8

"Staff Sergeant Hébert, phone call!" The shout came from the Commander's office. "You'll want to take this back here. I'm sure it's private."

The way the captain sounded made Joe's heart skip a beat or two. Joe thought of Ava. He dropped his pool stick and headed for the vacant First Sergeant's Office.

Joe lifted the receiver and cautiously said, "Staff Sergeant Hébert, Sir."

"Hi." The response came from a voice he had been longing to hear.

"Thank you, Lord," he mumbled. "Where in the world have you been? I was beginning to think I would never hear from you again." Joe sounded relieved and tempestuous at the same time.

"I am sorry. I have been busy and out of town for a couple of weeks." Ava stretched the truth.

"And you can't take time to call me? It's been almost five weeks. I called your office a half dozen times before they finally told me, you no longer worked there. They wouldn't tell me your home phone number. I've been over to the damn lunchroom several times, but of course, I didn't see you." Joe's exasperation could clearly be heard.

"I am sorry, Joe. I could not get away. It is not the fact that I have forgotten you. I think about you all the time," Ava sounded mournfully.

"Are you alright?" Joe interrupted.

"Yes, nothing broke."

"You're sure?"

"Yes, I am physically fine."

"Well, what gives? I don't understand!" His bluntness told her his feelings.

"If you want to see me, I will answer your questions Saturday."

"If I want to see you? See you! The Soviet Army can't keep me away from you! Do you want me to come to the school?" Joe couldn't believe his ears. "Of course, I want to see you."

"Are you going to Ramstein to skydive Saturday?" She asked, softly.

"I could, but I would rather be alone with you."

"You are sweet. However, I think I would rather go up in the plane with you, as we discussed the last time, we were together. Is that all right with you?"

"Sure, it'll be great! Somebody will be there, and we can catch a ride. We'll probably have to use a helicopter. Have you ever flown in a helicopter?"

"No. It will be exciting! Do you want me to bring anything?"

"I know it's August, but it can get cold ten to twelve thousand feet up. A good set of tight blue jeans and a sweatshirt should be sufficient. I'll arrange for anything else you may need. Oh, don't forget the running shoes."

"Okay, I will wear anything you recommend."

"No, bring it. You can change at the hangar. You know where to go?"

"Yes, I have been there before."

"When?" Joe quickly asked her. "Remember when I saw you last, you were going to compete? I was there. I did not think you saw me. I tried to stay out of sight of everyone. I was able to see you from a distance. I recognized your walk."

"I had no idea you were there. I looked but didn't see you. And then, I didn't hear from you for a month, and I couldn't contact you. You should remember; I take bombs apart. I always think in terms of the worst-case scenario for everything. In the bomb disposal business, you need to be a pessimist. To me, Murphy was an eternal optimist."

Ava chuckled, "Sure, pessimists do not wrestle alligators, jump out of airplanes, and play like Superman."

"Hey, since you aren't working, can you see me this afternoon? There's no problem for me to get away." Joe's voice turned cheerful.

"No, I am busy, and I must get off the phone. I am at home, and my husband will be here any moment. I will see you Saturday at whatever time you say."

"How about one minute after midnight, Saturday morning?" She could hear the impishness in Joe's voice.

"When?" Ava sharply asked.

"One minute after midnight, Friday night. It's Saturday morning. Never mind. I know your answer. But the earlier the better for me."

"How about ten-thirty at the hangar?"

"Then, ten-thirty is it."

"Joe, please understand. It was not you. You should know it. Well, by now, you should know how I feel about you."

"I thought I did. Thanks for reminding me though. I have worried and missed you, greatly."

"The same here, Joe. Again, I am sorry. I will explain, but for now, I must go. See you Saturday."

Ten-thirty came and went Saturday morning. Joe paced around the large hangar and parking lot as his pessimistic personality took over. He worried something had happened, and he may not see her again or worse. Those fears were somewhat relieved when he saw the familiar Fiat pull into the parking lot. At least his plans could be set in motion, he hoped. A quick jog led him to Ava's door as she opened it. Without a word they embraced with a long full-bodied hug.

"Hi." Joe breathlessly said. He released a breath he did not realize he had been holding. *She came, and nothing else matters.*

"Hi, back to you." She looked into his brown eyes with a tender smile.

"I see you followed my suggestion and didn't wear jeans or a sweatshirt. He admired her short, blue skirt. Did you bring them?"

"Yes. I am so late, and I am sorry. I have too many things to do." In frustration, she shook her head causing her ponytail to flip from shoulder to shoulder.

"You're here. That's the important thing, and you're going up with me! You don't know how good you look, and how I appreciate you coming." Joe had a huge smile on his face.

"You also look good. Look at you in your coveralls." She assessed him from head to toe.

"Jumpsuit. Okay, tightfitting coveralls and thermal underwear to help. with the cold." He smiled and consented willingly.

Ava looked around. "Where to now?"

"We have a beginner's class going on now, mostly safety stuff. You have time to change. I'll show you where the ladies' locker room is. If you need help, I'm available." Joe gave her his best classy grin and moved his eyebrows up and down.

Ava shook her head. "Oh, yes! It has been a while since I saw you and heard your innuendos. I think I can manage by myself. You can simply show me the way."

"A pair of jeans and a sweatshirt sporting a large German icon on its front, don't distract from your natural beauty." Joe mumbled to himself as she slowly approached him.

"Will this do?" She spread her arms and performed a pirouette as she came closer.

"Oh yeah! With you in it, it would do as formal attire. And yes, it'll work for a ride in a helicopter, too." Joe beamed.

"Good."

"Let me get you some gear you'll need. Afterwards, it'll be only a short wait before we can take off. It's a beautiful day for skydiving, and you'll love it."

Joe led Ava to the equipment room. "Most of the equipment here is privately owned. The rest belongs to the government. It's common for us to borrow each other's stuff. So, you can use whatever you want from here." He pointed in the direction of the equipment room.

"Okay." She walked over to the equipment.

"Try one of these. One should fit. If not, one of these two will." Joe pointed at the helmets to choose from on the table.

After selecting a black helmet, Joe helped her with goggles, gloves, and he pointed out a reserve parachute, which he recommended. "Wait, why do I need a parachute?" Ava stepped back and looked at Joe like he had blind-sided her. All color drained from her face.

"You are going up in a helicopter. Sometimes crap happens. It's a safety matter. When we go up, all the jumpers carry two chutes, a main and a reserve. This is yours. It's a reserve. I thought you might feel more secure." He used a very caring voice, trying to assure her.

"Joe, now you are scaring me. Maybe I should stay here." Ava suddenly became nervous.

"It's only a precaution. If something happens up there, I'm sure, with the two guys jumping with me, you'll be fine. If you want to leave it here, it's no problem; however, even the pilot and copilot will sometimes have parachutes." Joe, somewhat, stretching the truth.

"If something happens! How often does something happen? If something happens, what am I to do with this thing?" She anxiously and quickly ran the words together.

"I'll take care of you, but if anything happens, we'll have plenty of time to react. You do trust me, don't you?"

"With my life!" She squeaked.

"That's not the situation. But now, you mention it; do you trust me with your life?" He asked, hoping she would say the words he wanted to hear.

Ava looked at him in a way he had never seen, completely drained of emotion, and finally said softly, "With my life? Yes, Joe. I trust you. I trust you with my life."

The way she said it, and the tone of her voice struck Joe deeply. Finally, he spoke again. "Okay let's get strapped into this thing. It's called a Nutcracker by airborne troops, and its name and reputation are well deserved. Put your right leg through this loop, and your left leg through this one." He held the harness as she stepped into it. "Now, put your arms through each of these loops."

After tightening the straps and buckling them, Joe asked, "How does it feel? Too tight?"

Ava did a deep knee bend, stretched her arms above her head, twisted, and then slightly adjusted the straps. "I think this will do."

"Good. I'll help you with the rest of your gear, and then I'll introduce you to the two guys flying with us today."

Joe led Ava out of the equipment room to a far corner of the almost empty hangar, where two men were summarizing their safety class for new jumpers. After they concluded, the two walked over. Both wore jumpsuit like Joe's. One proclaimed loudly, "Staff Sergeant Hébert, this must be your new jumper!"

With her mouth ajar, Ava gave Joe a piercing stare.

"No, Sir." Joe said sternly, only a passenger. Without looking, he could feel Ava relaxing. "Ava, this is Captain Marks. He's an Air Force Captain, and this is Mr. Collins. He's a retired Army Master Sergeant. Guys, this is our guest and passenger for today." Joe emphasized the word passenger.

"And what a lovely passenger we have. You can call me Avery, if you please." Captain Marks extended his hand to her.

"Yes, Captain, I mean, Avery." Ava shook his hand.

"And you can call me, Top. Everybody else does, or you can call me anything you please." Mr. Collins reached to shake Ava's hand.

"Top, will do." Ava looked dubiously. "I thought Top was slang for First Sergeant." She looked at Joe for an explanation.

"You are right, Madam." Mr. Collins interrupted. "When I retired from the Army, people kept calling me Top."

"Okay, Top." Ava said cheerfully. "But drop the Madam. I am Ava."

"Captain Marks is an Air Force Academy graduate. If you don't know, it's basically the same thing as West Point. He may disagree. He pilots one of these jets which you see flying around here."

"I am impressed." Ava nodded her head.

"Well, don't be. Today we are jumping out of a helicopter, piloted by two Army hombres. The pilots are waiting for us, so we need to hit the head and get ready to fly. We'll meet you outside in a minute." Captain Marks nodded to the exit door.

"Sounds good. We'll meet you at the chopper. I need to pick up her reserve, and we'll be ready." Joe looked toward Ava.

Joe disappeared for a minute. When he returned, he brought a small package, no larger than a football. "This is the reserve we were talking about. I assure you; it's only here to make you feel safer and more comfortable. If you want to, we can leave it here."

Ava took a deep breath. "Joe, I'm getting nervous again, but I guess, I'll wear it."

"Don't worry and remember, I'll be there for you, always." Joe reassured her.

"You are sure?" Ava still had reservations.

"Yes, I pledge my life. Nothing catastrophic will happen to you. Besides, this little baby goes great with the rest of your outfit!" He connected it to her harness. Ava forced a smile and asked, "Did Pam go through this?"

"Yes, Pam had a lot of safety rules taught to her." Joe fudged the truth. "I want you to remember one thing. No matter what happens, don't panic. I'll say it again, don't panic. I will be there. The only thing you need to worry about is the parachute landing fall, PLF. It's how we hit the ground. When it comes to landing, bend your knees slightly, and keep your knees and feet together. I know fully well you can keep your knees together." He teased.

"You don't need to sprain an ankle or blow a knee out. Think about hitting the ground after jumping from six to eight feet high. Be prepared, and it won't hurt. You can try to roll by hitting your feet, knee, hip, and shoulder in order." Joe gave her good advice.

"If you are going to be a pessimist, I am going to be an optimist. I am not thinking about anything bad. Nothing bad is going to occur. Now, it is time to get this over with before I completely change my mind." She firmly proclaimed as she turned and stalked purposefully toward the helicopter.

With one-hundred, twenty-five miles per hour cruising speed, the AH-1D Huey helicopter's abilities made it a fast gun ship. However, on a good day, it could reach an altitude of nineteen thousand feet which makes it a super platform for skydivers.

During the ascent, Ava sat silently watching the three men talk. Their carefree attitude gave her comfort. Joe sat beside her, holding her hand. She could not understand what they were saying. They were yelling trying to communicate. Through the wind and the noise from the turbo jet engine, only a couple of feet overhead, she thought she heard Captain Avery ask Joe, "Are you sure about this?" Joe had replied positively.

Ava wished she had worn a windbreaker. The higher the altitude they climbed, the colder she got. Going from mid seventy degrees to what seemed like freezing gave her quite a shock. The open doors of the helicopter did not help. They allowed for a constant and brutal wind which cut through her sweatshirt and jeans.

Joe squeezed Ava's hand and put his face close to hers. "We are high enough. Top is going first. I am going second, and Captain Marks is going last," he said and stood up. The lack of headroom caused them to slightly bend over.

"Would you like to get a better look?" Joe yelled into Ava's ear and tugged on her arm to help her up. She felt Joe's hand grab her harness behind her back to help stabilize her.

Joe yelled again, "Be careful and move behind Top. You'll see the ground from there."

Joe held her tight guiding her toward the door where Mr. Collins stood. "When he goes, move over to make room for me. Look, you can see the runways. We'll be landing close to the hangers on the north end of it. You can't make the hangers out from this altitude, unless you know where they are." Joe continued yelling and pointed down.

Ava peeped around Top's side and looked down where Joe pointed. A sudden blast of dizziness flashed over her. "Yes, I think I can see it. From up here, everything is so green." She yelled, after looking up to find Joe's eyes.

In front of her, suddenly, Top's figure disappeared. Ava, again, looked into Joe's eyes. He mouthed, "I love you, Ava!" And he pushed hard.

Her mind began racing. A weightless and dizziness feelings were upon her. She experienced the sudden and strange loss of almost all sound, only a slight whistling remained. Her feet were astonishing in the big blue sky.

A sudden sick feeling engulfed her whole body. As quickly as it came, it disappeared, replaced with panic.

Damn, something did happen. I fell out of the helicopter. Even though, Joe said I would be safe, I am surely going to die today. Did he say he loved me? Yes, but no, I did not fall out. He pushed me! How long before I hit bottom?

Accepting her fate of dying, Ava's panic feeling eased, replaced by serenity and the knowledge, at any moment she would have to the answer to mankind's greatest question, what is on the other side?

While plunging toward the ground at nearly one hundred and twenty miles per hour, totally at peace, she closed her eyes. Suddenly, she felt something, a tap on her foot, and then another on her hip. When she opened her eyes, she saw a figure approached. Although, wind distorted his face, she could see Joe smiling.

Even after pushing me out of the helicopter, he continued to smile. She couldn't believe it. With one arm extended, he used his other to point at his eye, rubbed his chest, and pointed at her. She knew what he meant. Then he vanished, only to reappear.

Oh my God, he can fly, she batted her eyes a half dozen times. Then she noticed the other two figures flying with him.

Joe moved closer and then behind her, out of sight. He grabbed her harness. The movement caused them to begin a slow tumble. Joe inserted a strap inside her harness and coupled it to his. Their tumbling slowly ceased.

Ava felt Joe's arms wrap around her waist and her harness tightened around her chest. Suddenly, the two other figures were speeding toward the ground. She felt the harness supporting her entire weight. The whistling wind tuned to silence. Two parachutes opened below her feet, and she could see two hangers and a grassy field below them. She looked up and saw the large white parachute and blue sky. *It's the most beautiful thing I have ever seen in my entire life.*

She could see Joe's arms and hands reaching and pulling the steering lines and feel the parachute responding.

"How exciting is this! Remember to keep your legs together and slightly bent!" Joe shouted into her ear as they continued to descend toward the ground.

Ava did not respond. She looked down at the fast-approaching ground. Panic and fear had returned, and it consumed all her senses. Her feet finally reached Earth.

Ava's feet hit the ground a fraction of a second before Joe's, which caused them to tumble and fall hard into a pile. With him on top of her, the parachute crumpled around them.

Ava felt the ground and then all the parts of her body she could reach with Joe on top of her, and the parachute lines entangled around her.

"Are you okay? No broken bones, I trust," Joe said, nonchalantly while unbuckling the two harnesses. He helped her stand. Then, he removed his helmet and goggles and looked at Ava as if nothing happened.

Ava's fear at once turned into enragement. She stood erect and confronted him with a face Joe had never seen before. With narrowing eyes, and an index finger pointed directly at him, Ava screamed, *"Du Bastard*! You bastard! You threw me out of the plane, the helicopter! You, God damn, dumb son-of-a-bitch! How could you do that to me?" Then she shoved him backwards with both hands against his chest.

The two men jogging toward them stopped and headed away, toward the hangar.

"You could have killed me! What were you thinking? What did you have on your mind? I thought I could trust you!" Ava continued to unload on Joe.

"I was trying to impress you," Joe managed to say in his defense.

"Impress me! Impress me!" Ava lividly shouted. "You almost scared me to death. I told you; I did not want to jump. I only wanted to ride! Men, they cannot be trusted!"

"I--" Joe presented his dumbstruck face.

"I! All you can think about is, me, me, me." She removed her helmet, goggles, and gloves, and threw them at him. Then she began shaking all over.

"I--" Joe tried again to speak.

"No, do not come here with your crap again. You have no excuse! I thought I could trust you. You threw me out and almost scared me to death!" She used a lower voice, but anger still dripped from her words. Her whole body shuttered, profusely. "Now, look at me. I peed in my jeans! You are lower than a slug!"

Joe glanced down and saw her legs were wet. He realized he had never heard Ava say a curse word, and she called him things which would make a sailor proud. He knew he had screwed this up, royally.

"I do not know how I get myself into this type of situation. I knew I could not trust any man. All men want is to get into my pants. That is all. No, I should never have trusted you." Ava ran her hands through her hair as she nervously paced.

Joe came close to her. He tried to console her, but she pushed him back, pounding on his chest and shouted, "I hate you! I cannot trust you! I hate you, Ian! I hate you more than anything in the world! I hate...Oh, oh! What am I saying?" She cupped her face in her hands, turned away from Joe, and shook her head.

After a moment she dropped her hands and faced him. "Joe, Joe, I am sorry, am so woeful. I did not mean that." Tears began to stream from her swollen eyes and her knees buckled. She fell to the ground in a fetal position and stayed there, with her knees pulled to her chest and her head bowed.

Joe sat beside her with his hand on her back and said, "I'm terribly sorry" over and over, as Ava continued to sob.

After a long cry, the shaking eased. She raised her head, squared her shoulders, placing her hand on his cheek, looked into his eyes, and said, "Joe, I do not hate you. Not at all. I love you. You certainly know that."

"I do, now." He said and pulled her close for a moment. He then rose, offered her a hand, and help her to her feet.

"I cannot stand yet. My legs are too weak," she said, and sat back down.

Joe gathered the parachutes, strode over to Ava, and sat beside her. Saying nothing to each other, they sat there for a couple of minutes while she collected herself.

Finally, she spoke. "Joe, I apologize. I guess I took three years of frustration out on you. You did not deserve it, and I am terribly sorry. Now, help me up and get me out of this harness."

Joe jumped to his feet and did as she said, "We should walk and talk." Ava caught his hand and led him away from the hangar.

"We can't go far. There are places out here you'll get shot for wandering around." Joe waved his right arm around, pointing.

"Okay, we will walk in circles. I feel like circles are what my life has been. I know, I owe you an explanation for what happened. First, I want to tell you." She turned, pumped her arms, and faced him. She smiled and shouted, "It was great!"

She jumped into his arms, wrapped her arms and legs around him. "It was absolutely fantastic! It was better than sex! And now, I know why you like it." She kissed him, firmly kissed him with passion.

After gaining her feet she said, "I believe, I experienced every emotion that is possible within a few minutes."

She took a deep breath and continued. "It apparently overwhelmed me, and I lost control of myself, obviously, physically and mentally. Maybe the cry is what I have needed for a long time. Hopefully, it is over."

Only a couple minutes ago she hated him, now she loves me, and I get my first enthusiastic kiss from her. Women, so dubious. I wonder if I will ever completely understand her. He gathered all their equipment.

"Come on." She said and again pulled his arm.

"Joe, as I have told you, I have loved Ian all my life. Anyway, I am sorry about calling you Ian. I may always love him. I thought he was the love of my life.

When Ian broke my heart, I promised myself, I would never feel that way about another man. I have been true to the promise. I do not love my husband the same way I loved Ian. It is not within me. And then, well, then, you came along. I woke up, one Sunday morning, after we had been together the day before, looked into the mirror and told myself, Ava, you have a problem. You love and want that man."

"Was it about a month ago when you quit seeing me?" Joe seemed dumbstruck.

"No, that is another story, a story which will have to wait until tomorrow."

"Tomorrow!" Joe, again, appeared to be shocked. "You are going to see me tomorrow?"

"Yes, unless you have something more pressing, or you do not want to see me."

"No, Babe, no! I mean, yes, I want to see you. You know better." Joe looked slightly exasperated and exhilarated at the same time.

"I hoped so. Now, we should go to the hangar where I can change clothes. Can I take a quick shower there? I am in an unspeakable, shabby condition."

"If you let me dry your back, I'll find you a clean towel somewhere." Joe gave her a big grin.

"Not today, Lover Boy. I have experienced enough emotion for one day. Shall we go?" She gesticulated toward the hangar.

While she showered, Joe stored the burrowed equipment.

"You were quick," Joe said, when Ava appeared from the lady's locker room so fast.

"I feel better and more refreshed. It is amazing what clothes without urine and a cold shower can do for you."

"Yes, I know. Since I met you, I've had quite a few cold showers." Joe hoped she would catch the meaning.

"I thoroughly understand." She agreed.

"Would you like to go over to the NCO club and drink a beer, or glass of wine, or maybe something to eat? Heck, I bet you have never been to an NCO club."

"Regardless of my feelings about you, no, and no. Joe, I need to go home. It has been a very traumatic day. At one point, I thought I was going to die. And do you know what, I was at peace. I certainly am not ready to move on. I believe in God, and I know, He has a future for me. I need to lie down and get a perspective on life.'

"Wow, you're deep." Joe grinned.

Ava sighed heavily and smiled. "I know, especially coming from a dizzy, feather-brain blonde! Can I drop you somewhere?"

"No, I have to pack my chute and do some other odds and ends around here."

"Then, I am out of here. Is that correct American slang? How does ten thirty at the school, tomorrow, sound to you?"

"It sounds great! And Ava, I love you. I genuinely love you!"

"Thank you. And by the way, I understood your sign language up there at about seven thousand feet." She turned and walked away.

Before his knees weakened to the point he could no longer stand, Joe reached for the closest chair. He softly whispered, "Holy crap, what a day, what a day! I wonder what tomorrow will bring?"

CHAPTER 9

For the first time ever, Ava arrived at the school early. As Joe walked into the parking lot, he saw the familiar Fiat parked in the front of the school.

"Guten Morgan, Fraulein." Joe smiling as he opened Ava's car door.

"Good morning to you, too. But it should be Frau, not Fraulein. Remember, I am a married woman," Ava said, and began to drive.

Right, like I could ever forget, and It's the one thing I can't change. "Am I allowed to inquire about our destination? I didn't think about discussing it with you yesterday."

"I am taking you to the forest again, the one where we volks marched in, near Kashofen. I enjoyed the day immensely. I thought we could walk along the trail, among the trees, again. We can talk."

"As I have told you many times, I love the woods, and I'll follow you anywhere."

Joe reached over and placed his hand on her bare thigh. She wore cutoff blue jeans and a teal-colored shirt which was tied at her midriff.

"We should talk about yesterday. I could have been killed," Ava said sternly.

"Yes, you could have, but you weren't. You could've been killed the day before, or you can die today or tomorrow. In my line of work, I have learned; one can't dwell on dying. Someday, it will happen to all of us." Joe did not blink an eye as he spoke. "Besides, I told you; I wouldn't let anything happen to you."

"I know and would agree with you, if you had not pushed me out of the helicopter! However, do you agree that certain activities will hasten that someday?" Ava quickly glanced at him before returning her attention to the road.

"Of course. If you speed up to ninety miles per hour going over these hills and around these curves, it could certainly hasten that someday. But, if you are referring to yesterday, I don't agree.

"It would be reckless of you to do anything with explosives, while it's certainly acceptable for me. It's my profession, and I know what I can and can't do."

"Joe, you pushed me out of the helicopter over a mile high!" She looked at him and pointed up with her right hand.

"Yes, I did! But everything worked out fine." Joe's face remained fixed in absolute certainty.

"At the time, I did not think about it, but what would have happened if I had pulled the reserve?

"Nothing. Absolutely, nothing!" Joe quickly looked away.

"Nothing! What do you mean by nothing!" Ava almost shouted.

"Nothing means nothing. The reserve was a dummy. It was filled with rags."

When she glanced over at Joe, Ava almost lost control of the car. "You mean you pushed me out without a functional parachute?" Somehow, she managed to keep her response to a low roar.

"Yelp. Do you remember when I gave you the reserve? I expressly told you. It was only to make you feel better and safer. It worked, didn't it?

"If it had been real, we all could have been in danger. You didn't know, how to use a functional parachute. You can't imagine what a misadventures calamity could have happened? If you activated a real reserve, which is a real parachute, while we were inside the helicopter, we could have easily met our someday."

"I know you would try to save me. But how did you know you would be successful?" Ava's anger subsided.

"Because, like working with explosives, I knew what I was doing. After more than one hundred and fifty jumps, I know what I can and can't do when jumping out of an airplane. If I couldn't have saved you, Top or Captain Marks certainly would have.

"Not all skydivers fly alike. Top can fly slower than anyone in our club, while the captain can fly faster than anyone. Top, by going first, was able to wait on you and me, while the captain was able to catch up with ease.

Our first job was to stop your slow tumble, which I did, simply by bumping your lower legs as you rotated. If I had simply grabbed you while you were tumbling, we both would have likely started tumbling which would have made my job of coupling with you harder. You know the rest of the story." Joe answered in a very matter of fact and persuasive manner.

"But what if--"

"Oh, what if the plan failed?" Joe interrupted. "Then the someday would have been yesterday for both you and me. I would've gone down with you."

"So, you risked my life and yours without talking to me first? Do not ever do it again. Joe, I admit, I should have known, you would never let anything happen to me. But you do not make decisions for me. Never! Trust me, my poor response yesterday will seem like a cheerful beer tent during Oktoberfest."

"Obviously, you, freaking out wasn't part of the plan. However, I did like what you said, and how it all turned out at the end of the day." Joe shrugged with a smile and wink. "I promise. I won't make any more similar decisions for you."

"My actions surprised me too." She admitted and smiled back at him.

They continued their drive toward Kashofen. Upon arrival at the parking lot, Joe saw Ava had packed a lunch and an army blanket. They walked the same trail as before, noting the difference in the early spring and the summer foliage.

Ava asked, "Shall we try to find the place by the creek when we were last here?"

"Sounds good to me." Joe with his instincts, developed in the bayous of Louisiana, quickly led them to the place where he and Ava picnicked about three months previously.

Ava emptied the basket of brochen (bread), cheese, cold cuts, fruit, and wine. After Joe spread the blanket and reclined, Ava sat next to him and held his hand.

"Ava, it is so beautiful and peaceful here. You know I love the woods. Being close to nature is relaxing to me."

"I knew you enjoyed it here before. It is why I wanted to come back. I like the woods, but I am a city girl at heart." Ava spoke softly.

"I'm glad you did. This means so much to me. Thank you."

Ava squeezed his hand, sighed, took a deep breath, and spoke. "Okay, it is time. We need to get this over with." She instantly straddled Joe and kissed him passionately. It took less than a minute for their clothes to be scattered on all sides of the blanket.

At first, they experienced feeling of animalism passion and lust which had been building in both since the day they met. In a fleeting time, it turned into tender love making. The two bodies melted into one, with every cell in their bodies reacting like a shaken snow globe until both were joyfully rewarded.

After a while, there were exhaustion. Contentment and huge smiles showed on their faces. Laying there, still in each other's arms, Joe whispered, "It was nice. No. It was better than nice. I don't have the words to express what I'm feeling. Thank you. I needed your love for a long time. Did you hear the angles singing the hallelujah courses?"

Ava chuckled and retorted. "I thought it was lions roaring, or perhaps satin's hounds calling the adulteress vixen home."

"I doubt that, but my blood pressure must have elevated to stroke level. You are as hot as a high school cheerleader in the back seat of a car with the quarterback. I love you very much."

"I understand your feelings for me, and I am enthralled by them, in a good way. I feel exhilarated by your love." Ava whispered, as she stroked her hand across his bare chest.

Realizing he must have had his eyes shut for the entirety of their love making, Joe raised his head slightly to look at her nude body now lying next to him. "Wow, simply Wow!" He did not have the words.

They lay still, kissed, and held each other tightly for a while. Then Ava moved her hand lower. It created a joyous repeat performance, after which, they took a long nap.

"Oh, I was sound asleep," Joe said when he opened his eyes.

"I know, I watched you sleep. Can I get you something to eat?" She gave him a cup of wine.

"No, I'm not hungry."

"But you will need your strength." She said with a big smile.

Sipping his wine, he said. "You have already exhausted me. Do you have other plans?"

"Maybe. If you are strong enough!" She presented a large insatiable grin.

"I'm not about to give up. I have waited too long and wanted you too badly. You may have to carry me out of here, but I will take all you have to offer." He swallowed his wine down. "That will give me enough energy."

The next time he woke up, Joe said, "You're still here. I wasn't dreaming. Tell me, why today, not last month, next week, why here and now?"

"I am not here for long," she replied, but did not move. Her head remained on his chest.

Joe noticed a change in the tone of her voice and dropped it. "I know it's getting late, and you must get home. We'll have next week."

"Yes, Joe, it is getting late." She replied while lifting her head and sitting up.

Joe at once noticed tears in her eyes. "What's wrong? Did I do or say something, I shouldn't have, or did I hurt you?"

"No, No. It is not you or that simple. It is my problem. But okay, I'll get it out. Joe, you remember, I told you, we would talk about why, we have not been together in a month?"

Joe nodded and stopped her before she could continue. "Ava, if it is your marriage and you being a Catholic, and all, I don't believe you're going to die and go to hell, because you made love with me. After all, you were not married in the church. By some people's standards of the Catholic Churches, you're not married."

"You do not believe that. But that is not our problem. Joe, I will find time to manage those details with the church later. I simply could not tell you."

Joe demanded, "Tell me what!"

"There will not be a next week." She now sobbed profusely.

"What, why? I don't understand!"

Ava looked at Joe through her teary eyes and managed to say, "I will not be here next week. I will be in the States."

"In the States!" Joe's mouth hung open and a rush of depression flashed over him.

"Yes, I will be in the States, and today is the last time I will see you."

Those words felt like a hammer hitting him between the eyes. "No. This can't happen."

"Yes, it can, and it will. My husband received orders last month. He has been reassigned to Fort Benjamin Harrison, Georgia. He was selected to be promoted to full Colonel. He will be one of the Deputy Post Commanders or something like that. We are leaving, Wednesday. I will not see you again, and I love you, Joe. I have always wanted to go to the States, but not now. I do not want to leave you." She continued, now crying uncontrollably.

"I don't want you to go. You can stay, and we can work something out." Joe's mind rapidly sought a suitable answer.

"No, I must go! I thought you might say something like that. I have spent a month thinking about the situation, and I must go! This is why I have not seen you, and this is why I had to be with you yesterday and today."

"I can't believe it. This is why yesterday was so emotional for you." Joe wiped his face.

"Joe, I do not want to hurt you. You should know; I love you. I knew I could not leave without telling you, or without being with you like we were today. Now, we must face reality, get ourselves together, and get out of here."

As Ava drove Joe to his barracks in Kaiserslautern, they spoke extraordinarily little. Both were physically and emotionally drained, even more so than the day before.

At the barracks, not caring who saw her, Ava got out of the car and embraced and kissed Joe.

"I love you, Joe, and I will miss you."

"Not for long. Always remember. I love you, and I will see you in slightly less than six months. You have the units address and phone number. Write to me when you are settled, and if there is anything I can do for you over here, let me know." He looked into Ava eyes and kissed her forehead softly.

"I will. I promise. How are you going to see me at Fort Benjamin Harrison in six months?"

"Be assured, I will. I'm already working on it." He patted her on the butt and watched her drive away, knowing he wouldn't let her drive out of his life.

65

CHAPTER 10

"Enlisted personnel management, this is Specialist Jones, may I help you?" A female voice came through the receiver.

"Yes, this is Staff Sergeant Joseph A. Hébert. Is Sergeant Major Yates still in this office?"

"Yes, but now he answers to Mr. Yates," Specialist Jones replied.

"Mr. Yates, as in Warrant Officer or civilian?"

"Retired."

"May I speak with him, please?"

"In a minute, Staff Sergeant." After a short pause, the receiver came alive. "Staff Sergeant

Hébert, this is Mr. Yates, what can I do for you today?"

"Sergeant Major, I hope you remember me from four years ago. You helped me when I was thinking about joining the Army. I was trying to make up my mind whether to reenlist in the Navy, or transfer to the Army. I wanted to go to EOD school. You convinced me that the Army should be my home."

"Yes, of course, I remember you, Staff Sergeant. We only have a handful of Hébert's in the Army. Also, I'm sure you are the only qualified hard hat diver we have unless they are Engineer. So where are you, and why are you calling me?"

"I'm in Germany, in an EOD unit, and I should be receiving orders for a permanent change of station (PCS) soon. I thought I would call you and tell you where I would like to go."

"Staff Sergeant, if you're in Germany, and carrying an EOD military occupational specialty (MOS), you should know your next duty station will be Vietnam." Mr. Yates told a well-known fact.

"No, Sergeant Major. I'm going to Fort Benning." Joe asserted his position very firmly.

"You mean, you would like to go to Fort Benjamin Harris. The people in this office will determine where you are needed, and Vietnam is where you'll go."

"No, Sergeant Major, unless you send me to Fort Benning, you can discharge me from the Army.

"If necessary, I'll go there as a civilian. One way or the other, I'm going to Fort Benning in February." Joe asserted his demand.

"Oh, your enlistment is up, and you want to re-up for a duty assignment." Mr. Yates changed his story.

"Duty assignment and cash, Sergeant Major. The reenlistment bonus for a Staff Sergeant is close to six thousand dollars. Isn't it? If I'm staying in the Army, I'm not going to give that up."

"I understand, Staff Sergeant. I'll do the best I can to fill your request. You know the final decision will come from my superiors, and they don't like being dictated to."

"I understand, and thanks. You were extremely helpful to me before. I'm sure you'll take care of me this time."

"Why Fort Benning?"

"It's a personal reason."

"I see, Staff Sergeant. I'll pull your files today and get back with you early tomorrow morning by 0800 hours. Be prepared to answer the phone there at 1300 hours, your time."

"Can-do, Sergeant Major. Again, thanks." Joe hung up the phone.

The next day Joe did not have to wait long. He answered the phone when it rang at exactly 1330 hours. "EOD, this is Staff Sergeant Hébert. How may I help you?"

"Yes, Staff Sergeant, this is Yates, and I'll get right to it. The EOD folks are playing hardball. They want your butt in Vietnam. If you are in EOD, it's where you'll go. They say there isn't an open position at Fort Ben."

"Then I won't be assigned to an EOD position. I'll pull my hazardous duty volunteer statement."

Joe had prepared for this. He knew they could not assign him to an EOD unit without him volunteering to perform hazardous duty.

"You would pull your statement?" Yates couldn't believe this.

"I love EOD. But yes, in a heartbeat! Maybe later I can sign another statement and be assigned back into EOD."

"I don't see a secondary MOS listed in your military records. I'm sure you would be issued an infantryman's MOS."

"You can assign a paratrooper's MOS to me and assign me to the jump school at Fort Ben. I'm well qualified. I have approximately one-hundred sixty-five documented jumps. Eighty percent those jumps are free falls. I'll bet, over half of the Jump Master's at Fort Ben have less. I believe the school can use someone with this kind of experience." Joe had planned well.

"I'll talk with the school. I don't doubt your word but get me a copy of the jump records."

"They'll be faxed to you by this time tomorrow." Joe had easy access to a fax machine.

"If we can get the school's approval, you'll have your orders by Christmas. If you have not received orders by then, give me a call. And, Staff Sergeant, do not pull your volunteer statement. I'll manage EOD's threat from this end." Yates worked the angle like any good NCO, retired or not.

"Okay, Sergeant Major, I'll sit tight. But be sure to make those eggheads you work for, understand, I'm serious. It's Fort Ben or I'm out." Joe sounded emphatically.

"You know, this is poking somebody in the eye. Your name will be remembered." Yates wanted to be sure Joe knew the consequences of his actions.

"You're probably correct. I want to stay in the Army. But for now, I need to be assigned to Fort Ben." Joe restated his position.

"I've seen this situation before. Your personal reason must be a woman."

"Dumb guys don't get promoted to Sergeant Major. I'll be waiting for my orders. Thanks a lot." Joe hung up the phone.

Normally, three or four months would not be hard. However, the past three months had been exceedingly long and strenuous for Joe. Ava had written every week. He had not written to her. In her first letter, she asked that he not write to her, until she could provide him with a safe address.

Apparently, the time went slowly for her as well. Once settled in military housing, she found she had nothing to do and knew no one. There had been Officers' functions which she and her husband attended. But she felt out of place.

To alleviate her boredom, she took a job at the Post Exchange (PX). There, she had made friends with the NCO wives who worked there.

She had promised to call before Christmas, but as of today Joe had received no calls.

On December 2, 1967, exactly three months after speaking with Sergeant Major Yates, Joe received three copies of written orders in the mail. His heart leapt as he read; To: Staff Sergeant Joseph A. Hébert. You are assigned to the Fourth Airborne Training Battalion, United States Army Infantry School, Fort Benjamin Harrison, Georgia, effective February 1, 1968.

There was more to read, but that would wait until later. He laid the orders aside, took a deep breath, crossed his heart, and said, "Thank you, Lord. Thank you, Lord." Only two more months, Baby. Two more months. It struck him; *it will be only a month. I will take thirty days leave and see you shortly after the first of the year.*

He grabbed a copy of the orders and headed for Top's office.

"Joe, is that what you have been looking for? Have a seat." Top leaned back in his chair.

"Yes, Master Sergeant. As I requested, I report to Fort Ben on the first of February. I will take thirty days leave and hope to get out of here before the New Year."

"Joe, I know the Sergeant Major over at personnel. With travel time, I'm sure they can get you on a plane no later than the twenty-seventh of December."

"That would be great!" Joe took a deep, wishful breath and slowly exhaled.

"OK, Joe. Grab the leave papers, fill them out, and get them back to me, ASAP. I'll get the Commander to approve them."

"I'm on it." Joe stood to leave.

"Joe, remember, we start half days, for the holidays, a week from Monday. So, you don't have long to get ready to leave."

"Top. If my plane was ready, I could be on it tomorrow. Thanks for your assistance." Joe turned and left the office.

After lunch, on the last Friday, before the half day holiday schedule started, Joe was sitting at Top's desk, reading his newspaper. The phone rang. He lifted the receiver, placed both elbows on the desk, and reached for a pen to take notes. He said, "EOD, this is Staff Sergeant Hébert. May I Help You?"

"Joe, it is Ava."

A shot of adrenalin flushed over him. He felt the warmth affecting his entire body. He swallowed and said, "Ava!"

"Yes, Joe, and I still love and miss you."

He closed his eyes and said, "Thank you, God. Ava, your voice sounds great. And hearing those three words is refreshing."

Ava softly replied, "Yours as well."

"Oh, girl, you don't know how much I have missed you. As you should know, I love you. Thank you for writing every week. I think your letters saved my sanity."

"There was not much in them, but I had no news from you. I did not even know if you were dead or alive. You promised to see me around the first of February. Are you going to be able to come. I surely hope so. It is only six weeks away. I have been counting them,"

"Well quit counting weeks and start counting days. The good news is, I have my orders, assigning me to Fort Ben, with a reporting date on the first of February. Better news is, I have thirty days of leave approved. I'll likely see you shortly after the first of January. Everything depends on my flight from here. It hasn't been scheduled yet."

"Joe, you are not kidding me, are you?"

"Not about something as important as this. The next two weeks are going to be extremely long. I have already packed my bags, except for my fatigues and shaving kit. Of course, I didn't have much to pack. I only need my ticket, ten minutes to sign out, and an hour to get to Rhein Main Airport."

"Joe, I am at a friend's home. Write this number down and call it the minute you get to the States." She gave him the phone number and continued. "You can leave a message with my friend. I trust her. I have told her about you. She offered to let me call you from her apartment. I will reimburse her for this call. I had saved two roles of quarters to use when I called you."

"Ava, is there any way you can get away for a couple of days?"

"No. But I can see you while he Is working. I am sure that I can get somebody to take my hours at work. We can find time to be together, but not at night. I will find you a suitable motel close by."

"We will work it out when I'm there. But I need to go to Louisiana for a few days to see my mother." He did not tell her, but he would fulfill a promise to Pam by stopping by to see her for an hour.

"Joe, I need to get off the line. The overseas calls are expensive, and I need to be at work in thirty minutes."

"Okay, Baby. Thanks for calling. You know I love you. I'll see you soon."

"The same here. Love you. I'm looking forward to being in your arms. Bye for now." Ava placed the phone on the receiver.

CHAPTER 11

Joe stood in the middle of Friar Drop Zone, Fort Benning, Georgia, an unusually cool morning, for this time in the middle of August 968. A tropical storm churned in the Gulf of Mexico, which created gusts of wind from the south up to twenty-seven miles per hour. The airborne students' schedule had been compressed to get all five of the required jumps in before the wind conditions became too high and dangerous to jump. The high winds could cause the parachute to drag the students when they hit ground. The final plane had already taken off from Lawson's Field and would be over the drop zone within five minutes.

After the last stick had exited the plane, and all the jumpers were safe on the ground, Joe would have the rest of the day off for personnel time. He could hardly wait to see Ava.

Joe thought about how well things had been. The last seven months had been the best of his life. However, his EOD experience had taught him to always think about the worst possibility. The little voice in his head constantly reminded him, life could not always be these good, and dreadful things, happens. But as of right now, he would like to be with Ava more. He could take this life. Lately, he was seeing her three times a week.

He had seen Ava at least twice a week since his arrival from Germany the first week of January.

As promised, he first stopped in D.C. to see Pam for dinner. The next day he flew to Columbus, Georgia, Fort Benning. He spent four days in a motel, where Ava visited him every moment she could. He then went home to the Bayou to see his mother before reporting in at Fort Ben.

Pam looked great and appeared happy, even bubbly. She wore the shortest skirt he had ever seen on a woman. She told him, she was dating a law student, and she enjoyed college life at Georgetown. They only took time for dinner, wished each other good luck, and promised to keep in touch.

At home in Louisiana, he noticed his mother had aged during the last few years. Even more surprisingly, she had a man in her life. Joe did not meet him but approved of his mothers' relationship with him. After all, if his mother cared for a good man, why should Joe complain.

On reporting for duty at Fort Ben, seeing Ava at least three times a week elated him. He liked his new job as a Jump Master. He had visited the EOD unit regularly and knew all the guys.

He worked extensively with student paratroopers, consisting mostly of young enlistees and young officers. Because of his dedication, and his skydiving experience, his Battalion Commander appeared pleased with him.

Joe could not understand the lack of skydiving experience his fellow Jump Masters had. His encouragement to the NCOs to get involved, and his ability to teach skydiving fundamentals were promptly and pleasantly noted by the higher-ups. As a result, he could feel the respect from his co-workers.

Standing on the drop zone this cool August morning, Joe's attention turned, as he heard the roar of the twin engines of the C-119s approaching. The planes, Fairchild's flying boxcars, were developed and put into service in the late 1940s. Therefore, they were old and worn out.

The student paratroopers often complained about watching rivets fall out of the fuselage while racing down the runway before takeoff. As a result, they thought jumping out for the plane created the safest choice than continuing the flight. The planes had been pressed into service because the newer C-130s, which were previously used by the school, where now being used more efficiently in Vietnam.

Due to the wind conditions this morning, the planes were over the southeastern edge of Friar Field, at an altitude of fourteen hundred feet. The wind would carry the paratroopers to the desired area of the drop zone.

Joe watched as white parachutes began to pop open below and aft of each plane as the student jumpers bailed out. His attention suddenly focused on one of the paratroopers. His parachute did not deploy correctly.

"Oh crap, a Mae West!" Joe shouted and hoped the student had learned his lessons well.

He had. Joe saw the white reserve parachute, but it did not correctly deploy as designed. Joe sprinted downhill toward the area where a young paratrooper would hit the ground, hard. *Murphy's Law,* Joe thought as he could see the student jumper struggling with his reserve which refused to correctly deploy.

Joe could do nothing but watch and think the worst. Amazingly, only feet above the ground, the main parachute popped open and slowed the jumper's descent no more than five seconds before he hit the ground.

"Are you alright?" Joe spoke to the jumper as he reached the young man collecting his chute.

"Yeah, Staff Sergeant, air boune!" The reply came from the jumper.

"Pvt. Brown, you scared the crap out of me." Joe read the young man's name tag and rank on his shirt.

"Yas, Staff Sergeant, I's okay. It scaid me too. But de Good Loud took kare of me. The Good Loud hear me. He nos my work is not done. After I's jumped, I's count to fou and looks up, laks the sergeants taught me, nutting happun. I's look up agen and see druble. So lis pull dat razerve and it went poof. It went aut and den cum bak and waped round me. So, I's chunk it aut dare agen and de same ding happun." Private Brown gestured with his hands and arms as he told his story.

"Private Brown, you are one lucky SOB. If you had landed two hundred feet up the hill, you would've had major problems. Your parachute wouldn't have opened in time. Where are you from?" Joe investigated the blackest face he had ever seen. A face which could never be forgotten.

"I's from Lake Village, Arkansas. And, Staff Sergeant, dat good luck had nutten to do wid it. The Good Loud take kare of me all my life. I's go to church all day, erery Sunday, and on Wednesday night. I's read de Bible erery day, and I's pray erery day. I's nere use the Loud's name in vain, nere drank nor smoke nutted bad. And you nos, Staff Sergeant, ain't nun of dat dime been wasted."

"I won't argue with you. But now, you're through, and you have earned your jump wings. Where are you going when you leave Fort Ben?"

"I's goin' to Nam, Staff Sergeant, Ninth Division." Brown beamed with pleasure.

"Vietnam. I surely hope your good luck continues. Let's get your gear over to the buses. You have to attend a graduation ceremony, and I have places to go." Joe helped private Brown finish gathering the parachute and walked with him to the collection point.

Joe droves back to the main post. He had picked up his old 1955 Ford pickup truck when in Louisiana to see his mother in January. He had it tuned up and the tires changed. It drove perfectly.

He stopped at the PX for a bit of lunch and called Ava to make sure he could come over.

Joe parked his truck, a long block, away from Ava's residence. The red post sticker on his truck bumper, signifying enlisted personnel, would have stood out parked in officers' quarters where blue stickers prevailed.

As he always did when visiting Ava, he carried a clipboard and pen. He walked down the alley behind the quarters, pausing briefly to check occasional trash cans. No one would think oddly of an NCO checking to ensure a prompt trash pick-up. Upon checking Ava's trash can, he calmly walked to her back door.

The back door entered the kitchen of the red brick semidetached house where he saw Ava.

She wore a long light-blue terrycloth gown. Her long hair flowed below her shoulder blades.

"Hi, beautiful." Joe said, as he entered. He wore his fatigues uniform.

"Hi, handsome." Ava closed the door quickly behind them.

"Are you sure we're safe?" Joe cautiously looked around as he put his arms around Ava.

"Yes, he has a staff meeting this afternoon which will last a couple of hours. And he never comes home early."

"Then, I'll be out of here in two hours. The question is, what will we do for two hours?"

"We can sit in the living room and watch the soaps, if you like, or--"

"I like the or option." Joe interrupted and pulled her closer to him.

"Or we can sit in the living room and talk, or--" She tried to finish.

"I'll take the or option, thank you!"

"Or, we could go upstairs, and--" Ava said with a big smile.

"You have it! I'll take the upstairs option any day."

"First, remove those soiled boots. I do not need the dust all over my house. Place them by the door." She pushed him away and pointed at the floor and headed hurriedly upstairs.

Joe did as he was directed and followed her up the stairs, where he found Ava pulled the bed linens down. She was already undressed. "Lady, what do you have on your mind? I thought we were coming up here to sit and talk."

"We can sit and talk or do whatever you would like." Ava smiled broadly.

"It looks like I'm a little late for the party, but you can continue with what you're doing. And then, we'll decide what to do," Joe spoke with a burly voice, while pulling his fatigues off and dropping them on the floor just inches inside the bedroom door.

After making love, as usual, Joe wanted to take a nap, and Ava wanted to talk. Ava shook him and asked about his morning.

He told her about Private Brown and tried to nap again.

This time Ava asked, "What are you doing tomorrow?" Joe leaned on his elbow and looked at Ava, "If you want to talk, let's talk about something more meaningful."

"Okay, like what?" Ava sounded perky.

"Like, what are you doing for the rest of your life?" Joe looked seriously at Ava.

"The rest of my life? I'm not sure that I know what you mean?" She shook her head.

"I'm, I'm? You are becoming Americanized. This the first time I can remember hearing you use a contraction."

"Oh, God, what is happening to me?" She sounded flabbergasted.

"Yes, what is happening to you is exactly what I want to know. What is going to happen to you for the rest of your life? What is going to happen to us, you, and me?" Joe stared deeply into her blue eyes.

"You are serious! I have certainly given it some thought, but I do not know." Ava looked away.

"Ava, you know, I love you, with all my heart and soul. I don't like sharing you.

Before Ava could comment, they both heard a siren close by. "The MP's must be after someone." Ava glanced at the window.

"Don't change the subject. I want you all to myself. I want you to leave your husband. I can take care of you, albeit, not by Officer standards." Joe paused and listened to the siren as it got closer.

"Joe, I love you, too. You know that. And I have thought about leaving my husband. It would be atrociously hard and so messy." She stopped and raised up "What is going on out there? The siren is on our street. It is right outside."

"Don't worry about it. Whatever it is, it doesn't concern us. You're not getting out of this conversation because, something is going on out there. Yes, divorcing your husband will be hard and nasty. But it's doable. It happens every day, and we could be together, forever."

They both suddenly jumped at the noise coming from downstairs. "Ava, Ava, Ava, are you here!" A male voice yelled.

"Oh, God, it is McCoy!" Ava jumped up.

They could hear him climbing the stairs, taking two steps at a time.

"Go!" She waved at Joe. Still necked, she stood on her side of the bed.

Joe jumped to his feet, on the opposite side, where he remained until Lieutenant Colonel McCoy rushed into the bedroom.

"What? What, the hell! You bitch!" He yelled and headed toward Ava.

Joe stepped forward to confront the Lieutenant Colonel.

Ava looked at Joe and yelled, "Go!"

As McCoy reached her. Joe hesitated and then obeyed. Begrudgingly, he headed for the stairs and the door. Taking the flight three steps at a time, he could hear loud yells and something breaking. Then he opened the back door and took two steps out where he heard a child's voice. "Mama! Mama! The man has no cloths on!"

Then, Joe noticed the Military Police jeep, a fire truck, and smoke coming from the adjacent housing.

As he searched for the little girl whom he heard, he could see at least a dozen people staring at him.

Back inside, Joe realized he had to retrieve his cloths from upstairs, where the screaming and cursing were still raging. He moved his boots to the front door and crept carefully up the stairs. Ava and the Lieutenant Colonel, with his back to the door, were facing each other. Ava remained on her side of the bed, and they were still screaming at each other. Quietly and hurriedly, Joe gathered his fatigue jacket, trousers, and underwear. He again moved to confront the Lieutenant Colonel. Ava's eyes met his and she told him, "No!"

The Lieutenant Colonel noticed her look and turned to see Joe standing in the door. Rather than charging Joe, the Lieutenant Colonel headed for the nightstand on the opposite side of the bed.

Ava's nude body flew across the bed to attack him. Joe intuitively knew what it meant. Four steps later, brought Joe to the foot of the stairs, where he could put his underwear and pants on.

Before he could finish dressing the upstairs door darkened.

The deafening explosion splintered the door facing inches from Joe's head. His ears rang and the left side of his face and neck felt as if he had been attacked by a swarm of bees.

A second later, he dashed outside the front door, carrying his boots and running down the street as fast as he could.

After reaching his truck, he checked over his shoulder to be sure no one followed him. When satisfied, he jumped into his truck and pulled out of the parking lot. He noticed. the blood on his clothes and remembered the stinging sensation. A quick glance in the rearview mirror revealed a bloody mess, with splinters sticking in his face and neck. He did not drive far before pulling into another parking lot to collect his thoughts about the situation.

Now, his body shook, and he tried to think. *Will McCoy harm her? An officer and gentleman wouldn't. But McCoy? Yeah! Should*

I go back? No, it's out of the question. The SOB shot at me and barely missed! But more importantly his mind raced back to Ava. *Should I call the MP's or someone else? No, the MPs were outside with the fire trucks. They had to have heard the shot and the screaming and would have investigated. If the SOB intended to hurt Ava, the MPs would intervene in the struggle and protect her if they made it in time!*

Joe realized; he could do nothing for Ava. *But what can I do for myself is the question*, he pondered to himself. *After all, one of the Deputy Post Commander took a shot at me, maybe justifiably so!*

Does McCoy know who I am? No way to tell. If he knows, he knows. If not, nothing to worry about. How badly am I hurt? No gushing blood, so it's only superficial. Should I go back to the barracks? No, too risky. Where can I go? I don't know. I'll have to think about it. Where can I get first aid? Hospital? No, too many questions. Whom can I rely on for help? Only close friends. No one in the chain of command, only friends.

Joe now knew where to go. *Now, the easy questions were answered, the two toughest ones remained! How am I going to clean up the mess with McCoy? More important, what is going to happen between me and Ava?*

CHAPTER 12

The sign over the door read, 'Restricted Area Authorized Personnel Only'.

Almost as soon as Joe mashed the doorbell, a smiling young soldier dressed in fatigues, unlocked, and opened the door.

"Staff Sergeant Hébert, what the hell happened to you?"

"It's a long story. Is Top, the senior NCO, in?" Joe asked and sighed.

"He's in a training session." The freckled-face Specialist continued to look concerned.

"EOD training, pinochle, poker, or pool?" Joe tried to smile.

"Pool. Come on in. Let's see what we can do about getting you cleaned up." The Specialist led the way.

"Holy crap, Joe! What have you done to yourself?" The six-foot Master Sergeant asker with a Midwestern accent as he rushed to meet Joe. He and everybody else were dressed in fatigues and wore their hair high and tight.

"We can talk about it later. Can I get a shower and some clean clothes? Also, who' s your best doctor? I need to get these damn splinters out." Joe pointed to the left side of his face and neck.

"Specialist, get the first aid kit. You've got me for a doctor. But I recommend you go over to the emergency room. I know, I know, you have sense enough to think of that. For some reason you don't want to go get first aid. Maybe you should jump into the shower first. Then, I can see what I'm working with when I pull those splinters out." Top grinned at the thought of this. The smile accented his large nose.

"Thanks. That sounds fine. Is the captain in?" Joe nodded toward the captain's office.

"Yes, he's here."

"Ask the captain if he can see me before he leaves. Would you do that?"

"Sure, Joe. Now, get the dried blood washed off. I'll get you a pair of shorts to put on. After you get your shower, come to my office, and we'll get the stuff out of your face and neck. You don't have any in your ass, do you? We all would enjoy pulling them out and taking turns doing it." Top gave Joe an evil smile.

It took Joe longer to shower than he expected. He could not rub his neck. Running water over the dried blood took a while for it to dissolve. When Joe arrived in Top's small office, he wore only flip-flops and a pair of boxer shorts. Top had waited patiently with a quart of alcohol, bandages, and a pair of tweezers.

"Come on, sit in my chair by the window and lean back. I sent your clothes to the laundry. Your wallet, keys, and stuff are in the captain's office." Top brought Joe up to date.

"That's fine, and thanks. Let's get started." Joe sat down and accepted his fate.

It was not pleasant, but Joe had undergone much worse pain in the past. After a little while, Top said. "Okay, I think this will do. There is no need for stitches. Only three of those suckers gave me any trouble. I'm sure you know which ones I'm talking about. I hope I got all the splinters out. If they fester up, you'll know I didn't do a very good job. I still recommend that you go have a professional look at your neck. If there is something in it, and it starts moving around, it may cause you problems. That type of thing happens all the time, only to be found years later." Top stepped back and examined his work.

"Thanks Master Sergeant, it'll be fine, and I'm sure you did an outstanding job. I may have trouble when I try shaving tomorrow. I'm grateful I don't have manly whiskers. Anyway, I'll take your work anytime."

"I did the best I could with what I had to work with. Are you ready to see the captain?"

"Yeah, let's go." Joe slowly nodded.

"Come in and have a seat," the five-ten studious looking Officer waived them in.

Joe and Top did as they were directed by Captain Taylor.

"Joe, Top tells me you been trying to kiss a porcupine's ass, and you want to tell me about how the experience turned out."

"Well, Sir, it didn't exactly happen while playing with a porcupine." Joe tried to smile.

"I can't imagine what you need to talk to me about. You know, I would normally ask Top what I should say and do," Captain Taylor smiled and shrugged.

"Yes, Sir, I understand, but I have a problem. I think. Your collective wisdom will be helpful."

"Spill it. But first, you're not going to tell me, you've done something illegal. Assault, dope, or anything similar, are you? If so, I don't want to know." All smiles were gone from Captain Taylor's face which now showed seriousness.

"No, Sir, but it might be worse." Joe tried to smile again and shook his head.

"Okay, then, let's go. Let me have it." Top jumped in. "Let's start with, what happened to your face and neck?"

"It's the result of, I would guess, a 45-Magnum aimed at and intended for my head but hitting a door facing inches away." This time Joe spoke slowly with a serious tone.

The Captain and Top gaped, sat stunned, and motionless for a couple of moment. "A 45-Mag!" Top finally whispered. "This begs an explanation of who shot at you, why, and where? We already know, what and when."

"You came here, and not to the MPs?" The captain at once responded and adjusted his Army issued, black rimmed glasses.

Joe had both their undivided attentions. However, as the senior officer he directed his statements toward Captain Taylor. "Sir. I need friendly advice, straight thinking, not law enforcement. I know you're not in my chain of command, but that is probably good. Over the last few months, you've made me feel as if I was a member of your unit. I consider all of you very good friends, and right now, friends are what I need."

Top said, "Okay, but let's start with answering who did it, and we can go from there."

Joe looked at the two of them and gave them an answer, "Lieutenant Colonel McCoy."

Again, Top and the captain were stunned. Finally, Top swallowed and asked, "Who are you talking about?"

Before Joe could answer, Captain Taylor spoke. "It would probably be Lieutenant Colonel McCoy, who will be a Full Bull within the next couple of months. He's high up the chain. Joe, please tell me you're not talking about him or tell me you're kidding."

Joe grimaced, shook his head, and admitted, "He's the one! He's from the Office of the Deputy Post Commander."

"Okay, Joe, you probably shouldn't get me too involved. I might have to testify at your court martial. However, to give you my honest opinion, I need to know why and where. If you want to continue, I'll listen," Captain Taylor sounded cautiously.

"The answer to where it occurred is, it was in his quarters." Joe closed his eyes and exhaled, as he replied.

"It was in his quarters! What, the hell kind of business did you have in his quarters?" Top snapped.

"Well, it wasn't exactly business," Joe responded sheepishly.

"Not exactly business!" Captain Taylor sat straight up in his chair. "What do you mean?"

"Joe, you're a damn idiot! He should've put the bullet squarely between your ears. That way, it would've done no harm as you have nothing up there!" Top vociferously and stared at Joe with an incredulous look.

"Top, what are you talking about?" Taylor looked directly at him.

Joe leaned back in his chair and remained silent.

"Captain, there's only one reason for him being there. Joe got caught banging the Colonel's wife."

Oooh crap! "No wonder you didn't want to involve the MP's. They would have found a reason to put your ass in jail. On the other hand, I don't think they can get you for a UCMJ violation for fraternization or adultery. Since you're not married, and she is not in the service, there's probably no violation to the Uniform Code of Military Justice. Although, I wouldn't like to bet five to eight years in Leavenworth on it." The captain argued.

Joe finally spoke. "There are two things which are important here. I'm sure the MPs are involved. When the shot was fired, they were outside the quarters on another matter. They surely investigated. Secondly, the Lieutenant Colonel probably doesn't know who I am. Today was the first time I have seen him, and I don't think he has ever lay eyes on me before. Needless to say, he only saw me briefly, and I should add briefs less. He was not thinking right, and I'm sure he couldn't read my name tag, as I had no clothes on when he got his best look at me."

"Joe, you're right. You need friendly advice. You, of course, know what it's worth. You also need JAG advice. I don't recommend you obtain the advice from the local office here at Fort Ben."

Captain Taylor tried to be the friend Joe looked for and give him good advice.

"Captain, I know it's not quite quitting time yet, but I need a beer. I know there's some in your fridge."

Without hesitation Captain Taylor firmly ordered, "Top, make it a half dozen."

Joe and Captain Taylor sat quietly waiting on Top. When he returned with a six pack, Top demurely said, "Joe, I don't know what I can do for you. I know the Sergeant Major over at the Jump School, and I know the post, Sergeant Major. I can talk with them. I'm sure they'll do anything they can to help you.

"Hell, they might write you up for some kind of achievement award, especially if the lady we're talking about is the good-looking blonde who works at the PX. I think her name is McCoy and her husband is an Officer."

"Top, not so fast on talking with the Sergeant Majors. If we need their help, we have time for it later," Taylor used a placating tone as he rubbed his temples.

Right now, I think the fewer people who knows about this, the better. I think it would be smart to keep it this way for as long as possible."

Joe sat still and did not reply. He merely rubbed his bare thighs with both hands.

"Joe, like Top said, there's nothing we can do, except give you some logistical support: a place to stay, the use of a phone, and a shower until this thing blows over. As for my advice, it's simple, run as fast as you can. Get your ass off this post ASAP, and don't look back. I don't mean for you to go AWAL.

"Somehow go on leave, or better yet, get reassigned. It may not seem necessary, but eventually, the higher ups will learn who you are. When they learn your name, if they want you, your ass belongs to them." Captain Taylor astutely summarized Joe's fate.

"Thank you, Sir. That sounds like good advice to me. I feel shameful, sitting here in your office half naked, with a problem such as this one." Joe hung his head down, staring at the floor.

"No problem, Joe. Your EOD brothers are here to help. However, I recommend you stay away from our wives!" The captain jokingly admonished him. "You two guys finish the beer. I'm out of here." Captain Taylor stood and walked out of the office.'

Top and Joe stood as the captain walked out.

"Top, if it's okay with you, I think I'll stay here tonight. I'll call my company and tell the First Sergeant; I had a small accident and will not be in tomorrow. I'll think on the situation and make a decision later."

"Let's have another one, or two, or three, while we wait on your clothes. But don't get too friendly. I don't like being in the same room with a man who is half-naked." Top smiled and raised his beer.

CHAPTER 13

"Enlisted Personnel Management, this is Specialist Torres, how may I help you?" The Hispanic voice of a young man answered the phone.

"Yes, this is Staff Sergeant, Joseph A. Hébert, may I speak with Sergeant Major Yates?"

"One moment, please." Specialist Torres quickly replied.

Within seconds, Joe heard, "Staff Sergeant Hébert, didn't I speak with you a couple months ago?"

"It was last December, Sergeant Major. I called to let you know that I received my orders."

"How time passes. If I remember correctly, you extorted me into sending you to Fort Ben. You are there now, I trust?"

"Yes, Sergeant Major, that's why I'm calling you."

"To thank me, I presume. I don't need your thanks for doing my job, Staff Sergeant."

"That's not exactly why I'm calling you."

"Okay, Staff Sergeant, what do you need this time?" Yates' crisp voice sounded friendly.

"I need a transfer. I must get off this post. I understand, I'm not due for a transfer. But it is an emergency."

"Emergency! Everybody has an emergency when they call this office. When dealing with NCOs, you can hardly use emergencies without a woman in the same sentence. If I recall correctly, a woman is the reason you originally wanted to go to Fort Ben. If this is all you've got, you're wasting your time with me." Yates huffed.

"To be truthful, Sergeant Major, well... if I stay here, I may get killed or have to kill someone."

"Hébert, this sounds exactly like an emergency to me. But I need to know more. You haven't done anything stupid like an assault on somebody have you?"

"No, not at all. It's not quite so simple as you may think. it so happens, one of the Deputy Post Commanders, a promotable LTC, took a shot at me yesterday afternoon." Joe tried to be factual.

"Woe! If I heard you correctly, that's a real emergency." Joe surely had Yates' attention.

"You heard me correctly. Other than him missing, the good part of the story is, he probably doesn't know who I am, yet. Although, he'll find out sooner or later. I don't need to tell you; I need him to find out when I'm out of his reach."

"Are you sure you're not wanted by law enforcement? Is there a warrant out with your name on it? Sergeant, you must be honest with me. I don't need any aiding and abetting charges lodged against me."

"No, but as you suggested, it's about a woman, his wife."

"Damn, I knew it! You young guys will never learn. Well, it's done now. Yes, you need to get reassigned at once. We should be able to promptly manage it.

"Give me a second. I need to see whom I can call." The wait took only a minute before Yates returned to the phone. "Staff Sergeant Hébert, do you know First Sergeant Martin at your personnel office?"

I think I have met him. But know him, no, I don't."

"I'll give him a call. How can I contact you?"

"I'm at the EOD unit here on post. I have discussed this matter with the Commander and the senior NCO. Other than them, you are the only person with knowledge of the facts. And if it's possible, I'd like to keep it that way," Joe sounded wishful, as he gave Yates the unit's phone number.

"I'll do my best, especially with First Sergeant Martin. I'll tell him nothing. The story does not need to get out there at Fort Ben. All he needs to know is, he'll cut your orders right now as directed by Department of Army.

"You know we'll be sending you to Vietnam. That shouldn't bother you because, you would be going there next February."

"I thought Vietnam was in the cards for me. Can you get me back in EOD?" Again, Joe hoped for the best.

"I'm sure I can manage that. Right now, stay where you are. If you haven't heard from me within an hour, go over to Martin's office. I'll make sure he is expecting you. Oh, and start making plans. I want you on a plane, headed west tomorrow. So, get moving."

"I started making arrangements as soon as I saw the gun. And Sergeant Major, thanks."

"You have no need to thank me. It's what I do to put food on the table. Staff Sergeant Hébert, while you're over there, keep your head down." Yates hung up.

While waiting the hour as instructed, Joe talked with Captain Taylor and Top again. "I'm going to Personnel to see First Sergeant Martin to get my orders. It looks as if I'll be headed to Vietnam tomorrow, unless otherwise directed within the next hour."

"You're fast." Top jumped in.

"Yes, you must know somebody in Personnel Management." Taylor looked surprised.

"I talked to a retired Sergeant Major who works at DA's, Enlisted Personnel Management. He's pulled some strings for me before."

"Joe, what do you need from us?" Taylor looked sincere.

"I'm doing nothing, until I get orders in my hand. Afterwards, I need only to clean my room at the barracks, get my records, and sign out at the company. I'll need somewhere to leave my truck and personal possessions. I'd appreciate any suggestions." Joe looked back and forth at the two of them.

Top spoke. "I have forty acres of land and a large barn out at my place. You can leave your stuff there. I'll start your truck once a month. It'll help to keep it running while you're gone. I'll not guarantee anything else. You should be aware; I have some big ass rats out there."

Captain Taylor suggested, "You may also need a ride to Atlanta, to the airport."

"I'll arrange for it. If I have to do it myself, I'll drive you there." Top looked at Joe and nodded his head.

"Okay. You don't know how deeply I appreciate it." Joe nodded again.

"Joe, if anything else arises, all you have to do is say something," Captain Taylor said assuredly.

Joe leaned back in his chair. "Sir, maybe there is one more thing. Can you get someone over to the PX and see if Ava, Mrs. McCoy, is at work and if she is, okay?"

Captain Taylor quickly responded. "Joe, I thought you'd want to know. I've already checked. She's not at work and has not called the office today."

Not knowing Ava's situation did not settle well with Joe, but he had no other choice. Going to Vietnam may be his only way to get a transfer from Fort Banning, like it or not. For right now, this is the best for both of us. I hope and pray, McCoy hadn't done anything harmful to Ava.

Also important, I hope she understands that I'm not running away from her.

CHAPTER 14

Joe boarded the Boeing 707, at the Atlanta International Airport. He vividly remembered, a little more than 48 hours ago, he shared a bed with Ava. He had no idea about her current mental or physical condition. He knew of nothing he could do but worry and pray for her. He would have to go with the flow and fly to Oakland, California. From there, he would board a military contract airplane, along with well more than two hundred Officers, NCOs, and mostly drafted enlisted personnel, headed to Vietnam.

Once leaving Oakland, he had a flight greater than thirty hours remaining, counting stops in: Honolulu, Hawaii; a paradise island with a significant World War II history, an abundance of flowers, blue skies, and surrounded by the blue waters of the Pacific Ocean, Wake Island; another significant World War II site, which is an extremely small V-shaped island with a spectacular turquoise colored lagoon, and Clark Air Force Base in the Philippines; a major player and source of America's military power projected into Southeast Asia. Joe had nothing to do but think about Ava's condition and about going to war.

Most people think the Vietnam war started when the evening news began to talk about it in 1963.

If Joe's memory served him correct, one could certainly argue the war began years earlier when President Roosevelt refused Ho Chi Minh's request for help in countering the Japanese invasion of Vietnam. After the Japanese were ousted by the Vietnamese, the French returned with all intention of reestablishing control over French Indochina, or Southeast Asia. Ho Chi Minh would not hear to this, and war broke out between the two countries. Seizing the opportunity, China soon came to the aid of Ho Chi Minh.

In 1950, President Truman developed the Military Assistance Advisory Group (MAAG) in Vietnam to advise and help the French with military equipment, supplies, and accompanying personnel to staff the MAAG.

However, the French wanted to do it their way. General Henri Navarre, the Commander of the French forces did not want a strong standing Vietnamese Army (VNA). It would complicate France's interests, especially his seat in power.

After the French were defeated at Dien Bien Phu, their aspiration of a new French Indochina ceased to exist. This resulted in the country being divided into a communist North and a noncommunist South by the 1954 Geneva agreement. Soon, all French troops were out of Southeast Asia.

Because of the Domino Theory, whose thesis prophesied, if one country fell to a communist's nation, the neighboring countries will subsequently fall. Using this and the established authority of the newly formed Southeast Asia Treaty Organization (SEATO), President Eisenhower filling the void left by the French by sending in US military advisers. He increased the size of the previously established MAAG mission.

During the late 1950s, the National Liberation Front (NFL), better known as Viet Cong (VC), gained power.

South Vietnam's President, Ngo Dinh Dien, a Catholic, held religious differences with his Buddhist citizens. Dien essentially believed all the Buddhists population aided and abetted the VC. He took repressive actions to control this problem. His actions created a situation which threatened the stability of the region.

By 1962, President Kennedy had increased financial aid and the number of US military advisers and had created the Military Advisory Command Vietnam (MACV). He also had sent special forces troops into harm's way. VP Johnson had even visited Vietnam. Efforts were made to get Dien to control his administration's corruption and to implement political and economic reforms.

By 1963, the American Administration became furious with Dien's lack of progress and asked him to resign. He refused. After being advised by US officials Robert McNamara, George Bundy, Henry Cabot Lodge, Jr., and others, many people highly suspected President Kennedy gave permission for a coupe to overthrow Dien.

After President Kennedy's assassination, Vietnam became Johnson's war.

In 1964, the Gulf of Tonkin incident occurred, where the USS Maddox and the USS Turner Joy were reportedly attacked by North

Vietnam. The U.S. Congress authorized President Johnson to essentially wage all-out war on North Vietnam.

As the US forces built to more than three hundred thousand in the next four years, the US assumed and more of the war effort. During this time, press coverage of the war had created an adverse relationship with public support. As press coverage continuously damned the war effort, and public support continually decreased to the point of rioting in the streets. The Johnson Administration did not know whether they should crap or get off the pot.

This environment and circumstance are where Staff Sergeant Hébert found himself, flying five-hundred miles per hour over the South China Sea at thirty thousand feet, heading headlong into a war zone. After more than thirty hours, including stops of flying, sunset and darkness approached, Joe could see the Vietnamese coastline as the plane passed over it.

The pilot spoke over the intercom. "Welcome to Vietnam, Gentlemen. We'll be arriving in about fifteen minutes. Prior to landing, you'll notice a fast and deep descent. This is normal and nothing to worry about. Immediately after leveling off, we'll touch down. Afterwards, you'll be off the plane within ten minutes. With this information, I wish you all good luck, and may God bless each and every one of you."

Jor had flown over a hundred times, but the ear-popping descent was the steepest he had experienced. The long trip had taken its effect on Joe. He could smell his own body odor. His body ached. Even if it meant getting out of the airplane in a war zone, he wanted out. His thoughts were quickly directed to large flashes of distance, flashed of light. He wondered what they could be. The flashes repeated, maybe two per second for almost a full minute. After a couple of seconds delay, they started again, and again, and lasted for about three minutes. *Not artillery. The flashes are too large.* He had seen artillery shells exploding at night. His mind raced. *No, it's not artillery. Well, they're mysterious lights of war. I'll soon find out what they are.*

Joe's thought shifted to himself and about how and why he came here. *Oh, yes, I know exactly why I'm here, and I pray she is safe.*

As soon as Joe stepped on top of the tall mobile stairs to deplane, his first sensations were heat and humidity, sauna like, which felt the same as July or August at home, down on the bayou.

At the bottom of the stairs and on the tarmac, an NCO barked out directions. "Welcome to Bien Hoi. Follow the line into the hangar. You'll be divided alphabetically and given additional directions. There are light snacks available. Help yourself. Your luggage will be delivered to the hangar. Move on. We must get this plane ready to take our war heroes home. Move on!

Joe followed the directions to a large hangar. He found a cold hot dog, a handful of chocolate chip cookies, and a cold Coke. He headed for the line forming under the sign marked 'H'. Joee had not reached the line before he heard his name called, incorrectly, of course. "He Bert, Staff Sergeant Joseph He Bert." Someone called out.

Joe could see the soldier yelling at him. He was a tall and lean Sergeant First Class. He was dressed in jungle fatigues. As Joe approached him, he strained to read the NCO's name tag, but his EOD badge named him well enough. Anyone wearing the EOD badge was a friend.

After close enough to read his name tag, Joe loudly said, "Here, Sergeant First Class Johnson! It's pronounced A Bear." Joe reached out to shake the square-shouldered NCO's hand.

"Oh, yes, sorry about the pronunciation." SEC. Johnson shrugged.

"No problem. It happens all the time. If you please, call me Joe. You can probably pronounce that correctly." Joe lightly chuckled.

"Sure, Joe. I'm Darrell. I'm glad to see and meet you. You're my turtle."

"Turtle?" Joe looked confused.

"Yeah. My replacement. Replacements are slow to arrive. In about a week, I am out of here" Johnson happily announced his departure.

"Good for you." Joe nodded in a congratulatory manner.

"We got word yesterday that you were coming in." Johnson looked at him dubiously.

Joe did not bite. Instead, he asked, "What do I do from here?"

Pointing at the table under the sign with an H on it, Johnson Said, "I think you need to sign in at the Replacement Battalion. Since you have your unit assignment, you can turn around and sign out. Then, we'll collect your baggage. I have a Jeep. We'll go over to the front gate and hook up with others going to Long Binh. There's safety in numbers, especially after dark. We'll stay there for the night. Does this sound like a plan to you, Joe?"

Joe appreciated Johnson's politeness, but replied, "What do I know?"

"Tomorrow, we'll head south."

"Where to?" Joe looked at Johnson.

"To Dong Tam, where else?" Darrell shook his head at Joe's lack of awareness.

"Dong Tam, where's Dong Tam?"

"You seriously don't know? It's down in the Delta, close to My Tho, with the Ninth Division."

"No, I didn't know where it is. My orders simply read, that I was assigned to the 269 Ordinance Detachment. "Joe spoke while shaking his head.

"We received word yesterday about you coming. Nobody in the unit, or the EOD Control Center, knows you. Besides that, you're wearing a master jump badge, meaning you have more than sixty-five jumps, and coming from the Airborne School in Fort Benning, rather than from the EOD unit there. So, what gives?" Johnson asked in an apothegmatic manner, this time with authority in his voice.

"You don't know of me because, I have had only one EOD assignment. I was in Germany. I wanted out of the Jump School at Fort Ben. So here I am. You know the story." Joe looked around the hangar, anywhere but not at Johnson.

"Sure!"

Before he could say anything else, a flash of light, and a loud explosion, accompanied by a concussion wave ripped through the hangar. They both hit the concrete below them. Joe reacted a half-second slower than Johnson.

They heard second and third explosions, farther away.

"Anybody hurt?" Somebody yelled.

"We have one down over here." Another voice yelled from at least thirty yards.

"You okay, Joe?" Johnson stood.

"Yeah, but I was slow reacting to it." Joe hung his head.

"You'll learn. They were probably 122-millimeter rockets. The nearest one hit at least fifty yards away."

"I guess they were welcoming me to Vietnam." Joe smiled sheepishly.

"You'll get used to being mortared. At Dong Tam, we get hit at least twice a week, often as many as five or six times. There's nothing we can do to help here, so let's get out of this place." Johnson stuck his thumb over his shoulder toward the parked transportation.

Staff Sergeant Hébert signed in and out, as Johnson had said. He turned in his money, his greenbacks, for military pay certificates, MPCs, funny colored bills. Joe collected his duffel bag, and they headed for Johnson's Jeep, pausing to watch three fighter jets taking off on a strike mission in response to the rocket attack.

When they arrived at the Jeep, Johnson unlocked a chain which secured the steering wheel.

Joe asked, "What's all that about?"

"People steal Jeeps over here. We are authorized only one Jeep; we have three of them. It's called midnight requisitioning." Johnson grinned innocently.

They drove to the main gate leading of Bein Hoi and joined a line of other vehicles, two of which were Jeeps with M-60 machine guns mounted on them. The other vehicles were transporting troops and supplies.

Before pulling out, Johnson handed Joe a flack vest and steel pot, which had been laying in the back seat of the Jeep.

"We don't go off post without the essentials. You'll find our M-16s and ammo in the backseat. It's doubtful we'll need them, but you never know. I hope you can use it." Johnson looked at Joe for confirmation.

Joe put the flack vest and steel head gear on, loaded a magazine into the M-16, and said, "I have no problem with using shoulder fired weapons. So, I guess I'm ready for war!"

Johnson and Joe drove to Long Binh to spend the night at the EOD unit. After the customary meet, greet, and beer, Joe excused himself for a much-needed shower and bed. Joe did not wake until midmorning, at which time, he offered his apologies for being tardy.

"No need, we've all made the flight and know what it's like," Johnson said. "After you get a bit to eat, we can head south."

Joe replied, "I'll be ready in fifteen minutes."

"No hurry, we have plenty of time."

Less than an hour later, Joe found himself in the middle of Saigon, a bustling metropolitan area.

Because of the number of people, his first thoughts turned to New Orleans during Mardi Gras. But as a Third World country, it had different sounds and aromas.

Joe had never liked big cities and considered himself a Bayou Boy. The vast number of pedestrians made him uneasy. He literally could not count the number of motorcycles, and rickshaws which they found themselves in. The substantial number of military vehicles reminded him; they were in a war zone. A half dozen American uniforms, scattered among ARVN uniformed soldiers were readily visible. A sudden sense of lack of security came over him.

"They could take us out anytime they want to, couldn't they?" Joe said and adjusted his M-16 to a more ready position.

"Yes, but it's not likely. The only thing you need to worry about is some VC throwing a grenade into the Jeep."

"That kind of thing is just what I need to hear from you!" Joe replied sarcastically as he rolled his eyes.

"I hear you, Joe. But it's true and you do need to hear it. You are in a war zone. If you want a chance of going back home, you need to know what you're facing. Now, give me the radio's Mic. I'll check in with Control. You do know, of course, they have Operational Command over all the EOD units in country." While asking a stupid question, Johnson glanced over at Joe.

Joe reached into the backseat and grabbed the mic. off the M-46 radio and handed it to him.

"Scarlet O'Hara, Scarlet O'Hara. This is Course Jackal Two, over," SFC Johnson spoke, while pressing the button on the side of the Mic. He released the button and waited.

After a couple seconds, the radio came alive. "This is Scarlet O'Hara, go."

"This is Course Jackal Two. I have the package, and we're going home. I just wanted to let you know. Do you have anything headed my way? Over."

"Thanks, I'll relay the message and nothing going your way. Scarlet O'Hara, out." The radio went silent.

"Course Jackal," Joe commented. "I'm assuming that's our call sign, and Scarlet O'Hara is EOD Control. Also, you are the third ranking individual in the unit, and you don't always use correct radio procedures."

"You got it," Johnson said. "You're an adaptive learner."

"I know Control is here in Saigon, but that's all I knew about the units over here. I thought I had another six months, before I had to worry about deployment."

"You had to leave in a hurry?" Johnson tried to dig for information.

Joe did not answer but deflected, "Who's our Sergeant Major?"

"Sergeant Major Hicks. He came out of the Control Center in Texas."

"And who's the Commander?"

"Major Sparks, and I don't know him. I've never met him. The only time he came down to Dong Tam, I wasn't there. The captain likes him and talks to him sometimes on the land line.

Occasionally, Master Sergeant Scott speaks with him. "Scott is our Top. Oh, yes, he's colored. I guess we have to say black, today. He's an old timer, WW-2 and Korean War Vet. He stays in the office a great deal the time doing all the administrative work. The captain likes it this way.

"Scott is a big dude. I'd hate to anger him to the point of fisticuffs."

SEC Johnson continued to drive through Saigon, saying nothing, except to occasionally curse at the traffic and the hundreds of jaywalkers. After what seemed like an hour, the massive logjam thinned. Joe knew they were almost out of the city.

At the edge of Saigon, Joe noticed a large blue and yellow structure which looked abandoned. He nodded his head at it, "What's the story there?"

Johnson looked where Joe had showed. "It's an old Buddhist monastery. I believe it was closed a few years ago when the government cracked down on the Buddhists."

Out of the city, the road narrowed, and the terrain noticeably changed to flatter than north of Saigon. Rice paddies were tended by the local population, some using water buffalo. All the people were wearing coned shaped, light-colored headgear, white shirts, and black trousers which looked like pajamas. Joe thought the terrain and weather looked and felt like South Louisiana, only no cypress trees, alligators, or muskrats were visible. At least he hadn't seen any, yet.

Joe knew the Mekong Delta consisted of little more than rivulets, islands, and flooded plains. But it made up an enormous area, filled with rice and other fertile farmland. It encompassed about fifteen thousand square miles. It also was an important fishing region.

Joe spoke. "The people aren't very attractive, are they?"

"As a whole, no. But the longer you stay here, the better looking the women get. It's like a bar at night. The longer you stay and the more you drink, the better the women look. Don't be fooled by the look of some of the women you've seen. There's a lot of world-class beautiful women here. Frenchmen improve this country in ways. They sired a large population of fine-looking women. You'll see!" Johnson glanced at Joe with a broad smile on his face.

Joe shook his head and said, "I haven't seen any, yet."

"We'll be in Dong Tam in less than an hour. You can relax. This road should be safe during daytime." Johnson waved a hand in front of him to show the way they were going.

They passed a half dozen small hamlets with a dozen or so dwellings mostly covered with reeds. At the entrance of each hamlet, sandbagged bunkers with armed ARVN soldiers, maned with M-60 machine guns, guarded the road. A couple of hamlets also had tanks available. As they drove through the hamlets, SEC Johnson slowed down considerably and waved to the people. Waves and smiles were returned.

After passing through one of the small hamlets, SFC Johnson said, "I think we have a problem. This thing is pulling badly to the right. Crap, we have a flat tire. We'll stop at the next outpost. It's only a short distance."

They limped off the shoulder of the road when they came to the next hamlet. They found the right front tire had shredded, except for part of the sidewalls. ARVN soldiers, who were acting as lookout, started barking out commands from the sandbagged bunkers. More ARVN soldiers, who were heavily armed, and ready for action, came out of the reeded huts. They surrounded the Jeep like it was an intruder. Hébert could feel goose bumps all over his body, as the muzzles of M-16's drew down on them. Johnson showed no outward signs of nervousness.

None of the ARVN soldiers spoke fluent English, but they were able to help with changing the tire, for a small fee of course. They pointed to a puncture hole on the wall of the tire which was still intact. When they concluded that a bullet caused the hole, adrenaline dumped into Joe's body.

Johnson, again, showed no outward concern. He and Joe thanked the soldiers, shook their hands, and headed further south.

After a brief period, SFC Johnson said, "We're coming up to a small town, Tan An. The 9th Division has a rather decent size contingency there. We keep an on-site team of two people there to provide immediate EOD support, round-the-clock. The team stays rather busy as they often respond to incidents in the surrounding area."

"Is there a lot of action in this area?" Joe asked a sincere question.

Yes, quite a bit. We're coming up to a large river. We'll be crossing it on a one-way floating bridge.

"The VC took the original bridge out during Tet. It has taken a while, but the engineers are starting to work on a replacement. It should be a high priority. The floating bridge is a major bottleneck when convoys are running up and down this road."

As they crossed the river, Joe sat back and watched the Army Corps of Engineers in action, executing a major river crossing of more than a hundred yards. Joe surmised, "This is the same modus of operation as the Army used during World War II to cross the Rhine River. Also, Burnside's troops used the same method to cross the Rappahannock River to prepare for the attack on Lee's Army in and around Fredericksburg during the Peninsula Campaign.

"The information came from the only college book that I have ever read. One, on world history. I thought about reading another one, but never got around to it, yet. That is saved for one of those 'someday' things to do."

"Yeah, it's essentially the same, barges lashed together. I'd think the material they're using is basically the only difference." Johnson sounded as if he knew the subject.

"Well, if it works, don't screw with it." Joe seemed to end the bridge discussion.

"Exactly! There should be nothing remarkable between here and home, except the road gets worse, and we have to go through Ambush Alley, the last couple of mile of our drive."

Johnson's words brought Joe rapidly back to the present. "Ambush Alley!" Joe repeated excitedly and ominously.

"Yes, we lose all this open space which the rice paddies provide. The trees grow along the graveled road, a stone toss away in places. This means the VC can use cover and concealment extremely efficiently. Major ambushes, requiring a large force, are rare. But it's common for a lone sniper to shoot at passing traffic. So, we normally kick it in high gear going through there. The 9th Division sweeps the roads for mines every morning.

"What I'm telling you, Hébert, chisel this in concrete, don't go through there too early or too late. You don't want to be the first vehicle going out of Dong Tam in the morning or the last vehicle coming in after sunset." Johnson did not blink as he spoke, making sure his words hit home.

"Okay, it's a lesson learned. Ambush Alley, what a nice name!"

Joe wanted to ask, what time they would arrive, but Johnson reached for the Mic. and keyed it. "Course Jackal Base, Course Jackal Base, this is Course Jackal Two,"

A distinct pause occurred, before the radio crackled and popped, and then squeaked. "This is Course Jackal Base, go.

"Base, this is Two. We are about twenty minutes out. Over"

"I read, your ETA twenty minutes. Over"

"Roger. Over"

"I'll pass it on. Base out." The radio went silent, which allowed Joe to ask the question. "Twenty minutes to Dong Tam?"

"Yes, it's about thirteen miles. Thirteen miles to your new home."

CHAPTER 15

The single entrance into Dong Tam appearance was far from impressive. It had sand bagged bunkers maned by five-armed MP's who were guarding the checkpoint and examining every vehicle entering. Coiled barbed wire led away from the guard post on both sides. The mighty Mekong River flowed about fifty yards south of them.

The EOD facilities were approximately three hundred yards northwest from the entrance of Dong Tam. The facilities consisted of a small wood frame office and storage building, two well-sandbagged bunkers, a sandbagged rectangular squad tent used for sleeping, a small sandbagged round tent used as a setting room, and a wood latrine. A thick layer of reddish dirt covered everything. A jeep and a two-and-a-half-ton truck, bearing EOD markings, were parked outside the building.

As Johnson and Joe drove up and parked, they saw no one outside.

"The piss tube is over here." SFC Johnson motioned toward it.

As it had been a long, bumpy ride for the bladder, Joe followed Johnson without hesitation to the piss tube. To provide privacy, two sheets of plywood were staked on their edge, perpendicular on their long side to the ground. He noticed a buried fifty-five-gallon barrel, with approximately one foot of the cutout end sticking out of the ground. A screen covered the end of the barrel.

Johnson produced a stream of urine directed at the screen. Joe, with a large smile and an "Ahhh," quickly followed his aiming lesson.

"It's a larger hole than the eight-Inch tube which we used at the unit at Long Binh," Joe pointed out and sighed again.

"Yeah, we're first-class down here." Johnson smirked.

"You made it in!" Someone yelled from the screen door on the wood building.

"Yeah, no problem, "Johnson called back as he and Joe finished their business and headed in the direction of the door.

Johnson made the introductions. "Sergeant Hébert, this is Specialist Wheeler, our clerks' typist. If he wasn't the lowest ranked person in the unit, he would be running this place, as if he doesn't, anyway. He's mild-mannered and the go-to guy."

"I bet he keeps everything in order, regardless of rank." Joe seemed professional.

"Come in." Specialist Wheeler extended his hand to Joe. "With a name like Hébert, I bet you're Cajun." Wheeler stood a couple inches less than six feet and had short military cut dark hair. His jungle fatigue looked excessively wrinkled, but his boots were nicely shined. His accent placed him from somewhere in the South.

"You win the bet. Born and bred a Cajun." Joe entered the building and offered his hand. He noticed the walls were lined with lockers and there were three desks, a bunk, a filing cabinet, and two, six-drawer security safes. Behind one desk, a physical fit, yet noticeably graying hair, Black Master Sergeant (MSG) rose.

"Master Sergeant Scott this is Staff Sergeant Hébert. Sergeant Hébert, this is Master Sergeant Scott. Some people around here call him Buck." Johnson moved his head back and forth as he introduced the two.

Scott it's a pleasure to meet you. SFC. Johnson told me you made WW-11 and the Korean conflict. I'll look forward to hearing some stories from you regarding them," Joe held his hand out to shake Scott's.

"War, Son, War! Korea was a war for those of us who experienced it firsthand. It was a conflict for the people in D.C. And you won't be hearing any war stories from me. However, we're glad to have you onboard. With Johnson leaving, I thought we'd be down another man for a while." Scott did not smile as he shook Joe's extended hand but intensely studied his face.

"Well, I'll be asking about those stories anyway, and I'm glad to finally be here." Joe couldn't help but have a smile for Scott.

Scott looked over at Wheeler. "The captain is over at the Officers Club. Go get him. If I don't send for him, he'll be there until dark.

"Johnson, show Hébert where he can bunk,"

As Scott finished his directions, the back screen door burst open. "Johnson! Johnson, you back!" A very pregnant Vietnamese woman shouted as she came through the back door. Like 99 percent of the Vietnamese Joe had seen, she wore black pajamas like slacks and a white buttoned silk-like blouse. She ran up to Johnson and gave him a big hug. He embraced her and kissed her on the cheek.

"Sergeant Hébert, this is a Lein. She is one of our hooch maids." Johnson reached down to rub her stomach. "And this is mine. She is due to pop any day now."

"Hébert, I am good worker. I keep everything clean. I clean your boots every day. Every day, I make your bed." Lein smiled broadly and used rather good English for a Vietnamese. "I work hard, long time. You want anything, you ask me."

"Thank you, Lein. I'm sure you're diligent worker." She stood no taller than five feet and looked as if she weighed a ton.

Joe noticed a second Vietnamese female entered the back door.

Johnson said, "Joe, this is Baby San, the other hooch maid."

"You no touch! No touch! I cherry girl! I no like G.I. touch," Baby San stepped behind Lein. She was dressed the same a Lein and stood about the same height but weighed less than a hundred pounds. Her black hair was as long as Ava's blond hair. Joe rated her as looking genuinely nice, but not beautiful like Ava. *Maybe after a six-pack, she would look beautiful. This is what Johnson was telling me on our drive down here.*

"I'm sure you work hard too." Joe smiled and nodded to her.

"Now, since the introductions are over, Johnson will show you a bunk and locker. The captain will be here in no time. He'll want to talk with you. So be back in here in ten minutes, with your records in hand. If you'd like one, grab a beer." Scott looked and nodded at Joe.

"Joe, get your bags. I'll grab the beer. Come next door to the large tent." Johnson spoke as he genteelly patted Lien's back.

Joe did as he was directed and carried his bags next door to the squad tent. Sandbags, about four feet high, surrounded the tent except for the two entrances. It had somewhat clean plywood floors, and eight cots with white sheets covering them. Accompanying the beds were footlockers and wall-lockers, on each side of the cots.

The sides of the tent were rolled up above the sandbags for ventilation. Sitting on top of the footlockers were pairs of shined jungle boots. Johnson sat on one of the cots holding two beers. As Joe approached, Johnson leaned over and patted the cot in front of him. He said, "This one is yours."

Joe dropped his bags on the cot and took the beer. "Thanks."

"No problem. If you are wondering, we drink anytime of the day from breakfast until bedtime. Don't abuse the system, and remember you're on duty, 24/7. I've been here for a year, and I haven't seen any of our guys drunk during the day. Everybody here is typical EOD, very solid and will cause no problems, maybe apart from one guy. And I'll let you figure out who it is.

"Now, at night, Jackson, and me sometimes over drink...Am I supposed to say Jackson and I?" Johnson rolled his eyes.

"I don't think a real Coonass will judge anybody's English." Joe chuckled and pointed to the boots on the footlockers. "I presume this is Lien's work?"

"Yeah. Because of dampness and your feet's health, you change boots every day. Leave your dirty pair under your bed. The two girls do an excellent job. We chip in fifteen dollars every month to pay them. They're well worth every penny we give them."

"I would say it's true, especially in your case." Joe presented his wriest smile and raised his beer in a toast.

"Yes, but nothing goes on around here. I go into My Tho, sometimes a couple times a week, and spend the night with her at the ARVN compound. There are a couple of American soldiers stationed there. They take care of us. One of them is the MACV EOD advisor to ARVN personnel around here. He is stationed in My Tho.

"Factually, in total, there are more than nine thousand American soldiers currently serving in this kind of advisory capacity with ARVN units. They eat, sleep, and work with their troops daily. They earn their paycheck.

"Lein ensures no harm comes to me while I'm in town. When any of us are in My Tho with them, they're the boss. We listen to them as far as where and when to go, and what and what not to do. I trust Lein with my life, and she trusts Baby San. I don't know Baby

San very well. She has been here only a short time and talks only to Wheeler and Captain S. I guess they are the only ones here who hasn't grabbed her ass."

"Okay, thanks for the heads-up. I'll make sure I don't touch her. Changing the subject, Scott seemed extremely nice. For an old man, the guy looks like he could take us on. I presume he's a straight shooter?"

"Yeah, he could kick our ass if necessary. He treats us all, the same. The only question I would have with him is his abilities in doing EOD work. It's only because, I have never seen him in the field. I can't remember him going on one incident since he's been here. And he's been here a little over a month. But he's been in EOD a long time, now in his third war."

"Is there anything I need to know, before I talk with the captain?"

"No, he knows his stuff. I work as his partner all the time. Some of the others here don't necessarily like to work with him, but I would follow him anywhere." Johnson's retort sincerity in his words.

"Why? Why would anybody not like him?" Joe presented a suspicious face.

"Don't get me wrong. It's not that they don't like him. It's, he has a certain, something, about him. He can sometimes be extremely lucky. You know the type of guy who can hit an inside straight, two times in a row. He seems to be able to answer your question before you ask it. You may get the feeling he knows what you're thinking. I kind of like it, and we get along fine. I don't keep anything from him. If he chooses you as his partner, you'll be, I guess, lucky." Johnson gave fond feeling to in his description of the captain.

"Okay, let's get over there." Joe stood and motioned toward the screen door.

"You go. You're the one who must pass muster. I'll stay here and have another beer." Johnson remained sitting on the cot.

It only took ten small steps, from the squad tent to the office building. As Joe entered the building, he saw the sandy blonde headed captain standing in front of Scott's desk, talking with him.

Wheeler sat behind his desk with Baby San in a folding, metal chair beside him.

"Come in Staff Sergeant Hébert," the captain said while reaching out to shake his hand.

Joe did not reach for the captain's hand, but rather, he locked his heels, stood at attention, and like a robot made a sharp salute. "Staff Sergeant Hébert reporting, Sir."

The captain withdrew his hand awkwardly, and he at once returned Joe's salute. As soon as the captain dropped his hand, he again offered it out to Joe and looked at Scott. "Did you tell him to salute me?"

"No, Sir." Scott shook his head.

This time Joe took the captain's hand and shook it firmly. "Glad to meet you, Captain Summerville" All the men except Joe wore jungle fatigues and boots. Joe wore khakis and black shoes.

"Yes, glad to have you aboard. At ease, Staff Sergeant. We don't do a lot of saluting around here. Saluting is usually synonymous with trouble and an ass chewing. I mean trouble with me. Now, if another Officer comes in here, by all means give him your best salute." Captain Summerville smiled.

"Yes, Sir."

"Scott, take a break. You can talk with Hébert later. Wheeler, you, and Baby San can take your work to the sitting area, the small tent." The captain politely suggested, but they knew an order when issued.

They complied promptly and left. Captain Summerville took a seat behind the third metal desk, the one with only a double deck, in and out file, and a nameplate with Captain Summerville engraved on it. There were also a couple of papers in the in-file and none in the out-file "Sergeant, pull up a chair and have a seat, I'll take your military records."

Joe passed his military records to Captain Summerville and sat quietly for a couple minutes, as the captain thumbed through his records.

"Is there anything missing from your records or anything else which you would care to tell me about, Staff Sergeant?" The captain asked as he looked up and stared, what felt like a hole, into Joe's eyes.

"What you have there is pretty much all of my military life, Sir." Joe shrugged.

"You didn't answer the question that I asked you, Hébert." Summerville continued to stare at Joe with an authoritative manner.

"Yes, Sir." Joe replied and noticed a sharp contrast in the warm and congenial captain who minutes ago greeted him, and the cold and firm captain now staring at him.

"Yes, Sir, what?" Captain Summerville continued staring.

There it is. Johnson warned me about it. Joe silently felt anxious. "Yes, Sir. There is something you might as well know now, Captain. You'll learn sooner or later."

"Spit it out, Staff Sergeant!"

Leaving nothing out, Joe spent the next ten minutes explaining the events of the last few days. He detailed his road traveled by him and Ava from Germany to Fort Ben which ultimately led to his arrival at Dong Tam.

"You tell an interesting story. It's personal. And it answers every question that I was concerned about. I won't repeat your personal affairs. You don't have to tell anyone else. I know MSG Scott will ask you what's behind your sudden arrival. He's no dummy! He knows there's a story there.

If you want to, tell him I know why you showed up unexpectedly. Of course, you can tell him whatever you please. The bottom line is this matter does not concern me.

"What does concern me is, you are still wearing Band-Aids on your neck. Get over to the 9th Med. as soon as you can, and get your wounds cleaned. Anytime you have a scratch, get first aid ASAP. Infections are rampant over here. Do you understand what I'm telling you?" Captain Summerville wanted everything to be up-front and clear from the beginning.

"Yes, Sir."

"Next subject! I see you are wearing standard issued khaki with a white T-shirt. Around here you wear no white. None! Not even underwear. White makes a good aiming point. Regular fatigues are too hot, and they take too long to dry. The same goes for your boots.

You'll have to get jungle fatigues and boots. Scott will take care of you on this matter. Don't let him forget the black name tags." Captain Summerville leaned back in his chair.

"Yes, Sir."

"Now, what concerns me the most is, you didn't have time to do any necessary training for Vietnam. This is a different world over here There are two worlds, the real world and over here.

"As an EOD NCO, you know we are allowed only one mistake in our work, and the one mistake is likely fatal. There are a thousand mistakes you can make over here, not only related to EOD. Any one of them will get you, or someone else, killed. If you make the mistake, and I don't go with you, I'll have to write the letter to Mama. I'm not looking forward to that.

"It'll take time to get you oriented. As soon as you get all your gear, you'll pair up with me. Except for the crapper and the officers club, where I go, you go. As I'm sure you know, Johnson is leaving shortly over a week. He's been my partner since I came aboard. So, I need you to be ready as soon as possible."

"Yes, Sir."

"I find your SEAL training quite interesting and intriguing. I would like to hear about it. With this kind of training, you're well ahead of the average G.I. over here."

"Yes, Sir, I would like to think I am."

"And you are qualified as a Jump Master! Impressive! That and your SEAL training leads me to believe, you have undergone serious military cultivation.

"I'm sure you guessed; these are cherry wings that I'm wearing. I made my five jumps and no others. The Ordnance Corps told me their Officers were lovers, not paratroopers."

"Yes, Sir. I've heard the story, Sir."

"Hell, I can't take any more of this 'Yes, Sir stuff'. Let's get a beer. I'll buy. Oh, did anyone tell you about our bar? We keep a running tab, to be paid every month. We charge fifteen cents, each.

It covers the cost and gives the unit a nickel a can profit."

"Yes, Sir, and thanks."

"I'll keep your records and give them to MSG Scott for his review. He'll want to sit down with you, and afterwards, he'll take them over to the Personnel Office."

"Yes, Sir."

"Yes, Sir. Yes, Sir. I got hardly anything out of you, didn't I? Let's go and get that beer." The captain stood. "Any questions?"

"Yes Sir. Where do I find my 'welcome to scenic Don Tam and things to do', brochure? Joe could not help himself.

Captain S shook his head and smiled. "Come on. We had enough for today."

Joe followed him out the back door onto a small eight by twelve, wood patio. At the back end of the patio, a lean-to covered, what Joe thought was the unit's bar, a sheet of plywood nailed to two sawhorses. MSG Scott and Johnson were sitting at a foldable card table. Johnson stood, walked behind the bar, opened a cooler, pulled out two beers, and returned to the table. He gave them to the captain and Joe. "Thanks," Captain Summerville nodded.

"Yes, thanks. I need another one," Joe said.

Scott asked, "Well, Sir. Did he pass the muster?"

"Yes, and no. The only thing I found out about him is, what's in his records, and he knows how to say 'Yes, Sir'. You and Banks have some things to do with him tomorrow." Captain Summerville took a swallow of his beer.

"I expected you to say that. We'll get him straightened out." Scott looked at Joe with the patented Master Sergeant's stare.

"Where are Banks and O'Neil?" Summerville looked around.

"They went to the exchange a while ago and should've returned by now." Scott frowned.

Joe asked, "Where did you send Wheeler?"

"He and Baby San are over there." Captain Summerville gestured to the round, small six-sided tent. "For about an hour a day, Wheeler is supposed to help Baby San with her English. I think it's become more of a math class though. Wheeler tells me, by comparison, she is very gifted mathematically, but slow in English. He told me yesterday; she is competently working with linear equations and had never seen an X or Y before two weeks ago."

"Wow!" Johnson interrupted. "Hell, I hardly passed algebra in my senior year of high school."

"Nobody ever said you were gifted at anything." Scott laughed.

"Not true, not true! My Mama always told me; I was very gifted in the art of BS." Johnson laughed at his self-condescending statement.

"Well, now, I stand corrected. Your Mama was obviously correct." Scott swallowed a swig of his beer and continued. "Wheeler had better get her out here soon. It's time for the girls to go home.

Johnson, do you want to take them into town? We need to get ice.

Johnson shook his head, "No, maybe Banks and O'Neil would like to. I've driven enough for today."

Joe asked, "Do we have to provide transportation for them?"

"No. The 9th Division runs trucks to and from My Tho for the local labor. However, we often take them home, especially, when we need something from town." Johnson quickly explained the situation.

"Or a certain someone wants to spend the night in town." Scott looked at Johnson.

"Guilty as charged. I think, Banks and O'Neil just drove up." Johnson looked to the front where the Jeeps were parked.

"Wheeler! It's time to finish up!" Scott yelled toward the small tent.

"We'll be there in a few minutes, Master Sergeant Scott!" Wheeler yelled back.

"Now, we need to find Lein," Scott said.

"No, no. I hear." Lein replied from behind the administration building.

"Are you back there spying on us? Are you VC?" Johnson playfully asked her.

"Johnson, you number ten. You know; I no VC. You say not true. I no VC. I here, clean Captain S's boots." Lein stepped awkwardly upon the patio carrying a pair of boots, which she placed on the card table. "Clean boots, no?"

Summerville looked at the boots, "They looked clean to me. Thanks, Lein."

"You know; I'm teasing you," Johnson said while rubbing her stomach.

Joe asked, "When's the baby due, Johnson?"

"The way she's looking and moving, she was due yesterday or last week," Scott pointed out.

"Lein, I told you not to come to work until the baby arrives, didn't I?" Summerville asked her.

"Captain S, you know I come to work. When baby come, I no come. It comes soon. Moves all time." Lein frustratingly insisted.

"I don't want you to deliver it here," Summerville said, and continued. "And by the way, Hébert, everybody here calls me Captain S, and it's fine with me. I'm sure you know where the name came from."

"The babies come, when it comes!" Lein remained unyielding in her position.

"Scott, do you know how to deliver a baby?" Captain S was not smiling.

"No, Sir. But I think, mother nature does the work. All you do is cut the baby's cord after the baby and everything else fall out. Then someone must clean up the mess. That will be Johnson's job, if he happens to be here at the time. We better get extra first aid stuff and be prepared.

"Captain S, you ain't high enough on the packing order to run her off." Scott laughed louder than the others.

"We all know, Lein is the boss around here," Johnson sincerely stated.

"Well, here are our wandering boys," Scott pointed at Staff Sergeant Banks and Specialists O'Neil walking up.

Hébert stood and introduced himself.

"Glad you made it in," Staff Sergeant Banks acknowledged Joe. Banks was shorter and weighed fifteen pounds less then Joe. Joe was not into men, but he thought women would consider him a handsome, a brown eyed and dark headed hunk.

"I'm glad to meet you." Specialist O'Neil offered his hand. Joe measured him at five-eight and rather skinny. He would not push the scales over one-sixty. His Adam's apple was pronounced and attention-getting.

"Likewise, to both of you," Joe responded.

"Where have you clowns been?" Scott firmly asked them. "And don't tell me you have been to the exchange all this time."

"No, we ran into Colonel Fairbanks and Sergeant Major Laird from Division Artillery (DVARTY) at the exchange. The Colonel wanted us to go to his office and pick up a 155mm, ejection round. He wanted us to take it apart where he could see what was inside, Banks replied."

"You told him we couldn't do it, and it's not authorized by regulations, didn't you?" Captain S sternly looking at the two of them.

"Yes, Sir. I told him to call you. Then, I talked to the Sergeant Major, one-on-one, and we worked it out." Banks looked at Scott.

Scott quickly asked, "What did you get?"

"Ten sheets of, three-quarter inch, finished plywood." O'Neil answered with a big smile.

"Okay, what kind of ejection round is it supposed to be?" Scott nodded his approval.

"The Colonel told us, it was a propaganda round, containing leaflets telling the VC all kind of crap. It seems as if they have fired more than a thousand rounds throughout the Delta, and there's been no leaflets reported anywhere." Banks explained.

"There's definitely a problem somewhere," Captain S said. "And changing the subject, do you two want to make an ice run?"

"Well--" Banks tried to reply.

"Yes. Yes, you do." Scott answered for him.

"Since you put it that way. Yes, Sir, we do!"

"We'd love to!" O'Neil rolled his eyes.

"Wheeler!" Scott yelled.

"Yes, Master Sergeant Scott, we're coming" Wheeler popped out of the small tent with Baby San following.

"Baby San, I understand Wheeler is teaching you English," Joe looked into her brown eyes.

"Yes, Hébert." Baby San answered sheepishly, while standing behind Wheeler, holding his left arm with both of her hands.

Joe asked, "Well, what did you learn today?"

"I learned verbs." She replied, while easing out from behind Wheeler and dropped one hand.

"What kind of verbs?"

Baby San looked up at Wheeler, "What kind?"

"Tell him what we talked about today." Wheeler nudged her.

"I learn. I am, you are, he is, we are." Baby San said and dropped her other hand.

"Okay, enough of this. Banks, get the ladies out of here. It'll be close to dark when you get back," Scott demanded and motioned for them to go away.

"O'Neil, grab a cooler. Girls, you should be in the Jeep by now." Banks passed it downhill, and they all headed for the Jeep.

"Hébert, you need to get settled. I'm sure you'll want to hit the hay early." Scott continued getting everything in order.

"I can manage it. But it's been a long time since I ate breakfast. When and where is chow? Don't know how long it's been since I sat down and enjoyed a good meal."

"Johnson will show you where the mess hall is. By the time you get unpacked, they'll be serving dinner. You'll find the chow is sometimes good for a war zone. The poor grunts, who spend their days and nights in the bush, don't eat very well. Now, the Captain, here, eats at the Navy Officer's mess at times. They eat good."

"Rank has its privilege (RHIP)." Captain S interrupted. "All kidding aside, Navy officers do eat a lot better than the Army. Tasty food, with real silverware and china, served family style by Philippine servers, on a linen tablecloth, is hard to beat. Can you believe it?"

"Rub it in." Scott frowned.

"You do have to admit; I eat with you guys occasionally. I do it simply to stand in line waiting for food to be slopped on a plastic tray, to drink out of plastic glasses, and use terrible flatware." Captain S commented sarcastically.

"You didn't mention the good company and the intelligent conversation." Johnson grinned.

"Yeah, but I also forgot to mention the flatulencies and the vulgar language. And I didn't mention chicken, prime rib, and steaks, all with bones." Captain S tried to score last.

"You made your point Captain. But speaking of bones, Hébert, you have chewed on your last bone for a year, unless you get it downtown. And we're not talking about gay sex. They debone everything coming in here," Scott looking at Joe.

"Oh, and Hébert," Captain S said, "While we were talking inside, I forgot to mention one thing. You should have been taking Malaria pills for a couple of weeks before coming over here. You don't need to catch Malaria. However, you are less at risk here, on post, than in the bush. Things are different out there. They spray for mosquitoes on post."

"Yes, Sir. I'll unpack, eat, and turn in early."

"You have now met the entire unit, except for Staff Sergeant Jackson and Specialist Redding," Captain S mentioned.

"They make up the on-site team at Tan An. Remember, I told you the story as we were passing through Tan An." Johnson looked at Joe.

"Let's get moving. I want to look at Hébert's records, before dinner." Scott interrupted.

Johnson followed Joe to the squad tent and said, "It's not nice, but it's a place to sleep and hang your hat. At least it beats a rice paddy. After you've spent a night or two in the bush, you'll learn to appreciate this place. Clean sheets at night, and clean clothes every day is hard to beat in a war zone. We can get you a fan. It'll help with mosquitoes and your sleep."

This place is a dump. It's a dark, musty, smelly tent, surrounded by sandbags which are mildewed. Judging by the shape of the surrounding facilities, we're not being discriminated against.

I like to camp, and this place reminds me of an old hunting camp we used on the Bayou. Joe did not consider the terrible condition of the hunting camp too bad for a night or two-night stay.

The camp provided nothing more than a rundown shack on the Bayou with rustic old flea market furniture which had long since seen better days. But it looked like a Taj Mahal compared to this musty tent.

After dinner, Joe went to bed at the same time as the sun dropped below the horizon. Obviously, when his head hit the pillow, his thoughts turned to Ava. *God bless and keep you safe.*

I have one day down and a year to go before I see Ava again.

*****

The next morning Joe woke when Scott loudly barked, "Boy, did you sleep good?"

Joe rolled over, not totally awake, opened his eyes, stretched, and sat up. "Yes, except for the damn rooster crowing this morning at daylight."

Looking directly into Joe's eyes, trying to catch a clue, or note any body language, Scott said, "Something is wrong." He paused for effect. "Why are you here?"

Caught off guard with Scott's assertation, after a moment, Joe finally asked, "What do you mean?"

"What do I mean?" Scott snapped at Joe, questioning his remark. "Look, dammit, I've been in this man's army long enough to know, you are not here because you love EOD and Vietnam. There is more to the story, and it bothers me. I don't want anybody in this unit who doesn't want to be here… I have a feeling you are here not of your own choice. And furthermore, I have never known a young man leaving the Navy and coming to the Arny unless, there were mitigating circumstances. And do not hold anything back."

Joe could feel himself beginning to squirm, and he knew the big man could read him like a book. *The SOB is not dumb.* Joe opened his mouth to speak, but before the words came out, he heard Scott continued. "If you don't want, you don't have to answer. You are in my unit, and you are going to fly right, or I'll personally kick your ass. Understand?"

Again, Joe felt Scott's penetrating eyes, seeking any weakness. *But the game works both ways. His words are for effect only. Although the big man could get physical.* Joe felt he could take him.

Of course, it would never come to a physical altercation. *Scott is merely exerting his authority.*

"Master Sergeant Scott, I'm a team player. From what I can see, you need all the team-players you can get. You are correct. Like everybody, I have had problems in the past, but none of them were job related. I have discussed the situation with the captain. He has no problems with my background, and you'll have none with me."

"There was no doubt in my mind; you would respond like this." After a short pause, Scott continued. "I gave it thought last night. As soon as you are acclimated, you are going to be the captain's partner. Where he goes, you go. I do not want you answering to anybody except for him and me."

"Okay, I can manage that." Joe seemed to wake up.

"When you get your cloths on and eat, Banks will show you around post and get you processed. We will get you proper clothed, and make sure you can fire a weapon."

Scott turned to leave. Before he exited the squad tent, He looked at Joe with a smile and winked; "Don't fool yourself; you could never take me!"

Scott's decisive point enforced Joes's budding opinion. *This is no man to take lightly in any respect.*

After dressing and going outside, the next morning, Joe found Lein and Baby San squatting and working on dirty boots.

Lein washed the boots in a small pan, while Baby San applied polish. While Looking at Baby San, Joe thought, w*hat a lovely creature she is, with her long jet-black hair pulled back into a ponytail?* Her face was not quite as round or dark as the young girls he observed driving through Saigon. Her teeth were like pearls, and from what he could see, her eyes were doe-like.

Lein, on the other hand, was hardly pretty, by his standards, but she was not a crone. Her hair was chopped to above the shoulders. Her extremely round face, swollen from her pregnancy, was her dominant features. She had a very pleasant smile and appeared to be exceptionally cheerful. When you considered her circumstances, she would do in a pinch, as a late-night pick-up.

Neither girl was any more than five feet tall, and weighed no more than ninety-five pounds, when Lein was not pregnant.

After going to the mess hall for a late breakfast, Joe went into the office building, where he found Banks, and got a cup of coffee. Once he settled down with his coffee, he asked Banks, "Do you want to get me ready for war?"

CHAPTER 16

"Hébert, are you ready to do some work?" Captain S asked him, as he walked through the door. "You have been sitting around for what, seven days?"

"Yes, Sir, I'm ready to go. And it's been a week. Where are we going?"

"Down the road to My Tho. A barge, which looked shot up a little, anchored in My Tho late yesterday. While coming up the Mekong River, they were attack with rockets. They report, duds are on board. They want us to look at it. So, grab your gear and let's get your first incident out of the way."

"Yes, Sir." Joe grabbed his new gear, consisting of a steel pot, flack vest, M-16 rifle, a flashlight, and a belt which contained a canteen, his EOD tools, a first aid pack, and a full ammo pouch. He also grabbed a pack which held ten pounds of C-4 explosives, thirty feet each of time fuse and detonating cord, six fuse lighters, and a small wooden box of ten blasting caps. He should have separated the caps from the explosives but did not. "I'm ready to go."

He headed for the Jeep with his pack slung over his shoulder and his M-16 in his hand.

Captain S got the same gear. However, he chose an M-79 grenade launcher, with six 40-mm high explosive rounds, for his weapon.

Joe slid into the driver's seat and used the combination Scott had given him to unlock the chain securing the steering wheel. "Are you ready, Captain?"

"Let's go."

As Joe pulled away, Captain S nodded toward the two-and-a-half-ton truck, sitting next to them. "I surely wish someone would steal that old dog. It never starts when we need it. Scott tried to use it yesterday to pick up some plywood, but it wouldn't start."

"I assume, the plywood was coming from DIVARTY and was what Banks and negotiated for disassembling the ejection round. Shortly after I arrived, we discussed it.?"

"Yeah." Captain S replied.

"If you don't mind me asking, what did you find in the round?"

"You didn't hear?"

"No, Sir. As you know, I have been busy processing. I had to go to places like personnel and finance. I turned medical records in which resulted in three shots. Also, I had to zero my weapon and find uniforms."

"Well, Banks and Johnson removed the faze, the baseplate, and the injection propellant. There was nothing inside to see, except for a short piece of 2x4 wood." Captain S chuckled.

"A two-by-four?" Joe could not believe it.

"Yelp, and Colonel Fairbanks was livid. The two-by-fours were placed in the rounds at the ammo plant. When the projectiles arrive in country, the intelligence, (G2) people, are supposed to select and insert the proper pamphlets into the round. Obviously G2 did not take part in the supply chain. I don't know or care whose fault it was, but I would bet more than one Full Bull, or colonel, got a vicious ass chewing by a General.

"It's nothing for us to worry about. It's only a few extra dollars wasted." Captain S sighed and continued to shake his head.

"I would say a lot more than a few dollars were wasted. I bet the mechanical time fuses, used in ejection rounds, are quite expensive." Joe quipped.

"You're right. The manpower and the equipment used in the supply chain to get ammunition from the manufacturing facilities to our ammunition supply point (ASP) here are by no means a short drive." Captain S ended the conversation.

The bumpy, graveled, and dusty road to My Tho had potholes everywhere. Palm trees and other vegetation grew close to the road. On their right, there were a couple cinder-block buildings with ARVN guards and barbed wire guarding them. Also, a dozen or more hooches, reeded homes, part of them completely covered with thatch. Others, with thatched roofs and plywood siding, sat close to the road. Behind them lay the omnipotent Mekong River. It was a half mile wide.

They met a half dozen military vehicles on the road which usually had a significant amount of traffic.

On the outskirts of My Tho, a large road sign pointed to the route for convoy traffic. They read the words, 'No Convoys Allowed in My Tho', printed on the sign in English and Vietnamese. In total, they had traveled a little less than five miles to reach My Tho.

My Tho, an important Delta city, sat on the north bank of the northern most branch of the Mekong River. This close to the South China sea, the river split into three branches.

My Tho's originally founders when remnants of refugees fleeing from China's Ming Dynasty in Taiwan, in the late 1600s. The Japanese seized control of the city from French control during World War Two.

As a central hub of the Delta, My Tho supplied Saigon with fish, rice, and other agricultural products, such as vegetables, coconuts, bananas, longans, and other fruits.

Joe's only reference to Vietnamese cites were Saigon and Tan An. My Tho seemed to be neither.

The main street of My Tho ran parallel with the river. It compared favorably to the other two cities. Little traffic and fewer people make it less threatening.

Rusty tin covered the buildings, but a couple had asphalt shingles. Homes, and business establishments were painted green, blue, or yellow. Cinder block buildings showed unrepaired bullet holes and other signs of recent fighting. Joe knew there had been significant fighting here during Tet, and then again as late as April. There were also large shade trees with battle scars showing.

Local people were cooking on the street in what Joe considered a Vietnamese style outdoor kitchen. Their business consisted of a small charcoal fire in a metal container and two or three cook pots. They sold bananas and other types of fruit that Joe did not recognize. Bottles of Coke and beer, covered with ice, was for sale. The aroma and noise were the same as Saigon's, but nowhere near as prevailing.

When they arrived at the river port, they were quickly escorted, by ARVN guards, to the area where they found a moored single barge attached to a huge tugboat. The barge looked to be about forty feet wide and ninety feet long. *There must be other barges placed elsewhere*, Joe thought.

"What do you have for us today?" Joe asked the shirtless, overweight, bearded, balding, and obviously American man who greeted them.

The man ignored Joe's question, scratched his hairy stomach, and said, "Follow me, please. We took several rockets yesterday and some of them didn't go off."

"What's your name?" Captain S asked him.

"Dude, everybody calls me Chubby."

"You are a private civilian contractor, I presume?" Captain S followed up.

"You got it right, man." Chubby grinned and made a smacking noise with his mouth at the same time.

"Okay, Chubby, lead the way. And how do you know they were rockets?" Captain S needed any information available.

"Well, dude, I don't know for sure. But I've been up and down this river a bunch of times and have never been slammed as badly as we were yesterday." Chubby shrugged as he led Captain S and Joe onto the deck of the barge.

"Isn't everything flying fast through the air a rocket? I know you're the expert and all." Chubby made quotes in the air with his fingers. "Everybody knows you are." The look he gave Captain S suggested, he was not such an expert, after all.

Joe gestured to a round spot on the side of the barge, where bare metal showed, and asked, "Were you hit there yesterday?"

"Yup." Chubby retorted.

Captain S asked, "Do you have any of the frag from the exploding rounds?"

"Un-huh," He reached his into his pocket and retrieved small pieces of sharp metal fragments. The largest was oddly shaped, half inch long and wide. He handed them to Captain S.

After examining the frag, Captain S gave them to Joe for him to examine.

"You guys know what you're doing, don't-chu? I have experience with explosives. That's why I know we have some duds in those pallets." Chubby proudly smiled and pointed to the barge's cargo, stacks of tightly bound cases of can drinks on pallets.

"What kind of explosive experience do you have?" Joe curiosity spiked.

"For one thing, I blew up some gopher holes using bombs that I made. That was cool." Chubby puffed his chest as fully as possible, proud of himself.

Joe decided to take a leap and asked, "Do you also reload your own ammunition? I'll bet you load used brass."

"Yeah, dude. I do! How did you know?" Chubby looked at Joe, astonishingly. "Joe, you surely must be a kindred spirit, and you might even know explosives as well as I do."

"He's really smart sometimes. Now, let's take a look at those pallets." Captain S held back a laugh as he looked at Joe and shook his head in disbelief of Chubby.

"Dude, you can see right here. This is where the rocket went in." Chubby pointed to a hole about three inches in diameter. "Since it's only a hole, and there's no other damage, it didn't come out or explode. So, it must be inside the pallet of drinks."

While looking down, Captain S noticed the large puddle of orange liquid under his feet. He nodded to the source, and asked, "What's in this pallet?"

"Orange flavored drinks. Other pallets have Coke and strawberry on them. Those down there have cases of beer on them." Chubby escorted them to the pallets of beer.

Captain S and Hébert looked at one of the pallets holding beer and then looked at each other. Joe smiled first, but the captain smiled was wider. He whispered to Joe, "Bingo."

Captain S looked at Chubby, ran his hand over his head, and surveyed the cargo load. "I think we have duds everywhere."

"*Dynomite*! I knew it! I knew it!" Chubby jumped up and down while ringing his hands.

"What we'd like to do is get the pallets to a safe area where we can properly dispose of them. Chubby, will you get your captain to release them to us for our disposal? Ask him to type up a statement saying he is releasing them to EOD for disposal, because of potential explosive hazards within them. I'll sign it with your captain, and he should be relieved of any responsibilities."

Captain S looked around and did a little mental planning. "We'll arrange for some trucks. It'll be good if you or your captain can arrange for a forklift to load the pallets. What are we looking at, fifteen to eighteen pallets?"

"Ya dude. I'll tell the captain, and I'll get the forklift. I can drive it, and I'm not scared about working with duds." Chubby grunted and started waddling toward the tugboat.

"Joe, get on the radio. No, I'll do it. You look around more closely, and I'll call the unit."

Captain S walked back to the jeep and lifted the radio mic. "Course Jackal One, Course Jackal One, this is Course Jackal Six, over." Captain S spoke into the radio's mic.

"This is One, go." Scott's voice came through the radio.

"I need enough transportation for eighteen pallets at my location. ASAP. Over."

"Six, did you say eighteen pallets, and what is the destination? Over." The radio replied.

"One, roger on the eighteen pallets. The destination is your location. And One, this is a priority. Use every chip you have, to get the transportation here ASAP. Over."

"Six, can I ask what we you're dealing with? Over." The radio came back.

"No and give me a progress report in fifteen minutes. Six, out."

"Joe, how does it feel to hit a jackpot on your first incident?" Captain S grinned and pumped his fist.

"Great, Sir, great! I'm sure glad Chubby knows a lot about explosives." Joe mocked and could not resist laughing. At the same time, he noted the captain had used Joe to address him for the first time. "When Chubby tells him what you said about duds on his barge, the tugboat captain will gladly release the pallets."

"Be careful with the words you use. I did not tell him there were duds on his barge. I specifically said, I think, we have duds everywhere, which is a true generalization, not necessarily specific to his barge. Also, in the release statement, it will say potential explosive hazards, not explosive hazards.

"They will release the pallets to us for our disposal. Drinking the contents will meet this criterion," Captain S said with a sly grin.

"I like the way you think, Sir. As a matter of fact, if things keep going this well, I may like Vietnam." A grin spread across Joe's face.

"Joe, be assured, things won't always go well. This will be a good day, but it's not over, yet. You will have other good days. But you'll also have some hellish days now and then. You will see more bad days than good days. Now, I'll go find Chubby and see how he is doing with the release paperwork. You stay with the radio." With all the levity dropped from his statement, Captain S headed toward the tugboat.

"Yes, Sir." Joe went to the Jeep and relaxed.

Joe thought about Ava, until the radio blared, "Course Jackal Six, this is Course jackal One, over."

Joe fumbled with the mic., but finally found the key and said, "One this is, Oh, Oh, hell, I don't know who l am. Over."

"I know who you are. I presume Six is busy. Over."

"Roger, One. You can give me a situation report, or sitrep. I'll pass it on. Over."

"Tell him three, two-and-a-half-ton trucks are headed to your location with an ETA of approximately thirty to forty minutes. I'll keep trying to pin the time down and will be back with you when I learn something. Over."

"One, anything else. Over?"

"Nothing, except to tell you, you need some schooling, and you can give me a sitrep. Over."

"One, I don't need schooling badly enough to cross the captain. Over." Joe knew better than to bite on Scott's inquiry.

"You're already learning. One, out." The radio went silent.

Joe sat back and again tried to relax. This time making sure he did not dose. He knew Captain S would be back shortly.

"Has Scott called?" Captain S asked Joe, as he walked up to the Jeep.

"Yes, Sir. He called about five minutes ago. The trucks are lined up and will be here in twenty-five to thirty-five minutes.

"The tugboat Captain happily signed the release statement. We left the number of pallets blank. We'll fill it in and initial it after the pallets are loaded. He seemed more interested in the Vietnamese girl in his quarters." Captain S smirked.

"Sir, it sounds as if we have the keys to the bank." Joe schemed like a good NCO.

"Yeah, it's working out well, but I don't see anywhere near eighteen pallets which were hit and has holes in them." Captain S could think, but he did not think like an NCO.

"Captain, we need to alert the front gate about the trucks coming in. If you'll do that, I'll go find eighteen pallets which have holes in them. I noticed a loose piece of metal that will do the job." Joe smiled. He gave Captain S plausible deniability for what, they were about to do.

Captain S knew it. "Staff Sergeant Hébert, I like the way you think, too! I can see you're going to be an outstanding partner for me. You do know of course, I prefer beer over orange and strawberry sodas, don't you?" He chuckled.

"Captain S, while we have a few minutes, there is something I'd like to tell you. I sent a letter to Captain Taylor, the Commander of the EOD unit at Fort Ben, giving him my address. You know, he helped me. Captain Taylor told me to let him know where I am, and he would let Ava know, where I am."

Captain S nodded. "You're fine Joe. Thanks for keeping me informed about the situation. I know she is especially important to you, and you are worried about her. However, you cannot let the situation consume you. For the next year, you must bring your best game to every incident. If you do not, well, I don't have to tell you. You know the story.

"Don't worry, Sir. I'm a soldier first. I'll keep my head in the game."

They both went their respective ways. The captain drove to the front gate. Joe went to the barge where he retrieved the piece of metal which he had previously noted. It turned out to be a one-inch bolt, twelve inches long. He quickly went to work putting holes in pallets of beer, making holes of approximately three inches in diameter which looked like the so-called rocket holes.

When Joe heard the forklift approaching, he finished his last pallet, giving him a total of eighteen. Enough, he thought. No need to give them anything to think about. He replaced the bolt to its original place and went to meet Captain S and Chubby.

"I'm ready to rock and roll." Chubby hopped off the forklift. "When are the trucks coming?"

"They'll be here in about ten minutes." Captain S looked around. "Staff Sergeant Hébert, did you get a count on the pallets?"

"Yes, Sir. I counted eleven pallets of beer, two pallets of orange drinks, two pallets of strawberry, and three pallets of Coke with holes in them. Sir, rockets hammered these boys hard. If they were in the Army, they would receive some kind of metals for bravery." Joe managed to keep a straight face while reporting the count.

Captain S turned to Chubby, who now stood two inches taller and grinned from ear to ear. "Do you want to go count those pallets?"

"No, Sir. I trust Staff Sergeant Hébert. He's right. We got hammered yesterday."

Captain S nodded with great satisfaction. "Okay, then. Let's go and report this to your Captain, and get the paperwork finalized."

"I'll go to the front gate and wait on the trucks," Joe said.

Later in the afternoon, the last truck pulled out of the port. The three trucks had made two trips, each carrying three or four pallets each.

The tugboat captain finally made an appearance on the barge, but for only a minute. He told Captain Summerville, "I'm glad to get this stuff off my barge."

"I can understand what you mean, but my work has just begun. We'll start this afternoon to see what we must do." Captain S had to try hard not to laugh.

"Very well, and Good luck. Thanks for your help. I'm out of here. I have better things to do." The tugboat Captain turned and started to leave.

"Oh, Captain, before you go, I have one more thing. I'd like to commend your man, Mr. Chubby for his actions relating to this incident. You have an outstanding man there." Captain S nodded toward Chubby. "And Chubby, should this situation occur again, call us. We'll take care of your problem."

"Groovy mam. How do I contact you?" Chubby asked, while beaming with pride.

"You get on the horn, call Dong Tam EOD and tell them Chubby needs help." I assure you; we'll not forget you, Chubby."

CHAPTER 17

"I think the house can afford a few beers for all of us." Captain S announced, as he entered the office building.

"Damn, Captain. What a heyday! You have quite a haul of beer. How in the hell did you manage it!" Master Sergeant Scott acted bedeviled and excited.

"Before we get into that, we need to get some beer iced down. Hébert and I brought the ice. Scott, call all your card playing friends, or anyone who you want to impress, and tell them to come over here for a drink on the house. Tell them it's a going away party for Sergeant First Class Johnson. Don't mention the good fortunes we had today. If anyone asks about all the pallets, the storyline is, they told us, there is a possibility of a dud in each pallet. Stick with the story," Captain S ordered and turned to Specialist Weaver. "Get on the horn to Tan An and see if our guys can come down here for the night. Make sure you follow the storyline."

"Yes, Sir," replied Wheeler. He at once went to the radio to contact the on-site team.

Captain S asked, "Scott, have the girls already gone to town?"

"Yes, Sir, they left early. Lein was not feeling well. I would not be surprised if she's not back for a while. She's going to drop the baby anytime now."

"I'll bet you ten bucks; she'll be back the day after the child is born." Wheeler chimed while waiting on the radio.

"I won't take the bet." Captain S shook his head.

I should reword my statement. She should take some time off." Scott clarified his comment.

"I think we can all agree with that." Wheeler smiled and nodded.

"The last truck left a few minutes ago," Specialist O'Neil said, as he appeared in the door. "Banks is getting a small trailer to ice the beer in, and Johnson is taking the borrowed forklift back to the ammunition supply point (ASP). I could use some help to break a couple of the pallets apart."

"Sure, come on Scott. Let us see what we can do," Captain S motioned with an arm swing, and they headed out.

"It looks like we have some Schlitz and Hamm here!" MSG Scott examined a couple of the pallets.

"We have some Budweiser and Coors over here. I like Coors, but it's hard to get when you're outside of Colorado," Captain S bellowed.

"Yeah, I saw the Coors. There is a pallet of the Australian rotgut over there. I haven't looked at the rest of it." He pointed toward a pallet.

Scott said, "Let's get three cases each of Coors, Budweiser, and Hamm. We should not more than nine cases. That should be enough for thirty people. I do not think any more than that will drop by. What do you think, Captain?"

"Sounds about right to me. Let's get to it."

"Captain S, can you please tell me how you managed this? It's driving me crazy." Scott's curiosity got the best of him.

"You know how the incident was called in. Well, we were met by Chubby."

"Chubby?" Scott interrupted. He did not have a clue about Captain S's story.

"Yeah, Chubby, and let me tell you, he was chubby. He also knew about explosives! Apparently, he had made some homemade bombs to blast gopher holes." Captain S chuckled.

"Bombs and gophers make him an expert." Scott nodded.

"Chubby knew the pallets contained duds, because of the entry holes. Of course, he did not know the whole story. Chubby showed us a piece frag. He had picked it up. Hébert and I at once knew; a 90mm recoilless weapons hit them. The amount of liquid on the deck told us, the projectiles had exploded inside all the affected pallets, destroying no more than fifteen to twelve casas and slightly distorting the pallet's tightly bound shape. Chubby and his tugboat Captain insisted we remove the pallets. Of course, we were duty bound to dispose of the suspected hazards." Captain S could hardly control his laughter. "Oh, and we told Chubby how brave and wise he was, and if it happens again, to be sure to call us. I hope he calls next week." Captain S doubled over in laughter.

"If only we could be so lucky!" Scott nearly cried from laughing so hard.

Joe raised a beer, "To Chubby and all the other experts like him!"

After sunset, Captain S surveyed the guests and thought his estimate of thirty people seemed about right. He stood with Lieutenant Colonel Phillips; Commander of the 9th MP Battalion, Lieutenant Commander Davis, Commander of the Naval Support Activities at Dong Tam, Chief Warrant Officer Crawford, Commander of Dong Tam's ammunition supply point (ASP), and an artillery captain whom he had not met until recently.

Staff Sergeant Hébert stood with Staff Sergeant Jackson from their on-sight team, who pointed out the other guests: "Sergeant Major Donaldson, from the Division Support Command (DISCOM), and from the 9th MP Battalion, Sergeant Major App. The others sitting at the table with MSG Scott are Master Chief Petty Officer Willis, from the Navy Support Activities, MSG White, who ran the mess hall."

Jackson and Specialist Redding had made it to Dong Tam from Tan An only a minutes before the roads closed. Since the 'glad to meet you' statements, Jackson had been standing next to Joe, all the time running his mouth. Jackson did make one comment of which Joe took seriously. "The people you see here are friends of EOD. You can trust them. They will help you anyway they can. They know what our mission encompasses, and the unique hardships associated with it."

At the senior NCO table, they were discussing how Vietnam differed from the Korean War. All had served there. "I'll take the hot and humid weather over the snow and ice," Sergeant Major Donaldson said.

"I never got cold." Willis immodestly informed them.

"Only, because you kept your ass in a ship," White mocked.

"What I hated the most were those damn bugles the Chinks blew." Scott shook his head.

"Buck, you may be right there. I still hate bugles. My spine shutters when I hear one. Our soldiers have never faced wave after wave of a screaming enemy charging from all directions." White closed his eyes at the memory.

"One thing bothering me today is the quality of our young Officers. Part of them is outstanding, others are self-centered SOBs. Their main goals should be to take care of their mission and their personnel, not enhancing their careers. They think of no one, other than themselves." Scott's voice sounded full of disdain.

"Your comment goes for senior Officers, as well as junior Officers," Donaldson added.

"I'll echo what you said, but all this fragging of Officers is ridiculous! Also, part of our troops stays high on dope all the time. There are lots of sorry ass NCOs and enlisted personnel out there, too." White bemoaned the situation.

"I couldn't agree more. The Navy has their share of similar problems." Willis shook his head.

Scott added, "It's not a problem with EOD. Our young troops are better than the average. Sure, we have some immaturity, but if they do not have it all together, they don't make it through EOD school. We cannot allow problems in this field. Also, most of the NCOs have top-secret clearances and everybody has at least a secret clearance, some with secret restricted data clearances, and some other type of clearance which you can't even say out loud."

"You don't know how lucky you are." Donaldson looked at Scott.

"Oh, yes, I do know! We all know what your situation is. I bet you would give a month's pay to take your uniform off and give your man, Colonel Hollow, an old fashion ass whipping." Scott goaded Donaldson.

"Truer words have never been spoken." Sergeant Major Donaldson replied with a smile.

Meanwhile, at the Officers huddle, Lieutenant Commander Davis bragged about all the new construction on the Navy side of Dong Tam. "We're spending more than three million dollars on our new helicopter pad and hangers, new Officers and senior NCO quarters, and clubs."

"You're spending a lot of money!" Captain S could not believe the amount.

"By the way, Summerville, if you want one, we'll find a room for you in the new Bachelor Officers Quarters (BOQ) facilities." Lieutenant commander Davis looked at Captain S.

"No, thanks. For me, it's too close to the ASP." Captain S shook his head.

"You don't like the Navy side?" Mr. Crawford jumped in.

Captain S looked at everyone in the group. "You know better. But one of these days, Charlie's going to get the ASP. So far, I think they have hit five ASPs further North this year. If they hit ours, all those new shiny buildings will become rubbish in a single heartbeat."

"He's right about the ASP's north of us, Commander." Phillips spoke in a matter of a fact manner.

"Captain, I like you a lot, but you're talking a bunch of BS! It'll never happen your way. If what you are saying is true, the Engineers would never have approved the location of the buildings." Davis sounded anecdotally and defensively at the same time.

"Sir, I'll bet those brilliant engineers only looked at the soil integrity when they did the site inspection for your buildings. There's no way in this world they'd approve the construction of those buildings at the current location if they accounted for the ASP. Mr. Crawford, certainly you can see what I'm talking about." Captain S stood his ground.

Mister Crawford replied, "The buildings are really close. But we have thick berms around the ammunition pads on three sides. They will protect against blast waves."

"I'm not buying any of this." Davis refused to listen.

"Sir, I'm no engineer. But I do know what explosives will do. Furthermore, I have been in several ASPs in the states, and I've never seen a permanent structure within three quarters of a mile from any of the pads or bunkers. Hell, I don't feel safe here! You know, we would not be here if Colonel Hollow hadn't thrown my predecessor off his side of the base. I was told; he called us a nickel and dime unit." Captain S threw his hands up in the air in a, can you believe it, gesture.

"He's right, Sir. Hollow said it. I was there." Mr. Crawford added when the Lieutenant Commander looked at him strangely.

Davis replied, "If you don't feel safe where we're standing, and if it goes as you suggest, and we get hit, what are you and more important your people, going to do?"

"We're going to go and get in Lieutenant Colonel Phillips' back pocket. If and when the ammunition supply point, ASP, gets hit, he is going to need us badly." Captain S nodded to Phillips.

Phillips waved his hand. "Come on! Bring your guys! You won't need anything. Nobody will get any sleep for days. Commander, I attended a seminar on ASP explosions last month. What I carried away from the meeting was, when ASP's get hit, they can be major, but don't have to be catastrophic. It depends on what pads are hit, and how many of the exploding pads propagates from one pad to another."

While looking at Crawford, Davis said, "I would think, if the small arms pad is close to the new buildings, and if the really explosive stuff is further away, you have the best scenario. Am I correct, and is this situation not what we have?"

"Yes, Sir, this is what we have," Crawford retorted.

"Then I'll take it as a positive, and I'll not worry about it. Now, Summerville, I know you'll continue to eat with us and patronize our O-club." The Lieutenant Commander's tone changed.

"Oh, yes, Sir. Be assured, I will. The food is great and the two girls working at the bar look mighty fine." Captain S grinned.

Hébert escaped from Jackson and found refuge with Wheeler, who said. "These guys can put the beer down, can't they? I hope we have put enough beer on ice."

"We have plenty. They have to work tomorrow and will be leaving soon."

"Joe, what are we going to do with all the beer, especially if the guy calls us next week or the next? I'll bet the stuff will not last long sitting in the sun." Wheeler expressed his thoughts.

"I don't know how well the beer will hold up in the sun, but I'm sure we'll find a way to use it." Joe said as he took a sip of his beer.

"Well, I've been thinking about it. I think we should sell it." Wheeler looked pointedly at Joe.

"Sell it? For what, for a dollar a case?"

"No. You see this crowd. They look amazingly comfortable and relaxed. There is no reason we could not have this kind of gathering every night. We would need to add to the patio and make a real bar with at least five stools. If we could sell beer for fifteen cents each, we would get three sixty per case. Ten cases per night, gives us thirty-six dollars per day profit, less the cost of ice. Let's call the cost of ice, six dollars per day. I want to keep it round numbers.

"For a week, we have two hundred and ten dollars. For a month, it's eight hundred and forty-dollars profit. Again, that's a high estimate. I know we will not sell that much every night" Wheeler looked staunchly at Joe.

"Did you do those numbers in your head?" Joe looked astounded and wide eyed.

"Yeah, but what do you think about my idea of selling the beer?"

"I forgot, you have a degree in Banking, which means, you know how to count dollars and cents." Joe nodded in approval.

"Yeah, but what do you think about the idea of selling the beer?" Wheeler asked again.

"It sounds like a lot of work, and a lot of dollars. It doesn't matter what I think about it. You need to talk it over with Master Sergeant Scott and Captain S."

"Will you talk to them with me?" Wheeler meekly asked in a little reserved manner.

"Sure, but you don't need me. I can't add anything to what you told me. You aren't afraid to talk to them, are you?" Joe refused to believe this.

"No, but I--"

"So, are you a Coonass?" Specialist Redding, from the on-sight tram, interrupted as he walked up and placed his hand on Joe's shoulder.

"Trust me, born and bred, and proud of it. I've been called a lot worse." Joe replied in a proudly manner.

"You don't mind being called a derogatory name?" Redding asserted in a negative tone.

"A derogatory name? If you think calling a Cajun, a Coonass is a terrible thing, you are wrong.

All Cajuns are proud of their heritage. They have more to concentrate on than what others say or think about them. Some may take offense to the term, but I'm sure most wouldn't. Most could care less about something so trivial. It's not like a white man calling a Black man the N-word, even though, the white man may not mean it to be derogatory." Joe smirked and shook his head.

Jackson interrupted with a loud voice. "Sorry to interrupt, but I heard what you said. Tell me how a white man calling a Black man the N-word is not considered anything but derogative!"

"Why does it have to be derogative or demeaning? Growing up, I used the word a thousand times and never intended it to be derogative. I didn't ever dream the word inferred low class. I thought it was simply easier to pronounce than Negro, a perfectly acceptable word at the time. I believe it was first used by the Romans, in reference to their enslaved Black people's original home, Nigeria, rather than demeaning. How am I wrong?" Joe tried to explain his words.

"No, no, man. When white people use it, it's meant to put you down." Jackson demanded and pointed at Joe. Jackson stood about five-eleven and weighed one-seventy.

Redding said, "I agree, Black people have been held down. They all came from poverty, and it's hard for them to get out of impoverishment." Redding stood five ten and carried one-seventy.

Joe said, "Again, growing up, my nearest neighbors on the Bayou were colored. Therefore, my hunting and fishing friend were colored. I ate and slept at his house. He ate and slept at my house a couple of times a month. He was my best friend, my brother."

"Oh, I have a colored friend! All racists say the same thing." Jackson moved closer to Joe.

"Backup, man! Jackson, are you calling me a racist?" Joe held his hands up, in front of him, to make sure Jackson could not get any closer.

"Well, you sound like a racist." Jackson tried to force the issue and got closer. "You sound like Captain S when he's talking to me."

Joe calmly said, "To me, it sounds as if you have already had enough to drink."

"It's not what he's drinking, but rather, it's what he's smoking," Wheeler said sarcastically.

"Jackson, you need to get straight because you are becoming a nuisance and making a scene. I don't think you want to act obnoxiously." Joe did not want to sink to Jackson's level.

"I don't give a damn what you think! Nobody likes me or Redding. Why do you think we stay up at Tan An as often as we can? They do not like me because I'm Black. They don't like Redding because, his father is a Bird Colonel. Hell, Baby San, will not even look at me, but she looks at Captain S!" Jackson practically shouted.

"She doesn't like you because you won't take no for an answer! You will not keep your hands off her. As for Captain S, he doesn't touch her." Wheeler also remained calm but struck the important aspect.

"She likes you, hangs on you like a tick on a dog! And you must see the way she looks at the captain. Both of you are white, and I am Black! What does it tell you?"

"Poor Jackson. He was born poor, and nobody likes him because he's colored." Joe mocked and was a little cynical.

"Don't call me colored! I'm Black!" Jackson gave the appearance of someone seething.

"Black! For years, your people wanted to get away from being called Negro and wanted to be colored. Now, you want to be called Black. What, the hell, is next? Recently, I heard someone us the words, African Americans!

"I understand you likely came from poverty. I did, too. Someone told me you are from Chicago. I do not believe the poverty in Chicago is worse than on the Bayou. If you come to the Bayous of Louisiana, I will show you what poverty is. So, do not give me any of your BS! You wouldn't make it on the Bayou for twenty-four hours." Joe wanted his turn to be disdainful.

"Now, there's some BS," Redding scoffed.

"Look! I am the new kid on the block, so I'm taking a step back. However, be warned, do not ever get in my face again with your racist crap," Joe turned and walked away.

All the chatter continued, but the guests had thinned considerably. There were only ten people left when Banks, sitting in a chair at the end of the bar, began strumming on his guitar and shouted. "How about, we have a sing-along! Let's have a little, 'Detroit City'. I believe credit should go to, Bobby Bare and his producers."

Banks started singing and everybody sang-along.

"I want to hear you. Let's get louder!" Banks yelled, then started singing again. Everyone stood and started singing at the top of their voice. They bellowed the lyrics loudly.

When Banks sang the last stanza, everybody sang it over and over:

CHAPTER 18

The morning came early for Joe. After a late night of alcohol, song, and of course, exaggerated war stories, the VC had decided to show their muscle by lobbing in mortar rounds on two separate occasions. The rounds hit their favorite target, Charlie Pad, the helicopter pad on the north side of Dong Tam.

During the night, as soon as the mortars started falling, Staff Sergeant Hébert and Specialist O'Neil were called out of their bunker, where they and the rest of the team sought safety during the mortar attack. The call asked for help in crater analysis and fragmentation identification. Evidence collected at the crater would tell them which direction the mortars came from, while frag analysis showed the type of round. With the information and number calculation, counter-mortar artillery fired within a couple of minutes, targeting the area where the mortars were fired.

So, after a night of drinking and then working, Joe found himself rousted out of bed.

"Time to get moving, sleepyhead. As soon as Captain S arrives, you have work to do." Scott sounded as loud as a drill sergeant.

"What time is it?" Joe grunted and rubbed his eyes.

"It doesn't matter what time it is. Get your boots on. Your presence is requested back at Charlie Pad." Scott walked out.

It took Joe only a couple of minutes to get dressed and to get into the office building where Captain S waited patiently. "Two hours sleep?" Captain S asked Joe.

"Maybe, but probably less." Joe was not awake yet.

"They found a couple of dud mortar rounds you missed last night." Scott looked at Joe.

"We missed! I wasn't looking for duds when mortar rounds were falling everywhere. We were looking for small craters. When we found one, we were looking to get our ass out of there as soon as we examined it. We could have missed a Russian tank out there!" Joe strongly asserted, defending himself and O'Neil about the job they did in the early morning hours.

"Don't get riled up. It's not our job to find duds, or to do crater analysis. We do it because we can. You two guys did fine. If anything is said, I will cover you. Now, let's go see what they found." Captain S headed for the door as a phone rang.

Before reaching the Jeep, Scott followed them out the door. "Captain, Captain, it's Colonel Hollow wants to talk with you."

Captain S thought for a second. "It's probably about this thing. Tell him I'm gone. And ask him if you can pass on a message to me. If not, I'll call him back after we're through with this incident."

"Are you sure? Sir, you know how crazy he gets." Scott sounded worried.

"Absolutely, I'm sure." Captain S chuckled, as he and Joe drove away.

At Charlie Pad, they were met by a young Buck Sergeant. He offered Captain S a salute, which he promptly returned. "What do you have for us, Sergeant?"

"Well, Sir, I'm responsible for checking the petroleum pumps and fuel levels in the storage tanks. I was doing it and found a couple of duds from last night. I reported it to my First Sergeant, who reported it up the chain of command. They told me to meet you here."

"Okay, Sergeant, show me where they are." Captain S extended his arm in a lead the way gesture.

The Sergeant led them through the petroleum tank farm. The huge tank farm was made devoid of anything except for gravel and fuel tanks. The Sergeant pointed to a dud a couple of feet from one of the tanks and said, "This's one of them, and there's another one, two tanks further down the line."

"It looks like an 82mm mortar, with its fuze sheared off.", Hébert said.

A couple seconds later, he continued. "There it is," the fuze lay a couple yards away.

Captain S said, "It looks like a point detonating fuze. I wonder what broke it off."

"Look up, Sir. The round struck the side of the tank. It caused the long scar." Joe pointed to the side of the tank.

"Obviously, the round came in at an angle where the point of the fuze didn't strike the tank first. The front ogive of the round hit first and caused the fuze to break off. At that angle, the round couldn't penetrate the tank." Captain S guessed.

"That sounds possible." Joe nodded. "Let's take a look at the other dud. I think both the fuze and projectile could be extremely sensitive. The fuze contains the detonator, but after the impact the main charge may be a little more sensitive than normal."

They walked to the second tank, past where two rounds had exploded harmlessly on impact in the gravel covering the ground. They found another dud and determined its condition to be the same as the earlier one.

Captain S looked at Joe. "We can't take care of them here. We will have to carry them outside the berm around this petroleum farm and take care of them there. You take this one. I'll go back for the other one."

"Okay, you two get back out of the danger radius. I'll move this one down there." Joe pointed to the nearest berm.

After the two departed, Joe moved the projectile and fuze carefully to the designated area.

There he placed his items in a safe place, where they can safely explode them. Joe then went to search the other sections of the tank farm.

Captain S retrieved the first round and fuze and set them beside Joe's round and fuze. When Joe returned, Captain S told him, "Let's get our gear and take care of them."

"Not so fast. We have a problem, Sir."

"A problem, Joe. What kind of problem?" Captain S suddenly started worrying.

"It would be best if you let me show you." Joe led the way to a tank next to the end of the complex.

"Take a look up there," Joe said, while pointing to a hole in the tank. "The tank definitely suffered a hard hit, but we have no dud. We have a hole of entry, not a scar from an explosion."

"No projectile or fuze anywhere, and no evidence of an explosion on the tank. There is only one answer. The fuze and projectile are inside the tank." Captain S exhaled heavily.

Joe said, "I think, you're right, but this one is not all. Let me show you another problem. "There's the mortar." Joe pointed to a dud. "I can't find the fuze. It must be in the tank, sense the tank has a hole similar to the first tank."

"Crap, crap, crap! If this is all, let's go and find the Sergeant. We'll have to check the tops of each tank." Captain S took his cap off and ran his hand over his head.

"Sir, I haven't checked all the tanks. I'll do it while you're gone."

"I'm here. I followed well behind you." The Sergeant announced his presence.

"Sergeant, can you drain these tanks?" Captain S patted the tank they were standing next to.

The question surprised the Sergeant. "No, Sir, I can't do that!"

"Who can?" Captain S did not ask nicely.

"Well, I can drain them, but my Commander--" The Sergeant stammered and did not finish his sentence.

"Go get somebody who has the authority to drain these tanks. Be back here in no more than ten minutes." Captain S used his authoritative voice.

"Yes, Sir!" The Sergeant saluted and left in a double time trot.

Captain S went to the Jeep, keyed the radio's Mic., and spoke. "Echo Oscar Delta, this is Six, over."

"Go," a reply came from Master Sergeant Scott.

"Have O'Neil bring us some flashlights and an oxygen breathing apparatus. The OBAs were in storage for a while, so he should check it out. Over."

"Do you need Johnson? Over."

"No, he's too short. He only has two or three days left. I've told him not to leave there unless there's an absolute emergency. Anyway, he needs to spend time with Lein. She needs him. Over."

"Roger, I agree with you. O'Neil will be there in about thirty minutes. Jackson and Redding are still here. They'll head back later. Over."

"Thanks. Six out."

Captain S returned to Hébert's location. "You want to start checking the tops of all the tanks to see what you can find?"

"Okay, Sir, but I sure hope there's not a bunch of holes up there."

"Me, too. Be careful going up the ladders. Heck, I don't know what's up there, not even if they are flat or not."

"Nor do I, Sir, but I'll find out." Joe walked to the first tank which needed inspection.

Captain S waited only a minutes before he saw two people approaching. "Captain, this is my Lieutenant." The young Sergeant said as they approached and saluted.

"I was told, we need to drain a couple of these tanks," the Lieutenant said.

Captain S explained the situation, and the Lieutenant nodded. "I agree. You need to get inside the tanks. I'll have to check and see where the fuel can be transferred to. In the meantime, my Sergeant can check to see if it's possible to pump the fuel to nearby tanks. If he can, it will not take long. One good thing, no matter what we must do, we can continue working. You do realize we cannot empty them completely?"

"No, what do you mean by completely?" Captain S was not sure he liked the sound of this.

"I guess; they are designed to hold at least four feet all the time. I cannot pump much more out. I can't get them completely dry." The young lieutenant explained.

"Four feet!" Captain S nearly yelled.

"My SOP says four feet. I do not know if it's due to structural integrity, or contaminants. It doesn't matter, sense the pumps are set for only a little less." The Lieutenant shrugged.

"That's a problem. It's a real problem, but let's see what we can do. There is a utility hole on top, isn't there?"

"Yes, Sir. It's about twenty-four inches wide, and there's a ladder leading to the bottom. If it's okay, I'd like to see what we're dealing with, so I can report it up the chain," the Lieutenant pleaded.

Captain S understood. "Good. Of course. Come on, I'll show you. I have my NCO checking the tops of all the tanks to see if there is any kind of other problem up there. I have another EOD tech coming. He can help."

The young Sergeant reported, "Sir, I know the first tank contained less than 30 percent of liquid. I checked it, before I found the dud. I can have it empty in less than an hour. The other tank may take more than two hours to empty completely."

"Empty, meaning, there's still almost four feet of fuel in it." The Lieutenant clearly explained the situation to Captain S.

"I understand. Now, let me show you the two tanks with holes in them. Then, we can go back to meet my other man."

After surveying the situation and needing to report to higher headquarters, the Lieutenant excused himself. When he left, Specialist O'Neil drove up and asked, "What's up, Captain S?"

Captain S gave him a quick sitrep. "We should be able to go to work anytime now."

"Okay, but I don't think--"

"You get an at-a-boy." Captain S interrupted as they both looked at the OBA laying in the Jeep. "I had a brain fart. No, we don't need it in four feet of JP4 or whatever these choppers are flying on these days. But I'll take the flashlight."

"Thank you, Sir. I was worried for a moment." O'Neil sighed in relief.

Captain S smiled and said, "You were worried, if I knew what I what was doing! Truthfully, I initially thought the OBA could be used but then remembered it could not because of safety."

"Uh, Sir. I think I'll go find Staff Sergeant Hébert, before I get myself into trouble." O'Neil gave the captain a big grin, then quickly turned and walked away.

They met with Hébert, who reported that he had more tanks to check, and he had moved the third mortar outside the berm.

"Continue on, Joe. We'll be down there with the Sergeant." Captain S nodded toward the young Sergeant.

"I think she's about ready, Captain." The Sergeant reported as they walked up to him. "So, I can climb on top, open the manhole, and then go down a ladder?" Captain S did not have a warm feeling.

"Yes, Sir. If you would like to."

"If I'd like to? Hell no, I would not like to! But I must! It's my job." Captain S reached for the ladder and began climbing.

Once on top, he carefully maneuvered the slightly rounded surface. O'Neil followed closely behind on hand and knees. Before opening the utility hole, they paused to survey their surroundings.

To the south laid the mighty Mekong River, with two large Navy vessels and five smaller Riverine Vessels. The Navy side of Dong Tam was clearly visible. They were able to see the entrance to the post, the ASP, and the Navy Riverine basin. They tried hard and finally pinpointed the EOD unit's facilities.

On the west side, the fixed wing landing strip, with a burned fuel tank, stood out. Charlie had previously destroyed a large fuel tank with mortar fire. The landing strip had its own operational fuel tank like the one they were perched upon.

On the east side, they could see large trash dump and the defensive perimeter, with sand bagged bunkers and barb wire which lay in a cleared field about two hundred yards wide. Behind it lay Charlie's land and Ambush Alley.

The north end consisted of the petroleum farm, where the Captain and O'Neil were sitting, and the helicopter pad with more than a dozen helicopters, to include Huey, Cobra, a Loach, and a couple of Chinooks. They were protected by parallel mounds of dirt, revetments, used to deflect blast waves and protection from direct fire. Others were in the open. A large, cleared field, four hundred yards wide, lay beyond the defensive perimeter. From O'Neil's and Captain S's position, they were able to see Hébert checking out the top of one of the fuel tanks.

"I guess we can't put this off any longer." Captain S begrudgingly shook his head.

Specialist O'Neil opened the utility hole and exhaled, "I'll go down and take a look."

"Sure, you will, but no, it's my job. Before we go swimming, I'll see what's down there." Captain S took a breath and let it out, took another deep breath, then descended the ladder.

A moment later he popped his head out of the utility hole. "I can't see anything, but liquid down there. The hole of entry, where the projectile punched a hole in the tank, provides ambient light and can be used as a reference point. This utility hole and flashlight provide more light, but not enough to see anything. The good news is the fuel level looks to be shyer than waist deep. "

"Let me take a look." O'Neil moved toward the utility hole.

"Can you hold your breath very long? You won't be able to breathe down there." Captain S coughed and crawled out of the utility hole.

"We'll see!" O'Neil shrugged. After taking deep breaths, he disappeared down the ladder, only to quickly reappear. "I see what you're talking about."

Captain S moved over to the edge of the tank and yelled at the young Sergeant below. "Do you have all you can get out of this tank?"

"Yes, Sir. The other tank will be ready in about thirty minutes!"

"Okay, O'Neil, it looks as if we start skinny dipping unless you have a better idea." Captain S hoped he had a good plan.

"I was afraid you would make that decision." O'Neil replied, stood, and started stripping. "I'm leaving my drawers on."

"I don't know why, but I am, too, but everything else comes off. I think; we should come up with a plan of action."

"What do you have in mind, Sir?"

"We can use the light from the entry hole of entry like a clock's hand as a reference point. I'll go down, walk toward the light, trying to feel anything on the bottom with my feet. When I get to the edge of the tank, under the hole, I'll bear right one step and return to the ladder. Then, I'll repeat the action moving right as long as possible. When I go back down, I should be able to approximate the time, amount of area I previously covered. Maybe I can get to three o'clock. If necessary, the next trip down I'll start from there. When you go down you could do the same thing, only move left each time. We'll see how long it takes to cover the entire tank. Maybe we'll be lucky and find what we're looking for on our first trip down."

"Dream on, Captain!" O'Neil did not sound optimistically.

After deep breaths, Captain S descended into the tank wearing nothing but his briefs.

When the captain reappeared, he gasped for air and shook his head, saying no luck.

"Okay, Captain. I'll show you how it's done." O'Neil sounded cocky.

"Don't push yourself. We have all day." Captain S tried to catch his breath.

"I won't." O'Neil disappeared into the tank. After a minute, he reappeared, smiling, and holding up a mortar round with no fuze. "I told you, Sir."

"Why didn't you get the fuze?" Captain S flashed a grin.

"Come on, Sir. I had to leave something for you." O'Neil replied, with an emphatic smile.

"Okay, here we go." Captain S psyched himself up. However, like the time before, he returned shaking his head and empty-handed.

"Damn, Sir. Are you going to make me do all the work?" O'Neil teased and descended into the tank. This time he returned with nothing in his hands, except for the light.

After each of them had taken more turns down, Joe appeared atop the tank and asked, "How's it going?"

"We have the mortar round but no fuze." O'Neil functioned as cocky as earlier.

"This is getting old fast. My ass is beginning to burn, and I'm sure O'Neil is as well, since he had to go neck deep to reach the round,"

"You're right, Sir. This stuff is eating at me." O'Neil whined.

"The good news is there's no other tanks affected. Only the two we originally identified." Joe presented the good news.

"Good. I don't know how long we can take this crap!" Captain S grimaced.

Joe laughed and said, "Well, at least this is a moment to remember. Someday, I'll tell my grandchildren about the time when I saw two naked EOD guys sitting on top of a thirty-feet tall petroleum tank, in Vietnam."

"Why would you tell them someone such a story? You should tell them the truth." Captain S looked at Joe.

"The truth, what do you mean?" Joe softly spoke in a muddled voice.

"Yes, the truth. You can tell them about the three naked EOD guys on top of a fuel tank, working hard. This is correct, unless you want to go in with your clothes on." Captain S retorted with a mischievous smirk on his face.

"Oh." Joe cringed as he dropped his head. *Dumb ass, learn to keep your mouth closed.*

CHAPTER 19

"It's time for you to get in the tank. Down the hole you go, Joe." Captain S motion to the utility hole. "We've been over the entire bottom a couple of times, but we can't find the damn fuze."

"Okay, I'll go get it." Joe began removing his clothes. "Is the stuff cold? I don't like being cold."

"You may live through it." O'Neil replied sarcastically, as Joe started down the ladder.

In less than a minute, Joe reappeared with the fuze and asked, "What's your problem?"

"Where the hell did you find it?" Captain S couldn't believe his eyes.

"Right under the entry hole, up against the wall. And I see why O'Neil is wet up to his shoulders. I had to bend over in that stuff to reach it."

O'Neil emphasized, "Under the hole! Dammit, I stepped all around the area several times."

"So, did I. We simply missed it." Captain S tried to support O'Neil.

"Well, I have many years of experience wading around barefoot down on the Bayous of Louisiana. There, you had better be careful of what you're stepping on. If you step on a big cottonmouth snake or a mad logger head turtle, you're in trouble."

"Okay, okay, if you're so damn good, and know what you're doing, you can be first down in the next tank." Captain S looked at Joe and did not blink.

"Self, make a note, learn to keep your damn mouth shut!" Joe huffed and started putting his boots on and picking up his clothes.

The three walked to the second tank. They carried their clothes and flashlight and wearing only their boots and underwear. They met the young Sergeant, who asked, "Did you find what you were looking for?"

"Yeah, that tank is clean. We laid the mortar and fuze over there." O'Neil pointed to the tank they had cleared. "We only need to find a fuze in the next one."

"Is she ready for us?" Joe asked.

"Well, she's about empty. I may be able to get two or three more inches, but not more." The Sergeant shrugged.

"It'll be good enough," Captain S told him, and turned to his two guys. "Let's find that damn fuze and get through with this mess. I need a shower."

The three rotated, one at the time, wading in the fuel, searching for the fuze, for a half-hour.

"I don't understand, why we haven't found the damn thing!" O'Neil aired his frustration.

Joe replied, "What I don't understand is, how you two are still going. This stuff is burning like hell, and you two have been at it longer than I have. I don't know if it makes any difference or not, but your skin is a lot lighter than mine. Yeah, we can't keep this up. One more trip down for each of us, and if we can't find it, we'll call it quits. We still must take care of the mortars we have. That will take a while. I hope we'll have some skin left when we hit the showers." Captain S decided to end it after another try.

The extra trip in the tank produced no results. So, Captain S ordered, "You two take the mortar and fuze from the other tank and put them with the others. I'll go to the Jeep and get some of our toys. Then, I'll call Dong Tam Tower and let them know, we're making a shot in thirty-five minutes.

We don't need to knock one of the helicopters, flying around here, out of the sky. I think it's safe to say headquarters would frown on it."

The three checked their watches, removed their fuel-soaked underwear before dressing, and went about their task. Fifteen minutes later, Captain S joined the other two outside the berm with everything they needed to set the shot. Captain S prepared the explosive charge, while Staff Sergeant Hébert aided by cutting the time fuse.

After completing the shot's preparation, Hébert said, "Captain, we're ready to go."

Captain S checked his watch and yelled loudly in three directions. "Fire in the hole! Fire in the hole! Fire in the hole!"

Joe at once checked his watch and noticed the second hand and pulled the dangling metal ring on the fuse lighter. This caused a small pop.

The three took their time walking to the Jeep. Once there, Captain S took the radio Mic. and said, "Dong Tam Tower this is Echo Oscar Delta, over."

"This is Dong Tam Tower. Go."

"We have activity in your area, in roughly seventy-five seconds. Over"

"Roger. I can see you. It's a Go. We have no immediate traffic. Dong Tam Tower out."

After a couple of seconds, Captain S looked at his watch and said, "Now, Staff Sergeant Hébert, we'll see how good an EOD man you are."

"Well, sir, I'm sure I haven't done this as many times as you, but I do know how to measure and how fast time fuse burns."

"We'll see." Captain S looked at his watch. I have ten, nine, eight, seven, six, five, four, three, two, one, zero, -1, -2." The sound of a loud explosion coming from outside the berm interrupted him.

"I'll take it. Eight minutes, and I missed it by two seconds," Joe said while beaming.

"Not bad, not bad. Okay, you two check the shot. Hurry back. My scrotum sack is burning like hell." Captain S tried hard to stand still.

When the three arrived back at the unit, Staff Sergeant Jackson and Specialist Redding were ready to leave, going back to Tan An. O'Neil asked, "Did you two take care of the OBA canister while I was gone?"

"No, the canister is your business." Jackson shook his head.

"You knew I had to go, and I didn't have time for the canister to cool." O'Neil showed his anger.

"I'm going to shower. You three fight over this." Joe could not believe the bickering.

O'Neil announced, "I'm not fighting. I'm going to shower too."

Captain S said, "Jackson, Redding, you two left the canister sitting around all this time, knowing the thing is hazardous. What have you been doing other than following Baby San around like a hound dog following a bitch in heat? No, don't answer, get a tub of water, and put the canister in it. Be sure not to put large holes in the canister and be careful with the water."

"I know how to manage a used OBA canister. And I know how to take care of the water. You only talk to me like this because I'm Black." Jackson shot back.

"I know there was a Sir in there somewhere but skip it. Get it done and get on the road. We have to shower." Captain S left Jackson and Redding and walked into the office building.

"What the hell is wrong with Jackson? Everything to him is about race," Captain S asked Scott.

"He's got a hair across his ass because of Baby San." Scott appeared disgusted with Jackson, as well.

"This isn't all of it. Last night he all but called me a racist because, I made a reference to colored people. He rudely asserted that he was not colored, but Black. I don't even know how to carry on a casual conversation with him. And it's the same way with a lot of colored or Blacks, or whatever, people. He did the same thing with Joe.

"What has happened to the relationship between the two races? Growing up in Colorado, there weren't many colored people, so I don't remember this problem. I'm sorry, Top, I may be tired and hurting, or it may be my thinking." Captain S sounded frustrated.

Scott looked at him. "No, Captain, it's not only you. Hébert also had a confrontation with him about race last night. I'm Black, and you have never said or done anything which makes me think you harbor any prejudice feelings."

"What has caused the split in the races?" Captain S tried to understand.

"I don't know, Sir. I'm not smart enough to answer your question. But, as I told Joe, if I had to pinpoint anything, it would be the invention of the cotton picker."

"The cotton picker!" The wrinkles on Captain S's forehead showed his confusion. He would have never guessed such a response.

"Yes, Sir, before the cotton picker was invented and became popular in the South, most of us Black folks lived on the farm. We worked and were provided a house and were paid. It wasn't a lot of pay and not a good house, but a lot of hard work. The small farmers basically didn't have any money to pay their help. I know firsthand because, I was born and raised on a small farm like that.

"After the cotton picker became available, the farmer no longer needed the hands to work on the farm. So, most Black people packed up and moved to the city. There, people say, because there was no work in town either, we were provided a house and food by the government. The only thing the Black people had to do was make babies, and we do that extremely well. This makes things worse. People began to expect everything. They developed an attitude, and an angry heart.

"Mind you, not all Black folks were like this. They were simply poor like a bunch of poor white folks. Part of us were able to obtain work. But some, Blacks and whites, never learned to do hard work. Angry hearts and hard work should be considered mutually exclusive." Scott had obviously been on this pedestal before.

"This is too heavy for me to think about. I don't know if you're correct or not, but I did ask for your opinion. Thanks for sharing your thoughts with me. Now, I have to get a shower." Captain S headed to the door. He turned and asked, "Oh, I forgot to ask, how is Lein this morning?"

"She and Johnson have been sitting in the little tent all day. Wheeler and I went to check on them a couple of times. She was crying her heart out. He is leaving is going to be hard on her. I hope we don't lose her. She's been a good worker."

"I agree." Captain S turned and walked out.

The shower helped, but it did not end the burning. When Captain S returned to the unit, he noted Jackson and Redding had departed and had left the canister in a tub of water. He checked on Hébert and O'Neil who shared the same opinion of the shower.

"We better go over to the 9th Med. to see if they have anything that can give us some relief from this burning," Captain S told the other two.

"Let's go." They both anxiously agreed.

At the medical facilities, the first they noticed was three soldiers laying on stretchers. They had been wounded by a booby trap. Two with leg and arm bandages were conscious and talking about how they were in a fire fight, and what they were doing when the booby trap exploded. The third appeared unconscious.

"Hopefully, they have him medicated. His wounds don't appear to be any worse than the other two. I would guess; he suffered a great deal of blood loss." Captain S whispered and nodded toward the unconscious soldier.

O'Neil said, "I don't know, Sir."

"Captain Summerville!" The Orderly called out.

"Overhear. My two soldiers have the same problem as I do. Can we all three come at the same time? It may save you a couple of minutes."

"It won't bother me." The orderly shrugged.

After giving their name, rank, and serial number, the orderly listened to their problems and promptly took notes. Afterwards, he left saying only, "The doctor will be here in a moment."

Shortly thereafter, the doctor walked through the door, and said, "I understand you guys have a red ass."

"Sure enough, Doctor." Captain S spoke for all of them.

"Okay, drop them and let me see what you've done to yourselves."

The three did as the doctor told them and stood side-by-side with their pants and drawers around their ankles. When the doctor examined them, Captain S turned to Joe and asked, "Are you going to tell your grandchildren about this, as well?"

"If I had stayed in the stuff any longer, I may not have grandchildren to tell."

"Oh, your sex life isn't harmed. But your skin will be dried out. Once it stops burning, it'll start itching. I'll give you some lotion which will put more moisture back into your skin and help with the burning and itching. You can pull them up. The orderly will get your lotion." The doctor presented the news in a matter-of-fact way.

They complied, and the doctor handed each a slip of paper, "If there's nothing else, you can give this to the young man who brought you in here. And Captain, you did the right thing by bringing your men in. Don't hesitate on coming in regarding any wounds, scratches, or anything. Come see me. Infections can occur at any time here. Do you understand?"

"Yes, Sir."

Outside, the Orderly presented each with a plastic bottle of lotion. "This should take care of you. Don't forget to sign the register on the clipboard over there." The Orderly pointed to a small table between them and the three, wounded soldiers.

"What's it for?" Captain S asked, as O'Neil and Joe headed over to the table, ready to sign.

"It's for your Purple Heart."

O'Neil and Joe stopped and looked back.

Captain S couldn't believe what he heard. "Purple Heart for what!"

"You were wounded as a result of hostile action. You deserve a Purple Heart." The Orderly looked dumbfounded.

Captain S, Staff Sergeant Hébert, and Specialist O'Neil looked at each other and walked out the door without signing the register for an award which none of them felt they earned.

While walking to the Jeep, O'Neil vented his frustration. "Purple Heart! My God! With soldiers, half blown apart laying there, they want to give us a Purple Heart for having a red ass. It's not going to happen with me. I wonder kind of soldiers would have signed the paper an accepted the Purple Heart?"

"You may be surprised at the number. One of these days, we may have a Governor, Senator Secretary State, or maybe even a President who accepted such an award." Captain S shook his head.

Back at the unit, the three walked into the office building. "Master Sergeant Scott, if you need me, you can reach me at the O-club." Captain S turned to leave again.

"Not so fast, Sir. You still need to go see Colonel Hollow."

"Crap! What does the bastard want? Have any of our guys crossed his path in the last few days?"

"Nothing I know of Sir. But you know he's upset about something. He's not inviting you over for tea."

"Okay, if he doesn't run me off post, I'll be back shortly."

As he walked out, he heard Hébert asking Wheeler, "Is Baby San doing hers and Leins' work?"

Wheeler responded, "Yes."

Captain S walked to the Division Support Command (DISCOM) office covered approximately one hundred yards from the EOD unit. When Captain S entered, he told Sergeant Major Donaldson,

"The Colonel had requested to see me. Do you know why?"

"I can't say, Sir, but he's been waiting on you for quite a while. I'll tell him you're here."

Colonel Hollow's office looked like no other office Captain S had ever seen, a big, magnificent showplace. The desk, armoire, tables, bookcases, and chairs were all handmade from teak wood and were exquisitely carved. Captain S had been in the office before. He knew the furniture was the Colonel's prize possession, and it is important to him. It gave the feeling of being the finest in Vietnam, excluding none.

How, the hell, did he get teak wood over here? Captain S thought as he walked into the office.

The Colonel, slight in stature, sat behind his desk. He glanced up at Captain S, while tapping his West Point ring.

Captain S stood at attention in front of the Colonel's desk, saluted and said, "Captain Summerville reporting, Sir." The Colonel returned the salute but remained seated. "I called before 0800 hours this morning, telling your Master Sergeant to have you reports to me. And you ignore me until now, Captain!

"What is your excuse? Did you not get my message, Captain?" The Colonel growled.

"I got your message, but I have been busy, Sir." Captain S replied still standing at attention.

"Too busy to see me!" Colonel Hollow growled angrily.

"Yes, Sir. I had work to do." Captain S answered very clearly.

"What kind of work is more important to you than to respond to a Colonel's order?"

"EOD work, Sir."

"Dammit, Captain, from now on when I call you, you had better get your ass in front of me, pronto. Do you understand me?" Hollow roared.

"Yes, Sir, but--"

"But what, Captain!" Hollow yelled.

"But, if I have work to do, it is usually in response to Division Operation's, G3, or DISOPS request. Perhaps, we should speak with them or maybe the Division Commander, to reaffirm, whom I should respond to first." Captain S looked Hollow right in the eyes, daring him to say he should answer to him before the other higher ups.

"Are you threatening to go over my head, Captain?" Hollow remained firm.

"I'm not threatening, Sir. But as you know, you're not in my operational chain of command. If you have a problem with this, we need to resolve the issue."

"There's that chain of command question again. You will show me respect! You are an 0-3, a Captain. I'm an 0-6, a Full Colonel, you got it! But that's not why you're here. I understand you had quite a party last night, making a loud noise, singing, and yelling. Now, don't tell me that I have no authority over that!" Hollow snapped. "This is my Post."

"Well, Sir, we're located on the Navy side. Activities such as you describe should fall under Lieutenant Commander Davis's authority. However, if we were disturbing anyone on your side by singing, I would like to know who could not understand a soldier or sailors relaxing and enjoying themselves. If you direct me and my troops to curtail singing at my unit, I'll do so, but I would expect my guys would be sitting in the IG's office the next day."

"You're threatening me again, Captain!" Hollow snarled.

"Not at all, Sir. I'm trying to explain the situation. My predecessor told me; you had a problem with my unit because of the operational control issue. He said you moved us to the Navy side, because you could not force him to sit on a court-martial board. He also said, something to the effect, you told him to take his nickel and dime unit off your post. If you still harbor this kind of prejudicious feeling about me or my personnel, we need to work it out." Captain S never raised his voice.

"Well, never mind, but I want to know what you are going to do with all those pallets, you have stacked up next to my fence. I understand they may be hazardous." Hollow looked for anything to intimidate Captain S with.

"As you know, Sir, three strings of barb wire separate the Army side and the Navy side. The pallets are on the Navy side. I'm sure they present no danger to anything on your side of the fence.

Lieutenant Commander Davis has not objected to them being there. As for as what I'm going to do with them, I'll take them apart as time permits. They were reported to me as possibly holding an explosive hazard. You should be prepared, there may be more coming, in a couple of weeks. If you have a problem with my time frame, maybe you can provide me with some personnel to help work to advance the process."

"You know I don't have the resources to do that! Now, how is your young Specialist Redding working out for you? I was at the Academy with his father, who is now at the Pentagon." This time, Hollow spoke with more of a normal dignified voice.

"Specialist Redding is one of my young men. Most of the time, he stays at Tan An. His and an NCO"S presence there significantly cuts our response time to incidents in the area. We can support the Second Brigade much better from there."

"Good. I know he's doing an outstanding job. Now, get your ass out of here." Hollow swept his head toward the door, singling the end of the conversation.

"Yes, Sir." Captain S saluted, did an about face, and left the office.

Sergeant Major Donaldson, like any good NCO, stood at the door in a position where he could hear the conversation going on inside the office. As Captain S passed, Donaldson winked and whispered, "Good job, Sir."

"Thanks. I think I handled the situation rather well. At least he didn't threaten me with a court-martial."

The short walk back to the unit gave Captain S a chance to reflect on what had occurred. The Sergeant Major rightfully accessed his performance. He had done a respectable job. He had not given an inch to the pompous SOB.

He wondered if Hollow understood what a thrashing he had taken.

Captain S knew that he would never again give way to the Colonel or worry about his power.

Hollow will surely try harder to make life more miserable for me. If he finds a way to cause problems, so be it. This knife cuts both ways. Regardless, I'm on offense now, and I'll find a way to get him.

"Scott, I'm back, and I'm going to the O-club." Captain S said, as he walked into the office building.

"No, no, not yet. One more thing you need to do. But first, how did it go?"

"Ask your buddy, Donaldson. I'd like to know what he says," Captain S replied with a smile.

"I'll do it. I'll ask him," Scott stated and moved to the door and called. "Wheeler! Hébert! The captain is back from his meeting. He'll see you now."

"What's this about?" Captain S asked.

"Wheeler, wants to talk to you about an idea. Hébert is here to support him. I'll let them do the talking."

When they came in, Captain S looked at Wheeler. "What's this bright idea you have, Wheeler? It must involve Baby San."

The comment did not faze Wheeler. "No, Sir. It's about money."

Captain S blared his eyes which wrinkled his forehead and nodded. "Money! Well, I wasn't expecting this kind of response. Pull up a chair and let's talk about money."

Joe set up the situation by saying, "Sir, Specialist Wheeler mentioned this to me last night. I told him it sounded like a clever idea, but he needed to talk with you. I'll let him run with it from here."

"Master Sergeant Scott, scoot over here. I don't think you want to miss talking about money.

"Now, Wheeler, it's your ball. Run with it." Captain S nodded again to Wheeler.

Wheeler presented his idea about selling the beer, essentially the same as he had discussed the previous night with Hébert. He concluded by saying, "The bottom line, Sir, if we can get the beer free, the only cost is our labor and ice. We have enough talent here to scrounge the needed materials. So, what do you think?"

"I'm thinking, lots of enjoyable work for maybe twenty dollars a day. I think it's a no brainier. I say, let's go for it! Of course, I'll have to run it by Lieutenant Commander Davis. I don't see a problem. What do you think?" Captain S turned to Scott.

"It sounds good to me, but we'll need to enlarge the patio and build a nicer bar. As soon as we can get the twelve-by-twelves for a foundation to extend the patio, we can move right along with the rest of the project. The twelve-by-twelves are hard to come by, but we have decent connections with the Engineers. They can possibly help."

"Okay, let's put it together. I'll leave it there. My ass is still burning, and a couple of scotches will help. You guys are the only thing standing between me and a glass of scotch, and two good-looking bartenders." Captain S announced his intentions as he stood.

"Oh yeah, Master Sergeant Scott, I haven't seen Banks all day. Put him in charge of the project and tell him to warm up his voice and guitar for tonight. We're going to sing and sing loudly to boost morale."

Captain S couldn't help himself. He intended to poke Hollow as hard as he could.

CHAPTER 20

"Wake up! Wake up! You get up now! I have do work," Baby San said loudly, while standing at the foot of Joe's bed. He knew at once he had overslept. Due to a weak stomach and a pounding head, missing breakfast would be no problem.

"Oh, last night was late and encompassed a lot to drink. Don't get upset and frown at me. It messes up your pretty face," he told Baby San.

"I not pretty. I cherry girl."

"Yes, you are attractive." She dressed as always, white top and black pajamas.

"No, I not. You get up now!"

"Okay. But, yes, you're still lovely."

"You get up now. I do Lein's work. I work, work, work, all day."

Joe stood, wearing only his briefs. This did not bother him or Baby San, as she and Lein had often seen all the guys wearing nothing but their underwear. "Is Lein here?"

"Yes. She here. She no work. She cries. Johnson go States tomorrow. She sick. Have baby soon. She cry, cry, cry, all day."

Joe dressed and went outside. "Hébert, come here!" Johnson called with a high volume from the small tent.

"Good morning," Joe said, when he saw Johnson and Lein sitting in the small tent. "How are you feeling, Lein?"

"No feel good. Johnson go home. Have baby soon. No more Johnson."

"Yes, Johnson will go home tomorrow. He has orders, but you'll be okay." Joe tried hard to reassure her.

"Johnson come back Vietnam after war. Get me and baby. We go States. I love Johnson." Lein looked at and touched Johnson's face.

"And I love you." Johnson leaned over and kissed her on her cheek. "Staff Sergeant Hébert will take care of you."

"I surely will." Joe nodded.

Wheeler called, "Hébert, are you out here?"

"Yes," Joe replied.

"The captain wants you."

"I'll be right there." Joe went to the office. "Good morning, Sir, Master Sergeant Scott."

Captain S spoke. "I hope you enjoyed your morning nap because, we have to go to work. It seems as if, while during an early perimeter sweep at a firebase, they found a couple of ready-to-go rockets pointed at them. They wanted EOD to check them out for booby-traps. Banks and O'Neil are taking care of that. They have been gone for an hour. DISOPS just called on another matter.

"A unit out in the Plain of Reeds found a bunch of stuff to include a five-hundred-pound bomb. It sounds as if they may have stumbled across one of Charlie's makeshift ammo plants." Captain S brought Joe up to date on the incidents.

"Sir, how are we on time?"

Captain S looked at his Seiko watch. "The 3rd Brigade's Commander and his command-and-control chopper (C&C) will be at Charlie Pad in about fifteen minutes. They want us on site, ASAP. Apparently, the area is quite active, and they want to pull their personnel back."

"Sir, if you're wondering, I know, I'm a little slow this morning, but I'm ready to go." Because of his obvious hangover, Joe tried to reassure his commander.

"Ready or not, there's no difference. We're going! "They reported a bunch of stuff which worries me. It could be anything. We better take enough C-4 for several shots, also some extra detonating cord, and don't forget more time fuse. Get it together, and we're out of here."

"OK, Captain."

"Sir, I want to let you know, I had a little talk with Sergeant Major Donaldson last night," Scott cut in, while doing his paperwork and not looking up from behind his desk.

"I saw you two talking. What did he say?"

Scott did not answer, but glanced up at the captain, smiled, and gave him the thumbs up.

Joe asked, "What's this about?"

Captain S looked at Joe. "Nothing to concern you, Hébert."

He then redirected his attention. "Master Sergeant Scott, I had a talk with Lieutenant Commander Davis last night. When Banks gets back, have him get busy building us a larger patio and bar. We're going to keep singing."

"Yes, Sir. It sounds good to me," Scott replied.

"Staff Sergeant Hébert, are you ready to go?" Captain S sounded authoritative be saying, "Get your ass moving!"

"In a moment, Sir. I'm practicing my singing." Joe began singing one of his favorite Cajan songs.

"Ugh, you need a lot of practice." Scott grunted.

Captain S and Staff Sergeant Hébert arrived at Charlie Pad as the chopper landed. Joe carried an extra twenty pounds of explosives. As they approached the chopper, they leaned forward and placed one hand on the top of their heads to steady their steel pots. Their other hands covered their eyes, protecting them from debris kicked up by the prop wash. As they stepped up into the helicopter, they both noticed the Full Colonel, 0-6, obviously the Brigade Commander, sitting in the right seat beside the pilot.

The two door gunners adjusted their M-60 machine guns mounted on stands on each side. An onboard NCO pointed to two seats and yelled above the roar of the engines. "Take your seats!" He then gave Captain S a helmet and yelled. "The Colonel wants to talk with you."

After buckling up, the chopper lifted off, nose down, tail high, and headed west. The Mekong River spread out below and to the left of them. Captain S replaced his steel pot with the helmet given to him by the NCO and spoke into the helmet mic. "Good morning, Colonel, it's a great day to fly." Captain S sounded cheerful.

"It surely is, Captain. But it's been a long night for some of our boys on the ground. Early yesterday, we received information about unusual movements out there where we're going. It'll take us about thirty-five minutes to get there. We inserted a Company there short afterwards. After wading around in those reeds all day, we made an unusually heavy contact with Charlie at 1500 hours. Of course, we pounded the area with artillery and air support from the Air Force, as well as our helicopters. That silenced the opposition.

"About 1800 hours, our boys found a small well camouflaged structure which apparently contained an US 500-pound bomb, several buckets of something, and an assortment of homemade devices.

The boys at once secured the area but did not touch anything. They were afraid of booby-traps. Booby-traps are why you're sitting here, Captain."

"Yes, Sir. This is what they reported to us. However, I do have a couple of questions."

"What do you need to know, Captain?"

"I was wondering about the security of the perimeter, specifically how far it extends outwards. The bomb is going to throw frag a long way. Maybe a half mile. It's probably unrealistic, but the farther the perimeter is pushed out the better. The second thing is, are you going to leave us out there?"

"I'm sure the security line is nowhere near half a mile out. It's probably more like a hundred yards. I'll alert my on-site Commander. He'll have to push out farther or dig in. He can make that decision, better than I can. He'll have to know five to ten minutes before you do your thing."

"That won't be a problem. This could take us thirty minutes, or two hours. It depends on what we encounter. How about the second question, Sir?"

"Don't let it worry you. I won't be on the ground, but I'll be in the area. We'll pick you up and take you back to Dong Tam. My boss, the Commanding General, has repeatedly said, if his EOD assets were not available when he needed them, and he finds out they were left twiddling their thumbs somewhere, heads will roll. I intend to keep my head. And while on the subject, if you have this problem with anybody in my brigade, contact me immediate. I'll resolve the issue."

"Okay, thank you, Sir."

"No problem, Captain. Now, lean back and enjoy the ride. It's an order." Captain S could not see the Colonel's face, but he knew it wore a smile.

They could see nothing but a plain of green reeds for miles and miles. After what seemed like longer than thirty-five minutes, the helicopter descended and started circling. When the door gunners brought their weapons to a ready position, Captain S and Joe knew they had reached their destination.

"Captain, as soon as we depart, you'll be met. Hang tight. Our guys will come to you. Good luck, and we'll see you soon." The Colonel spoke through the helmet.

The NCO who had given Captain S the helmet gestured for him to remove it and yelled, "Watch your step. It's a long drop through the reeds!"

Gray smoke suddenly appeared from the sea of green below. Captain S and Joe rose to their feet. "Sir, I'll go first," Joe yelled, and he stepped toward the door.

The NCO yelled. "Anytime!"

Joe sat down on the deck and placed one foot on the landing skid of the chopper. He pushed off. His foot slipped, and he fell eight or nine feet, landing on his left shoulder. Captain S followed and landed on both feet. They both looked up, as the helicopter quickly disappearing.

"Joe, are you alright?" Captain S put his hand on Joe's shoulder.

"Yeah, I'm more embarrassed than hurt." Joe assured his Commander. He stood and rotated his left arms. "I'm going to be a little sore, though."

They looked around and saw nothing but a green wall around them. The field of view gave them about five feet at best. Looking up, they saw the helicopter had disappeared into the blue sky. Suddenly, the noise from the chopper completely diminished. "Man. One could get lost here in a second. There's no directional reference point." Joe looked around, everywhere.

"Yeah, I'd hate to be here on a cloudy day."

"It would be like being lost in a fog. You can lose all sense of direction in fog in ten seconds, even if you are the best woodsman or seafarer in the world and feel like you have a profound sense of direction. If you're on a lake in the fog, it'll humble you in seconds. I'm speaking from experience."

"I can understand that." Captain S nodded.

"Not necessarily, unless you've been there and experienced it." Joe insisted.

"Are you guys, okay?" A distinct New York accent sounded, accompanied by a rustle in the reeds.

"I think so," Captain S answered while searching for a face.

"There you are." The voice replied. This time it came from, at best, a filthy and unshaven figure approaching through the reeds. "I'll show you where the bomb is. Follow me."

Joe noticed the guy did not say Sir, much less bother to salute Captain S.

"Don't get too far ahead of us," Captain S said.

"I won't but follow the trail." The New Yorker replied.

"What trail?" Joe asked while looking down to see what looked like a small muskrat trail. "Okay, I see it. How far?"

"About seventy-five yards."

Along the way they passed a wallow area. It was slightly large enough for three filthy infantry men to sit and smoke.

"Good morning, troopers." Captain S acknowledged them as he passed.

"Morning," one of them replied, with no 'Sir' following.

"It's only a little farther." The New Yorker told them.

They walked to within five paces of an Infantry Captain and his radio man, before seeing them. They were accompanied by two riflemen, one standing and one lolling, trying to take a nap.

"Good morning, I'm Captain Higgins." The captain introduced himself and offered his hand.

"I'm Sandy Summerville. This is Staff Sergeant Hébert."

Hébert saluted the captain, who did not return the salute, but shook Joe's hand. "Unless you're trying to get me identified as an officer to Charlie, I don't recommend a lot of saluting in the field. Even a Louisiana man, I presume, should know this." He scolded Joe.

Taking his tongue lashing, Joe looked embarrassed. "Yes, Sir. What gave Louisiana away?"

"The name, of course. Now, the structure with the bomb and other stuff is right up the trail." Captain Higgins turned and led the way. The radio man followed in line behind him. Then came Captain S and Joe. The three infantry soldiers followed.

"You'll notice a trail which had previous traffic running perpendicular to us. We followed it for a short distance yesterday going in both directions. None of the trail can be seen from the air. We had quite a little skirmish down the left trail. It was like they were trying to protect something important to them. This is the only thing we found." Captain Higgins gestured to a short structure covered with mud and live reeds.

The ground under the structure had no vegetation. There were chairs and two workbenches with hand saws, wood mallets, and buckets on them. The structure consisted of a wood roof. It was about eighteen by thirty-two feet, with no walls, only support poles on each side and down the middle. Metal scrap lay in piles. A large bomb could be seen under the left side of the structure.

Captain S asked, "Has anybody walked inside this thing?"

"Yes, we have one stupid trooper. He didn't touch anything and quickly retreated. We're well disciplined when it comes to booby-traps or something like this.

"There's been a lot of traffic up and down this trail." Captain Higgins pointed to the trail about two feet wide. "I'm sure it's safe, but I wouldn't set a foot off of it. We prop-washed the immediate area and trails looking for Charlie, but you can't see anything from above unless it moves."

Captain S told Higgins, "Okay, in case we screw the pooch, get your men back and in a prone position."

"I can't do anything more for you regarding security. Hell, Charlie is likely to be laying right there, ten feet away, looking at us." Captain Higgins gestured to the green wall of reeds.

"I understand. We'll try to watch and listen as we go through this thing. Have someone check on us every ten minutes. Make sure they announce themselves first. Staff Sergeant Hébert, here, had some sniper training and is a very good shot." Captain nodded toward Joe.

"Staff Sergeant Hébert, I know Louisiana has a lot of reeded Delta. However, you don't have anything like this, so be careful." Captain Higgins looked at Joe and smiled.

"No. We have nothing anywhere near what this stuff is, and that sniper training is worthless here. The reeds must be at the least twelve feet tall. I can't even see the sky."

"Good luck, I'll see you when you say, it's time." Higgins turned and walked down the trail.

"It's only you and I, Tonto." Captain S said in an informal manner. "Let's see if we can find some stuff left by the bad Indians."

"I don't see anything that bothers me from here. The soil looks solid and packed. There's no sign of disruption." Joe nodded to the interior of the structure.

"Good observation. So, from what we can see from here, we don't have to worry about stepping on something nasty. I hope you have a flashlight in your pack. It's a little dark in there."

"As a matter of fact, I have two. I always try to carry them." Joe dropped his pack.

"I'll take the left side. You take the right side. We can cover the area on our hands and knees." Captain S accepted a flashlight.

"Okay but watch above carefully. It's likely one of those five-foot two-inch bastards strung a monofilament fishing line next on the ceiling, knowing a six-foot American man would have to bend over to move around in here. There's no way the ordinary man should see it. Speaking of that, look there." Joe shined his light at the ceiling about eight feet away.

"Oh, yeah. Good call." Captain S directed his light at the ceiling. "Tonto has good eyes. Once you have seen fishing line with a light on it, you can't miss it the next time. Without the light, it may have killed us."

"This one was easy to spot. If there is a next one, I hope it's as easy," Joe spoke softly.

"The little reflection runs all the way across, and it's taught. It's holding something back, which is not good for us. Check your side. I'll check mine. We'll find out what kind of surprise Charlie has for us." Captain S started moving to his left.

Joe carefully stepped to the right end of the monofilament line and quickly reported. "The line is tied here, so you have the goodies on your end."

"Thanks, we both know what I'm looking for. And here it is. It's tied to a pole with dried reeds. I'll secure it. The device is homemade. Okay, it's safe. You can reel the line in now." The captain secured the device.

"Okay, good job Ke-mo Sah-bee," Joe replied, using the same informal manner the captain had used and pulled the monofilament fishing line in his direction. "One booby-traps down. Now, let's look for the *City of Lost Gold.*"

"I would not advise touching the table, chairs, or the buckets. I don't believe we'll find gold in those buckets. I'll bet there's nothing in them other than some golden colored explosive and scrap metal. I see nothing on my side between me and the bomb." Captain S quipped.

Joe replied, "I have some 81mm mortars neatly stacked over here, also an AK-47 and some scrap metal. I think I see another line blinking at me at the far end, in the corner. The line is down low. There's probably something on the other side of it."

"Be careful moving forward, and don't touch the table, and definitely not the AK. It's souvenir bait." Captain S informed Joe.

"I have nine mortars. I'm not touching them." Joe announced his intentions. "It looks as if the only hazard to all this scrap metal is dropping it on our toes. They have been saving the metal for a reason. The scrap looks as if it's mostly from 105mm and eight-inch projectiles, with the explosives missing from them."

"Coming in!" A recognizable New York accent voice called from ten yards out.

"Come on! Stay on the trail and don't touch the shack." Captain S yelled back to him.

"Captain Higgins wanted to know if you guys needed anything?" The New Yorker asked.

"No. Tell him, if all goes well, this thing will be history in about thirty minutes. Check back in fifteen. Then, I can be more precise about the timing."

"Okay, Sir, I'll tell him."

Joe said, "It's a nice AK. Are you sure you don't need a souvenir for something? It's good trading material."

"I don't need it badly enough for what it might cost. Besides, I think, we have four already. You have not been here long enough to find them. We also have a Chinese made machine gun. They were in a small cache, which we destroyed about six weeks ago. We have a small amount of ammunition for both of the guns."

"Sir, regarding the AK, I appreciate you placing such a high value on my life. And no, I haven't seen the weapons. All this scrap metal on my side appears to be the same as you described. But there's definitely a trip line in front of me and there's a box behind it, in the corner." Joe moved slowly forward.

"What do you mean, a high value on your life? I was talking about my life. You screw up over there; I go with you." Captain S chuckled while moving on his knees.

While examining the bomb, Captain S continued speaking. "It looks as if, Charlie has been sawing on the bomb, and I see a little freshly disturbed soil under it."

"Be careful, Ke-Mo Sah-bee. I'm sure a rat dug under it, a two-legged rat, about five feet tall. I'm moving to the trip line." Joe moved slowly.

"If the rat has a nest under the bomb, He can keep it. I'm not disturbing this baby." Captain S knew not to touch the freshly disturbed soil.

"This trip line only goes halfway across. It's slack, so I'll take care of it. The payload is over at the edge of the reeds." Joe moved toward it. "It's an M25 grenade. The line is attached to the carter key. I'll fix it. Okay, the pin can't come out now. It's safe, but I'm not moving it. We'll take care of the grenade where it is."

"Sounds good to me, Tonto. I've looked overhead and haven't seen anything. In fact, I see nothing else on my side. I'm backing out and I'll check the buckets on the table."

"Okay! I'm checking the box to see what's in it. Uh, oh it looks like an Easter basket full of large eggs." Joe sounded surprised.

"What you got, Tanto?"

"Ok, Ke-mo Sha-bee. I have bomblets. Blue 3B's, compliments of an US Air Force cluster bomb. All these things are probably duds. There's probably twenty in the box."

"Don't touch, backout, and check the buckets on your side. Mine look like they contain chunks of explosive from the projectiles which are now scrap metal."

"Okay, Sir."

Captain S waited while Joe checked the buckets, crawled out, and stood. "Oh, this feels better." Joe stretched and exercised his left shoulder.

"Is your shoulder bothering you?" Captain S seemed concerned.

"No, I'm good to go. It's nothing a few beers won't fix when we get back to the unit." Joe continued stretching his arm.

"Let's get this shot set up where we can get out of here."

"Okay, I'm--" Two distant explosions interrupted Captain S. "They were about three hundred yards away."

Before Joe could answer, small arms fire broke out nearby. They hit the ground ready to fire, Joe with his M-16 and Captain S with his M-79. Captain S suddenly realized the worthiness of his M-79 in this terrain. Because once fired, it would take distance for the 40m round to arm.

After laying on the ground for about five minutes, they heard the New Yorker call, "I'm coming in!"

"Come on!" Captain S answered back.

"Are you guys, okay?" The New Yorker asked, and lay down close to Captain S.

"Yeah. Do you have any idea what the shooting was?"

"No, Sir. Second platoon guys are over there. As soon as it started, I was sent here."

After the firing had completely stopped, they laid motionless, except for swatting bugs, for a couple more minutes.

The New Yorker said, "It's over. I doubt it was anything. If they had real contact, there would be artillery shells landing over there by now, and most likely, Cobras would be overhead."

"We have started setting up the shot. It'll take about ten minutes. Go back and tell Captain Higgins, we'll be ready then. After we pull the pen, we'll leave the area. And eight minutes later, we'll hear a loud bang. Tell him to make sure; there's no helicopter traffic in the area. And Soldier, how far can I walk down the trail that you came down?" Captain S planned his escape strategy.

"The captain is about two hundred and fifty yards down the trail. I don't know how far it goes." The New Yorker explained.

"Okay, go tell your Captain what I said, and then come back. I'll wait for you."

They were finishing setting up the shot to take care of everything they found, when they heard, "Coming in!" This time, Captain Higgins called out.

"Come on, Sir," Joe said loudly.

"I wasn't expecting you. I thought you'd have headed over to the fireworks," Captain S said.

"No need to worry." Captain Higgins shook his head.

"We're about ready to get out of here. Do you have any idea what the shooting was about?"

"The second platoon Sergeant said somebody saw something. After yesterday, everybody is still trigger-happy. Out here, it's best to shoot first and ask questions later." Captain Higgins explained the situation.

"I understand. We have this thing ready to go. After we pull the pin, we'll have eight minutes, give, or take a few seconds. Can we get far enough down this trail before it goes?"

"Sandy, we can move rather fast. I'll give our troops an eight-minute warning, followed with a one minute, and then, fifteen seconds warning. At this point, we can all grab grass roots. We should be okay." Captain Higgins nodded.

Joe asked, "What about anything flying overhead?"

"I'll give the Colonel an eight-minute warning, and they can worry about any other aircraft. I'm sure he'll be monitoring my radio as well as several others in the area. He has that capability."

"Are we ready to go, Staff Sergeant Hébert?" Captain S looked at Joe.

"If you did your part correctly, I think we are." Joe couldn't resist teasing his Commander.

Captain S asked, "Do you want the honors? If you think I messed up, and this thing doesn't go right, you can be responsible for the mistake. "Captain S gave Joe a big grin.

"That's all right, Sir. You know the senior man is responsible for the final step of any procedure." Joe's smile turned downright cheesy.

"I know what the regulations say," Captain S told Joe, and ask Captain Higgins. "Are you ready?"

"I'm as ready as I can get," Captain Higgins nodded.

"Alert your troops," Captain S said. Then, he yelled, "Fire in the hole! Fire in the hole! Fire in the hole!" He pulled the ring on the fuse lighter. "Let's go!"

They headed down the trail at a nice pace, not running or jogging. Two infantry soldiers led the way, followed by Captain Higgins, the radio man, Captain S, Staff Sergeant Hébert, and the New Yorker. The radio man spoke into the mic. "Seven minutes. Next update at one minute prior to the detonation."

Three, different Rogers was received.

The trail bent left and right, with straight-a-ways no more than twenty feet. The reeds encompassed them and allowed only glimpses of blue sky above. They continued their pace while checking their watches only occasionally.

"One minute," Captain S announced the remaining time.

The radio man echoed, "One minute." Then came, Roger, three more times.

"Fifteen seconds, get on the ground." Captain S advised.

Again, the radio man passed on the time, and they all hit a prone position.

"Nine, eight, seven, six, five." Captain S called out loudly, but no one heard the five because of the loud explosion, and the noise of frag tearing through the reeds. "Is everyone okay?"

Three Oks were heard.

"Get me a sitrep," Higgins commanded. The radio man at once keyed the Mic. and said, "Sitrep." It took a couple of seconds before the third response came back, but they all reported, "No problem."

"Let's go see what we have left," Joe said. This time he and Captain S took the lead.

No signs of the mud-covered structure were visible. Instead, there were three craters, one larger than the other two. A four-bedroom home could be placed, where only a few minutes earlier stubby reeds stood. The odor commonly associated with an explosion permeated the air.

Captain S proclaimed, "I think we had a good shot."

"If anything got kicked out, it's laying where it will never be found," Joe replied.

Captain S turned to Captain Higgins, who actively examined the large crater, which looked about three feet deep, and said, "I think we're through here. Can you fetch us a taxi?"

Captain Higgins turned to his radio man and said, "Raise the Colonel. Tell him the EOD team is ready to depart."

CHAPTER 21

"Good morning, Phillip," Joe said, calling Wheeler by his first name, as he headed to the coffee pot. "Is it through brewing, yet?"

"It's finally finished," Phillip replied. "Why are you up so early?"

"I can't sleep. My shoulder ached all night. The first step out of the helicopter, yesterday, was a big one. Busted my ass. Are you always in this early?"

"Master Sergeant Scott, or me, are usually the first ones here every morning. Of course, I sleep in here quite often, more correctly, nearly all the time. The first thing we do is get the coffee pot going." Wheeler shrugged and then continued talking. "Captain S said something about you taking Johnson to Bien Hoa today. I thought you may be leaving early."

"Well, it won't be too early. First thing, I'm going over to the 9th Med. to have my arm and shoulder checked. Hell, the way this thing hurts, I'm not sure I can even drive. I was hoping someone would drive me over there. Maybe you can take care of Johnson." Joe rubbed his shoulder.

"We'll see what the boss says. I wouldn't mind getting away from the desk for a day or two. All I do is monitor the radio and phone, and of course type. Oh, and I'm stuck with the accounting duties for the unit's slush fund. The job will get larger and more time consuming with the bar proceeds increasing daily. We're up to fifteen people charging now, and I tabulate all those daily."

"It sounds like you're busy, and you didn't mention tutoring Baby San."

"Tutoring Baby San is a pleasure. She's an extremely smart sponge. I would bet her IQ is off the charts. For someone with no formal education, it's hard to believe how fast she has come in such a short time." Wheeler seemed to light up when he talked about her.

"I'm sure you've done an outstanding job there. I know you have a degree in banking. What school did you attend?"

"I went to UT. Tennessee, not Texas. My father's a banker, so it's only natural for me to follow in his footsteps."

"Your father owns a bank! I've never known someone who owns a bank.

"Yeah, a couple of small ones in Chattanooga." Wheeler nodded and turned to see Scott walking in. "Good morning, Master Sergeant Scott."

Scott asked Joe, "What are you doing up this early?"

"I'm talking with the banker. I was about to hit him up for a loan, and then you walked in."

"He's tight. I've been trying to get a loan since I got here, without any luck, I might add. Now, I'll ask again, why are you up this early?"

"I need to see someone about my shoulder pain." Joe continued to rub his shoulder.

"Yeah, I saw you favoring it yesterday. When you returned, I asked Captain S about it, and he told me how you got hurt. Well, go on. This time of the morning it won't be too busy. All the sick call people will be showing up later." Scott poured his coffee.

"There's a little problem. I can't drive and shift gears with one arm."

"Let's finish our coffee, and I'll drive you over and drop you off. You can get a ride back or walk. It's not far over there." Scott had an answer for everything.

When Staff Sergeant Hébert arrived at 9th Med., he noticed there were a couple soldiers ahead of him, and the three stretchers which held wounded soldiers a couple of days before were not there. After an extended wait, the orderly took notes as Joe told the story from the day before and the sleepless night.

When he finally walked into the doctor's office, he had another few minutes' wait.

"Staff Sergeant Hébert, I remember your name from a couple of days ago. It says right here on your chart, you saw me because you had a red ass. It also says you banged up your shoulder yesterday," The cheerful doctor said, as he entered the room.

"Yes, Sir. You about summed it up."

"First things, first. Drop your drawers and let me see your red ass."

Joe did as the doctor ordered.

"It looks like you still have a few red spots, but there is nothing to worry anyone. You can pull them up." The doctor watched Joe carefully and wrote notes.

"It looks like your shoulder is not broken or out a socket, probably just bent. I doubt there's a tear in your rotator cuff. If you are not better within four days, we can take another look. I'll give you some muscle relaxers and a sling. No driving or drinking, and extremely limited duty after taking the pills."

"You're not going to examine me?" Joe queried the doctor incredulously.

"Sergeant, I did. You dropped your trousers and got them back up. I noticed you flinched because of pain. But if you want me to twist and turn the sore shoulder, I will. I can tell by the way you move; you're only bruised and stretched.

"This note will keep you on limited duty, for three days. The pills will help relax your muscles. I'll say again. You can't drive or drink alcohol while taking them. If you are not better in four days, come back to see me. We'll check the rotator cuff for a tear. If you have no further questions, give this note to the guy outside."

"I have no questions, and thanks." Joe took the paperwork from the doctor.

The orderly helped Joe into a sling and gave him the muscle relaxers. "Take one now and one every twelve hours. Be sure to sign the paperwork, by the door, for your Purple Heart."

Joe took his pill, and the bottle. He said, "On the Purple Heart thing, no thanks. I don't need a Purple Heart for being clumsy and careless."

Joe decided to take his time and walked back to the office, passing the Riverine Basin on his way. As a small but active naval port in every respect, it serviced assorted types of boats in its maintenance facilities.

When Joe walked into the office, Captain S asked, "Are you going to live?"

"Yes, Sir, as long as I take these magic pills." Joe shook the pill bottle and handed Captain S the limited duty papers.

Captain S took the paper and properly crumbled and tossed it into the trash can. "What does limited duty mean to you? Don't answer, it doesn't matter. I have my own interpretation. However, those pills make some people silly and drowsy. Let me know if you have a problem with them. Have you ever taken them before?"

"No, Sir. But I don't expect any problems."

"Banks will take Johnson by himself. First, we must get Lein to turn him loose of him. Since you're on a no-go status, O'Neil will stay here. I don't like Banks being on the road by himself coming back, but hell, we do what we have to do, solder on." Captain S laid it out.

"Johnson's bags have been in the Jeep for fifteen minutes," Scott told no one in particular.

Captain S ask, "Wheeler, did you give Banks the money to buy the amplifier and speakers?"

"Yes, Sir, Wheeler replied."

Scott stood, and said, "Let's go put their butts in the Jeep and get them moving."

"If we don't, they'll be here till noon." Captain S led the way out the door. Joe followed.

Joe looked at Lein sitting sadly with her head down and not crying for the first time in two days.

Baby San sat beside her and held her hand. Joe noticed Lein's white knuckles. He knew physical or mental problems could cause it and wondered if they were due to pain.

Johnson stood and told the others he needed to go. He bent over and helped Lein to her feet, hugging her and said, "Take care of yourself and Junior. You'll hear from me, and I'll send Staff Sergeant Hébert some more money for you. He'll help take care of you."

"Bye Johnson. I know Hébert take care of me." Lein spoke softly and glanced toward Joe.

Joe wondered why, neither said, "I love you."

They all went ahead to the Jeep. Lein, with the aid of Baby San, brought up the rear slowly. Everyone said, "Bye" and Johnson said, "Keep your heads down. I don't want to hear bad things about any of you."

As the Jeep drove off, Lein said, "Bye, Johnson," repeatedly, in a soft voice. As she and Baby San headed to the small tent; all the guys went to the office.

"Now, it's done, let's see if we can get some work done," Scott firmly demanded.

Captain S asked, "What time are the Engineers delivering the twelve by twelves?"

O'Neil answered, "Sometime around noon."

Scott said, "Okay, let's start getting this place cleaned up. I think Baby San has her hands full for the rest of the day. She can use some help."

"I don't think the shit has been burned in the last four days. O'Neil, you take care of it. Take Staff Sergeant Hébert with you. The rest of us can sweep, mop, and clean up the trash." Captain S looked at everyone.

"Yes, Sir. Come on Hébert. I don't think you've had the pleasure, yet." O'Neil patted Joe on his back.

Joe followed him to the outhouse. "This has only been done a couple of times since you've been here. All we do is pull the shit pot out. It is half of a fifty-five-gallon metal barrel, like this." O'Neil demonstrated the process by lifting a drop door on the back and pulling the container out and away from outhouse.

"Shit stinks!" Joe waved his hand in front of his face.

"Yeah, especially after three or four days in hot weather! We pour a gallon or two of diesel into the container and drop a match in like this." O'Neil started the fire.

"It's usually done earlier in the morning. When there's no breeze, the smoke goes straight up. As you can see, with this breeze the smoke is going to head right for the mess hall. Oh, no! And toward Colonel Hollow's office. Oh crap!" O'Neil said loudly.

"Well, it won't be the first time, and probably not the last time, Captain S will get a good ass chewing." Joe smiled and shook his head.

"This will take about ten minutes at most. I'd better warn him."

"Tell him to blame it on me. I'm the new NCO in charge, and it's my first time. What's he going to do to me, send me to Vietnam?" Joe laughed.

"I'll tell him, but I doubt he'll use you as an excuse. Hollow, will still blame Captain S." O'Neil shook his head and went inside to report their culpable actions.

As it turned out, Captain S did not give too much thought about the situation. "Don't worry about it. Another ass chewing will give me more motivation to develop a plan to get even with the SOB. We should have a couple of minutes before the smoke makes it over there."

"Mark the time. In no more than ten minutes, the phone will ring requesting, no demanding, your presence at DISCOM headquarters" Scott chuckled.

"It wouldn't be so funny if you were the one standing there and wanting to punch him." Captain S frowned and glared at his Master Sergeant.

"I'm sure your ass is like Staff Sergeant Hébert's and mine, still a little sore from a couple of days ago He's going to get some tender meat." O'Neil laughed under his breath.

"It's getting to be routine."

They were giggling when Baby San interrupted them by standing in the door, with her mouth open, arms extended, and eyes wide open.

Wheeler spoke first. "What's wrong?"

Baby San said something in Vietnamese. Then clasped her face and finally said, "Come, Lein."

Scott, closest to the door, dashed outside, while the rest followed closely behind.

Joe, still outside, saw the commotion and quickly followed.

Within seconds Scott knelt in front of Lein who sat on the couch with legs spread, grimacing, and holding her lower abdomen. "You'll be fine Honey," Scott said softly, and then looked toward everyone peeping in the door. "Her water has broken!"

Captain S asked, "Are you sure?"

"I'm sure. I have been here before."

"What should we do for her? "Captain S sounded a little nervous.

"We need to get her somewhere soon. It's not going to happen in the next few minutes. At least I don't think so. There's always the exception. Since this is Leins' first time, it should take a while."

Scott remained calm and explained his expectations.

Baby San, now at Leins' side and speaking Vietnamese to her, presumably, gave Lein support. Lein let out a strong sigh. "She had a contraction. Let's see how long it takes before the next one. What do you want to do, Captain?" Scott looked at him. "I don't think the 9th Med will accept her. We need to get her to My Tho soon. How soon depends on how fast we can drive with her."

"It's a plan. Help Baby San get her to the Jeep." Scott made the decision. Someone had to take control.

Captain Summerville took it from there. "Wheeler, get your gear on and in the jeep. You're going with Staff Sergeant Hébert and me. Yeah, you're going! Joe, you can ride shotgun. You may not be able to shoot a gun, but you can carry a weapon in a show of force. I'll drive."

"If need be, you know I will use it," Joe said and headed to gear up.

Captain S said, "I surely hope we don't have any delays on the road. But that could be is a good thing."

Scott asked, "What's that, Sir?"

"When the SOB calls, you can tell him I'm not here. I'm sure it will tickle him to death and make his day." Captain S laughed.

"I'll manage it," Scott replied.

"One more thing. With only you and O'Neil here, if something comes up, you'll have to take care it." Captain S looked seriously at Scott.

"I know, Sir. I don't mind. You folks like all the adventure of going here and there to save the world. Some of these guys think I'm too old and scared to go on an incident. I don't care what they think. You've seen my records. You know. I've been there, done that, and can do it again if necessary." Scott sounded sure of himself while at last letting off steam about the subject.

"Yeah, I have, and I understand. I respect you and appreciate what you do and have done. I have all the confidence in the world in you." Captain S placed his hand on Scott's shoulder.

"Captain S, I appreciate you not telling anybody about my records. Now, shut your mouth and get on the road. The girl could hatch any minute!"

CHAPTER 22

"I'm out of here." Captain S turned to leave. By the time he gathered his gear and got to the Jeep, Wheeler, Baby San, and Lein were cramped in the backseat. Joe sat in the shotgun seat.

"We better hurry. She had another pain, or cramp, or whatever they are," Wheeler said.

They had not made it to the front gate before Lein had her third contraction. Obvious in pain, she panted while sweat rolled down her forehead. She and Baby San continued speaking Vietnamese. The guys had no idea what the girls said but knew both were loud and excited.

Baby San climbed out of the backseat and sat on top of the radio. Lein reclined, leaning on Wheeler, who had his arm around her, supporting and holding her completely limped head. Lein let out another loud cry, or more of a scream.

About three miles down the road, Wheeler yelled, "We have blood, Sir!" Less than thirty seconds later, he yelled again. "Oh, crap! Lots of blood, Sir! We better stop and check it. This bouncing around is not doing her any good."

"Okay. There is a hooch up ahead of us on the right. I'll pull over there. Hébert, keep your eyes open." Captain S carefully scanned the road. He pulled off in front of the reeded hut and turned his attention to Lein. Joe went to the front right fender and assumed a watch position. Wheeler removed his arm from Lien's neck, pushed both front seats forward, and moved to the rear right fender. There, he also assumed a watch position.

"Baby San, we have to pull her pants down to her ankles and see what is going on. I need your help," Captain S cautiously said.

Baby San did as was directed. She straightened Lien's legs out over the two folded front seats and began helping Captain S pull her wet pants down.

Lein cried and screamed with pain.

"Damn you, Johnson! You haven't been gone thirty minutes. Damn you, Johnson!" Captain S knew he had seen better days than this.

"What do you have Captain?" Staff Sergeant Hébert asked, while looking over his shoulder.

"Damn you, Johnson. Unless Vietnamese women suddenly developed lots of pubic hair, I think I see a baby's head. Joe, get back here and help!" Captain S bellowed.

Lein screamed louder, and Baby San continued speaking Vietnamese to her, constantly.

"Let me change the last remark. We do have a baby coming! Damn you, Johnson!" Captain S said loudly and excitedly.

"The other day Master Sergeant Scott told us, all you have to do is catch the baby, cut the cord, and clean it up." Joe gave advice but stayed exactly where he stood.

"Come back here and catch it." Captain S looked harshly at Joe.

"No, Sir! You are there. You catch it!" Joe stood his position.

"You don't tell me, no! I'll fire your ass! You can walk the point for some infantry platoon and take your orders from a Second Lieutenant." Captain S seemed beyond excited at this point.

"First, you won't do it! Secondly, I won't be walking point. I can shoot better than 98 percent of the people over at the sniper school. They could use me. Besides, what happened to Ke-mo Sah-bee and Tonto, since yesterday?" Joe remained calmer than Captain S, which did not say anything.

"Sergeant, get over here and catch this baby! Come catch this thing! I've never held a baby. Damn you, Johnson!"

"I haven't either, Sir! I see this as the same as a ticking bomb. As you and I discussed yesterday, the regulations state, the senior man does the last and most dangerous part in the render safe procedure, the RSP. It's your job!" Joe went nowhere near Lein.

Captain S demanded, "Damn you! It's an order! Come and get this thing!"

"Sir, you know, I'm on limited duty because of a bum shoulder! I may drop the baby and hurt it. That magic pill has made me woozy" Joe did not move, no matter what Captain S threatened. He looked at Captain S and shook his head, no.

"Damn you, come--"

Wheeler interrupted Captain S. "Will you two babies quit arguing? Captain, get out of the way! I'll do it! She needs help, and you two are worthless. Get out of the way! Now! Go watch and don't let Charlie shoot us." Wheeler pushed the captain aside.

Joe and Captain S looked at each other and quickly assumed a watch position at the front and rear of the Jeep, respectfully.

Wheeler said loudly, "I need something clean. What's the cleanest thing we have?"

Everyone looked around but no one spoke. Baby San unbuttoned her white blouse, took it off, and handed it to Wheeler, as the three guys watched.

"Thanks. She's about here. The head is out. I need your first aid packs. Baby San, you get them?" Wheeler remained calm and firmly in full control.

Captain S and Joe removed their first aid pouches and gave them to Baby San who, now, stood topless, except for her bra.

Lein screamed, this time louder than before.

"I got it! I got it! It's here! I got it! He's here!" Wheeler sounded excited, and the baby started crying. "Boy, you don't need a spanking!"

Captain S and Joe suddenly appeared over Wheeler's shoulders, forgetting about their security duties.

"He's ugly," Joe said.

"He's bloody," Captain S replied.

Baby San, now standing beside Captain S, still talked to Lein, who looked almost unconscious.

Captain S removed his fatigue shirt and stepped behind Baby San. He wrapped it and his arms around her and held her tight.

"All right, this is the big one. Anybody got an idea about cutting the cord? I've seen dogs chew and lick them, but I don't think that's an option. Will one of you please watch the damn hooch and present some semblance to security. We don't need Charlie to burst out, firing an AK-47." Wheeler admonished the others.

"Your knife is probably cleaner than ours," Captain S said.

Wheeler cut the cord and cleaned the afterbirth off the baby as best he could. He wrapped Baby San's blouse around the baby and handed the swaddled baby to her. "I would keep its face and eyes covered. The sun can't be good for him."

Wheeler turned his attention back to Lein. Using the bandages from the first aid kits, Wheeler wiped her, trying to stop the blood loss. "She's still bleeding some. We better get her to a doctor." He removed his fatigue shirt and covered her.

The remaining two-mile drive down the gravel road bounced them around rather roughly. Lein became more alert, but still in pain and could not hold her baby. Wheeler, now bloody and wet all over, supported her. They pushed forward and finally reached their destination, a small, whitewashed, cinder-block house.

"Okay, here," Baby San pointed. She still wore Captain S's fatigue shirt and held the baby, which remained wrapped in her blouse.

Joe and Captain S helped Baby San out of the backseat.

"I'll need help getting Lein out," Wheeler said. With considerable effort, the three guys stood Lein on her feet, but due to weakness she couldn't support herself.

"I'll carry her in." Wheeler lifted Lein and headed for the door with Baby San and the baby following. "I'll be back in a few minutes, Wheeler called over his shoulder."

"Damn. I'm tired. Stress can be a bitch," Captain S sighed and sat down in the driver seat of the Jeep.

"Me, too." Joe exhaled. He returned to the shotgun seat to its normal position and looked around. "Ke-mo Sah-bee, your ride is filthy."

"I know, and it stinks too. You have any ideas?"

After a moment Joe replied, "I noticed a small boat ramp at the port the other day. If we can find a bucket to dip with, we can get most of this crap out, at least cleaner."

"We'll try it after Wheeler gets back. I had better let Scott know what's going on." Captain S reached for the mic.

"Echo Oscar Delta, this is Six. Over."

After a moment, the radio responded. "This is One. Over."

"One, shortly after our departure, we had another passenger suddenly appear. It took us a while, but we are now at the original destination. Over."

"All, okay? Over."

"I think so. Mom is weak, though, and he has strong lungs. Over"

Good, Six. How long will you be there? Over."

"I have no idea. Anything going on there? Over."

"Six, the Engineers came earlier than expected, and we got the call we were expecting. Over."

"One, I'll manage the colonel when I get back. Over."

"Six, you are on a questionable incident. You don't know when you can get back. You haven't been here since early morning. I'll handle the call. Over"

"One, I see your logic. I guess you can truthfully say all of that, depending on what early means.

"Six, I'll manage it. It'll be my pleasure. Over."

"Thanks, One. You know where you can reach me. Six, out."

Master Sergeant Scott lay the mic. down and turned to O'Neil. "You'll need to take care of the Engineers. First, call Personnel, and get me an appointment for an official photograph. It's time for me to upgrade my personnel file." He then called Sergeant Major Donaldson and told him about the captain, and he would be over to see Colonel Hollow in an hour.

An hour later, Scott entered the DISCOM building. "Well, Buck, you should impress him. Clever idea," Sergeant Major Donaldson told Scott when he walked in. "I'll tell him you're here."

Master Sergeant Scott stood at attention, tall and sharp, in his dress greens. He saluted and said," Master Sergeant Scott, reporting, Sir."

Colonel Hollow briefly looked up, returned the salute, and growled. "I didn't call for you. I called for Summerville."

"Captain Summerville left early this morning, and I don't know exactly when he'll be back. I thought; I'd come over here and answer any questions you may have, Sir."

"You know, damn well, why I called, Master Sergeant," Hollow said roughly, this time paying more attention to Master Sergeant Scott.

"I think so, Sir."

Hollow did not promptly reply, rather he stared at Scott's left chest. It was covered with seven rows of ribbons, including, among many, a Purple Heart with two oakleaf clusters, which showed he had received three purple hearts, an Army Achievement Medal with three oakleaf clusters and a V device, which indicated valor. On the top row set the Army Distinguish Service Medal, second only to the Medal of Honor.

"I see you made WW-2 and Korea. For a Black, enlisted soldier, your awards are very impressive for the times. They didn't give Black enlisted awards like yours to everybody."

"Yes, Sir. Thank you," Scott replied.

"Are you here trying to impress me with all your medals? If you are, you did."

"No, Sir. I'm on my way to the Personnel office to get my official photograph taken for my file.

"If you called to talk to my commander about the smoke this morning, I'm the ranking NCO, and I'll take full responsibility for what my young men do. However, in this case, I believe the Good Lord is responsible for sending the smoke this direction. Sir, I can do nothing about it," Scott spoke, in a matter-of-fact manner.

"Don't get smart with me Master Sergeant. I'll let this situation slide, but don't let it happen again.

"Yes, Sir."

"Master Sergeant Scott, I understand you play a little poker from time to time."

"Yes, Sir, I do." Scott, still standing at attention, briefly nodded.

"Do you win?"

"Sir, if I lost, I wouldn't play."

"I bet you wouldn't. You're dismissed."

Scott saluted, did an about-face, and exited the office. Sergeant Major Donaldson was in his customary position, wearing a big smile. "He wasn't expecting the real Buck," Donaldson said softly.

"I think I caught him by surprise." Scott asked, "What in the world is wrong with him?"

"He's simply a wrathful man, taking his anger out on others. He thinks the DISCOM Command is beneath him, and he won't get a star because of it. In hopes of getting one of the Brigade Command positions, he extended his tour of duty. As you know that command would be a real steppingstone to the star. Obviously, the General didn't give him the Brigade. Hell, he may even extend again. Dumb SOB!"

When Captain S, Staff Sergeant Hébert, and Wheeler returned to the unit, they found Scott, and O'Neil working on the deck extension. Scott had changed his clothes, back into his fatigues.

"Master Sergeant Scott, are you taking your frustrations on out the nails."

"No frustrations to take out on anything, Sir. But I'm glad you decided to come home." Scott dropped his hammer and went indoors. The others followed.

"Not frustrated? It must've gone okay then," Captain S took his seat.

"I told you; I could manage it. I'll bet I did better than Larry, Curly, Mo, and Tinker Bell, managing our little pregnant lady." Scott sat behind his desk.

"Assuming you are talking about the three of us, we didn't have any problems. We took your advice and let Lein do all the work." Joe spoke up and held his head high.

"Yeah, right! However, the Captain may have ruined his sex life, at least as he knows it. I don't think he had one to start with." Wheeler laughed.

"You're correct, wheeler, on both accounts. The bottom line is, the little rascal and Mama are doing fine. We left them at the Doctors Office. I'm sure Lein will be home before dark. Baby San said they could get a ride. You know they never want us in their neighborhood. I understood, Baby San will stay with mom and baby tomorrow morning and then come to work later if everything is okay. I don't know when we'll see Lein again." Captain S summarized the events.

Scott replied, "There's nothing going on here, except the captain from transportation brought a grenade over. He said, he had found it in his Jeep and didn't know where it came from. I haven't taken time to check it out."

"This sounds like it falls outside the bounds of limited duty." Joe smiled, retrieved the grenade, and went outside. Within seconds he returned and handed the striker, spoon, and detonator to Captain S.

"The delay element is missing." Captain S said, "He's one lucky captain. If he had tried to throw the grenade, it would've detonated an inch off his fingertips. Scott, will you call his First Sergeant tomorrow and pass the word along?"

"Yes, Sir. I know I'm old, so I don't understand the young troopers today. Hell, if you want to get rid of an Officer, you shoot the sucker, nobody else gets hurt." Scott looked at Captain S and smiled.

"Master Sergeant, are you trying to send a message to me or something?" Captain S looked directly into Scott's eyes.

"No, Sir. I'm simply stating well-known facts." Everybody gave Scott a good laugh.

"I'll take the grenade back, Sir, and I'll take care of it and the detonator." Joe reached for it.

O'Neil said, "Hey, back to the baby boy. What did she name him?"

Since Wheeler was in the Doctors Office with Lein and Baby San when it went down, I'll let him answer." Captain S retorted and chuckled.

Sensing something, O'Neil asked, "Well, Wheeler, what's the story?"

"Lein, insisted on naming him, Samuel Johnson Wheeler!" Wheeler grinned.

"Wheeler! Boy, what have you been doing behind Johnson's and my back? I had no idea!" With a huge smile, Scott berated him.

"Yeah, I want to hear this, too! I would've sworn, and bet last dollar, you had not touched a woman since you have been here. Now, I find out you are a daddy. A daddy!" O'Neil patted Wheeler on his back. Congratulations!"

"A wolf in sheepskin. From now on, I'll have to find more work for you, Boy. The next thing we know, Baby San will show up with a big belly," Scott proclaimed and laughed.

"Hey, it's not like what you're thinking! Let me finish." Wheeler tried to defend himself.

"I've heard enough. I'm writing to Johnson tomorrow." O'Neil laughed so hard he could hardly get it out.

"Wait, let me finish, there's more to this story!" Wheeler joined in the laughter.

"There's more! This, I have to hear this! Did Sam get some too? And who in the hell is Sam?" O'Neil asked over all the laughing.

"Please, let me finish with my story," Wheeler cried while trying to compose himself. "Since I carried Lein into the doctor's office, the Doctor assumed I was the father and wrote it down. Then he wanted two more names. Remember, Lein had recently gone through hell. She said, Samuel Johnson. We all know where Johnson came from--"

Scott interrupted, "Okay, you sound somewhat reasonable to me, but what about Samuel?"

"Now, we have another story. I asked her the same question. She answered me by saying, it's what, Captain S wanted."

O'Neil shouted, "Damn! Am I the only one around here who's not banging Lein? The captain's also holding out on us. I want to hear some more about this."

"Well, you see, during the birthing process, Captain S was cursing Johnson with every other word out of his mouth. You should know, Lein doesn't think our illustrious and righteous Commander would ever curse. She was in bad shape. She, instead, thought he was calling the baby, Samuel Johnson. I didn't have the heart to tell her, he was saying 'Damn you Johnson'!" Wheeler finally got it out.

"Oh, hell we need a drink. We need a drink, bad." Captain S declared.

Joe proclaimed, "Yes, we do! Hell, I need a bunch. I haven't been here two weeks, and let's see. I've scalded my ass, fell out of the helicopter, and helped deliver a baby. Maybe not deliver a baby, more like, I refused a direct order. I helped make a beer hall any

Bureau of Narcotics and Dangerous Drugs, BNDD, agent would be proud of, refused two purple hearts, and last but not least, met some great teammates."

"Hear, Hear!" Scott shouted. "Let's drink!"

Joe enjoyed the commonality and the levity the unforeseen situations had brought. Thinking about Johnson and Lein, he couldn't help but think about how long it had been since he had seen Ava. *God, I miss her and hope she's safe.*

CHAPTER 23

12 Nov 68

Dear Mom,

First, let me apologize for not writing sooner. It has been nearly three months since I spoke with you, telling you I was going to Vietnam. You know, I am a terrible writer, but I should have contacted you before now.

Secondly, please be assured, I am well and perfectly healthy. Remember the old rule about no news is good news. In the case of those of us in Vietnam, the rule is paramount.

I am in the Mekong River Delta, south of Saigon, attached to the 9th Infantry Division, at a place called Dong Tam. As I told you the last time we spoke, I am back in EOD, and I am loving it. We are doing an important job. Basically, we are saving the lives of innocent people.

I know you sometimes watch the evening news. Don't be alarmed by all the combat you see. I am not involved with anything such as that. In fact, I haven't been shot at. I haven't even fired my weapon. Please, don't worry about my well-being. If something happens to me, you will know about it from the Red Cross or an Army Chaplain within hours.

I trust; you and your new guy are doing well. I'm sorry, if you told me, I forgot his name. As you know. I wish you the best. You were alone for too many years. Write to me and let me know how you are doing. Also, let me know what's going on down on the Bayou. Do you know if there are any of my old classmates over here?

As we get no local news from home, anything would be welcome. We do get a daily dose of news coming from Washington's propaganda machine. I'll reserve any further comments on what is coming out of there. I'm sure you understand how I feel.

Sitting here thinking about home, makes me hungry for your cooking. A good plate of your bouillabaisse or a good court bouillon would put a big smile on my face. Thinking of food, will you send me a couple of things? Tabasco and Filét would be good. With that, I can get the other makings for a good pot of gumbo.

Mom, please take care of yourself. There is nothing I can do for you. But if I can help you, in any way, you know I will.

Let me hear from you soon. And have a good Thanksgiving.

Oh, tell my stepfather hello for me. Always remember, I love you.

Bon Dieu te benisse, and *Laisse les bons temps rouler.*

Luv ya, Joe

*****

18 Nov 68

Dear Pam,

I may not be the last person you were expecting to hear from, but I'm sure this is a surprise, especially the return address. Yeah, I'm in Vietnam. I've been here for more than three months, and no, dammit, I haven't won the war, yet! I'm still working on it!

I hope this finds you well, and trust school is going great for you. I surely hope you are not one of those hippies who are marching and protesting in the streets. I trust you have better things to do.

To answer your unverbalized question about why I'm in Vietnam, I think you will like this. Putting it simply, I got caught with my pants down, literally down! Maybe I should say off. Had his shot hit a couple inches to the right, Lieutenant Colonel McCoy would have killed me!

Yelp, you're right. You can sit back down now. A miss by two inches is still a miss.

It's not a long story. He missed. I ran. In fact, I ran twice, the first time with no clothes on. My first effort to escape was exposed by a four or five-year-old girl, whom I surely scarred for life. I had to return inside to retrieve my forgotten pants. That is when the shot was fired.

Careful now, I can see your hazel eyes dancing.

I ran all the way to Dong Tam, in the Mekong Delta, south of Saigon. This happened a little more than three months ago. Now, you know I'm fine, you can start laughing. Oh, I'm sorry, you already are!

My only regret over the entire situation is, I fear, I have lost Ava. She did not return to work after the incident, and I have not heard from her since. Yes, there was a fight, a physical fight between Ava and the Lieutenant Colonel. I wasn't involved in it, and I don't know for sure, but I don't think she won. I heard only one shot, the one intended for me. Remember I ran, and I can run fast if necessary.

Ava worked at the PX. A couple of EOD personnel have checked regularly for me. They have been told she is not there but is still considered employed. They keep me informed, but three months is a long time to be on vacation. To say I'm worried about her is an understatement.

As for Vietnam, it's like home, South Louisiana, in many ways. It is hot and humid, swampy, rice patties everywhere, and has copious mosquitoes.

As for the job, I'm back in EOD, and it is great! We have at least two incidents a day. During three years in Germany, the best or worst incident I worked on was an overturned truck of ammunition. Over here, that is absolutely nothing. Booby-traps are our biggest concerns. I work on at least two per week in addition to myriads of ordinary incidents, the blow in place or simply pick it up type. The work is sometimes challenging, and so far, I've enjoyed it.

To give you an example, we were called to check out three VC bodies which were suspected to be booby-trapped. Snipers had shot them the previous night. The bodies were not recoverable until the next morning. This is when they called us to check them out. Sure enough, the area around them was booby-trapped. We had to search the bodies. Thank goodness, they were not booby-trapped. But we found a slew of VC classified documents on one of them. In my three months here, I have responded to dozens of incidents like this.

One thing I like is, the 9th Division gives us great support. They fly us out to the incident site, wait on us, and then, they fly us back. This is big around here. It means, I get to sleep between two clean sheets every night, rather than in a mosquito infested, rice paddy.

I almost exclusively work with the captain. It simply worked out this way. I inherited the job. He was paired with the guy whom I replaced, so we kept it rolling. The captain is a Duke graduate. This alone tells you he is intelligent. He is also easy to get along with. Also, he is good at what he does. He nearly always selects the best incidents for us.

Can you believe I am talking about an Officer like this?

He is lucky, one of those guys who steps in a pile of crap and ends up smelling like roses.

One day when we were late coming in and got back after dark, his first stop was the crapper. About the same time red flares started popping. This meant we were getting mortared. Everybody got in bunkers except the captain, who stayed in the outhouse. One of the mortars landed within twenty feet from where he was sitting with his pants around his ankles. The four-by-four-by-eight-foot outhouse was hit with about ten pieces of frag. The captain was not touched. It all honesty, it had to be divine intervention.

He is steady. I have only seen him off tune one time. He was unable to manage the job, and he had to be replaced by our clerk typist. To be honest, I could not manage the job either, but this is a different story for another time. It can wait for our old age.

Another thing I like is the nightlife! No. No, it's not what you're thinking. We have a party every night. We built a nice outdoor bar, and we sell beer to our guests, usually twenty to thirty Navy and Army guys every night. One of our NCOs is an outstanding musician and singer. He will make big money with it one of these days. I think he is better than Barry Sanders.

We sit around at night drinking, singing, and telling war stories. As for as the other nightlife you were thinking of, there has been none of it. But I think one young lady here has had her eyes on me for a while now. I think she is hungry for my body.

Now, you know what is going on in Vietnam. Tell me, what is going on at Georgetown, especially about a certain law student that you once mentioned. He has probably been replaced by another one by now. It is okay but stay away from the slimy politicians. You know, of course, I am kidding.

Pam, you are a big part of my life. I think of you often, and I treasure every moment we spent together. This will never change. And if there is one thing in life, I am sure of, it is our friendship will endure for scores of years, if not for our lifetime. Take care and let me hear from you. Happy Thanksgiving.

Laisse les bons temps rouler.

Joe, from over here.

CHAPTER 24

"Staff Sergeant Hébert, hey, wake up," Wheeler said while shaking Joe. "Get up. You must go. Captain S is on his way."

"What, what's going on? Man! It's still dark outside!" Joe questioned him with a grumpy mood.

"We have a downed chopper, a short distance off Ambush Alley. They want you there, *pronto*. I have the coffee pot on." Wheelers stood back from the bed to make sure Joe raised up.

"Okay. The damn rooster is crowing, so I know what time it is. I don't know why Scott keeps him around."

Wheeler replied, "He told me it reminds him of his childhood on the farm."

"Okay, I'm up now. I'll be in the office in a few minutes." Joe rubbed his hand over his face.

Ten minutes later, Joe walked into the office, "Good morning, Sir, and Happy Thanksgiving. This is an effective way to celebrate; isn't it?"

Captain S got right down to the matter at hand. "The coffee is brewed. The 9th MPs are sending over a couple of gun Jeeps to escort us to the incident site. They should arrive here in any minute. So, we don't have a lot of time."

"It didn't take you long to get here. I presume they have a security force on-site waiting for us?" Joe sipped on his coffee. "Oh, what would I do for a cup of café au lait."

The caption continued. "When they contacted Wheeler, they were trying to extract the pilot from the area. They didn't know his status. Due to the time of day, they were not expecting any resistance. This is the reason for the rush. We don't want to give Charlie a chance to organize anything. He obviously knows we're coming."

As Captain S and Staff Sergeant Hébert drove out of the gates of Dong Tam headed toward My Tho, the eastern skies were red. The sun was not yet in their eyes. A short three quarters of a mile drive and a left turn brought them to the infamous Ambush Alley, which one never wanted to travel at this time of day. Ambush Alley ran parallel with the perimeter of Dong Tam's eastern side.

Between the Ambush Alley and Dong Tam lay the small hamlets of Bien Duc, which was VC infested. Both Captain S and Joe were on high alert. The two MP gun jeeps escorting them were also on their toes.

A short drive north brought them to three, two-and-a-half-ton military vehicles, pulled off the east side of the road next to and in a rather dry rice paddy. They followed the lead gun Jeep as it parked near the trucks.

Captain S had scarcely placed his feet on the ground before a figure appeared in front of him. "Good morning, Sir, I'm Lieutenant White."

"I'm Captain Summerville, and this is Staff Sergeant Hébert. What is the current situation?"

"I have a couple of fire teams at the chopper. We have retrieved the two bodies. Both were dead. My directions from DISOPS are to tell you to blow the electronic components and the munitions you find."

"This sounds reasonably viable. What does the overall security look like?" Captain S questioned.

"Iffy, at best. We've asked everybody, the locals, to evacuate the area, but you know how that goes." The Lieutenant shrugged.

"Well, keep the evacuation effort going. I have no idea what armament was on the chopper. It could be nothing; or it could be heavily armed. Do you have any idea how people live in and around the area?" Captain S knew that he needed all the information he can get.

"No, Sir, not at all, and I don't fancy having my men running around looking for them."

"I agree. You're taking us in, aren't you?" Captain S cocked his head.

"Yes, Sir. Of course, I'll lead the way." Lieutenant White waited until Captain S and Joe gathered their gear.

As they entered the tree line on the west side of the road, the big red ball in the eastern sky could now be seen. They followed an elevated trail, about a foot high, through the woods. It was raised to provide a walking path during the wet season.'

The lack of full daylight prevented them from seeing the hamlet. They met a dozen old men and women, and young children walking in the opposite direction they were going. Presumably, they were evacuating the area.

When they reached the helicopter, Joe announced, "Nine minutes in, Captain."

"Got you." He slurred and turned to Lieutenant White, "This will take a while. Your men have been all around here, right?" Captain S pointed at the ground.

"Yes, Sir. If you're thinking booby-traps, it should be safe."

"Good. Go ahead and do what you have to do but leave me someone to watch our backs."

"You got it!" The Lieutenant pointed to one of his soldiers. "Private, you stay and keep your eyes and ears open."

Joe, who had walked around to the opposite side of the crash site, suddenly shouted, "Oh, crap!" He darted back to where Captain S stood.

"What is it? What's the matter?" Captain S asked Joe as the shooter sprang to an alert position.

"Oh, he, ah. He scared the crap out of me!" Joe felt embarrassed.

"What is it?" Captain S asked again.

"He's the biggest damn hog I've ever seen in my life! Crap!" Joe pointed at a hog that looked the size of a living room couch. The hog now looked ferociously at the three of them.

"Wow, he's huge," Captain S said, as the soldier moved closer to them.

The soldier asked, "Do you want me to put him down, Captain?"

"No. Keep an eye on him, and if he acts threatening, shoot his ass," Captain S said, and noticed for the first time a reed hooch about ten feet beyond the hog. "Check the hooch!"

It took only a minute, for the soldier to report, "The hooch is clear, and the hog is staked out.

He's not bothering us. It looks as if he's simply a big pet and is harmless."

"Good. Look at the balls on him. What a monster! Still, if he moves, shoot his ass," Joe said with a firmly held conviction.

No, Tonto, Since I've thought about it, he has enough to worry about. When we blow this stuff, we'll surely kill him, and we'll likely knock the hooch down, too. Let's see what we can do about the situation. It sounds like a challenge to me."

"Oh, Ke-Mo Sah-bee, did you notice there's no M-60s?" Joe pointed at the remains of the chopper.

"We took them out with the bodies," The soldier quickly said.

"Oh, good. We don't have to worry about them opening up on us." Joe seemed relieved.

"Tonto, come over here and look at this. It's a 2.75-inch rocket pod with only about eight inches of the rocket motors exposed. It's carrying nineteen rockets. I forgot the nomenclature of this thing." Captain S shook his head.

Joe looked at the item and said, "There are several nomenclatures for these pods. The warheads are our concern. I'll bet the entire pod is intact. Naturally, the war heads are two feet deep in the ground, and the ground is as hard as concrete. The bastard is going to be hard to dig up. You check for the electronics, and I'll start digging."

After placing C-4 charges on every piece of electronic equipment he could find, Captain S returned to where Joe used his knife to dig around the rocket pod. "You're not making a lot of progress, are you?"

"No, Sir. This may take longer than we expected. We need to expose the whole rocket pod down to the warhead to ensure that this thing goes properly. I'm not sure a shovel would help."

Already tired and disgusted with all the digging, Joe stood and stretched.

Captain S thought for a minute. "You know, if we hit this thing hard enough with sufficient C-4, the rocket motors will detonate rather than burn."

"Yes, Sir. But your operative words are 'hard enough'. What is hard enough? And if we don't hit it hard enough, we'll have flaming rocket motors going everywhere." Joe pointed the facts out as if Captain S did not already know them.

"These pods usually come in pairs, one on each side of the chopper, but not always. If there were two, I wonder what happened to the other one?" Captain S started looking around more carefully.

"Sir, I have no idea. There's enough light now for you to search the area better, but don't get out of sight of the gunner. I'll keep digging."

"Okay, Tonto," Captain S replied, and started searching the area, only to return in a couple of minutes. "I didn't find anything resembling a rocket pod. But I took a good look at the hog and hooch. I want to try to kick everything away from them, to give them a chance."

"Heads up! Movement!" The soldier called out and knelt, weapon ready.

Captain S and Joe grabbed their weapons and faced toward the movement.

"Easy. It's a couple of women," the rifleman announced, as two elderly women approached them. "They don't appear to be hostile, but who knows?"

The two women paused momentarily and looked at the three GIs. After the private said, "d*i di*", go away, he waved his hand for them to leave. They continued on their way.

Captain S said, "Okay, they got the heart rate up. Let's go with what we have and get our ass out of here."

They quickly placed C-4 as far down on the rocket motors as they could, keeping the hog and reeded hooch in mind. Then they connected it with the detonating cord, previously placed by Captain S, leading to the electronics in the down chopper.

Captain S said, "Nine minutes out. Let's say six minutes to call Charlie Pad, and alert everyone else, and to account for the uh-ohs."

"Sounds about right to me. Fifteen minutes coming up." Joe started measuring the time fuse.

"Private, can you find your Lieutenant?" Captain S asked.

"I'm not sure I can, Sir. But I can give it a try."

"Mark your watch. We'll pull the pin in two minutes. This means, you have seventeen minutes from now, and this thing is going up, no matter what. I would like for you to try to find your Lieutenant, and anyone else, and inform them of the time of the explosion. Can you, do it?"

"Yes, Sir!" The Private responded.

"When the seventeen minutes are up, I want your ass back on the other side of the road with anybody you find. Do you understand?"

"Yes, Sir."

"Okay, look at your watch. Seventeen minutes from now, this thing is going up. So, get out of here, go." Captain S genteelly pushed the Private.

Joe spent the next two minutes checking the shot. With fifteen minutes left, he yelled the customary three, "Fire in the hole," and pulled the pin.

They both took a last glance at the hog as they headed out. Joe said, "Good luck to you, Buddy."

"He'll need it," Captain S said.

"What are the odds-on having roast pork tonight?"

"Ninety-eight percent. I'd say." Captain S responded.

"Some pulled pork may be good." Joe glanced over his shoulder as they left the area.

"Not from him. The old boy is too tough and too strong. I tell you what though, if somehow, he lives through this, I'd say, it would be the best job we've done."

"The best ever. Two percent is not a good survivability rate. It's like rolling snake-eyes, twice in a row."

When they walked out of the trees and crossed over the road, they saw a crowd of approximately thirty locals standing with the MP's. "It looks as if they got most of them out." Captain S perceived.

"Let's hope. Joe responded automatically.

At the Jeep, Captain S contacted Dong Tam Tower. "This is Echo Oscar Delta, be advised we have a hot shot, I repeat a hot shot, approximately one kilometer east of your position. It will go in five and a half, minutes. Over."

"I read, five and a half, minutes. Over." The radio responded.

"Roger."

"I'll take necessary procedures."

"Thank you. Echo Oscar Delta out."

Captain S sit down at the edge of the rice field, about six feet away from Joe. He looked at the faces and hands of the old men and women. *They must have a hard life and aged early.*

An old man, with reddish-black stained teeth and lips, sat in a wheelchair and chewed betel nuts. He stared at Joe from about twelve feet away. The children were children, beautiful in every respect.

Captain S asked, "Time, Tonto?"

"Two forty-five, Sir."

No sooner than Joe spoke the time, they heard it. Looking up they saw an OH-6 helicopter bearing down on them from the east.

"Oh, crap!" Captain S ran to the radio.

"Dong Tam Tower, this is Echo Oscar Delta, we have a bird in the air.

You better get him off us. Over."

After a distinct pause with no answer, Captain S said, "Dong Tam Tower, did you read me? Over."

There was still no answer. The helicopter started circling overhead, obviously concentrating on the crowd below. Captain S estimated the arc taken by the chopper could put it over the incident site when it exploded.

"Dong Tam Tower, this is Echo Oscar Delta. Over."

"We have a visual on the bird. He's not checking in and has not responded to us. Can you get his attention? Over."

"That's the problem. We have his attention. He's circling us. It looks as if he'll be over the shot when it goes, in about thirty-five seconds. Over."

"I'll keep trying to contact him. Dong Tam Tower, out."

Captain S returned to his earlier position.

"Fifteen seconds, it's going to be interesting Ke-Mo Sha-bee." Joe had a little anticipation in his loud voice, as they watched the helicopter arced toward the blast area.

"Ten, nine, eight." It looked like a New Years firework demonstration, flaming rockets piercing the sky upward. Their visual senses were fixed on the helicopter which rolled over and headed down between the road and the tree line. Their hearing senses noticed a wisp, wisp, wisp sound getting louder, so loud the visual senses of the helicopter gave way. They did not see the helicopter when it hit the ground. Instead, they focused on the flaming object headed their direction.

With everything moving in slow motion, neither Joe nor Captain S at once reacted. Joe thought. *I sure hope there's no warhead on that thing.*

The rocket motor landed, without a warhead, between them and the old man in the wheelchair.

People screamed and ran. Four or five women fell upon Captain S and Joe which restricted their movement. As the rocket motor lay burning, both knew there were in no danger. Their eyes were more focused on the old man in the wheelchair with the burning rocket motor at his feet. Looking at it, his eyes blared. His hands grasp the wheelchair so tight his knuckles were white. His chewing increased intensively, and reddish betel nut juice flowed down both sides of his mouth. As he sat there, helpless, he rocked back and forth. They were sure this amazing image would be imprinted in their brain for a lifetime, an image, worthy of a Norman Rockwell painting.

The Lieutenant tried to help by pulled the women, who had grabbed Captain S and Joe, away where they could get to their feet. Both returned their attention back to the old man. Captain S gave way to let Joe roll him behind one of the two-and-half ton trucks.

The helicopter had made a hard landing. Two people, one GI in uniform and one civilian, casually dressed, were now walking around. "I'll check on them out," The Lieutenant told Captain S and headed for the down chopper.

"I'll call the tower and let them know." Captain S walker toward the radio.

"Dong Tam Tower, this is Echo Oscar Delta, over.

"Go." The radio answered with no hesitation.

"He had a rough landing, but from here, it looks like two people walking. My guess, there is nothing major wrong with them. I can't speak for the chopper. Over."

"Thanks, I'll pass it on and take appropriate actions. Dong Tam Tower, out."

Captain S said, "Okay, it looks as if no one here is hurt. Come on Tonto, let's go get some roasted pork."

After arriving back at the blast site, they noticed the grass hooch still stood, and the pig, standing watching them approach. "I'm amazed!" Stunned, Joe had a flush of goose bumps over his body.

"Wow, Tonto, we're good! In fact, we're damn good! No blood, and I can't see an iota of difference in the hooch. I can't believe it!"

Joe investigated the rocket pod crater. "I think everything went."

"It looks good. I'll check the electronic components. You go and do a close check of the hooch and the hog." Captain S nodded toward the beast. "No, no! Oh, excuse me, I'm supposed to add a Sir behind my comments. You go check your electronic stuff. I'll check the hooch and hog from here. Man! He may be mad. Extremely mad."

Walking back down the trail, Captain S put his arms over Joe's shoulder and said, "Tonto, we're good. As it ended up, we had no real problem with the rocket pod nor the electronics. Mission accomplished."

"Yeah. It's the best job we've ever done, no doubt," Joe started singing.

Once reaching the road, Joe paused to take one last look backwards and said, "Uh-oh."

"What?" Captain S turned around. "Oooh, crap!"

"Oh, it's at least fifteen." Joe quickly counted.

"I'm sure we can't see them all. I can hear Hollow now." Captain S grimaced.

"Think of it this way. We saved the hooch and hog." Joe tried to be optimistic.

"Yeah." Captain S sighed, completely deflated from his jubilant attitude moments before.

They stood looking at the plumes of smoke boiling out of the trees as the thatched dwellings, downrange from their shot, burned.

"Sir, how long is it going to take for you to pay for an entire hamlet? You know, all those grass homes, you burnt down, will be rebuilt with Uncle Sam's mahogany plywood. Oh, and don't forget to add in the helicopter that you shot out of the sky." Joe patted Captain S on the back.

Captain S pinched his fingers over the bridge of his nose and shook his head. Then he held his head up, "I'm not going to worry about it. You know I get paid the big bucks. I can easily cover the cost in, let's say, a hundred years."

"Now, let's go eat some Thanksgiving turkey."

CHAPTER 25

"The best EOD job ever," Replied Joe when Master Sergeant Scott asked him how it went.

"We saved a hog, as large as two desks, and a grass hooch...But!" Captain S said, while dropping his gear and settling behind his desk.

"But?" Wheeler asked.

After Joe's dissertation, Scott excitingly proclaimed, "You knocked a helicopter down!"

Captain S clapped his hands, "Smack down! And burned down a hamlet! Is it too early for a Scotch? Nobody hurt, but it was a rough landing for two men in the helicopter."

"How are the ladies and little Sam this morning?" Joe changed the subject.

"They're busy as ever. You know, I didn't initially approve of letting Lein bringing the baby to the office with her, but it has worked out well, once the daddy learned how to change diapers." Scott nodded toward Wheeler.

"I don't mind changing my son's diapers," Wheeler boastfully replied. "With him in the small tent, he doesn't bother anybody. Although, I'd bet if Colonel Hollow knew about him, he'd have a hissing fit."

Captain S looked at Scott. "You're right there. Where are Banks and O'Neil?"

"Division artillery. DIVARTY called. They have a hung round in an eight-inch howitzer. It's pretty simple, so they should be back for lunch."

Captain S asked, "Have you heard from Jackson and Redding? Are they coming in for Thanksgiving dinner?"

"Sir, they are staying in Tan An. If nothing happens, they'll be here tomorrow afternoon and stay until Sunday."

"I guess I'd better go wish the girls a Happy Thanksgiving." Captain S headed for the small tent where he found Baby San shining boots, and Sam sleeping.

"Good morning, Baby San," Captain S sit beside her.

"My name is Mai Ly. You think I am baby. I am no, not a baby. I am not a baby!" She strongly emphasized her point and corrected her English.

"I know you're not a baby, but--" Captain S seemed caught off guard when Baby San interrupted him.

"You think I am ugly baby. I am not a baby!" She dropped her brush and pointed her index finger at Captain S.

"Baby San, you arc not ugly by a long shot." Captain S stood his ground.

"I am ugly. You no like me." She now sounded dejected and dropped her head.

"No, Baby San. You are not ugly. You are pretty." Captain S placed his hands on her cheeks and pulled her face toward him and looked into her doe-like eyes. "I do like you, a lot."

"You think I pretty!" She asked excitedly. This time with eyes wide open. "I surely do," Captain S said softly and sincerely. Baby San smiled and said, "I think you pretty, too."

"Thank you." Captain S dropped his hands.

The smile left Baby San's face. "I cherry girl. You think; I am baby."

"No, I don't!"

"I no baby!" She firmly took his hand and placed it on her breast. "I have tit, tit." She then moved his hands, down to between her legs, which were spread because of the boots. "I bleed here. I no baby."

Captain S moved his little finger and quickly found her clitoris. She jumped but did not remove his hand. A second rubbing got the same response.

"Good morning, Captain S." Lein said entering the tent.

Captain S quickly moved his hand away, hoping Lein had not noticed. "Good morning Lein. Happy Thanksgiving to you."

"Thanksgiving means nothing to Vietnamese." She brushed him off.

"I know, but it means something to us." Captain S tried to be cheerful.

"Where my Hébert?" Lein moved to check the baby.

"I left him in the office, but he may be at lunch. You know; Thanksgiving dinner is big for us."

"I know. I never eat turkey." Lein checked Sam's diapers and sat beside Baby San.

"Baby San, have you ever eaten turkey?" Captain S looked at her.

"No, I no eat turkey," she replied. She did not look up from her job of brushing the boots.

"I'll make sure you have some turkey to eat. As a matter of fact, I'll go to lunch now, and I'll bring you some turkey." Captain S rose and departed from the tent."

He returned in thirty minutes, with two paper plates full of turkey breast, and dressing, only to find the two girls were already eating. "Turkey good. Taste like chicken." Baby San looked up from her plate and smiled.

"Chicken many dollars in Vietnam." Lein informed him.

"I know chicken is expensive here, but duck is cheaper here than in the States. Well, you two enjoy, I'm going to the O-club,"

He had finished his first Scotch and ordered his second, when he heard Wheeler call his name from the door of the small Navy O-club. "You are needed at the office. We have visitors."

"Anybody I know?"

"Yes, Sir. It's the SEAL team. They were here before."

"Yeah, I remember." Captain S gulped his drink down quickly and walked to his office where he found the SEAL team waiting. "Well, hello. Good to see you again."

"If you've forgotten, I'm Lieutenant Armstrong, and this is Petty Officer First Class Teddy, Ted Butler."

Armstrong looked like a congenial, hansom, six-foot two inches man, with light brown hair. He weighed slightly less two hundreds and presented an outgoing personality.

Butler, on the other hand, looked like a wiry, sinewy, five foot eight inches at best, brown eyes, and dark-brown haired man. He had a reserve and quiet disposition.

"Of course, I haven't forgotten. What are you doing at Dong Tam?"

"We had a meeting with some of your operational people. We have a little time to kill. So, we decided to stop by and say hello. We're on our way out. I hope you don't mind?" Armstrong addressed his comment to Captain S.

"Not at all. I'm glad you did. Have you had lunch?"

"Yes, we ate over at Division Headquarters." Armstrong informed Captain S.

"Well, how about a beer? They're plentiful around here. There's a hell of a story behind our acquisition of beer. I'm sure you would appreciate it. Stay and have one or two, and I'll tell you the story." Captain S tried to enticed Armstrong.

"I'll get the beer." Scott started to get up.

"No, we'll sit outside. They haven't seen our new addition. Shall we?" Captain S led the way outside.

Sitting in the shade under the canopy covering the bar, Captain S told the story about Chubby and his barge. "We're now on the third load of beer. We have beer, coming out our ass. In fact, we dumped a pallet of the Australian stuff in the river a couple of weeks ago. It does not agree with the sun."

"What's all the commotion about? A guy can't sleep in the middle... I'll be damn!" Joe astonishingly said while standing in the middle of the patio. "I'll be damn!"

"Hébert! What the hell are you doing in Dong Tam? I always wondered what happened to you." Lieutenant Armstrong rushed to Joe and gave him a manly hug.

"What's this? Old lovers or something." Scott seemed bemused and looked back and forth at the two of them.

"Old lovers? No, but we've done about everything else imaginably together. We've had some good times, and some awful bad ones. We've been to hell and back together."

"Yes, Captain, I mean Lieutenant." Joe shook his head. "I've been in the Army too long. Yes, we experienced quite a bit together."

"Joe, I'd like you to meet my partner in crime. This is Ted Butler." Armstrong motioned toward Butler.

"Glad to meet you, Butler," Joe reached out to shake his hand.

"You want an ear?" Butler put his hand into his pocket to retrieve a black and disfigured, but still recognizable ear. He offered it to Joe.

"This means he likes you, Joe. Sometimes he doesn't talk a lot, until he gets to know you. Then he plays with your mind. It's a game for him." Armstrong grinned.

"It's great seeing you, Sir! Team Two, I see. You two haven't been over here too long, have you? Sit down. I'll get the beer." Joe went behind the bar.

"Yeah, Team Two. Team One needed help! We do a bunch of work here in the Delta. And we're damn good at it. We have Charlie so scared; he thinks there's a Special Operator behind every bush." Armstrong took a chair. He was obviously proud of the job they were doing.

Captain S spoke up, "I know Staff Sergeant Hébert had some SEAL training. Is this how you two know each other?"

"Yeah, we were in the same class. Joe would have surely finished first in the class, as a sniper, if his little secret had not been discovered. He was outstanding at everything we did, especially with weapons.

"We ran a thousand miles together, did a hundred thousand pushups, carried logs and boats for miles, swam untold number of miles, and fired every small arms weapon in the world. He's damn good at it.

"Did he tell you the story about hunting ducks with a single shot, twenty-two rifle when he was nine years old?"

"No, but I'm more interested in his little secret." Scott looked at Joe and then at Armstrong.

"They don't know?" Armstrong looked sheepishly at Joe.

"No, we're in Vietnam. It's not like it would be a problem here." Joe said.

"Go ahead and finish your story." Joe looked at Armstrong and nodded, "Tell them. It's nothing to be ashamed of."

"One night we were laying in the cold surf with our arms interlocked. I was on one side of Joe, and a guy named Jefferson was on the other side. We knew Joe couldn't take cold water, and we had tried to cover for him. Anyway, after laying there, Joe turned into a board. I'm not talking about teeth chattering cold. I'm talking about literally stiff as a board. He still would not quit. When we were called out of the water, Jefferson, one of our teammates, and I pulled him out.

"When the trainer saw us, he told us to drop him. We did, and Joe hit the beach like a rock, arms still folded. The medics took him away. It's the last we saw of him." Armstrong explained and looked at Joe. "You never officially rang the bell or quit, did you?"

"Nope. They simply told me I was through. It's called, Raynaud's Phenomenon. It's worse for me than most people. It simply means my genes don't like cold weather. Although, I was stiff, I wasn't as stiff as a board," Joe explained.

"The story is interesting. Thanks for sharing it with us. I knew, from his medical records, Joe was cold intolerant" Captain S nodded.

"It cost the SEAL's a good sniper, and I salute you, Joe." Armstrong lifted his beer to him.

"Wow, dude! That smarts!" Butler toasted his beer to Joe.

With O'Neil and Banks now standing beside Joe, Banks said, "What's this, a party, and we're not invited?"

"I think you guys met the last time they were here," Scott said.

"You know it, dude!" Butler nodded his head.

After the third beer, and an hour later, Captain S got up. "I better not have any more. I can see it now. My entire team will be drunk on their ass by dark."

"We need to be going anyway. I have important business to take care of, starting around 1600 hours at the ARVN compound. I don't need to be drunk for this meeting. Besides, everybody knows the Navy can out drink the Army. We don't need to prove it today." Armstrong smiled.

"My ass, Armstrong! But we'll shelve this dispute for another day. What kind of important business is going on, or can't I ask?" Captain S inquired.

"Poker game!" Armstrong replied in a matter-of-fact way. "What else?"

"A poker game! I'm sure the Navy doesn't have anything better to do in a war zone. However, poker is important to some of us." Joe mocked and looking at Scott.

Armstrong asked, "Why don't you come with us to My Tho, all of you? You'll see how it's done."

"I'll go, if he'll let me." Joe looked at Captain S.

"Not without me, you won't. Master Sergeant Scott, those big guns haven't gone off all day, and I haven't seen any air traffic. So, the 9th Division must have shut it down for the holiday. I don't see why Joe and I can't take some time off.

"We may, or may not, be back tonight. If it gets too late, and we can sleep, at the ARVN compound, we'll stay there. We'll let you know." Captain S quickly made a command decision.

Scott asked, "You want to give those two girls a little break and take them to town a little early?"

Captain S shrugged. "We might as well. Tell them to gather up the baby and drag Baby San away from Wheeler. We'll get on the road."

"Cool, man," Butler chimed in.

"Same old crappy story; leave all the work to Banks and me." O'Neil smiled and shook his head.

"You and Banks stay sober. Somebody needs to be able to work, "Captain S told him and stood.

CHAPTER 26

"I'm not putting my money on the table to play poker. Now, change the game to beurre, and I'll gladly put some money down," Joe stated as the poker game began.

"Well, you sit over there with the ladies and watch the men work." Armstrong looked at Joe, trying to shame him.

"I'll do it. I'll sit here with all five of these fine ladies. We'll sit and watch you idiots foolishly lose your money." Joe displayed sarcasm with Armstrong about the money, but not about the ladies.

Lein and Baby San insisted that they come along. With it still more than three hours before dark, they had sufficient time to get themselves safely home. The other young ladies were girlfriends of the men who were playing poker or staffing the bar.

In addition to Summerville, Armstrong, Butler, and three senior NC0s, who living in the billets in which they sat, were playing.

The girls talked and laughed in Vietnamese. They apparently were teasing Baby San. Each had a beer in their hand. Baby San had to be prompted by the others to take her beer. Her facial expressions told Joe she apparently did not like it.

Joe closed his eyes and relaxed. After all, the day had started early for him. When he opened his eyes, he saw Lein feeding the baby with no effort to hide her breast. Butler, no longer at the table, talked with the girls in somewhat fluent Vietnamese.

Joe jumped up and headed to the outhouse. He noticed the sun disappearing below the horizon in the western skies.

Back inside, he pulled Lein and Baby San outside. "We have to go. I'll take you home."

"No, no. We stay here," Lein said.

"No, I'll take you home before curfew." Joe shook his head.

"We stay here." Baby San agreed with Lein.

"No, let me get Captain S." Joe called for Captain S to step outside.

When Captain S joined them, Joe said, "They don't want to go home, yet. And it's too late for us to get back to Dong Tam."

"We're staying here. They have a couple of rooms we can use. Lein, Baby San, we need to get you out of here now, before dark." Captain S looked seriously at both girls.

"No, we stay. It okay" Lein nodded.

"You're sure that it's, okay?" Joe asked.

Lein reaffirmed, "Yes, Chi Bich say, we stay. Okay."

"Chi Bich, is one of the girls inside?" Captain S asked.

"Yes, Chi Bich say, okay. I stay with Hébert. Baby San stays with you." Lein looked at both men quickly.

Captain S and Joe looked at each other, and then at the two girls. Lein held her head up looking back and forth at them. Baby San's eyes were initially looking down, but they finally fixed firmly on Captain S's eyes.

After deep breaths, and noticing the sudden dryness in his mouth, Captain S said, "Tonto, it looks as if the decision has been made."

After a pause, Joe said, "I guess so, boss."

"Call the unit and confirm, we're still at the ARVN compound, and we'll see them tomorrow morning. I'm going back to the poker table. Are you coming in?"

Back inside, Baby San took her original seat and joined the girl's conversation. Lein picked up Sam, and she and one of the girls disappeared out the back door.

Joe sat beside Butler, "I see you speak Vietnamese fairly fluently."

"Yes, a little and a little Spanish.

"This is my second tour, and I've had some formal training. I can get my message over on some things, mostly after it has been repeated several times."

"Are you two staying here tonight?" Joe noticed how Butler's personality had changed.

"No, Joe. We're going over to Colonel Neueng's place. He calls it his hotel, but it's only a two-story villa. The first floor is reserved for ARVN soldiers and the second floor for Americans or other nationalities. It's usually first-come, first-served for the clean beds. Have you met Colonel Neueng, the Commander of all the ARVN MPs here in the delta?"

"Yes, he dropped by the unit one afternoon. He seemed friendly. He brought us a couple dozen crabs and prawns which I cooked. That prawn looks like a long-legged crawfish. We don't have them down on the bayou."

"Yeah, he's friendly like that. He told Lieutenant Armstrong the reason he puts the Americans on the second floor is, if the VC hit the hotel, they'd have to get through the ARVN troops to get to the Americans. Yeah!" Butler did not necessarily sound convincing.

"I guess he doesn't understand what RPG's will do to the second floor of a building."

Butler changed the subject. "So, you were in Lieutenant Armstrong's SEAL class?" This question led to a discussion of SEAL stories which lasted for a couple of hours. From the conversation, Joe quickly learned, Butler faked the dumbness that he tried to project.

"I've had all the poker I can take in one day." Armstrong stood and moved away from the table.

"It's about time, Sir! If we're going to get a bed, we need to move up the street. I don't want to sleep on the hard floor." Butler seemed relieved when Armstrong expressed a readiness to leave.

"This is coming from a guy who never complains about sleeping, ass deep, in mud-holes, no less!" Armstrong looked at Butler.

Captain S asked, "Are you guys going to be safe driving around this time of night?"

"Yeah, it's only about seven blocks. We've done it before. But we need to go. Joe, it's great seeing you and knowing you're doing fine. We never know where we'll be tomorrow, but we'll see you soon."

After they left, Captain S looked at Joe. "Joe, we need to find our rooms. It's been a long time since, 0430 hours this morning."

"I show you." Lein said. She had returned an hour ago, without Sam.

"Good night, gentlemen," Captain S said, turning to the small group still at the poker table.

"The same to you, Sir," a reply came.

"Okay, Lein, show us the way." Captain S motion for her to come. After walking down, a narrow, dark hall, Lein stopped and said to Captain S, "You here." She pointed at a door. "Hébert here." She pointed to the door across the hall.

Captain S opened the door and stepped into the dimly lit room. Baby San came in right behind him and closed the door. Until this moment, he doubted he had the correct understanding of their earlier conversation.

"Baby San, are you sure about this?" He looked down at her.

"Yes, I am sure." She said, and stepped past him and pulled the top sheet, covering the standard issue military, twin-size bed, down. Only a small ceiling bulb provided light. A wall locker, small table, and chair were the only other furnishings.

Captain S placed his gear on the small table and turned to see Baby San had already removed and folded her white blouse. He sat on the edge of the bed to remove his boots.

After removing her black trousers, Baby San folded them and placed them with her blouse on the table next to Captain S's equipment. Wearing only her bra and panties, she crawled between the sheets and lay close to the wall.

Captain S quickly joined her, wearing only his briefs.

Across the hall, the room appearance looked the same as across the hall, but other things were different. When Lein entered the room, she at once removed all her clothes, dropping them on the floor. She then helped Joe in removing his clothes and boots. She gently pushed him on the bed and lay on top of him. Nothing needed to be said by either of them. Joe closed his eyes and fantasized about Ava, as much as he could. He soon learned he had a tiger in bed with him.

Back across the hall, Captain S kissed Baby San on the forehead and pulled her on top of him. He then unsnapped her bra. She removed it and tucked it next to the wall. Captain S kicked the sheets back and removed her panties and his briefs, leaving them at the foot of the bed. Baby San pushed up far enough to see his erection. "Oh, I die!" She said in amazement.

"No, you will not die." He tried to comfort her.

"I die, for sure!" She sounded unsure and scared.

"No. You won't die." He reassured her and tried to spread her legs. "At first, it may hurt a little, but not for long."

"I no can do. I die. You big."

"No, I'm not big. You've never seen a naked man before, have you?"

"No, never see. I cherry girl." Even in the dim light, Captain S could see Baby Son's blaring eyes.

"I know, but you'll be okay. You'll like it." He said and spread her legs far enough to get himself between them, but not into her. He tried several times, but it wouldn't work.

"Oh, I die." She said again.

"No, I will not hurt you. Well, it might hurt a little, since it's your first time." He rolled her off him and got on top of her. "You have to spread your legs, a little." When he got into position between her legs, he moistened himself with saliva and pushed hard for a time. When her nails dug deep and painful into his back, he knew he had broken through and stopped pushing so hard. He began to gently move slowly.

"Are you okay?" He asked while looking at her.

"I okay. I no die." She answered with a deep breath but kept the tight grip on his back.

During the night neither of them got a large amount of excitement out of the experience, nothing but relief and pain. They practiced on her moving a long time.

When morning came, Captain S sat up and crossed his legs. The sheets, with blood everywhere, looked as if they had come from a slaughterhouse. The stinging, in his back and shoulders, told him a great deal of the blood belonged to him.

Baby San sat up and looked down at him. Covering her mouth with one hand, and pointing down at him with the other, she said excitedly, "Oh! I do. I broke? It hurt? I sorry!"

Puzzled at first, he finally realized she had only seen him with an erection. "No. It's okay, it's normal. You didn't hurt me." He grinned and stroked the side of her face.

"It, okay. No broke? For sure?" She paused, looked at him with wide eyes and said softly, "No more boom, boom?"

"No, it's okay. I'm fine." He tried, quite unsuccessfully he thought, to explain the functional operation of a penis.

CHAPTER 27

A few days later, Wheeler called from the office building's door, "Staff Sergeant Hébert, can you come here for a minute?"

"I'll be there shortly." Joe yelled back from under the hood of the two-and-half ton truck which he had been working on all morning, trying to get it started. Frustrated, he slammed the hood down and went inside.

Joe asked, "What's up Phillip?"

"You have mail."

I never get mail. It must be from Pam. He did not think it would take long for her to respond to his letter.

Joe took the letter, but before he could open it, Scott asked, "Did you get it started?"

Joe exhaled loudly. "No. Banks, O'Neil, and I worked on it all morning. They quit about fifteen minutes ago. They're probably over playing with Sam."

"Or maybe playing with the girls." Scott shook his head.

"Master Sergeant, I'm nowhere close to being a mechanic. I sometimes work on my old pickup truck back home. But I can't find anything wrong with that old dog. I guess it's simply worn out." Joe threw his hands up in disgust.

"You're probably right. We've had it in maintenance several times. They get it started and bring it back. The next time we need it, the damn thing won't start. I've put in a request for a new one, but we'll never get it. Vehicles lost due to enemy actions, combat losses, take priority."

"Do you have any ideas, what else I can try to do with it? I'll take any suggestion."

"I don't know. I guess, if you can't do it, you can't do it. Go tell one of those boys next door to come see me." Scott motioned toward the small tent.

Joe found both Banks and O'Neil standing over the table playing with a cooing Sam. "Are you two torturing him?"

"No. We're tickling him. Well, it may be torture to him, but he surely seems to enjoy it," O'Neil said, and he continued his evil deeds.

"Think about it. Other units have dogs, cats, snakes, monkeys, or anything as pets, or mascots. We have Sam." Banks beamed with pride.

"I guess he has replaced Scott's rooster as our mascot. Speaking of Scott, he wants to see one of you." Joe moved his index finger between the two men.

"I'll go," Banks said and left. Joe took his place in the cooing pew, and asked, "Where're the girls?"

"The last time that I saw them: they were cleaning the patio and bar."

"Damn, I almost forgot," Joe mumbled to himself, remembering his letter. He walked out, headed to the seclusion of the large tent. There, he lay down on his bed and ripped open the envelope expecting Pam's blistering response.

He read:

30 Nov 68

Dear Joe,

I was able to get your address this morning. I am sure you know; I am shocked; you are in Vietnam. I hope and pray you are in good health. I have not had a chance to ask about you, as I only returned from home five days ago. I spent three months in Landau.

Joe's heart suddenly skipped a beat. He sat upright, grabbed the envelope, and looked at the return address, which he had ignored before. The rush of blood to his head caused dizziness when, he read, Ava McCoy. His entire body quivered. He returned his attention to the letter.

I spent the three months in Landau recovering from three broken ribs. I am doing fine now, and I am as sassy as ever. I returned to work yesterday.

It was twenty minutes before lunch, when, I noticed a young soldier in the PX wearing an EOD badge. I asked him if he knew you. He said he did. I introduced myself to him, and he said his Commander had something for me.

It was not thirty minutes, before Captain Taylor was standing before me with your address. He assured me; you were physically fine when you left for Vietnam.

As I had found blood on the wall and door, I was pleased to hear of your safety. I will say nothing more about this or anything else for now. I will wait until I hear from you. I must confirm, it is you with whom I am corresponding.

As soon as I hear from you, I will write again. I will stop and get this in the post. To assure you it is Ava, who is writing to you, I will say one thing. As soon as I saw you staring at Cinderella's Arrival, I knew you were a tender, loving, and caring man.

Ava

*****

Anxiety caused Joe's heart to continue its pounding. Tears streamed down his face, and he shook like a leaf on a tree.

Joe mumbled, "Oh, dear, God, thank you. Thank you. She's okay. Three broken ribs. That SOB. I'm sure he did it."

Something is wrong. What is she not saying, and why is she not telling me if there is a problem to worry about?

Joe remained lying and read the letter three times. He smelled it for any faint hint of aroma, and tried to get his emotions under control, which took a while. Afterwards, he reached for pen and paper.

6 Dec 68

My Dearest Ava,

What a joyous feeling is racing over me right now. After reading your letter, I am not sure that I can write a cognitive sentence, but I'll try. Your letter has brought tears to my eyes, and there is no way I can express the feelings which it has stirred in me. I'll simply try to give you a short update and get this off to you today.

First, I am physically, perfectly fit. I hope you will understand; mentally and emotionally, I am a wreck right now. After I have time to get over the pleasant shock of your letter, it will certainly correct itself.

As for the blood on your wall, it was caused by splintering off the door facing. I had a couple of scratches on the cheek and neck, but nothing serious.

After being shot at, I thought it best to get out of town, as far, and as fast as I possibly could.

By getting back into EOD, the Army was duty-bound to help. They needed every warm bodied EOD qualified person they could find over here. We stay busy seven days a week.

What is surprising, it's not extremely bad here. Most people hate it, as I'm sure, I would if I were walking in their boots. However, I find it challenging. Maybe it's because of the hardships I experienced as a child. Part of the people around me have had it too soft for their entire life. Well, enough of that.

Ava, I don't know what I can tell you, but be assured, I love you more than anything on earth. Every night, since I last saw you, I have asked God to bless you and keep you safe. After three months, I was about to give up on even hearing from you. My only lifeline to you was the knowledge that the PX still considered you as an employee. Because of this, I knew, eventually you would be back.

I will not rotate back to CONUS, the States, until August, not for almost nine months. It's a long time to be away from you. However, if you love me, as I love you, we will get through this. We did it before. We can do it again. I'll stop for now and get this in the mail where you can receive it one day earlier.

I want you to remember, as we were passing through the five-thousand-foot level, I knew if you died, because I threw you out of a helicopter, so would I die that day. I also knew, if we lived, someday, we would have the opportunity to be together as one, for years, hopefully eternity.

My rejuvenated heart is pounding, caused by anticipation and possibilities of a lifetime with you at my side.

As you know, I love you.

Joe

*****

While still wondering what bothered her, he sealed the envelope. He could not figure it out. As he headed to the office, he found solace in knowing that Ava always stayed secretive about everything. She absorbs information, from and about others, like a vacuum sucking up dust.

However, she is still noticeably silent when it comes to her affairs.

Back in the office, Joe handed the letter to Wheeler and asked, "Can you get the letter out this afternoon?"

"Sure, Joe, no problem."

Over his shoulder, Joe heard Banks ask, "Master Sergeant Scott, is this what you need? It's a pristine Chinese made 82mm mortar, with fuze."

"Yeah, I'll take it." Scott nodded and reached for the mortar round.

Banks asked, "Is there anything you would like to share?"

"No. Nothing to bother you." Scott at once put the mortar round in one of his desk drawers.

"Haven't you learned yet? He doesn't dish out anything to anyone," Wheeler chimed.

"Sometimes we all have to learn things over and over. I'll go back to my babysitting job; thank you," Banks replied, while feeling petulantly.

Scott stopped Banks. "No, you and Hébert can clean the Jeeps. I think I saw grass growing in them."

"They're slightly dirty, but not very dirty." Joe complained.

Scott snapped, "Are you telling me, I don't know grass when I see it?"

"No, Master Sergeant. I think I'll shut my mouth and go wash and clean the transparent grass out of the Jeeps." Joe laughed.

"When you two boys finish with the Jeeps, you can take the girls home and bring back some ice. Of course, you'll have to wait until Wheeler is through panting over, I mean, helping Baby San, with her English lesson.

"I think we're going to have a good crowd tonight. We're supposed to have some new blood for the poker game. Now, get out of here and pretend you're doing something productive! Captain S will be back from the O-club any minute now. He needs to find you doing something, other than scratching your ass." Scott pointed to the door.

When the sun faded away and the crowd gathering, two tables of five poker players had been dealing for at least thirty minutes. Scott and O'Neil were in hog heaven with their money pile growing. Wheeler, as usual, maned the bar. Banks warmed up his amp and electric guitar.

"I understand you got some mail today," Captain S leaned over and bumped Joe as they sat at the bar enjoying a cool one.

"Yeah, thank God," Joe showed visible relief.

"So, it was from her, the Lieutenant Colonel's wife?"

"Yes, Sir. I was about to give up on her. She went back to Germany for three months. That's why I haven't heard from her."

"Well, I'm glad you finally received some news. But are you going to be, OK? You were uncommonly quiet this afternoon." Captain S kept his voice as low as possible so others could not hear their conversation.

"I'll be fine, Sir. I was a little shaken by her letter. She's hiding something. Then, I had to take Lein and Baby San to town. I think I felt like a philandering husband in Lien's presence. In a way I wish that had never happened." Joe looked guilt ridden.

"Don't let it bother you. Lein is a strong, quality person, and she needs you."

"Yeah, I know, and nine months, before seeing Ava, is a long time."

"You can do the time standing on your head. The past three and a half months haven't been bad, have they?"

Joe rubbed his hand over his head and answered. "No. It flew by quickly. Staying busy is the key. Sitting around here, the last few days with nothing exciting to do, gets old in a hurry."

"Don't worry about it. The Old Reliable, the 9tn Division, will gear it up soon, and we'll be going steady afterwards.

"Oh, did you think about R&R? You'll be eligible for a week of R&R after three more months. You could meet her somewhere. Did you say her name was Ava? You could meet Ava in Hawaii. Most married men meet their wives there. Single men usually go to Bangkok or Sydney. You need to--

Joe interrupted Captain S. "Are you saying, I could go to Hawaii in three months?"

"I'm saying there's a possibility. The earlier you get your request in, the earlier you'll get orders."

"Damn, you mean I could see her as early as late February." Joe thought positively.

"Joe, before you request orders for Hawaii, you need to make sure she can, and will, meet you. If she can't meet you in Hawaii, I think you'd rather be in Bangkok or Sydney's. In Bangkok, you can have your choice of a couple thousand women, two or three at a time, if you would like. In Hawaii, you may not even get laid."

"If she can, I think she'll be there. I'll find out and let you know."

"Good. Wow, look over there! Two Round Eyes!" Captain S nodded toward two nurses, dressed in light-blue scrubs, who were standing by the poker table.

"I haven't seen a white woman since I got here." Joe admired the nurses.

"Don't get your hopes up. Two doctors are probably escorting them."

"No, they won't be interested in a lowly Staff Sergeant like me. Now, a good-looking EOD Captain may be a different matter." Joe patted Captain S on the back.

"Oh, I like the way you think, Tonto. I have 0 percent chances sitting here and 1 percent over there. I'll give it a chance. I remember a hog with only a 2 percent chance. He beat the odds. Meeting them in this environment will be nice. I hope we never meet them in a professional manner. I hear they, the nurses over here, do an outstanding job. But I don't want them working on me." Captain S grinned and headed toward the nurses to introduce himself.

With Banks singing his version of Johnny Cash's, "Ring of Fire," and Captain S trying to make time with the two Round Eyes, Joe sat at the bar by himself. A young, filthy, Navy Petty Officer eventually joined him. He got Joe's attention by correctly saying, "Hello Staff Sergeant Hébert."

Joe looked at his name tag which read LeBeau.

"Hello, back to you LeBeau! What part of the Bayou are you from?" Joe showed great interest and thought, he finally met someone with a common background whom he I could talk with.

"Actually, I'm from Natchez, Mississippi. I'm redneck, not coonass."

"Nobody's perfect! LeBeau sure sounds like a Coonass to me. Maybe you're a half-breed? Half coonass, half redneck?" Joe picked at LeBeau.

LeBeau smiled at Joe. "Nope! I'm 100 percent redneck, and proud of it!"

"Good for you," Joe returned a big smile. "Master Sergeant Scott is from the Greenville area of Mississippi. It shouldn't be far from Natchez."

"Greenville is up in the Delta part of Mississippi, across the river from the southeast part of Arkansas. I don't know exactly how far it is."

"Well, you live north of I-10 and have a Mississippi draw, so you must be a redneck. I've seen you around. What do you do?"

"I'm a diesel mechanic. I keep those boats, over there, running." LeBeau nodded toward the Navy Basin.

"I should have guessed." Joe looked LeBeau up and down in a perfunctory assessing manner, noticing the grit under LeBeau's nails and on his clothes. He stood a little less than six feet and weighed about one-eighty. It was hard to tell if his hair was dark or simply dirty.

"Yeah, I should apologize, but I can't keep clean," LeBeau defended himself.

Wheeler moved from the other end of the bar and placed a beer in front of Joe. "Will you take this over to Master Sergeant Scott?"

"Yeah, give me one for the captain. I'll take him one too." Joe took the beer and excused himself.

He delivered the drinks hoping for an introduction to the nurses, but none came. He went to the other table and asked O'Neil if he would like a beer. "No, after this hand, I'll be joining you at the bar. 1 have enough of these gentlemen's money." He smiled like a cat who had swallowed a canary.

"You're going to take our money and run?" Mr. Crawford, the ASP commander, complained.

"You're right, Sir." I like taking Officers and Senior NCOs' money." O'Neil continued his grinning.

"Well, get up and go. Let someone else sit down. Someone who's not so damn lucky." Master Sergeant White dismissed him.

After three hours of drinking, the crowd had shrunk considerably. The doctors and nurses were gone. Those still present slurred their words. Five resolute poker players were still hard at work. LeBeau, still held down the bar as one of the last stragglers.

"I've never figured out exactly what you do, except for partying," LeBeau looked at Joe, who had returned to the bar earlier.

"Partying is our main job. We like to train regularly. We're dedicated." Joe did not crack a smile.

Captain S and the other EOD guys had joined them. He patted his left breast pocket. "LeBeau, you see this badge on my chest? It's an EOD badge. You know what EOD is? I'll give you a hint. It's not a rocket pilot's badge like some people think."

"I know what Navy EOD is." LeBeau looked at all of them.

"Are you sure you're not from the Bayou?" Joe asked, in a manner which suggested, like the others, he had too much to drink.

"Army EOD does the same thing as Navy EOD. We're simply better! We know how to disarm any munition in the world, from small arms rounds to the largest nuclear weapons. Some say we're experts at doing the most dangerous job in the military." Oneil proclaimed proudly.

LeBeau said, "I thought so. Tell me, what is a flechette?"

Captain S asked, "Is this a quiz? If so, I need another beer! A flechette is a small metal dart, used for anti-personnel purposes. Think of it as a modern day, old-time shrapnel round."

"How do you know about flechettes? Where did you hear about them?" Joe asked LeBeau.

"I have an 81-mm mortar flechette round. and I wanted to know what it is."

"There's no such thing as a flechette mortar." Banks shook his head.

Captain S turned and squarely faced LeBeau. "Let me manage this situation. LeBeau, besides being dingy and dirty, you don't know what the hell you're talking about. There is no such thing as a flechette mortar. The principal will not work. You drop a mortar round down a tube. The round going up and explodes when it hits the ground.

"If you fire a mortar, an indirect round, up and eject low velocity flechettes, it would be like raining toothpicks or small nails. It would do little harm other than scratches. They must be fired directly at its target like a big shotgun. When you eject flechettes the correct way, you have thousands of small nails flying at high velocity. My man, the flechettes will nail your ass to a tree, and excuse me for slurring my words."

"I don't know anything about all of that, but I do know, I have an 81-mm mortar flechette, Sir!" LeBeau emphatically and emphasized the Sir.

"No, you don't!" Captain S shouted.

"Would you like to bet, Sir?" LeBeau quickly replied and raised his nose.

"I want to get in on the bet." O'Neil perked up.

"I don't have any money to bet, but I'll bet you a favor." LeBeau showed his confident.

"A favor. What kind a favor?" Captain S seemed surprised by LeBeau's comment.

"I'll do anything around here you want me to do, wash your jeeps, pick up trash, or get--"

"Jump on this Captain!" O'Neil chimed in before LeBeau could finish his sentence.

"And what do you want from me?" Captain S cocked his head.

"Sir, I want to sleep in your bunker. I don't mean to move in and all that. I mean a bed-role and pillow."

"Well, I could offer you the bunker, but there's no such thing as an 81-mm mortar flechette round."

"So, if it's a bet for a favor, I'll go get it," LeBeau got up to leave.

"Go!" Captain S motioned him toward the Navy Basin.

Banks huffed, "I wish we could have had this bet yesterday. We would not have had help to wash the invisible grass out of the Jeeps this afternoon."

"Yeah, what a dumb prick." O'Neil laughed.

Joe said, "Let's have one more and call it a night. He won't be back,"

Banks grabbed his guitar and shouted, "One more song, and we're out of here. Banks started singing their favorite song, "Detroit City."

It took LeBeau about five minutes to return. As he walked toward them, they all could see the mortar round in his hand. O'Neil asked, "What you got there, LeBeau?"

LeBeau placed the mortar round on the bar in front of Captain S and said, "What is this, Sir?"

"Uh-oh!" O'Neil grunted.

"I might not be as smart as you EOD types, but I can read, some. It says right there, 81-MM, mortar flechette, test round. LeBeau pointed to each letter painted on the gray mortar round.

Shocked, Captain S picked it up, passed it around, and said, "It looks as if we've been had. Although, I don't understand."

"Yeah Captain, you surely have." O'Neil chuckled while emphasizing the word, you.

"I understand," Joe said, while lifting his head as to show knowledge.

Captain nodded and said, "LeBeau, you can sleep in the bunker. I apologize for my derogative comments directed toward you. Wheeler, give this man a beer on me.

"Now, O'Neil, what do you mean by 'you surely have'?" Captain S looked at him.

"I think I see egg on everybody's face." Banks looked around while replying for O'Neil.

"Joe, what do you mean by you 'understand this'?" Captain S looked harshly at Joe.

"It's a Navy thing, Sir. If you remember, I used to be in the Navy. If you recollect, they fired the cannons on old ships with lanyards. Our river boats have mortars. They drop a round down one of their tubes, nothing happens until someone pulls the lanyard. This gives them the opportunity to lay the mortar to a horizontal position before firing, like a big shotgun."

Captain S frowned and narrowed his eyes at Joe. "If you're so damn smart, why did you let me make an ass of myself? A great partner you are!"

"Some partner I am! Hell, you wouldn't even introduce me to the Round Eyes tonight. You want to explain that?" Joe quipped right back, in a respectful manner, of course.

"After your news today, I didn't think you would be interested."

Joe quickly changed the direction of the subject by saying. "To be honest with you, Sir, I didn't understand about the mortar either. Not until I saw the round. Anyway, we all should know not to bet with a guy from Mississippi named LeBeau. You can't trust a Cajun who claims he's a redneck!"

After everyone congratulated LeBeau, they went to their respective quarters.

*****

When Captain S reached his Batchelor Officer Quarters, BOQ, red flares started popping overhead. "Charlie Pad is getting mortared again. No need to worry, I know LeBeau is neatly tucked away in the bunker. But he should go back to the unit," Captain S mumbled to himself. *I better go back to the unit and make sure everything is OK.*

When he arrived back at the unit, the shelling had stopped. "Banks and O'Neil are out doing frag analysis and we took a hit, Sir," Scott reported to Captain S.

"What do you mean by, we took a hit?" Captain S pondered Scott's statement.

"Yes, Sir. The old two-and-a-half-ton truck took a Chinese made mortar right on top of the hood. It looks like a combat loss to me. Now we can get a new one." Scott grinned ear to ear.

CHAPTER 28

14 Dec 68

Dear Joe,

It was a relief to hear from you so quickly, two letters in one day. I notice you wrote them on different days.

I am sure you are concerned. I did not tell you anything in my first letter.

I have filed for a divorce, and my lawyer told me not to talk to anyone about anything concerning my marriage. You are certainly not simply anyone, but I must know with whom I am corresponding. You cannot imagine what my soon-to-be ex-husband can do. Writing fake letters is nothing.

I am certainly not innocent in the eyes of the law, or in the eyes of God. However, his actions have caused him major problems. I mentioned my three broke ribs but did not mention my three days in the hospital. In case you are wondering, I did get a couple of good licks in. His shot at you probably saved my life; because within two minutes after he fired it, two MPs were standing in my bedroom. Due to his rage, they carried him away in handcuffs. I was able to walk, only with help from the MPs. They helped me down the stairs. There, I saw your blood on the wall. They called an ambulance to take me to the hospital.

The first thing I did, was to contact a lawyer to get a restraining order against him. It was done while still in the hospital. I was surprised at how easily it was conducted. When I returned to my house, I found it had been destroyed. He had taken his personal possessions and trashed everything else. Of course, I reported the condition to the MP's and my lawyer.

The bottom line is, even after my culpability, I am viewed by the court as the innocent and defamed party. In other words, I have him by his balls! About his balls, did I mention, I managed a couple of good licks?

As for Lieutenant Colonel McCoy, I have not seen or heard from him since then.

When I returned from Landau, my lawyer informed me; McCoy was requested to resign his commission. He is now considered retired. I have no idea as to his whereabouts. He probably returned to his home state, West Virginia. What I do know is, he will never forgive me, nor will he give up the fight. He will use every underhanded trick to get any advantage and revenge on me.

As for me, I am fully recovered and getting plenty of daily exercise. I am currently still in my military quarters, but I will have to give them up by the first of January. So, you know what, I will be doing over the holidays. I have found a small apartment a short distance off post. I will keep my job at the Exchange and keep my PO box. If you want to, you can write to me every day.

In one of your letters, you said, you could possibly get a week off and go to Hawaii at the end of February. You wanted to know if I would be interested in joining you there. The simple answer is yes. Hell yes! Wow! Hawaii would be wonderful! I have one concern. It is for your health. My concern is not about you live through the war for the next three months, or so. It is your health once you reach Hawaii that I am worried about. Remember, I said, I have been and will continue to work out daily. You had better be in shape, or when I am through with you, you may not make it back to Vietnam. I think you can imagine what I'm thinking about, without my elaboration.

Joe, I am so thrilled and thankful that you are well and happy with your job. Please, rest assured; I will be counting the days until we are together again. Hopefully, it will be no more than three months, but if it is nine, I will be waiting for you. One more thing, at five thousand feet, I was confused. I was thinking, if he loves me like he said, then why did he throw me out of the helicopter? Thank you for answering the question for me.

I think the phrase in Vietnam is, keep your head down. Joe, keep your ass down.

Merry Christmas to you. I love you,

Ava

*****

16 Dec 68

Dear Joe,

It was wonderful hearing from you. I was surprised to learn that you are in Vietnam. However, I was not surprised with the humorous events leading to your unexpected departure from Fort Ben.

I must admit; I have not laughed so hard in years. I cannot stop chuckling when visualizing your butt naked escape.

On a more serious note, I hope you and Ava can work it out. I knew the instant that I saw you look at her, you two are made for each other.

I also enjoyed your war stories. Please write and tell me more. We get a heavy dose of the big picture over there, but your personal and unique daily experience is more interesting and informative. You asked about my man. He is the big news from me. My fiancé and I will be married on 26 December.

We are going to Cancun, Mexico for our honeymoon, to celebrate New Years. Can you imagine it? If I did not tell you before, his name is Stephen Rivers. I will be Mrs. Rivers! It sounds like Mississippi River. Doesn't it? Anyway, he has one more semester in law school. And then, he will take the bar exam. He is already looking for a job here in D.C. Despite being a lawyer, he is nice.

As far as my studies in international affairs, I am progressing well but still have a year to go before finishing. I am not sure, if I told you, but my area of emphasis is Central and South America.

I am so glad that I collected a lot of those basic courses while in the Army. My biggest task is learning fluent Spanish and the history and culture of all those countries down there.

Now, about the local feelings about the war, there is absolutely no support for it from anyone that I know. People do not, and do not want to understand why we are in Vietnam. You know where I am on the subject. I believe in the Domino Theory, and we must try to stop the spread of communism anywhere and every way we can. If we do not, they will govern all of us. However, this war is tearing the country apart and costing us dearly in terms of money and casualties. What makes it bad, I believe, if the damn politicians would turn it over to our military, the war would be over in two months. I could ride this horse all day, but you know what I would say.

Of course, Nixon has a plan to get us out of the war, but he will not tell us what the plan is. Maybe we will learn about it sooner or later. Damn politicians! They are all the same.

I am sorry about the delay in writing back to you. Things have been rather hectic for me, preparing for the wedding, and taking tests before the Christmas holidays.

Joe, thank you for your kind words about me and our relationship. I, too, continue to have warm feelings about you. Our past is over, but it will forever be a part of my soul. I would not change a bit of our relationship. Our future, as you said, will be a lasting friendship for both of us. So, let me hear from you. Stay safe, and Merry Christmas. With love,

Pam

16 Jan 69

Dear Pam,

The news of your marriage is a welcomed surprise. I never suspected you would settle for one man, when you could have all the men in the world you wanted. I sincerely wish you the best for today and tomorrow. Stephen must be a fantastic catch, or he and his family are filthy rich! You know I'm kidding. One way or the other, he is a lucky man to have you as a lifelong partner.

My news is also good. I finally heard from Ava! She went back to Germany for a while. She is now doing well. Someday, I will tell you the rest of the story. I hope to see her in Hawaii in February.

I will be due R&R then. I have already requested orders. Here's hoping they come through, ASAP.

Both Ava and I now write nearly every day. But I never tell her about anything going on over here. I don't want to worry her. I know you can take it. This makes my letters to her pretty short.

After the Thanksgiving holidays, things here relatively slowed down, nothing more than booby-traps, and small stuff to take care of. Charlie has been laying low and has a challenging time concentrating his forces. Every time he gathers into a force large enough to fight, the 9th Division takes them down. They are not like the Germans and Japanese during World War II. The VC only fights when they want to. There is talk about Charlie and him organizing and getting himself supplied for another run this coming Tet.

Even though he got his ass badly kicked last year, the propaganda in the good old US press unfortunately told a different story. It was reported like Rushen propaganda. Unfortunately for us, perception is paramount on the streets. Reality counts for little.

Captain S was emotionally down for a couple of days. He lost a good friend New Year's Eve night. It was a Captain whom he knew in EOD school. He was shot in the back by one of his own men.

No one thinks it was anything other than an accident. However, there has been more than enough fragging incidents over here where young troops take out their Officers. I'm sure you know what it means.

What's the general opinion with the college groups about Nixon's chances of doing something significant over here?

Let me give you a war story. A couple of days ago, we got a call to respond to a downed F-105, Wild Weasel.

They reported the pilot screwed up and put it in the ground, and I mean in the ground. When the Captain and I arrived at the site, we found a black and burned-out area which would expect. Wreckage was laying around a big hole. We could see the pilot still in his Martin-Baker seat, five feet down. Someone had brains enough to know there were ejection rockets attached to the seats. Not knowing their condition, they called us.

If you don't know, there are a lot of aluminum and magnesium, and fuel in an airplane. Heat and magnesium produce more heat, at high tempter. So, the two men, albeit dead, looked in decently good physical shape for being baked in their seats. Regardless of what a Mortician will tell you, freshly burnt human flesh is the worst odor in the world! The stench seems to influence every cell in the body. Anyway, we decided the propellants in the rocket motors presented no hazard, and the locking device had held the seats in place. We called for a helicopter to lift the wreckage holding the pilots' dead bodies, and what was left of the seats out of the hole. Things went well until the pilot's head, still wearing his helmet, fell off his shoulders and rolled between my feet. I could see his eyes looking at me. The combination of this, and the stench was overwhelming. And yes, Dear One, I lost my cookies! I know it wasn't manly. It took me two days to get the stench out of my nose.

I know many people think human burned flesh don't stink. It may not be true once it's cool but not for fresh, sizzling flesh.

Oh, did I say one war story? Let's try another little lighter one. It's the dry season here, although we have an occasional shower. The rice fields are mostly brown and dry except for ditches.

Captain S and I were out giving booby-trap safety classes to infantry types. At an intersection, we had to stop for a convoy to pass by. On the side of the road were three young boys, probably eleven years old. They were fishing. They were using bamboo poles, more than twenty feet long, and line the same length as the poll. Over here it's common to see boys fishing in ditches around rice patties, but this rice patty was dry! The boys simply cast their lines out into the dry rice field and gently pulled the line in through the stubble.

Captain S verbalized our thoughts. He said, 'We are over here risking our lives for people who are so dumb they fish in dry rice patties!' We laughed as the convoy passed. Then, we became worried. The boy's fishing expedition may, in fact, be a distraction for an ambush. Well, the question was answered quickly. Get ready for this. One of the little twerps caught a fish. I swear; he caught a fish out of a dry rice patty! When we got back to the unit and told the story to our clerk, Specialist Wheeler, he informed us that the boys had caught a walking catfish. Look it up! Can you believe there is such a thing as a walking catfish? Those critters are not found down on the Bayou.

Enough for today. By the time you get this, you will be accustomed to married life. Again, good luck and God bless you and yours.

Laisse les bons temp rouler.

Vacationing in Vietnam, Over Here, not Canada

Joe

PS: I just realize, I'm writing to a married woman. I certainly don't want to cause any problems.

CHAPTER 29

"Hébert, get your gear, we have to go," Captain S popped his head into the small tent, where Joe sat on the couch, holding Sam. Lein sat with them, while taking a break from her work.

"Coming, Sir," Joe replied, and placed Sam in his new crib which the unit had built for him. Sam, close to six months old, moves around and pulls up. Therefore, Sam had needed a larger crib.

"Bye, Joe. Come back safe." Lein reached for his hand.

"I will." Joe replied with a gentle squeeze and then headed for the office.

Captain S informed Joe, "We have a bomb not far from Ben Tre. It's reported only as a big bomb. Because of enemy fire in the area, the American people who reported the bomb from second-hand information. They didn't get close enough to identify it. They have a platoon sized unit waiting to escort us into the area. It sounds as if this could be fun. They're holding a helicopter for us at Charlie Pad."

"Captain, the area down there is rough. So be careful," Scott seriously vocalized.

"Don't worry. We'll have some of the finest in the Riverine Force for protection." Captain S waived his hand and walked to the Jeep with Joe on his heels.

The helicopter headed southeast, crossing the northern branches of the Mekong River. Rice patties, endless canals, natural waterways, and jungles were all to be seen on the horizon. They were looking at Ken Hoa Provence, an area which Vietnamese legend referred to as the Head of the Dragon.

When the Mekong River flowed out of the highlands of Columbia into the eastern part of the Vietnam Delta, it split into three major branches, which resembles the head of a dragon. Over thousands of years the river changes its course, due to the flatness of the low-lying terrain.

The legend of the Dragon states, 'He who controls the mouth of the dragon, controls the Delta'.

The French had occupied the area during the middle of the nineteenth century and helped its economic development. However, World War II brought the Japanese, who killed the large landowners and destroyed the economy. The Japanese were thrown out by the Viet Minh, who proved the foundation for the Viet Cong, (VC).

The enormous number of natural waterways and human-caused canals made it easy for the Viet Cong to transport people and supplies. The banks and dryer land had dense undergrowth, which made hiding people and material easy. The area, home for more than three hundred small hamlets, consisted of thatch houses with dirt floors, and no plumbing or electricity. The unsophisticated people made this region a prime recruiting ground for the VC.

Captain S and Joe knew the environment they were flying into, right into the Mouth of the Dragon. When the helicopter descended toward what they thought would be their destination, they noted a half-dozen 105mm howitzers and mortars sitting in landing crafts, Mike Eight boats, in the river. The howitzers were also on platforms, sitting in rice fields. They could easily tell; a couple of the howitzers were firing.

When they landed in the rather dry rice patty, less than fifty yards from the Song Ham Luong River, the Mouth of the Dragon. They were met by First Lieutenant Gates, who escorted them away from the helicopter. He, like everybody, carried weapons and was dressed in jungle fatigues, steal pots, and flack vests. After the introductions, Gates briefed them on the tactical situation. "We must consider the entire area hostile. My platoon is part of Bravo Company, whose mission is to seek and destroy VC in this area along the river." Gates held a map in his hand. "We have been informed by the locals. They found a large bomb right here." Gates said. He pointed at a spot on the map. "We are here. This morning, one of my squads was trying to recon the area, but they had to withdraw because of hostile fire. Artillery has pounded the area well. We now have the entire platoon together, with Tiger Scouts. We are ready to move forward as soon as you're ready to go."

"Lieutenant, we're ready now. But it's just less than three kilometers in a straight line, half of which is wooded jungle. Are we going to be able to get there and back before dark?"

"Sir, without any trouble, we can make it easily. If you're thinking of your ride out of here, and I don't blame you if you are. We can get them to pick you up almost anywhere."

"Okay, fine. You read my mind." Captain S felt better, but thought the Lieutenant looked years younger than he and Joe. He realized a year over here should be counted as a dog year, seven years.

"Then, Sir, with your permission, we'll begin moving," Gates started folding the map.

"You don't need my permission. I may outrank you, but this is your platoon. We're the boss. We're no more than a piece of equipment which you're responsible for. Now, when it comes to explosive devices, Staff Sergeant Hébert or I will be the boss."

"Roger!" Gates nodded, turned, and yelled, "Move it out Sergeant First Class Luckey!"

They headed east, down-river in a single file, led by two Tiger Scouts, Vietnamese soldiers dressed in idiosyncratic striped uniforms. Captain S and Staff Sergeant Hébert knew the Tiger Scouts were good. The scouts had an outstanding reputation among US troops as someone who knew the area and were loyal and trustworthy. Captain S did a quick count of twenty-nine American soldiers.

Gates looked at Captain S and Staff Sergeant Hébert. "I'm going with the first squad. You can join me or step in line anywhere you wish. I'm sure you know that Charlie likes to shoot at the radio telephone operator (RTO) and the people around him. They know he's obviously with the commander." Gates smiled as he talked.

"Well then, we'll stay back a few yards." Captain S thought, this is one of the easiest decisions I've made sense being in Vietnam.

They had walked well less than a quarter of a mile when they left the rice patty and entered the undergrowth. Even though they were using a well-traveled trail, visibility remained no more than thirty feet forward and ten feet to each side. It did not take too many wide leafed vegetation to totally obscure one's vision. Word quickly passed from the front to the back to watch for booby-traps. The Tiger Scouts had recommended they not go down this trail, but the lieutenant decided to use it. Otherwise, they would have to move north and go a couple of miles further.

Captain S and Joe found themselves whispering to each other, while listening and reacting to every sound and movement from the right or left. Their eyes constantly searched the ground before they placed a foot down.

The noise from an explosion, and the subsequent screams of pain, caused an immediate reaction from everyone. They drop to the ground in a prone position. Captain S and Joe looked at each other. Joe whispered, "Booby-trap!"

Captain S nodded and said, "We better check it out, there may be others." They moved forward as quickly as possible, hunched over, until they reached the area where the detonation occurred.

Gates and his RTO were kneeling beside a soldier laying on the ground, obviously in pain. Another man was examining hos blood spotted trousers. The RIO was requesting a Dust Off. They responded back, "Twenty minutes out."

Captain S asked, "Is there anything we can do?"

Gates shook his head. "No. We have one with multiple frag and one with minor frag wounds. I need to go back up front to the head of the column."

"Minors frag wounds! What an oxymoron?" Joe whispered and moved closer to the soldier laying on the ground, with a dozen small drops of blood on his arms and legs. His shirt and flack-vest had been open, allowing his chest and abdomen to be checked. Joe could see no blood there but did notice a couple drops on the top of his shoulder and neck.

The least severely wounded man said, "I only have three stinging spots on my right leg, and one on my arm. There is, basically, little bleeding."

Joe turned to Captain S, "M-25 grenade."

Joe knelt beside the man lying on the ground and said, "It looks as if we have a few minutes to wait. Why don't you rest your head on me?"

"Dat be good," the man said.

Joe sat down beside him, with his back propped on a large banana tree. "This may hurt a little, but I think you'll be a little more comfortable afterwards." Joe pulled the man's head and shoulders across his lap. "How are you," Joe looked closely at the man's face for the first time?

"Dat be fine, Sergeant. Dat's bedder." The man's voice seemed more at ease.

Joe suddenly realized he had seen this black face before and pulled his shirt to read the name tag. "Brown. Brown, I met you before."

"You has?" The soldier squirmed, trying to see Joe's face.

"Yes, at jump school. I was there on your last jump, and helped you collect your parachute, after your malfunction."

"It wus you? I's be God damn. How you remember me?"

"I could never forget your face. You are one Black dude."

"I's sho is." Brown tried to nod and chuckle.

"How's your pain? You seem to be getting better."

"It huts some, but I's feeling bedder."

"It looks like a grenade got you. You're leaking from several small holes, but you don't appear to have any big holes, and none in vital areas unless they got you in your pecker." Joe tried to add levity to make Brown forget about his pain.

"Dat's good. I guess, my pecker is okay." Brown managed a smile.

"It looks like the Good Lord is still taking care of you." Joe remembered Brown's comments on the landing zone.

"No, Sergeant, only luck. Tere ain't no Loud. If dere wus, dere won't be no Vietnam. No Good Loud would let dis God damn place be."

"I thought you never cursed and went to church every Sunday."

I's did, but no mo. I's don't believe in Him no mo." Brown tried to shake his head.

"Well, I do, and I'll say a prayer for you."

"Won't do no good." Brown continued to shake his head.

"Don't move. At least you have your ticket out of here. The doctors will patch you up, and you'll be fine. You'll be back in the States in a couple of days."

"I's don't wanna go home, yet."

"I thought you would want out of this hell hole." Joe seemed confused about Brown.

"I's does but not rat now." Brown slightly shook his head.

"Why not?" Joe looked puzzled.

"I's wanna see dat God damn Lieutenant dead before I's leaves here." Brown sounded serious.

For the first time, Joe looked up and caught Captain S's eyes. He had been listening to the entire conversation. Both now looked as if they had been hit with a baseball bat.

"Why do you want him dead?" Joe looked back at Brown.

Brown snapped, "Dat SOB dun got too many good men hut and dead!"

"That is war. People get hurt and killed in war. Charlie, out there, is pretty damn good at killing people." Joe tried to ease Brown's temperament.

"Tis not dat. It wus him. VC put up a dat sign. It says, do not use da trails. Dat Lieutenant, what he do? He says we go down dat trail. Tis like dat erery day. He nere lessens to nobody." Brown's face showed a disdainful expression.

"Don't work yourself up. You do not need to get your heart rate and blood pressure up. The Dust Off will arrive within fifteen minutes. It won't be long before you'll be pampered by a good-looking nurse and an ugly doctor. We probably need to get you back to the rice patty where the helicopter can land. Do you think you can manage it?" Joe tried to paint a more positive picture for Brown.

"I'll check and see what's going on," Captain S said, and steadily moved forward until he met Lieutenant Gates. He and the RTO were working their way back to the wounded men.

"Before you ask, they're inbound, be here in ten minutes. We need to get in the open and be ready to pop smoke." The Lieutenant told Captain S.

"Lieutenant, we'll help move Brown. The other guy can make it on his own."

Joe and Brown were still talking when Captain S got back to them. Captain S interrupted. "Tonto, you and I will help Brown back to the clearing. The chopper will be here shortly. Let's get him moving."

With Joe under Brown's left arm and Captain S under his right arm, they were able to get Brown back down the trail to the accessible area, the same time as a purple smoke grenade popped. The Dust Off came straight in from over the river. Joe and Captain S laid Brown on a stretcher provided by the medics. Captain S returned to the edge of the jungle, where Lieutenant Gates stood, talking on the radio. Joe stayed with Brown as the medics began working on him. He held Brown's hand while the medics administered the IV. "You take care of yourself and get back in church. One of these days, I'll come visit you in Lake Village. I remember. You're from there. I expect to find you in church." Joe admonished Brown. Within seconds the chopper lifted off, heading north.

When Joe joined them, Gates told Captain S, "We're pushing on. The Tigers have worked their way a couple hundred yards further up the trail with no trouble. The other two platoons in the area have met no trouble. My Company Commander told me to keep moving."

Captain S said, "Let's go. We're still with you."

Gates returned to near the front of the line. For the next hour, the pace slowed, due primarily to the fact, somehow two Tiger Scouts and eight soldiers, to include the platoon leader, had somehow missed the trip line which Brown managed to find. Captain S suspected something when, he saw Gates standing by the trail. He asked Gates, "Are you waiting on us?"

"Yes, Sir. I want to let you know. We have covered a little over a kilometer." Pointing at a map Gates said, "We're here at this natural waterway. The Tiger Scouts tell me, the water is not deep, but we'll need a short break on the other side, once we get everybody over. As you can see, we have almost three quarters of a kilometer before we reach the next clearing. It's another rice field.

"Once, we cross the field, we'll have a little under a kilometer to our objective. We can make it with some time left for you to do your work."

"Is there any reason for a break? We're already moving rather slowly, and we're not halfway there, yet." Captain S asked the Lieutenant.

"You don't know? You've never crossed this type of water, have you?"

"I've waded through several low areas and ditches up to my ass, most of the time with dust blowing in my eyes," Captain S seemed defensive.

"Then you should know. But if not, you'll find out. If neither of you two smokes, you may want to follow close behind the RTO. I'll go first." Gates smiled.

Captain S looked at Joe in a questioning manner.

"I don't know, Sir." Joe looked to be as confused as Captain S.

The warm water, with a soft bottom, quickly became shoulder deep, deep enough for the RTO's radio to momentarily dip underwater. He held the radio Mic. and his M-16 above his head.

Captain S and Joe had removed their packs holding their time fuse, fuse lighters, blasting caps, and other items. They held them and their weapons above their head.

When they finished crossing the thirty-yard-wide waterway, Gates waited for them. "Keep moving. I'll catch up when the last man is over."

"We had no problem. Any ten-year-old Cajun boy can do that walking on his hands,"

"Good. I'll see you in a few minutes." Gates smiled at them again.

They passed the word 'Rest' up the column. The soldiers sat and faced opposite directions and began removing their boots. Gates and the RTO joined Captain S and Joe, the guy sitting closest to Joe took his shirt off.

"Holy crap!" Joe softly shouted and looked at Captain S, who searched for an excuse for such an outburst. "Leeches!" Joe pointed to the now shirtless soldier.

"Now you know why we rest after going through this type of water. If you don't have them bum a cigarette. When you make it hot for them, they'll release themselves. They won't give you any problem. Remember what they were used for, long before penicillin." Gates was not smiling now.

Captain S and Joe stripped off all their clothes. They borrowed the RTO's cigarette. By gently touching the burning cigarette to the leeches, they disengaged and fell harmlessly to the ground, leaving only a red spot on their victim's skin. Captain S had nine, while Joe had fourteen leeches on them.

"I see leeches have good taste. They Prefer sweet, authentic, Cajun, NCO blood, instead of a mixed-breed Officer blood. If you asked me, it makes them pretty smart." Joe teased Captain S while trying to make light of the situation.

"Or they simply go after the weakest target. But what I see is a bunch of white and black butts and dangling dicks, with their flack-vests and helmets lying on the ground, and their weapons propped up against banana trees. I see a great opportunity for Charlie to score some major points."

Gates nodded. "Your point is well taken, Captain. We cross these waterways daily, sometimes two or three times a day and have never experienced any trouble. Besides, those two Tiger Scouts are good at knowing when Charlie is close. They say they can smell him."

After removing all the leeches and getting his clothes back on, Gates moved forward. It took only a minute or two, before the order to 'Move Out' went down the line.

Captain S whispered to Joe, "You know those two Tiger Scouts who can smell Charlie, too bad they can't smell booby-traps. They surely missed the one that got Brown."

Twenty minutes later, the underbrush became less dense, and the trees were more mature and taller. Captain S thought they should be nearing the clearing Gates had pointed out on the map.

The loud explosion behind them caused and immediate reaction. Everyone hit the ground.

Captain S and Joe's eyes met. Another explosion, this one coming from the head of the column, confirmed their thoughts. Joe said, "Those were not grenades, simply too loud."

M-16s began firing along the entire column. The third, fourth, and fifth, explosions confirmed their thoughts of RPG's. This meant they were under a full assault. Leaves and limbs above them began falling. Joe fired first at movement, followed closely by Captain S launching a 40mm grenade from his M-79. The explosion from his round could not be distinguished from the other explosions up and down the column.

Joe's became concern for his Commander. Joe had undergone extensive training for exactly this scenario, but surely the Captain, an Ordnance Officer, had not. A look in his direction resolved this concern. Captain S merely lay on the ground pumping round after rounds out into the endless jungle. Joe saw no anxiety in his demeanor.

Joe spent two magazines, and started on his third, when he realized, he only had two magazines left. He thought again of Captain S. He knew the captain only carried a dozen rounds, and hoped he would not spend them all at anything moving in the jungle.

As the sounds of battle somewhat diminished, the sounds of agony from a soldier up the trail were heard. Other soldiers were chattering, but they were quickly drowned out by a larger explosion which could not be seen. A couple seconds later, more loud explosions ripped a hundred yards out. Frag tore through the jungle tearing trees apart.

Joe had been through a dozen simulated artillery barrages before, but they had prepared him for this. *In fact, no safe training method could be anywhere near this realistic.*

A quick glance by Joe back at Captain S, revealed a smiling face. Captain S lay in the dirt looking at him. He winked and gave a thumb up.

As abruptly as the barrage had started, it ended. The ensuing, eerie quietness did not last long.

Voices from up and down the trail were heard, but most were indistinguishable.

Almost out of nowhere, two helicopters appeared overhead, a Cobra and the other a smaller egg-shaped Loach. This was the famed hunter killer tandem which had become both common and successful. The VC knew, if they shot at the little one, an OH-67, the large skinny one, a Cobra, nicknamed the snake, would come down and kill them. The Cobra usually carried an automatic 40mm grenade launcher, a 7.62 Gatling gun, and thirty-eight 2.75-mm rockets.

Captain S and Joe continued to lie as low as they could. When they looked at each other, this time Joe smiled and gave the thumbs up.

On occasional a single shot or two, or the burp of the Cobra's Gatling gun, were heard. After a while, the soldiers began to stir, others standing, kneeling, or sitting, while others remained in the prone position.

Joe decided he had laid down long enough and started to rise, only to be startled. He changed his grip on his M-16, clicked the selector switch to the fully automatic option, gently eased the muzzle forward, four or five inches. After nervously finding the trigger again, he squeezed and shouted, "Crap, holy crap!" He emptied the rest of his magazine. Everybody nearby sprang to an alert position. A couple of guys fired into the jungle at expected danger.

"What!" Captain S frantically looked around.

"Snake, a damn snake!" Joe shouted and jumped to his feet. He reloaded and backed up. "The damn thing wasn't more than a foot from my nose. It scared the crap out of me! Look at me. I'm shaking like a damn leaf. Man, I don't like snakes!"

"Charlie's out there, shooting at you, and you smile. You see a little snake, merely trying to make a living when his world gets turned upside down. He is scared, and you freak out and shoot him. What kind of a Cajun are you? Sit down, man, before you get your ass shot off!" Captain S chided Joe.

Before he could sit, they saw Gates walking in their direction. "What's the excitement back here?"

"I'm sorry, Sir. I got a little excited and turned loose on a snake." Joe pointed to the ground.

Gates used the muzzle of his M-16 to scratch through the vegetation and come up with a small green snake. "Okay! It looks like a two-stepper."

"What the hell do you mean a two-stepper?" Joe questioned the Lieutenant.

"Well, Staff Sergeant, it looks like you did the right thing, because if this pretty little thing had bitten you, you were only two steps from the Pearly Gates." The Lieutenant educated them on their creepy crawler friend.

Noticing Gates' bloody shirt, Captain S asked, "What's going on up front?"

"We got hit pretty hard. One KIA, another with a major leg wound, and a couple with minor scratches. I must get to the back and see how they're doing. Hang tight here until we can get it together. I'll be back in a few minutes" Gates moved down the line.

"Crap, I hate snakes." Joe looked at the dead snake. For an unknown reason, he felt as if the vegetation was enveloping him.

"Don't worry about the snake. You sent him back to hell. If I was, he, and lived here, given the chance, I'd bite somebody's ass. But I'm not worried about a snake. I'm more concerned about Charlie biting our ass. We don't know what's coming next," Captain S stated firmly and apprehensively.

It only took a couple of minutes, but it seemed like an eternity before Gates and his RIO returned.

Joe asked, "How is it back there?"

"Two hurt. Both are bad enough to get evacuated out of here. They were extremely lucky. They could have easily been killed. I must keep moving. My captain told me to push out into the jungle a hundred meters and get a body count! The enemy's holy body count! Numbers are all the bastard sitting safely back at Dong Tam think about. He doesn't seem to think about my body count. To be honest, I don't know; it may not be the people at Dong Tam. It could be the damn politicians in Washington! This is the problem. They must have something to justify all the money they spend over here. Enemy body count is the measuring stick, and we'll give it to them, right or wrong." Gates fumed as he walked away.

"Wow, the young man sounds frustrated, fed up, and angry," Joe said firmly.

Captain S nodded toward Gates, as he left, and responded. "Can you blame him? Forgive me, but I'm beginning to understand where Brown's anger came from. The only problem is his anger was misplaced. Brown was striking out at the first one in the line who happened to be the Lieutenant."

"Yeah, Gates is simply taking orders, and it's eating him up inside." Joe shook his head.

"It's not our problem, though. We're here to check out a big bomb," Captain S made quotes in the air with his fingers.

They sat for a couple more minutes, waiting to hear the command to move out. Finally, the orders were passed back. The squad leader announced, "We're to move off the trail, north, away from the river in five minutes, search for Charlie, and signs of enemy KIA's. We want to move in line for a hundred meters. At which point, we'll return to this trail and continue with our mission from there."

"We're screwed! We should wait here, right?" Captain S spoke quietly and looked at Joe for his comments. He hoped no one else heard his statement.

Joe kept eye contact. "No. No. Unfortunately, we can't. We must join them. There's safety in numbers. The only thing we'll have to worry about is Charlie refilling this area. There won't be any booby-traps out there. Back here, by ourselves, we're subject to anything. We must stay with the numbers, no matter what."

"Dammit, I know it! But still, this sucks! It's BS, and I don't like it. I have a bad feeling about this, so be careful, Tonto." Captain S continued his rant. "Politicians running a war? You might as well let a toddler fly a commercial plane. The result is the same, a lot of people die who shouldn't. Did I mention this sucks!"

Joe did not like the idea either. He had learned to trust Captain S's intuitions.

When the time came, they moved into the jungle where visibility decreased to at best three meters. They saw nothing but green in front of them. Movement deliberately slowed. After a while, shots sounded from their right, the head of the line, then all along the line.

"Crap, how can they see anything to shoot at?"

"Sir, they can't. Unless they're shooting at snakes!" Joe tried to alleviate stress.

After the firing settled down, orders to do an about-face and return to the trail were passed along.

Once they arrived at the trail, without seeing anything and killing nothing but time, Captain S and Joe waited. Finally, they saw the RIO coming their way, this time with a Sergeant First Class.

"Captain Summerville, I'm Sergeant First Class Luckey, the platoon Sergeant, or I guess now, the Platoon leader. Lieutenant Gates is dead, and I am the Senior NCO."

The shocking news caused anguish and anxiety. Captain S asked, "What happened, or does it matter?"

"What matters, Captain, is you're the senior man here and the only Officer. I reported his death to the company commander. I need to know if you would like to take over as the Platoon Commander. No, let me restate it, Sir, would you please take command of the platoon? Before answering, I want to tell you, I know you are not infantry, but I also know, they don't let anybody become an EOD Officer. I know you are no dummy, Sir."

"Luckey, what I know is, we're in deep doo-doo, and I don't have the experience needed for us to get out of here, alive." Captain S stated his honest opinion.

"I disagree, Sir. You're our only hope. You don't have to worry about what the bastard on the other end of the radio says. They don't write your report card, and you can tell them to shove it!" SFC Luckey encouraged Captain S while presenting facts.

"Sure, what you say is correct. But there is such a thing as the Uniform Code of Military Justice, and the UCMJ doesn't take violating orders by a superior lightly. I don't need a court-martial." Captain S frowned at Luckey. "Insubordination is serious business in the Army, even if the orders come via the radio."

"Yes, Sir, it is. But we need to get out of this place alive for it to happen." Luckey reminded him of the other possibility.

"Captain S, he's right. You can do this. I don't know Sergeant First Class Luckey, but I can see how he's thinking only of his troops. You know I would follow you to hell and back. If you feel you're not up to snuff on the tactical aspects, I know you well enough, you'll listen to Luckey. So dammit, Captain, get a grip and tell the man you'll take command!" Joe berated his Captain like any good NCO would in a comparable situation.

"Okay, Joe. Luckey I'll do it. But dammit, after you inform the Company Commander, you don't get more than ten feet away from me!" Captain S knew having Luckey so close couldn't be the smartest tactical decision, but he wanted to do everything he could to get the man out of this jungle. And Luckey, obviously, had a wealth of experience to lean on.

"Yes, Sir," Lucky replied, and turned to the RIO. "Get the Company Commander on the horn and give the Mic. to your new Platoon Leader."

The RTO did as he was directed.

CHAPTER 30

"This is Summerville. I am the ranking Officer on-site, and I'm pissed! Right now, I don't give a damn about radio security. Charlie knows where I am, and you know the situation here. I am here on a special mission. With more than one hundred of the 9th Division's finest, I intend to complete the mission and get this young man out of here safely. Then, you can have this unit back. I would appreciate your cooperation and support. If you have a problem with this, I'll be glad to talk with your Commander. Over." Captain S spoke frankly into the mic.

"Summerville, I don't know--"

"Breaker, Breaker, I'll take this," the radio squawked. "Summerville, did you run across some loco weed down there, and do you know who this is? Over."

"This is Summerville. I know who you are. We have no loco weed, but we have a load of ugly arrows here. Over."

"Roger. Be advised, you may have more arrows than you can count east of you. We have inbound traffic headed your way. Also, we have more artillery assets allocated to you. More air power is standing by if you need it. Do you understand what I am saying? Over."

"Yes, Sir, I'll find them and flush them out, and you can kill the bastard. Over"

"That's the right way to think. In the meantime, if you need anything, I'm right above you. Out."

Captain S handed the mic. back to the RTO. He took it and asked, "Sir, can you count?"

"That's not important. What we need to worry about is, Charlie's ability to count. Now, we must get the wounded moving forward. Tonto, find one of those Tiger Scouts and ask him how far and how long it is to the next clearing. I want to move out of here fast. We're sitting ducks, here."

Captain S turned and pointed to Luckey. "You, go to the end of the column and tell everybody to close it up and start moving forward, fast. I would bet anything. Charlie will be slamming this area any minute now. And you can forget about the ten-foot distance between the two of us."

Captain S turned back to the RTO. "Let's go up front and find the maimed."

When they reached the wounded, they found one man with a leg injury and two dead bodies.

"Who's the squad leader here?" Captain S looked around.

"I am, Sir." A young Buck Sergeant reported and stood up.

"This wounded man has been laying here for thirty minutes. Get two men on him and assign two men to carry the dead. Do it now and get moving forward. You take the point with the Tiger Scouts. Any questions?" Captain S spoke, in an authoritative manner.

The Sergeant replied, "No questions, Sir," and started moving.

Joe appeared and reported, "We are approximately five hundred meters from the clearing."

"Okay, get them moving forward. The rear should already be closing it up. I want to be in sight of the clearing in less than ten minutes. But don't let anybody set a foot in the clearing until the Dust Off gets there. I don't want to be seen by anyone in the tree lines across the field. Kick the Tigers' ass if they don't move fast!" Captain S made sure everyone could hear him.

"Yes, Sir," Joe replied.

"Tonto, be fast, but be careful." Captain S spoke softly.

"Thanks." Joe nodded and ran forward.

"Get me a status on the Dust Off," Captain S turned to the RTO.

A minute later the RTO replied, "Dust Off holding ten minutes out."

It took Luckey only a couple of minutes before he returned and reported, "We have two hurt pretty badly back there, but with help, they're walking."

"I want to be clear of this area ASAP! The front of the column is moving fast. You go up there and keep the wounded man moving. I'm sure he's hurting rather badly. I'll wait for the rear to catch up and try to help them move faster. Staying in the rear, I sound like a typical Ordinance Officer, don't I?" Captain S smiled at Luckey.

"If it works, it sounds fine with me, Sir." Luckey returned the smile.

"One other thing SFC Luckey, if you need him, my NCO, Staff Sergeant Hébert, is a well-trained and a steady soldier. Any questions or any recommendations?"

"You're doing fine, Sir. I'll be the first to tell you if you're not."

"Sure, as long as I stay out of your way, I'm doing fine. Now go. Leave the silly young Officer in the rear." Captain S shoved Luckey with his hands.

Bringing up the rear, the two injured men were not far behind. They both had shoulder wounds and were moving as fast as they could. Three soldiers followed. A young Sergeant saw Captain S and rushed over. "I'm the Third Squad Leader, Sir."

"Is this the end of the column? Is there anybody behind you?" Captain S eagerly questioned the young Sergeant.

"We're it. Nobody is behind us, Sir."

"You're sure, everybody's accounted for?" Captain S intensely questioned him. He wanted absolute accountability. He did not want to unknowingly leave someone behind.

"My eight are, Sir," the Sergeant assured him.

"Sergeant, I simply want to make sure. I'm not questioning you or ragging on you."

"I understand, Sir."

"Look, Sergeant, we need to move as fast as we can. We've been in this area way too long. Charlie knows where we are. Now, if you were Charlie, what would you do?"

"I see where you are coming from, but these guys are hurting and have lost a lot of blood."

"I know, but ask them, if they would rather hurt a little more or die. If necessary, I'd be glad to carry one of them." Captain S laid their options out without sugarcoating it.

"I hope that's not necessary. I'll try to speed them up." The Sergeant went to talk to the wounded soldiers.

After a couple of minutes, the soldiers had not picked up the pace significantly. Captain S approached the men and said, "I'm sorry guys, we have to move faster."

The men quickened their pace to the point where one of them almost fell. When his knees buckled, Captain S caught the wounded man's good arm and wrapped his arm around him. "Let me help you soldier. The bird is waiting for you a short distance up the trail. The medics will give you a couple of shots of good drugs, and you won't hurt anymore. Give me four or five more minutes of pushing hard."

The young Sergeant supported the other wounded man and said, "Come on, Tom. We can outrun the captain, can't we?"

They heard the Dust Off, before they saw it. It was still on its approach to the cleared rice field. The only soldiers in sight were in the open were two dead bodies and the soldier with the leg wound. Purple smoke boiled up beside them. Captain S looked around trying to find someone but saw no one else.

"Here we are." The squad leader loudly said a couple seconds later.

Once the helicopter landed, it did not take long for the medics to begin working on the leg of the wounded man. Captain S and the squad leader passed their wounded men to the medics, who put them on stretchers and into the chopper. Captain S turned his attention to the two corpses, one of which had half of his chest missing. "He was probably hit with a RPG," Captain S mumbled to himself.

He knelt beside the other body, Lieutenant Gates. He had a small exit hole in his throat. Captain S's thoughts returned to Brown's words. He again softly mumbled to himself. "The SOB. I wish I could find the one who did it. What has happened to these people?"

Captain S stood and turned around to find Luckey standing nearby. "Where is my man?" Captain S asked harshly.

"Sir, your men are dispersed in a defensive position along the edge of the rice field. As for Staff Sergeant Hébert, he's at the end of the defensive line with our Tiger Scouts, about one hundred meters over there." Luckey motioned north, in the direction away from the river.

"What can you tell me about this?" Captain S scrunched his face and forcefully pointed down toward Gates's body.

"Nothing, Sir. I was nowhere near him." Luckey shook his head.

"Is this why you wanted me to take command?" Captain S spoke sharply and caustically.

"No, Sir! I thought-- I was hoping, you could do a better job than I could." Luckey had sincerity in his words, and he expected the captain knew it.

"What a damn shame. What a waste," Captain S said, shaking his head, and gritting his teeth. He quickly turned and went to find Joe. Luckey following closely on his heels.

Captain S had not reached Joe's position when the helicopter lifted off, and when the first of a couple dozen mortars exploded three hundred meters behind them.

With the rumbling sound of counter mortar fire coming from 105mm howitzers somewhere in the distance, Captain S asked for directions to Joe's position from one of the young soldiers hiding along the edge of the open field.

"How's it going?" Captain S asked Joe when he found him.

"I don't know, but I'm sure it's better here than back there." Joe gestured over his shoulder toward the sound of incoming mortars coming into the area they occupied ten minutes earlier.

"Yeah, we got it right, there. However, we must think about our next move. To be frank, I'm not exactly sure about what to do." Captain S quickly looked toward Joe. "Tonto, the only thing I know for sure is, you and I are spending the night in the bush!"

"It's a given!" Joe smirked.

"It looks as if we have approximately thirty minutes of light left. If we're going to move, we better get at it." Luckey tried to give sound advice.

"We're going to move, but to where and when are the questions? I'm sure their mortar crews will have us pinpointed soon. Speaking of mortar crews, I would guess four or five tubes were used for the last barrage." Captain S surmised the number.

"Only three. I think; they are across the river. The counter mortar fire went over there. I would not bet it hit anything, though. Thank goodness. They don't have good communications. It'll likely take them an hour to adjust to our current location." Luckey wiped sweat off his face.

Joe asked, "Luckey, how do you know it was only three crews firing?"

"Other than the fact, I have been out here a longtime, and I have heard a lot of mortar fire. You may have noticed; there were no more than three explosions in rapid secession, without a second or two pause between them. A good mortar crew, and Charlie have them, can get them off in about four seconds. And I know some mortar crews have good communications, but my experience tells me this bunch don't."

"So, you think we have an hour before they'll hit this area?" Captain S looked around.

"At least. I'm sure they saw the Dust Off and, someone is sitting in the tree lines across this field. They are hoping that we'll keep going. Also, our counter mortar fire could have been close enough to make them nervous. If so, they are moving their mortar tubes and digging them in right now. However, they probably have already prepared sites." Luckey educated the two non-infantrymen.

"This sounds reasonable to me. Do you have the map of the area?"

"Yes, Sir. Here it is. I took it off the Lieutenant. There are smeared drops of blood on it. I'll show you where we are and where we were supposed to go."

"Staff Sergeant Hébert, come take a look with us. I want your opinion of the situation. No offense, Luckey, but I know how this man thinks and value his opinion." Captain S moved closer to Luckey.

"None taken, Sir. All opinions are welcome." Luckey nodded and briefly smiled.

Luckey gave a quick map orientation, which included the locations of the Company Commander, the other two platoons, and the planned rendezvous point, which they reported as the bomb's location.

Captain S said. "We'll have to give our situation some thought. Luckey, I want you to do something for me. If I'm wrong about anything which is going to get us killed, damn it, tell me! And tell me why I'm wrong. If I make a mistake and you know it's a dumb decision, and you don't speak up, shame on you. If you tell me we should not do something, and I do it anyway, it's on me. Understand?"

"Got you, Sir. What do you want me to do now?" Luckey started to admire this young Captain.

"I want you to split the Tigers. Put one on each end of the defensive line. I don't know which way we are going. But when we go, it will be fast. I'm hoping that we can outrun the bastards and lose them. I want you to get the troops paired up, keeping the squad's integrity. I recognize the problem with bunching together, but it's going to be extremely dark until midnight when the moon comes up. When we move, we are going to be quiet, and we don't want to lose anyone. If you have a problem with this, get it off your chest now." Captain S challenged Luckey.

"It's different, but if we're careful, we may get away with it." Luckey looked up thinking it over.

"If I understood the Battalion Commander Correctly, assuming I talked to him on the radio, he agrees with you, Luckey. Charlie is waiting for us east of here on the other side of this rice field. Personally, I'm sure he inflated his capabilities the same as I did. The actions back there were simply meant to push us across the field and into the open. If you are correct about their mortar crews, we'll want to move shortly after dark. Also, we better find a safe nest before moonlight. One more thing, do we have any night vision equipment?"

Luckey replied, "The Second Squad leader has a Starlight Scope. It's not standard issue or mounted on a weapon, but you know how it is. We've used it before."

"Okay, let's tell our guys to keep quiet and smoke now if they want to. After dark, we'll see what happens."

Captain S turned to Joe. "Well, Tonto, how are we going to shake these bad Indians who are after our scalps?"

"I don't know, Sir. But if we're going to see the sun come up tomorrow morning, we better find a way. The first thing we should consider is what Charlie will do. If I'm Charlie, and knowing our current location, I would deny you the use of the trail we were on.

It continues to the other side of the rice paddy. I would set up my ambush site to make sure we never get past this clearing. He knows that we're expecting to be hit in the open field. I would also set up spotters and runners for communications purposes along the tree line of this rice paddy."

Captain S said, "That sounds similar to what I'd do. Tomorrow morning, being optimistic, we're still alive. We must find a way to our bomb without going down this trail. Charlie will still be there unless they find us somewhere else. I guess we need to talk to our Tigers."

"I'll get one." Joe left and returned with a scout in a couple of minutes.

"Joe, you've been talking to them. Make him understand, we want to be tucked in by midnight, somewhere that will allow us to reach our target before the sun rises."

"He speaks some English and knows the area, so he can help." Joe showed the map to the scout and explained the situation to him. The scout pointed to a trail leading into the rice paddy northeast of where they were going to find to the big bomb.

"No booby-traps." The scout said, pointing to the trails.

Joe asked him, "You're sure?"

"No booby-traps. OK for sure. Many people walk." The scout nodded in affirmation.

"How about this one?" Captain S pointed to a shorter trail through the narrow part of the jungle, separating the two-rice paddies from where they sat and the next one northeast of them. It was further north than the other trail but shorter.

"Okay, no problem." The scout shrugged.

"There is no problem, to get through after dark?" Joe looked at the

scout questionable.

"Dark night. Maybe, okay to find," the scout said, while shrugging his shoulders again.

"Thank you, Thank you. You can go now." Captain S dismissed the scout and said, "It looks as if we have a plan."

Captain. I like the short trail." Joe said.

"The plan has one major problem. When we move after dark, how do we keep Charlie where he is, and keep him thinking we' ae still here. I am assuming Charlie is over there and waiting on us?" Captain S presented their problem while nodding across the rice paddy.

"Somebody's got to stay behind and show their ass." Joe exhaled.

"And the somebody is who, and for how long?" Captain S hung his head. Somebody who is extremely disciplined, in decent shape, and doesn't get lost in the dark. As for how long, we'll need to think about it. We better run this by Luckey. I want to keep his support and trust. He seems decent and cares about his people." Captain S wanted to keep Luckey informed about everything.

"I agree, and I'll go get him." Joe eased away.

When Joe and Luckey returned, darkness quickly approached, meaning almost too dark to read the map, Luckey said, "I got the troops paired up. And I told them to never lose their partner,"

"Hold on a second and look at this map, while you can still make out some features." Captain S pointed to the trails on the map. "I plan on us getting to the center of this rice paddy by 2400 hours. To do it, we must use this short trail through the woods, northeast of us, to get to the next rice paddy. The Tigers tell us the trail should be okay. We can rest and nap in the paddy until a little before dawn. When we can see the ground, we're walking on, we want to be entering the next trail which will take us to the bomb. Give me your opinion." Captain S pointed at the map as he talked.

"It's a long way around. It is just less than two kilometers at night, Sir? I'll check the Tigers to make sure they can find the first trail." Luckey seemed a little apprehensive.

"Can it be done? Traveling two kilometers at night, with no sound and no light will be tough. If not, and if they don't have the strength left for the distance, we're in big trouble. It's our only option of losing Charlie. Hopefully, they think we are a larger unit and will be expecting us to cross this field we're setting next to.

"What worries me is, when Charlie hit us back there. They hit the rear of our column first, after letting everyone walk right by them. If they counted, it means somebody out there knows our real strength. I hope the information hasn't reached their Commander, yet." Captain S elaborated on his thoughts as he rubbed his chin.

"How are we getting twenty-four men, counting ourselves, out of here without them knowing it and following us?" Luckey presented the major concern.

"We're going to show them four and make them think they are looking at more." Joe's large smile could barely be seen.

"What he's saying is, as soon as it's dark enough, we move out, leaving one Tiger and three volunteers. And no, you cannot volunteer. I need you with me. The four will stay and keep Charlie entertained until, we're well down the road. They will leave here in time to reach us by 0100 hours.

"If you think we can pull this off, you need to find four volunteers." In the dim light, Captain S searched Luckey's face for any emotions or reaction.

"Make it three volunteers. I'm staying," Joe announced.

"No" Captain S snapped.

"Yes, I am. Think about it, Sir. I'm the most qualified person here to get this rearguard out of here safely."

"Most qualified?" Lucky looked and sound puzzled but it could not be seen.

"Yeah. Yeah, he is. Trust me on this one. Luckey, go find three more heroes and tell your guys to eat if they have anything, and to smoke, if they have them. Noise is okay, but only a little. Right now, I want Charlie to know we're here. Maybe they'll bring up reinforcements after we're gone. Have our guys ready to leave in thirty minutes in a column of two abreast." Captain S had no emotion in his voice.

"I'm beginning to think we can pull this off," Joe said with false optimism.

"I hope you're right, Tonto. Otherwise, when Charlie comes after you, your fear of snakes is going to seem like a child's fear of clowns. So how do you plan to make them think the entire unit is still here?"

"Simple, we keep smoking and occasionally make a little noise. Most people don't know how far a lit cigarette can be seen on a clear night. Before we leave, we'll go back into the jungle, a short distance, throw a grenade or two, and put some tracers in the sky. In the meantime, I'll set up some booby-traps that will be waiting for Charlie when they decide to look around." Joe made it sounds simple enough.

"I hope we're far enough down the road that we don't hear the grenades, but maybe we can see the tracers. You think 2130 hours is about right to leave here," Captain S asked his friend.

"Hopefully, Sir, we'll be able to keep the rouse up that long, and they don't decide to mortar us. Ther have waited this long to mortar us, so now, I doubt they will. If worse comes to worse, we'll work our way back down the trail to our starting point from earlier today. If we leave here at that time, coming your way, we should make it by 0100 hours with ease. The four of us can move faster than all of you can move."

"Hell, Joe, if we go balls-to-the-wall, we can be in the middle of the rice paddy by the time you leave here. It depends on various things. We'll take the Starlight scope with us. You can try to get somewhere close to the middle of the field, and we'll find you. We'll use Tonto and Ke-mo Sah-bee as passwords. Make sure you find some more ammo if you haven't. Someone removed the ammo off our dead and wounded. More important, you get there safely. It's an order, damn it! I know you don't always follow my orders to the letter., but in this case, I'm serious about it. I'm not writing a letter to your mama or your lady friend."

"Sir, have no fear. Remember, I've been shot at before, and I can run fast." The way Joe said it, one would think he looked forward to the long night ahead.

"Make sure you do. Now, Specialist RTO, I know you have been listening to our conversation. Get on your horn, and let the Battalion and Company Commanders know what we're doing. We don't need them shooting us up. Use your best Indian talk. Charlie may be listening, and we don't want him to understand. If he figures out our plan, we've seen our last sunset."

Captain S and Joe told each other good luck again and moved away in different directions.

CHAPTER 31

SFC Luckey had formed the unit into a compact column-of-two. A unit which earlier in the afternoon had stretched more than a hundred meters in length, now stretched no more than a hundred feet.

He had warned his troops, if he heard a word, he would personally gag every one of them. They all understood what one well-placed mortar round, or one tripped booby-trap could do. They readily complied, due to necessity, rather than Luckey's threat.

A single Tiger Scout walking point. SEC Luckey, with the Starlight scope, and a soldier followed him. There were two pairs of shooters in front of Captain S and the RTO. A squad leader, tasked to make sure there were no stragglers, brought up the rear of the formation.

They moved out of the jungle into the open field, heading north, and making sure not to get anywhere near the far tree line. They hoped, Charlie, sitting across the rice field from them, did not have the Soviet version of night vision. Some VC units did, although they weren't as good or plentiful as theirs.

The Starlight scope used passive technology, meaning it did not emit any kind of electronic signal. It amplified reflected light such as moonlight, starlight, and sky glow. Weighing only approximately eight pounds, it intensified light up to thirty thousand times into green images. The user could see the same distance as if using a conventional scope. Although, movement caused the scope's images tend to blur and ghost.

Joe lit six cigarettes, two each for himself and his two heroes. Each kept the cigarettes lit and moved, giving the illusion of six moving people. One hero went fifty meters north of the trail just off the edge of the rice field. Joe remained at the end of the trail, while the second hero based himself equal distance between them.

One Tiger Scout took a position fifteen meters into the rice field and functioned as a listening post.

This sequencing continued, with a couple of well-timed sneezes, until 2130 hours, when Joe made his way back down the trail. He did not get as far as he had planned, but hopefully, far enough to give Charlie something to think about.

After throwing two grenades and emptying two M16 magazines, he moved carefully, skirting the booby traps he had previously placed, back to the open rice field to join his heroes.

They headed north in the same direction as Captain S had gone.

Since Joe had not seen or heard any sign of trouble in this direction, his confidence level had grown. *The area in front of us is clear. At least, It appeared clear two and a half hours ago.*

Captain S and his people had sufficient light from the heavens for the Starlight scope to work perfectly. The green tone in the scope, on the right weapon and in the right hands, is a deadly instrument. They took a short break before leaving the rice field and entering the dark and narrow trail leading to the second clearing. During the break, the Tiger checked and reported the trail could be used.

Captain S looked at the illuminated dial on his Seiko watch. It showed 2345 hours. "Can we be so damn lucky to pull this thing off?" He mumbled to himself. A second peep, this time over his shoulder, revealed no sign of Staff Sergeant Hébert. "I'll worry about it later." He again mumbled to himself and headed onto the jungle trail.

As they appeared from the trail into the second rice field, Luckey whispered, "I don't see anything ahead of us, Sir."

"Good, let's move out there about three hundred meters and call it quits. I want to go as far as we can but still be able to see any movement coming out of this area."

In the middle of the second field, the troops lay in pairs facing in opposite directions, predominantly along a dike eighteen inches tall which ran through the field.

Captain S congratulated each one of them on their performance on the march and asked them to still be diligent in their efforts of night security.

SFC Luckey told them, "One man in each pair will sleep for two hours while the other will remain alert. If I hear you slap one of these bloodsucking mosquitoes, I'll bind your hands to your back, and I'll personally castrate anyone whom I find asleep who should be awake."

By 0100 hours, faint snores could be heard along the line.

"Captain, you need to get a little sleep," Luckey whispered.

"That goes for you, too. I slept until almost 0700 hours this morning. Damn, was it this morning? Anyway, I bet you were up well before then. You sleep, and I'll wait on my man."

"I have, as you call them, two heroes out there. Ain't no way I'll sleep until they're in. And remember, they're all yours," Luckey reminded Captain S. of his responsibility for all the soldiers.

"So, what do we talk about, Nixon's secret plan to end the war?"

"How about I start with something a little more local." Luckey gave a short, soft laugh. "It seems the last mortar attack a while ago, on the empty trail behind us, struck home with our guys. To a man, they credit you with getting them out of there. They feel, had it not been for you, they would have been--"

Captain S quickly interrupted Luckey. "It was not all my doing, and you know that."

"No matter. Right now, you can do no wrong, Sir."

"What's the earliest you would expect our guys to get here? The worried captain asked."

"Oh, they could be here anytime. But realistically, another thirty minutes to an hour. They can, and will, move faster than we did when, we crossed the first field. This assumes a balls-to-the-wall approach." Luckey rose up for a look through the starlight scope. Then whispered, "As expected, nothing."

"Okay, about Nixon's plan." Captain S wanted to keep talking to keep his mind off Joe.

"Close your eyes, Captain. You should cover your face with your flack vest to keep the mosquitoes from feasting on you. If you need it, you'll have time to put it back on. I'll rest a few minutes and then move back closer to the trail and wait for them."

"I can do that, and you can rest." Captain S moved to get up, but Luckey grabbed his arms and stopped him.

"No, Sir. You can't, and I don't have to explain this one. Now close your eyes. I'll go get our guys and wake you when we return."

Luckey, admonished the captain in a way only a senior NCO could get away with.

Luckey and one infantry soldier left from the formation, but not before reminding the last pair of men in line of the passwords.

Captain S closed his eyes. The RTO's snoring could be heard, but his snoring did not cause Captain S's lack of sleep. His mind raced with, *What ifs.* His watch reported in at 0145, 0200, and 0215 hours. "They should be here by now. 0230 hours, damn! I shouldn't have let him stay. 0245 hours, crap! We should have heard something by now. 0300 hours, I need to do something, but what? 0315 hours, maybe they used Plan B and went out the other way. 0330 hours, where, the hell, is Luckey? The moon will be directly overhead of us any minute now. 0340 hours, crap! Do I have his mother's address, and what about his lady, Ava?" He hoped the men couldn't see him squirming around, as he mumbled.

He heard a slight noise before he heard Joe's whisper. "Captain, Captain we're here."

"Is everybody, okay?" Captain S quietly rose up and looked around.

"We're fine, everything went as we planned."

"What took you so long? I was expecting you more than two hours ago?" Captain S sounded concerned.

"We had a little trouble finding our way. We walked past the trail leading to this field and fiddled around way north of it. We went all the way to the other trail." Joe said begrudgingly. He hated acknowledging his flaw. "You do know it's hard to see at night!"

"You two stay here. I'll move up to the point with the Tiger," Luckey whispered to them.

"Okay, but make sure someone is using the Starlight scope and remember we want to be moving when the sky begins to lighten."

"Roger, Sir. You guys get some rest."

"Tonto, sit close to me where we can keep our voices down, and cover your face with your flack vest."

Joe stretched out perpendicular to the small dike. "Oh, it feels good. These mosquitoes should have almost two hours to feast on us before we move out. Who would've thought Vietnamese mosquitoes would think American food was so good?"

"Hell, Tonto, we may die of blood loss before Charley kills us."

"Speaking of getting killed, are you sure Lieutenant Gates was offed by one of his men? The thought of him getting shot is thoroughly irking me."

"I'd bet a month's pay against a nickel he was. Brown's words were chilling and foretelling. They're still echoing around my head. I can't seem to get it out of my mind. Believing anything else would be stretching all credulity. I surely wish there was some way to find out who pulled the trigger on him." Even in a whisper, Captain S's tired voice sounded somber.

"Sir, you know, this will never happen. No way. He's simply another casualty of a war.”

Captain S asked, "By the way, did you hear what the body count was?"

"I was told they counted three bodies, but they reported fifteen because of the blood they found."

"Oh, hell, Tonto, we're not going to sleep at all. Let's talk about something more pleasant."

"Sir, we're lying here hungry and filthy, in a mosquito infested rice-paddy, in a war zone. You can't even see three feet in front of your face. What pleasant things do you have in mind?"

"Oh, come on, Tonto. This should seem like heaven to you. All these mosquitoes, the humidity, not to mention the snakes sounds like south Louisiana to me." Captain S chuckled. "But all kidding aside, I was glad to see you finally got your orders for Hawaii. Sorry they weren't for February, but the first week of March isn't bad."

“Ke-mo Sha-be, what other pleasant subject can we talk about?"

"What else but women! You haven't told me whether or not Lein is any good in the sack."

"Well, you mentioned two pleasant thoughts for sure. A one-word description about Lein would be Tiger. When I'm on top, her moves are so extreme, sometimes I have trouble staying there. The way she gyrates her pelvis should be kinetically and anatomically impossible for a ninety-eight-pound woman, if she weighs that, she's extremely strong and has a vigorous sexual appetite. I don't get a lot of sleep when I'm with her. Of course, it's only been three nights. Now Sir, what about Baby San?"

"You know. We were in the bedroom across the hall to yours on those three nights. But I'm one up on you. One afternoon when I was supposed to be at the O-club, Baby San and I went to my BOQ for a quickie. Can you imagine what Hollow would do with this information?"

"Uh, UCMJ time." Joe laughed.

"Yelp. I must stay away from it. Anyway, a brief description of our love making would be not great. She's young and hardly moves at all. I think it'll change with more experience. Also, I feel guilty and lucky at the same time. Lucky, because she chose me. I know the only reason she did was because of my rank. Women, of all ages and parts of the world, are attracted to men with power. No matter their status in society."

"Don't sell yourself short there, Captain."

"I'm not. That's a fact. But I feel guilty because I know she cares more about Wheeler than me. And Wheeler is flat out in love with her. In fact, when I look at Wheeler, I feel slimier than pond scum. I like her, but at this point, I can't say, I truly love her. However, I'm not turning her down when she throws herself at me. I do care deeply for her, and the feeling seems to be growing. That may end up being a problem for me."

"I know about the guilt feeling. As far as vigorous sex goes, Lein's as fine as it gets. If not, I couldn't take anything better. But there's a difference between raw sex and making love, regardless of the hardware. I make love with Ava, and I'll take it any day. When we're together, it's not necessarily all a genital thing. Don't get me wrong, we can be primal, but there's more to it. It's about the heart and every cell in the body. I would guess; some people have never experienced true love." Joe remembered what it felt like to hold Ava and how long it had been.

"Joe, I can truthfully say, I haven't. I don't think I have loved anybody like you described. Sure, I have had girlfriends, but not one that totally engulfed me. However, Baby San is extremely sweet. The more time we spend together the feeling seems to grow."

"I know what you mean about Phillip. He pants when Baby San is around. And she cares for him, too. She simply doesn't know it, yet. She's only thinking of your body and learning about her body and life right now."

Captain S could not see Joe's smile, but he thoroughly understood and agreed with his words.

"I surely hope the other guys don't find out, especially Wheeler." Captain S said in mock horror.

"I try hard to keep my hands off Lein while at the unit, but she cannot hide her expression and feelings. She doesn't even try."

"You know--"

"Captain, Captain. We have a problem!" Luckey interrupted, maybe a little too loud.

"What is it, Luckey?" Captain S quickly sit up.

"We have movement headed our way."

"Tonto, go alert the troops. Tell them to be ready to move. Now! Go ahead, Luckey."

"It looks like at least six of them coming from the north."

"Time before they are on us?" Captain S looked at his watch.

"Four minutes, Sir."

"Recommendations?"

"The best I can see, they're moving directly toward where you and I are right now. We could easily take them out, but it would tell Charlie where we are. We could try to move the whole line left. This would be easy, but it would leave our flanks exposed. We can swing our right end around."

Luckey couldn't see Captain S's astonished expression.

"Do it. Have them keep close and no firing unless Charlie starts it. No matter what, not even if they step on one of us. Understand? We don't need a fight." Captain S ordered, adamantly.

"Yes, Sir." Luckey said and grabbed the first man he could reach on his right and whispered, "Wheel back, pass it on, and hold fire." The message went down the eastern part of the line.

Captain S did the same thing to his left. He could hear feet shuffling, the sound of movement. It sounded loud but he knew it could not be heard a few feet away.

They continued moving backwards until they heard, "On the ground in one minute," passed along the line. Shortly, there were no sounds to be heard, except for each man's beating heart and breathing. Suddenly, they heard a grunt, and something in Vietnamese, then, total silence engulfed them again.

Captain S looked at his watch, five minutes had passed since the troops were alerted. He knew all the soldiers on the ground were watching the seconds tick off. At the eight-minute mark, they've passed. "Hang tight," came down the line. A couple of minutes later, "Relax, they're gone."

Captain S heard the rustling noise of men standing, and Luckey telling the guys to move back to the dike. Luckey said, "Captain, I'll be back in a minute, after our guys are settled."

Joe reached Captain S before Lucky came back and said, "Man, it was close and exciting."

"Exciting hell! It was worse than the shoot out this afternoon! At least I could see something then.

"Sir, has your heart rate slowed down, yet?"

"I think so, Joe. But I may be wearing brown pants tomorrow." Captain S laughed at himself.

"No, I know better. It wasn't as bad as you think. Not as bad as the damn snake! I can still see him, only a few inches from my nose." The moon gave sufficient light for Captain S to see Joe moving his hand in front of his face like a dancing snake.

"No, it wasn't bad. Not at all," Luckey said as he eased close to them.

"Not bad for you! Crap, you could see! I'm totally surprised no one shot at an imaginary noise. Hell, I heard all kinds of noise. What was the loud grunt we heard?" Captain quietly asked.

"One of the VC stumbled over the dike," Luckey replied.

"The important thing is, we held it together." Captain S sighed.

Joe asked, "How close were they?"

"I'd say thirty feet. And there were eight of them. All carrying two RPG's and an AK. They looked as if they were ready for a war." Luckey's voice sounded crisp.

"How convenient, since they're in a war zone." Captain S mocked, and then added, "Did they go toward the trail we were planning on using tomorrow morning. I mean this morning?"

"If they keep going straight, and I think they will, they'll go well west of our trail. And, about our trail, before all this action, I was talking to the Tiger Scouts about it. There are reeded huts with a small clearance there. I don't know how many, more than five, and less than ten, is what I was told by the Tigers."

"Crap, we're walking right into a hamlet in a VC controlled area. Will, this crap never ends?" Joe bemoaned the situation.

"One piece of good news is, they don't think the bomb is too far in the jungle. They think it's located close to one of the hooches." Luckey added.

Captain S replied, "Well, great, but we've had an experience with explosives close to a reeded home. If true, we caught a break. We don't have to go back into the jungle."

"Yeah. And maybe we'll get the opportunity to burn down another hamlet." Joe quipped.

They couldn't see Captain S's roll his eyes. "Okay thanks, Luckey. I trust you can tell time and figure out how long it'll take us to get there. I want to be standing outside one of those hooches before anybody in there moves."

"Yes, Sir. You need to get a little rest. I'm going to pass the Starlight scope back to its owner and have him wake me at 0515 hours. Tomorrow, or this morning, will be interesting." Luckey stood and left.

CHAPTER 32

Before leaving the nesting area in the middle of the rice field, the RTO gave higher headquarters a sitrep. Headquarters seemed particularly interested in the enemy movement during the night. They had received similar reports from other sources. All the movement appeared to be moving in the same direction. They were headed southwest of their current position into the area where they were twelve hours ago.

At dawn, they could distinguish outlines of eight reeded homes only meters away.

The troops had been told to not shoot first unless necessary. They entered the hamlet, this time with space between them. The only thing moving, other than them, was a flock of nervous ducks. Not even a dog barked. Captain S expected to hear a rooster crow at any moment but remembered there were few chickens to be found in Vietnam. Luckey and one of the Tiger scouts were standing by a palm tree near the center of the hamlet, with Joe nearby. Other troops, with the other Tiger Scout, had moved further down the trail.

A minutes after the last soldier entered the hamlet, a woman appeared at the side of her home. She never looked up, and after emptying a pan of water, she returned inside. A child, in one of the hooches, deeper in the clearing, cried. A second woman walked around her home. A small boy ran into the cleared area and started urinating. Finally, a woman screamed and started yelling something in Vietnamese. The entire hamlet exploded with activity. A young man, carrying an AK-47, sprang from one of the hooches and passed only a yard from Captain S. Joe quickly tackled and disarmed him.

The Tiger Scout near Luckey yelled something in Vietnamese. The Scout further down the trail echoed it. As quickly as the clearing had filled with excited people, it emptied. A moment later, an elderly man appeared, and then a second, this one not as old. The Scout, standing in the clearing, yelled at them, and the two men began walking toward him. They talked for a moment, before the

Scout motion for Sergeant Fist Class Luckey to come over. After another talk, they gestured for Captain S to come over as well.

Now, standing in the clearing, Captain S understood, the men in front of him were the hamlet's chief and his son.

Captain S told the Scout, "Ask the chief if there are any VC in his hamlet."

"No VC, no VC," the younger man asserted.

"Are you sure? We are going to check all your homes," Captain S said. The Scout relayed the message.

"No VC, no VC," the man nervously said again.

"Ask him what this guy is," Joe approached with the bound young man, whom he had tackled. He was more a boy than a man, not over fifteen.

The old man stepped toward the bound young male, slapped, and kicked him, and then spit on him. "VC," he said.

"Tell him, we are here about the bomb, and we'll dispose of it. Tell him, we're going to search the hamlet, and if we find nothing, we will not hurt anybody or destroy anything. Tell him if any of us are harmed, we'll burn the hamlet." Captain S kept his eyes on the chief.

The Scout relayed the comment. The old man first frowned and then smiled and nodded. He then turned to his son and said something to him and then addressed the Scout.

The Scout repeated the comments. "He said, we can search the village. His son will lead the way, and he'll show you the bomb. He wants you to follow him."

SFC Luckey directed his men to wait on the chief's son before entering any of the dwellings. They were to look for VC, weapons, and manholes. They were to be careful and not to break anything.

Joe passed his prisoner off to one of the Tiger Scouts and told the Scout to question him. Then he, Captain S, and two soldiers and followed the chief. The second Tiger Scout started questioning the young teenager.

They could see the large, elongated, silver object through the jungle from twenty yards away. Joe and Captain S looked at each other and shook their heads. The old man pointed at the object and said, "Boom," while gesturing with his arms and jumping up and down.

"Ask him if this is the bomb and if it's the only one." Captain S looked at the Scout.

The Scout did as he was directed. After the old man answered, he said, "Yes, bomb. No more bombs."

Joe spoke first. "Damn, two dead, four with major wounds, and several minor wounds. For what? For what, Dear God?"

"For a wing tank." Captain S sounded disgusted. "Damn, The Almighty!" He threw his hands up.

"No boom," Captain S told the old man. "No boom! Come, come." He walked over to the wing tank and kicked it. "No boom."

The old man walked over to the wing tank and kicked it. "No boom!" He excitedly proclaimed while shrugging his shoulders.

Joe said, "Sir, let's get our ass out of here and see if we can get a ride home. I'm going to be sick. And from a good Catholic who attends Mass regularly, I can't understand this loss and my feeling."

"I'm ready to move," Captain S replied.

The sun popped above the tree line as they reached SFC Luckey. Joe told him, "It's not a bomb. It's a wing tank. Have you found anything, yet?"

"No, Hébert, not yet. We're still looking."

"Specialist RTO, tell the boss, our mission is complete and to pick us up ASAP, Captain S ordered."

After talking to headquarters, the RTO reported back to Captain S. "They want you to stay here for a while. They've been waiting for our call. They're going to hit the area west of us hard and want us to act as a blocking force in case any VC come this way. Then, they'll pick us up. Action to start in five minutes."

Captain S called for SEC Luckey and gave him the information. "You know what to do. Take the Scouts and let the people know what to expect."

"Has our guy over there given us any information?" Joe motioned to the young prisoner.

"Nothing." Luckey shook his head.

Joe, Captain S, and the chief walked over to the prisoner, who now sported swollen eyes from the slapping the Tiger Scout had given him. Joe stopped the beating and asked if he had talked. The Scout reported negatively.

"Bring him over here. I'll communicate with him and explain things to him. Tell him I'm crazy and like to do terrible things to VC. Tell him I'll cut his head off and eat his liver."

The Tiger Scout translated as Joe spoke. Joe removed three feet of det cord from his pack. He connected it and other items together and wrapped the det cord around the prisoner's neck to measure. He then removed the det cord from the prisoner's neck and placed it around a nearby banana tree, inches above the ground.

When the first artillery round hit the ground west of them, Joe told everyone to back up and yelled "Fired in the hole" three times. Less than a minute later, and after the loud crack of the det cord, the banana tree lay on the ground.

Joe calmly walked over to the prisoner and gave him his best cheesy smile. He then reached in his pack and pulled out three feet of det cord and went ahead and connect the necessary assessors while continuously smiling at the prisoner.

"Reiterate to him; this man is crazy!" Captain S shouted to the Scout, over the artillery fire. The scout rattled off the translation.

Joe wrapped the debt cord around the prisoner's neck and told everybody to get back. The prisoner lost his bladder but said nothing. Joe, then, yelled "Fire in the hole" three times, and gave the prisoner a big smile and a pat on the cheek, and ignited the time fuse. Joe had taken no more than three steps when the prisoner started screaming, but Joe continued to back away.

Captain S yelled, "Staff Sergeant Hébert, you can't do this." Joe simply licked his lips and smiled at the prisoner.

The prisoner, now, yelled faster and louder. Captain S went to the prisoner. He cut and removed the det cord.

"Tell him if he doesn't talk, I'm leaving him to the crazy man." Captain S turned and walked away. From further than thirty yards away, he could still hear the boy talking.

The artillery barrage lasted for almost ten minutes. When it lifted, three hunter killer teams worked the area over.

Luckey had spread his men out, under cover and concealment, along the south side of the opening and trails leading into the dense foliage. On two occasions, VC tried and failed to escape the carnage occurring west of them. They were not as lucky as those crossing the trail deeper into the jungle, where none of Luckey's men were dispersed.

At 0915 hours, the RTO reported to Captain S. "A relief force is on its way. It'll be here shortly. The choppers will drop the force and pick us up."

Captain S found his Tiger Scout and told the chief, who had been at his side every minute, to expect. "Tell him I thank him for his help, and I'll give him the wing tank. He can use it for water.

"By placing it on poles and catching rainwater, he can have running water."

After the translation, the chief smiled and hugged Captain S and shook his hand. Captain S removed his boonie or bush hat and placed it on the old man's head. "Tell him he is now a *Dai uy*, a Captain." Captain S had replaced his steel helmet for the soft bush hat when evert had settled down.

The old man smiled and yelled something to one of his flocks. A minute later, a young girl ran up to the old man and gave him a traditional cone shaped, Vietnam head gear. He, in turn, handed it to Captain S and spoke to the Scout.

"He said, you will need a *mu rom* to protect your head from the sun, and you are now a friend."

When the choppers arrived, the relay of troops went smoothly.

Back at the firebase, where they were nearly twenty-one hours before, SFC Luckey and his RIO, approached Captain S and Joe. "That's your ride coming in now." He looked and pointed toward an inbound chopper. "Before you leave, the men want to thank you." He looked toward where they had gathered into a small group. "You didn't ask, but we got nine of them, nine real ones, laying on the ground, beside the trail. Some likely got away and will be dead by dark."

"Good!" Captain S replied, as he and Joe walked toward the gathering of troops.

As they approached, the troops stood and saluted, something which is not common in the field.

Captain S stopped and looked at all the faces. "At ease men! SFC Luckey tells me; you want to thank us. Let's get this straight. It's Staff Sergeant Hébert and I who need to thank you. We asked you to do nearly impossible things, like a column of twos crunched together crossing a rice patty and doing a wheel maneuver, all in a combat environment, and other things that's certainly not tactically sound. It would get us thrown out of any infantry school. Your response on every occasion was far above what could be expected. Heck, I'm surprised; SFC Luckey didn't intentionally leave us out there in the dark, rice paddy. He's a great leader. You have a right to be proud of him, and of yourselves. So, thank you for getting two Ordnance guys out of such a hell hole. Thank you!"

Every one of the soldiers passed Captain S and Joe, shaking their hands, smiling, and saying thanks. Captain S looked directly into each of their eyes searching for a murderer hidden within but found no clue.

The chopper landed, and as they approached it, Joe asked Captain S, "Do you truly believe I would have blown the VC's head off?"

Captain S put his arms around Joe and said, "Tonto, you know, I couldn't sleep with anyone who would do such a thing. Besides, I've probably set up a thousand explosive shots, but I have never set one up without a blasting cap."

"Damn, I thought, I got it by you." Joe huffed and shook his head.

CHAPTER 33

"No, I'm not going back there, unless ordered of course. Are you giving me a direct order?" Joe filled his coffee cup with one hand and held his favorite inert grenade in the other.

"Joe, it was only a question. I've seen enough of that place, and everybody associated with it for a lifetime. Almost twenty-four hours was too much for me. I simply thought you might want to go back. I'll send Banks and O'Neil, instead." Captain S smiled, leaned back in his chair, and propped his feet up on his desk.

"It's a different Army. A young Sergeant telling his Commander what he'll do or not do," Master Sergeant Scott growled, while not looking up from his paperwork.

"You know better, Master Sergeant, and I know Captain S does as well. Sure, I'll go, but to be honest, I don't want to. We went twenty-four hours without food, and I've had only eight hours of sleep since we left here two days ago. I'm sorry. I'm not awake yet." Joe sounded frustrated with the idea that he may have to return to the Head of the Dragon area.

"You're awake enough to toss that grenade around. I've seen you playing with it before. Why are you always throwing it around, Scott asks?"

The short answer is, I don't have a baseball. It's a habit I picked up as a kid. I lay in bed at night, tossing a baseball up and catching it. Besides, it's good exercise, good for your hand-and-eye coordination and grip. You know it's safe. It's the one I disarmed shortly after arriving here." Joe tossed it up, caught it behind his back, quickly twisted the head off and replaced it.

Captain S shook his head, turned, and motioned to the tent where Banks and O'Neil were. "Wheeler, go make sure those two sleeping beauties are up and dressed. Tell them they're needed at Charlie Pad in thirty minutes to take care of a cachet which was found at the same place where Hébert and I were yesterday and the day before."

"Hey, I'm beautiful but not asleep," Banks proclaimed while walking in the back door. "What's going on to get everybody up so early?"

"I'll go get O'Neil." Wheeler excused himself.

Scott answered Banks' question. "We received a call at daylight wanting EOD personnel to go back to the same place Captain S and Staff Sergeant Hébert were for the past two days. It seems after they left the area, a fresh company was inserted into the area near the hamlet. The company met strong resistance. But what's important is, they found a cachet. They want us to check them out for booby-traps. If the truth were told, I think they want us to blow some bunkers. They're too smart to ask us to come blow them. They know we would tell them to call the Engineers. Regardless, we must go. And when I say, we, I mean you and O'Neil."

"O'Neil is moving, and a Jeep drove up," Wheeler said coming in the back door.

No sooner than the words rolled off his tongue, a Lieutenant Colonel walked through the front door. He stood six feet and looked about one- eighty pounds. He wore jungle fatigues.

"Attention!" Master Sergeant Scott barked, and they all reacted quickly and assumed the position of attention. Captain S moved to meet the Lieutenant Colonel. He saluted and said, "Captain Summerville, reporting, Sir."

The Lieutenant Colonel returned the salute and said, "At ease men. So, you are the Summerville whom I was speaking to on the radio day before yesterday, the one who took command of a platoon of my troops. I'm Lieutenant Colonel Abraham. Glad to meet you, Captain." The Lieutenant Colonel extended his hand to Captain S.

"If you're the guy who thought I was high on pot or something, I guess I'm your man. May I offer you a cup of coffee?"

"With sugar, please." The Lieutenant Colonel nodded and walked over and shook hands with everybody.

"You're the NCO who was with Summerville. I recognize your name, Hébert." Lieutenant Colonel Abraham recognized Joe's name.

"Yes, Sir. I'm the co-conspirator."

"I only have a few minutes. The chopper is waiting on us. I thought I would give you a ride to Charlie Pad. You did get the request for more EOD support, didn't you?" Abraham sipped his coffee.

"Yes, Sir. We got the request, but I have a previously scheduled commitment. Staff Sergeant Banks, here, will be going with you."

"That'll be fine, Captain. Can we talk alone for a minute before we leave?"

"Yes, Sir. But if it's an ass chewing, as far as I'm concerned, they can hear what you have to say. Captain S gestured his hands to the rest of his unit.

"Hardly, Captain, I assure you." Abraham halfway grinned. He then turned to Scott and said, "Please," and gestured for them to go elsewhere.

Once everybody left the office, Abraham took a seat behind Scott's desk, "Please sit down. Let me tell you my first thought when I preempted your radio call to my Company Commander. I thought you were probably drunk. Then, I realized you were talking to Charlie more than to me."

"I certainly didn't want to come across as pompous or arrogant. If he was listening, I simply wanted to make Charlie think we were a larger unit. If I could convince him of that, I thought they would stay off our backs for a while." Captain S explained his actions.

"Once I understood you weren't drunk, I knew what you were trying to do, and I commend you for it. At first, I didn't know for certain; your plan was to keep Charlie off your back, as you say. What I do know is, your actions got those boys out of harm's way without more casualties. You were essentially surrounded by a much larger force than yours. If you had hesitated, you certainly would've been wiped out. For getting them out of there, I have recommended you for a Bronze Star for achievement. I also sent a personal note up to the division Chief of Staff. I'm sure he'll see it gets passed to your operational chain of command, the guy who writes your report card."

"Sir--" Captain S started to speak.

Abraham held up his hand, stopping Captain S. "Wait a minute. The young prisoner you captured had no rank, but he was one of their runners. Therefore, he knew, and gave us, a half dozen locations where VC gathered. We're working on those locations as we speak. Everything shows his information is correct. I don't know what he meant, but he kept saying he would tell us anything, as long as we keep the crazy man away from him."

"The crazy man would be Staff Sergeant Hébert. What I started to say before was, you are giving me credit that I perhaps don't deserve. Everything I did was discussed with and essentially approved by SFC Luckey. He had the respect of his men. So, without him, we would not have been able to safely get out of the situation."

"I understand Captain. "Abraham nodded.

"Wait a minute, Sir. I must tell you about my man. Without him and his specialized training and actions, I promise you we would not have made it. The situations were extremely labyrinths. Sergeant Hébert's became the catalyst of the operation. Enough credit cannot be given to him and the two heroes, or volunteers to stay behind." Captain S lauded his men.

"Sir, I doubt that I have to tell you everything that went down. I'm sure you have been thoroughly briefed, and you have spoken to some of the soldiers." Captain S stared at Abraham.

"I have, and what you are saying coincides with what they said." Abraham nodded.

"Sir, what I'm trying to get you to understand is, I will not accept any medal unless the two NCOs receives the same recognition," Captain S spoke with great conviction.

"I should have expected such a comment from you." The LTC studied Captain S's face.

"While I have your attention, there's one more thing, Sir." Captain S's voice changed. It became harsher.

"Wait? Never mind, let me guess. Lieutenant Gates?" Abraham leaned back and folded his arms.

"Yes, Sir." Captain S nodded.

"I talked with SFC Luckey. He briefed me and told me you thought Lieutenant Gates was shot by one of his own men. Is he correct?" Abraham looked Captain S in the eyes.

"You're right, Sir. I do. I would bet my left testicle on it, and it tears me up inside. I knew him only a couple of hours. But, from what I saw, he was an outstanding young officer. His men didn't understand him. What they perceived as his idiotic orders, were in fact issued by people upstairs. And with no disrespect, Sir, it includes you. I wouldn't be surprised if up to 20 percent of his troops would have taken that shot, if given the chance." Captain S kept eye contact with Lieutenant Colonel Abraham.

"You're making an extremely serious allegation, Captain. Can you support any of it?"

"How about a man lying on the ground with no fewer than twenty frag holes in him saying, he didn't want to go home, 'before seeing the God Damn Lieutenant dead'?"

"I need another cup of coffee, Captain." The Lieutenant Colonel headed toward the coffee pot.

"Help yourself, Sir, I have had plenty."

"Captain, I came here this morning, because I thought you may have something to say to me. You have expressed yourself exceedingly well, and I hear you. I hear, we, as an Army in combat, have a big problem. Neither you, nor I, have the rank to influence the situation. Be assured, the people who can influence the situation are fully aware of, and are concerned about, the fragging issue. What I can do is ensure this individual case is highlighted. You know that's not enough, and there's nothing we can do unless someone comes forth. Captain, you also know that will not happen." Abraham poured himself a half cup of coffee.

"No, it won't, Sir, and what a damn disgrace." Captain S shook his head.

"Is there anything else you want to share with me?" The LTC asked.

"No, Sir. And I'm sorry if I was brazened." Captain S stood and faced LTC Abraham.

"I respect your honesty. If your men are ready, I need to get out of here." Abraham quickly gulped his coffee.

"I'll get them in here. I'm sending you two, Banks and O'Neil."

As Abraham started to leave, he shook Captain S's hand and said, "Thanks. I'll take care of the NCOs, and Captain, if you ever need a job, I'll have one for you."

"Don't say that unless you mean it! Colonel Hollow is always after my scalp. If he had the authority, I would be out of here, yesterday." Captain S jerked his thumb like a baseball umpire calling strike three.

"Hollow! Never mind!" Lieutenant Colonel Abraham regained his professionalism and left, following the EOD team.

*****

As they were driving away, another Jeep drove in. "Well, how about this? What are you two doing here, especially this early?" Captain S asked.

"We came to see you, of course," replied Lieutenant Armstrong, as he gave Captain S a chest bump and started in.

"I have a couple of fresh ears if anybody wants one." Butler patted his pocket.

"As far as I'm concerned, you can keep them." Captain S grimaced.

"That goes for me, too. Come on in. I think we can find a cup of coffee for you," Joe said as he led them into the office building.

"Do you think we can find some chow somewhere?" Armstrong rubbed his belly.

"Yes, Sir. Of course, if we can get Master Sergeant White, our mess Sergeant, to feed you. I'm sure, Master Sergeant Scott can arrange it. We haven't eaten, yet. I'll get Scott, and we'll go over to the mess hall," Captain S turned to find Scott.

After settling around the table in the mess hall, Butler grunted, "SOS on toast. That's all the Army serves for breakfast?"

"It's certainly not like the Navy's fresh fruit and a choice of eggs benedict or prosciutto frittata, with gourmet coffee." Scott looked at Butler and took a big bite of his breakfast before continuing. "But Shit on a Shingle is hot and better than the troops in the bush have."

"Listen to you!" Butler grinned.

"Yeah, but that kind of gourmet stuff is, what people in the fleet eat. It's not what you two are accustomed to eating." Joe looked at Armstrong and Butler.

"For sure?" Armstrong played with his SOS.

"We got a rare taste of your life a couple of nights ago. We had to spend a night in a rice paddy. It isn't commonplace for us," Captain S said.

"Other than the mosquitoes, I doubt it resembled anything like our life," Armstrong insisted.

"If you have a soft, stimulating job anytime soon and need some help, I'd like to go with you." Joe's eyes sparkled with anticipation and excitement.

"Not without me, you don't." Captain S looked sternly at Joe.

"You think you could manage it, Sandy?" Armstrong asked, in a macho way.

"He can take it." Joe emphatically stated.

"I know you can, but are you sure about him?" Armstrong pointed his finger at Captain S, while looking at Joe.

"Yeah, I think so." Joe nodded and took a big bite of his SOS.

"Thanks for the rousing endorsement, Tonto." Captain S said sarcastically and sipped his coffee.

"Well, I'm impressed." Armstrong took Joe's endorsement seriously.

Scott shook his head and said, "You don't have to worry about my candy-ass doing anything so stupidly. I sleep between nice clean sheets every night. The only thing better would be sleeping on top of those sheets with my big-butted Black woman."

"With any color woman!" Armstrong clarified the comment.

Butler looked at Scott. "Candy ass, my ass! You can sing that song if you want to, but you're far from a candy ass. Your physique and movement paint a different picture than your words."

"Now, I'm impressed by your observation," Joe said while looking at Butler.

"So, what are you two guys doing over here this early? I know you didn't stop by simply to check out our health or to eat this SOS with us." Captain S raised his fork in a toast to everyone.

"Hell, there are only two things a man should think about, poker and food. You have already eliminated one of those." Realizing his mistake, Armstrong stopped and looked at everyone at the table. "Maybe I should have added women to the list."

"Poker and food? What's wrong with you? Do you think a woman is only an afterthought? Women are foremost on most normal men's agenda," Captain S replied with a big smile.

"With all kidding aside, we have a meeting this morning. We should be free for lunch and anytime thereafter. We will find a poker game," Armstrong said.

Joe waved, and said, "Sir, come back as soon as you're free. Butler and I can eat lunch over here. Master Sergeant White will probably be serving fried bologna, or maybe cold bologna. You and Captain S can eat at the Navy officer's mess. They'll probably be serving T-bone or lobster. I think pheasants are served only on Sunday."

"I'll be here for the T-bone or lobster." Armstrong laughed.

Scott said, "Forget the Officer's cuisine. How does a man get invited to one of those games?"

Butlers shook his head and commented, "Yeah, I bet you need an invitation to a poker game. Sing me another song."

"No, but I do have to go. There's never an end to the Army's paperwork." Scott stood and excused himself.

Joe said, "Master Sargent, if you need me, I'll be in the sack, that is, if Lein and Baby San let me."

"I'll be over in a few minutes." Captain S looked at Scott.

After Scott's departure, Armstrong said, "I didn't want to say it in front of Scott, but we are staying at Colonel Neuner's place tonight. We saw him last week and promised him we would. I think it's a feather in his hat when he can get Officers to stay there. I'm sure. You and your ladies are welcome."

"You were right about Scott, and I think we could probably put up with Neueng if necessary. Thanks for the invitation," Captain S replied.

"Oh, hell, I'm going to need some serious rest, for sure." Joe Smiled.

CHAPTER 34

Master Sergeant Scott showed no concern or suspicion, when the four with Lein and Baby San drove away early, in the afternoon. Wheeler, however, had concerns about Baby San missing his tutelage. He had recently introduced her to basic trigonometry learning how to factor quadratic equations. He was extremely pleased and surprised with her advancement.

Once in My Tho, the girls had to find Lien's nursing friend for Sam. He couldn't go hungry, nor could he occupy Lien's every minute tonight. But they still refused to let Captain S and Joe go into their neighborhood. Instead, they chose to meet at a restaurant, found on the river.

Captain S and Joe drank, Vietnamese beer, The girls had hot tea. They all chose Lien's favorite rice dish, talked, and laughed. If it were not for Captain S and Joe's dress, and their weapons hanging on their chair beside them, one would think this could be a dinner date anywhere in the world. The guys insisted the small pieces of meat in the dish came from a dog. Of course, the girls denied it. Afterwards they walked toward the ARVN compound.

A fierce battle had raged through the streets of My Tho about a year ago, during the Tet Offensive. Buildings and trees still bore scars from the fighting. Every other commercial establishment, what few there were, seemed to be a bar catering mostly to ARVN soldiers. The girls became excited when they came to an apparel store selling women's clothing. In the small picture window, which would be overwhelmed by windows in a 1950's store in Small Town, USA. They saw a bright orange Vietnamese outfit, an *ao dai*. It was the type of garment worn at unique events or semiformal affairs such as special holidays or a dress-up date. Lein simply drooled over it and kept saying, "Too much, too expensive."

Joe put his arm around her and said, "How much is it?"

"Too much. Not know. Maybe thirty-five dollars." Lein shook her head. "Too much. No can do." Lein continued shaking her head and resisted as she followed Joe into the store.

Baby San said something in Vietnamese and began helping to pull Lein into the shop.

Inside, they were told, "Fifty dollars, American," by the owner.

Joe haggled. "Twenty-five dollars, Vietnamese."

"Forty dollars, military pay certificate (MPC)," the store owner counter offered.

"Thirty dollars, Military Pay Certificate, MPC, finish." Joe moved his hands through the air like a knife.

"No can do." The owner frowned and shook his head.

Joe took Lien's arm and walked toward the door.

"Okay, okay! Thirty dollars, MPC. "The owner folded.

"You buy for me?" Lein expressed surprise as Joe pulled his wallet out.

"Sure. It's not for me." Joe grinned at her.

Lein first covered her face with her hands and then wrapped her arms around Joe's neck and gave him a full body hug. "Thank you. Thank you."

"You set the bar pretty high for me, Tonto." Captain S turned to Baby San and asked, "What would you like?"

She asked, "You buy for me?"

"Baby San, find something you like. I'll buy it." Captain S took her hand.

Her expression showed, no one had ever bought her a gift, especially, such a lavish gift as anything in this store.

"I not know. I do not know." Baby San corrected herself and looked around. "You pick."

Captain S started looking for something. "Here is a pretty pair of high heel shoes."

"Pretty yes. I no wear. I will not wear." She shook her head at the misuse of the English language.

Captain S looked at the proprietor and raised his hands behind his neck and pulled them forward. "Necklace?"

"Oh, *vong doe co*." he said, and led Joe to a counter where he placed a large briefcase, or small trunk on top. The man opened the container and pointed. "Necklace, *vong doe co*.

In the container, they saw an assortment of jewelry, from extremely used, others slightly used, to looking new. After consideration, Captain S pointed at two items. "Forty dollars, MPC, for the two and finish. No more."

"Okay, forty dollars, MPC."

"Baby San, come here and close your eyes and turn around." Captain S crooked his index finger at her. She did as he said. He slipped a small dainty gold necklace, with a gold cross, around her neck and snapped it. "You can open your eyes now."

The owner provided her with a small mirror which she held up to her face. Looking at herself, she said nothing. Tears streamed from her eyes. She went to Lein and showed her the cross and hugged her. Now sobbing loudly, she lunged toward Captain S with open arms.

A half dozen blocks down the street, they found Armstrong and Butler at the poker table with the now familiar crowd. The lady friends were in their customary positions on the sofa and were chatting away.

"You started without me, I see," Captain S said, as he pulled up a chair.

Joe, not wanting to play cards, sat next to the girls and watched their interactions regarding Lein and Baby San's gifts.

It took Lein only a moment to disappear out a door, carrying her wrapped present. She reappeared a couple minutes later wearing the orange *ao dai*, adorned with what Joe thought were mother-of-pearl beads. All heads turned in her direction.

"Wow! What a little color can do for her', Joe mumbled. For the first time he saw the radiant beauty in Lein. Not a beauty contest winner like Ava, but most definitely a real keeper. One could do a much worse. *Money well spent. You are a lucky SOB. You'll be richly rewarded later.*

After a short while, Lein disappeared again. When she reappeared, she wore her regular uniform, black pajama trousers and white shirt. She sat softly on Joe's lap and snuggled close.

The poker game did not go well for the two Officers. This gave them the excuse to leave early.

Armstrong surrendered first, and said, "Are you guys ready to get out of here?"

"I have enough of your money for today." Butler acted extremely smug.

Joe said, "I've been ready since we got here."

"Okay, it looks as if the cards aren't going to change. So, where are we going? We still have an hour of sun." Captain S looked at his watch.

"We can leave the Jeeps here and walk over to Neueng's place. They'll be more secure here. It's only a few blocks away. On our walk over there, we can pick up some beer, for later."

The four guys and their ladies strolled back up Dong Le Lot Street, sometimes holding hands, skipping, and laughing. They talked all the way in a carefree manner, trying to forget they were in a war zone. Before they turned left onto Dong Le Phi, two blocks from Neueng's hotel, they randomly selected a bar across the street. They ordered beer, this time for the girls, too, and continued their conversation. After the second round of beer, they ordered two each to go. As they walked out of the bar, Armstrong pointed to a building straight across the street and two blocks down where Dong Le Phi dead ended, and said, "That's Neueng's place down there."

Armstrong and Butler had stayed at the hotel a half dozen times, Captain S and Joe were a little surprised at what they saw, a large two-story, blue, cinder block building, setting off the street. It had wire mesh supported by a steel frame running from the roof to the freshly poured concrete sidewalk. The mesh protected the entrance from anything thrown in and looked strong enough to cause an RPG to detonate, keeping the explosion away from the building. There were gates, on both sides of the protective mesh, which could be closed and locked. They could see sandbags stacked along the edge of the roof. Three jeeps with QC markings, Vietnamese MPs, where outside on the edge of the street and could be seen from a distance. Two of them were mounted with M60 machine guns. The third Jeep sat between the two, gun jeeps.

"The dude is serious about his security." Joe pointed out as they approached the building.

"Yes, and our luck hasn't improved. If you see the Jeeps here, he's here." Armstrong did not sound happy.

"Get ready for some teeth and grins." Butler sounded as happy as Armstrong.

As they entered the wire mesh-covered area, they saw the spit-shined Colonel Neueng. He and two other ARVN officers were standing near the front door. "Hello, Colonel Neueng," Armstrong said and the five saluted.

"My friend, Lieutenant Armstrong, and my friend, Captain Summerville, how are you today? It is good to see you. I hope you are here to spend the night." The words came off his lips like he was singing.

"We are, Sir. And it's good to see you as well," Armstrong replied.

Joe noticed he and Butler were ignored. *No lowly enlisted attention here.* He also noticed Baby San stepped behind Captain S, trying to hide. He checked out Lein's reaction. She had taken a couple of steps to the side and approached an ARVN Lieutenant Colonel, or another rank in another branch of service.

Joe did not know ARVN Senior Officer's ranks or uniforms. Anyway, he wore a different uniform. Joe turned his full attention to them. He wished he could understand their discussion, but the body language looked universal. Although there were no smiles, he knew they knew each other, and he suspected, they had mutual feelings for each other.

"I must go now. I am a busy man. If you need anything, I will be here at 2100 hours. I am here at that time every day," Colonel Neueng said, trying to dismiss them.

"I will do it, Sir. But I'm sure we'll be fine," Armstrong replied and saluted again. Now, facing Captain S, he said, "Come on, let's go upstairs."

After pausing a moment for Lein, they went into the entrance where they saw two staircases, one on each side of the entrance, and a large extra wide hall where six, huge ARVN soldiers, likely at least six feet tall, were sitting playing cards and drinking beer. The four doors on each side of them were closed. Six girls were sitting in chairs at the far end of the room. They were obviously with the cardplaying men.

"I'm told the right stairs lead directly to the roof. We use the left side. The second floor is ours. The stairs there, also, continue up to the roof." Armstrong informed them.

The second floor looked like a mirror of the first floor. Captain S and Joe chose rooms which were painted off-white and had white sheets covering single beds. Each had a straight-back chair, and a table with a water pitcher and bowl. At the end of the extra hall were two toilets and two showers.

Joe followed Armstrong and ask, No girls for you two?

"No. We have in the past, but no longer. You don't know what you are getting when you pick one up one of the locals. I brought a book to read."

"Hey, there have been some changes since we were here last time." Butler seemed surprised.

"And what can that be?" Captain S couldn't see anything which looked like an improvement.

"Before, the tables had no water or bowl." Butler said without cracking a smile.

"Its first-come first-served here, so we better claim a room if we want one," Armstrong said.

"We already have one neighbor." Butler pointed to a locked door.

After entering his room and removing his pistol belt and flack-vest, Joe told the others, "I'm checking out the rooftop."

"I'm coming, too." Captain S started to follow him.

"Go ahead. I've seen it." Armstrong waved his arm.

Joe led the way up to a small door which opened outward to a flat tax and gravel roof. The sun had set, but they could see sandbags were stacked around the entire roof, with each corner receiving a double layer built into a fighting position. A small, knee-high picket fence ran down the middle of the roof. A large black barrel with pipes set at the far back end of the building.

"Talk about segregating the guests. He doesn't want any association between the ARVN guys and us." Joe appeared astonished at what he saw. He pointed to the fence.

Captain S replied, "It's obvious. There must be some reasoning, but I don't understand."

"I wonder what the black thing is." Joe pointed toward a black barrel at the other end of the building.

Captain S retorted, "It's a solar hot water heater."

"Oh, crap, Sir! I should have known. What I do know is, this place can be defended against a small army with RPG's." Joe swept his arm around.

"If crap happens, I'm coming up here." Captain S liked all the sandbags.

"Sir, I'm going to let those guys downstairs do their thing. They look really big and capable."

"I noticed that, Joe. Speaking of downstairs, what's with Lein and the guy she was talking with?"

"I'm surprised that you noticed. Colonel Neueng had his head up your ass so far, I did not think you noticed her. But to answer your question, I don't know. However, I'll find out."

Back on the second floor, they found Armstrong and Butler talking to their neighbor. "Hello, I'm Captain Summerville, this is Staff Sergeant Hébert." Captain S offered his hand.

"I'm First Sergeant Farmer, from the Ninth Finance Company. Glad to meet you, Sir. I'm the guy who makes sure you get paid every month."

"Apparently you're doing a good job! We haven't had any kind of problem."

"Knowing there are some fighters next door; I can sleep better tonight. I don't know if you two Ordnance guys can fight, but certainly the other two are fighters." Farmer laughed.

"We may not be able to fight as well, but we can take care of booby-traps and duds better than them." Joe simpered.

"Master Sergeant Scott is your man, isn't he?" Farmer looked at Captain S.

"Yes, he is. Do you know him?" Captain S seemed more attentive.

"I've been in a few poker games with him. I don't suppose you guys would have any interest in a friendly game?"

"Don't think so. I've already taken my beating for the day," Armstrong grimaced.

"We only have two beers apiece, but I'm sure we can share." Joe offered Farmer a beer.

"I've got a whole cooler full. So, you have more than two if you need more." Farmer pointed at the cooler setting close to his door.

"Thanks, we'll see you out here, or we'll knock on your door!" Butler replied.

"Okay. I have some more business in here." Farmer stepped toward his door. "Look, if there's anything I can do for you. Let me know."

The four guys sat around a table in one room drinking their beer and talking about the war. The girls huddled in an adjacent room with their respective beers. After a while Joe said, "Will, you excuse me? I'm going next-door. I can't take it any longer. I have to talk with Lein."

When Joe entered his room, he said, "Baby San, please excuse us for a minute."

When she left, Joe continued. "Lein, I need to know something."

"What wrong?" Lein sat on the bed next to him.

"I hope nothing. I'm concerned though. The man downstairs. You know him well, don't you?" Joe took her hand.

Lein slightly dropped her head, "Yes, I know him."

"Do you mind telling me about him?" Joe tried to find her down cast eyes.

"No, I tell you." She hung her head, further, and then raised her hands to her face.

"Well, tell me," Joe spoke crisply.

"I know. Long time. When young. My family and his family friends have land and money."

"His family and your family had money," Joe repeated.

"Yes, my family no money now. His family, lost money, land."

"I understand. Go on."

"He my, my good friend. He go away. His name is Chi." She spoke softly.

"He went away how long ago?" Joe now noticed tears in her eyes.

"Long time, maybe five, six years. I think, I think he no come back." Lein shook her head.

"Good friend, does this mean boom-boom?"

"Good friend, yes, boom-boom, one boy, I love him. He go away. I think he no come back."

"One boy. Do you mean he was your first boyfriend?"

"Yes, first. Then Johnson, then you. I think he no come back. Johnson no come back."

Joe swung his feet up onto the bed and propped on the wall. Lein snuggled under his arm in a fetal position. "Johnson couldn't come back. You know that."

"He loved me. I know. Johnson no loves me. You no love me."

"You know; I care for you. I like you very much," Joe's voice softened, and it sounded caringly.

"You no love me. G.I. no love Vietnamese girls. Love girl in States," Lein said while sobbing.

"Lein, I have a girlfriend back home. You are a good person, and as I said, I like you very much. But you know, I must, also, go home, someday."

"You buy me pretty today." She looked up at him.

"Is today the first time you have seen him?" Joe wanted to know more about the man wearing a different uniform.

"Yes. No see, five years, maybe six."

"Maybe, you will see him again soon." Joe lay down next to her and faced her.

"No talk about him." She gently kissed Joe and snuggled again.

After a soft knock on the door and sticking his head into Joe's room, Captain S asked, "Hey, are Baby San and I interrupting anything?"

"No, we're simply talking. Come in." Joe rolled over to his elbow.

"I thought you might want another beer." Captain S handed Joe and Lein one. "Before long, they'll be too hot to drink."

Joe replied, "Whoa, Baby San, you are on your third. Can you manage it?"

"I can. I am not a baby." She smiled and raised the can up to her lips.

"I don't think she had more than one at any time in her life." Captain S smiled at Baby San.

"Sir, you better not let her have any more to drink, she may sleep all night. I don't think you want her too sleepy."

"I no sleep. I will not sleep tonight. I will do other things!" The beer emboldened Baby San.

"Way to go, Baby San! Wheeler is doing a good job with your English." Joe looked at her and kept smiling.

"I am learning good. Well! Good! Oh, I don't know which one to use."

"Don't let it bother you. It's sometimes hard for us, too." Captain S kissed her on top of the head.

"Okay." She took a big swallow from her can.

"Baby San, before you get too relaxed, tells me why you don't like Colonel Neueng." Joe looked at Captain S.

"I no like him. He is a bad man."

"Why is he bad? Has he hurt you?" Captain S sounded sincere and concerned.

"No hurt me. He hurt others."

Joe asks, "Is this all you can tell us?"

"He is bad!" Baby San had her head lowered.

"Lein, I see you have been crying. What have you two been talking about?"

"We've been talking about Lein's old boyfriend!" Joe answered for her.

Lein blurted out "We talk about G.I., no love Vietnamese girls."

"Okay." Captain S raised an arm in surrender. The other one, he wrapped around Baby San.

"I have to go to the head." Joe jumped up and headed out the door.

"Chicken!" Captain S said as he passed.

The two toilets had private doors, but Joe noticed the two large showers resembled his high school football team's open showers. Each had enough room for six people. They had dark-blue tiled floors and white walls with blue accent tiles, and a common opaque, plastic, privacy curtains.

When going back to his room, Joe saw the cooler sitting outside of Farmers room. "Well thank you, First Sergeant," He softly whispered.

"Is anybody ready for another cool one, compliments of Farley?" Joe asked, while walking back into his room.

"I am." Baby San raised her hand.

Joe said, "Baby San, I'm so glad to see you smiling and happy. You cried all afternoon."

"I cry, but I am happy. Captain S give me a pretty cross." She hugged him.

"Lein was all smiles this afternoon, but she has tears tonight. Baby San shed tears all afternoon and is smiling tonight. I don't know how to handle this. So, let's get drunk, and laugh." Joe raised a beer in cheer.

"Sounds good to me. I'll tell Master Sergeant Scott to invite Farmer over for drinks on me," Captain S raised his beer.

"Me too." Baby San replied.

Captain S asked, "Me too, what?"

"Me too. Me too. I don't know." Baby San slurred her words.

"Me too. She wants to get drunk." Lein tried to explain.

"I never get drunk." Baby San giggled.

"You no can say that tomorrow." Lein managed a smile.

After another beer, Baby San began to melt. Captain S said, "I better throw her in the shower and try to get her awake."

"Do you think you can keep her awake?" Joe asked.

"I surely hope I can. We'll be in the shower for a while."

In a couple of minutes Joe and Lein heard the other two heading to the shower. Baby San squealed, while Captain S tried to keep her quiet.

"We go shower." Lein stood and quickly removing her clothes.

"You want to go with them?" Joe showed surprise.

"Two showers, okay?"

"Okay. But we have no towels." Joe stripped naked.

"No problem." Lein looked out to the door and ran for the shower with Joe close behind.

When they pulled the curtain back, there stood Captain S and Baby San under the same shower head. "Oops," Joe said, and stepped into the other shower stall pulling Lein with him while Baby San made a half-hearted effort to hide behind Captain S.

"Oops, I'll show you oops." Captain S followed them into the shower where, Joe had turned into.

Lein giggled loudly and darted to the shower with Baby San.

Joe began chanting, with Captain S joining in. "I smell the blood of a Vietnamese gal, I'll grab her boobs and take her to bed."

They both, mimicked the well-known jingle and repeated the jingle over and over while walked into the shower with the girls. The four of them jumped around laughing, squealing, and played grab ass.

After a short while Baby San stopped. She grabbed Captain S, and said, "Today I cry. Tonight, I laugh. I shower. Now, it is time. We make boom-boom!"

"Oh, yes, but you may die," Captain S mockingly said.

"No. No. I will not die tonight. Lein, tell me what to do. You may die! You die for sure! " Baby San drug Captain S out of the shower.

CHAPTER 35

"Man, I'm leaving Sunday for five days and nights in Hawaii, to meet the most beautiful woman in the world, so you better not get me killed. If you do, I'm going to come back and haunt your ass!" Joe sounded adamant as he looked at Armstrong.

Armstrong and Butler had just driven in. They had a mission to conduct tonight. They needed Joe's help. Of course, Joe had agreed to go with them.

"And how are you going to do that?" Butler asked.

"Oh, man. I'll get my mojo and jeu-jeu and conjure up some of the Bayou's best voodoo in the world. I'll get Rougarou, a swamp beast, on your ass."

"You can't do that, for real?" Butler sounded as if he wanted to believed Joe.

"Oh, I don't know. I've heard him speak about his knowledge of voodoo before, and something about Rougarou. In case he can, what do you say, if he wants to go with us, let's not get him killed?" Armstrong looked at Joe trying to give him an out.

Captain S cut in, "He's not going without me. I told you, and I mean it!"

"Sandy, dammit! I'm not comfortable taking you. A single mistake might cost us the mission, not to mention yours and our lives. Hell, can you even swim? Can you use a weapon? Can you move quietly? Can you do anything? You know, useful?" Armstrong stared at Captain S.

"So be it. Staff Sergeant Hébert stays here." Captain S snarled, while standing his ground. He realized he took a somewhat childish position.

"He can swim. I know he's done some scuba diving before. A while back, he showed me his scuba-diving certification, his PADI certificate. Also, we have moved around some at night without getting shot." Joe defended his friend and Commander.

"You know there's a hell of a lot more to it." Butler looked sternly at Joe.

"Okay, dammit! If Joe thinks you can do it, so be it. We desperately need a shooter to cover our backs. I know Joe can manage that. Sandy, I'm telling you now, you are extra weight. You better not slow us down. We can't afford to wait for you." Armstrong stared at Captain S, again.

"Speaking of weight, we can use the fourth man. We have a long way to walk. Actually, we may move a little faster with him." Butler tried to add something positive to the situation.

"You're right. One way or the other, this operation is time sensitive, and we're going to take care of it tonight. We're going to get 10 o'clock Charlie's mortar team. Let's go inside where we can lay the map out, and I'll explain the mission to you." Armstrong motioned to the door.

Less than two hundred hours earlier, Armstrong and Butler had come to the EOD unit asking if they had a pristine Chinese mortar. They needed one to send to China Lake, in California, to have it changed. The modification simply changes the round where, once it's dropped into a mortar tube, it would instantly detonate. Of course, Captain S had provided them with the requested mortar.

"The turnaround time from China Lake was impressive," Joe said.

"Yeah, China Lake does a good job at supporting us. I'll bet this round stayed there no more than four hours before they put it out the door back to us." Armstrong nodded in agreement.

"If I needed something along this line, I would have to turn to Picatinny Arsenal in New Jersey. I would expect the turnaround time to be more like four weeks for an urgent request."

"Sandy, if you ever need anything remotely similar to this, let me know. I'll get China Lake working on it. Now let me show you what our plans are." Armstrong spread a map across Captain S's desk.

The plan looked and sounded extremely simple, but all four knew it would be physically challenging and would take all their strength.

"We'll take a short flight across the river and drop-off. There, we'll cross some shallow water with undergrowth and work our way to the riverbank, where we wait for a sampan. Think of it as a large

Vietnamese rowboat. It'll be carrying mortar rounds to supply the mortar team who has been hitting Dong Tam at 2200 hundred hours every night for the entire month of February and before that, nearly twice weekly for the last year.

"Then, we'll kill or capture the VC in the Sampan. There should be only one man. If there is no blood loss, we'll provide some, making it appears as if the occupant had been killed. We'll replace one round of his cargo with our China Lake modified round and set the sampan adrift, hoping it'll be picked up down-river about a half mile away.

"An informant has told us where the delivery point is. We don't want to be to close, nor to far from that point. Too close, they hear us. Too far away, the sampan may never reach its desired location. It may hang up on the bank or float out to far in the river.

"They are supposed to rendezvous at midnight. Shortly before setting the sampan adrift, we'll fire a few rounds off to let the guys downstream know the carrier is under attack. Then, we'll book it back to the drop-off point and wait for sunlight and a helicopter. Any questions?" Armstrong looked at the other three men.

Joe spoke. "Captain S and I have been over in that area. It's nothing but wet mud, and extremely thick stuff. Can we make it to the river in time?"

"I'd prefer the drop-off point be further away, but yeah, we should make it in plenty of time. If the stuff is as thick as you say it is, we'll swim down the natural waterway which essentially separates two islands. We may want to do this anyway. It would be quieter but would put us closer to their rendezvous point." Armstrong explained his planning.

"Okay, for arguments sake, let's say one of us doesn't know what he's doing. Finding the river doesn't concern me. It's a big river. Getting back to the starting point is another matter. If I'm correct, the drop-off point will be a small spot in an otherwise large jungle, or whatever you call the thick stuff. How do we find it?" Captain S moved his finger around the area on the map.

"It'd be easy during daylight. At night it's more challenging. I'll drop some crumbs on the way. We can follow them back to the drop-off point. If we get lost, we'll get in the waterway and stay there. If Charlie doesn't find us first, the helicopter will." Butler made it sound simple.

"Thanks," Captain S said sarcastically.

Joe said, "I don't want to speak for you three, but I think I'll skip any drinking this afternoon and take a nap."

"That sounds good to me. I'll take a nap, too. Butler always wants to sleep. I trust you have cots we can lay our heads on." Armstrong looked at Captain S.

"Sure, we can find a bunk for you." Captain S said.

"First, let's walk back to the Jeep and check out some things." Armstrong motioned for them to follow him.

At the Jeep, Captain S spoke first. "Four pairs of flippers, and four masks, with snorkels?"

"What's wrong, Sandy? You didn't think for a second that you were staying here, did you?" Armstrong looked at Captain S and raised his eyebrows.

"I should have known you three would play me like a fish. I never had a chance." Captain S shook his head.

"We wanted to make sure you had no doubts about going with us." Butler patted Captain S on the back.

"Oh, nice toys." Joe said, picking up a sniper rifle with a Starlight Scope. "And two of them."

"I assume you're familiar with the scopes." Butler looked at Joe.

"Yes, I went over to the sniper school about three weeks ago and fired a few shots off. They're better than what I used during SEAL training."

"Technologically, they've come a long way in a short period of time. How about you, Captain?" Butler looked at Captain S.

"I've held a Starlight scope in my hands and peeped through it on one occasion. It probably saved lives."

"In the hands of a good shooter, like Joe, this thing is a life taker." Armstrong emphasized the word taker.

"I'm sure they'll do us a lot of good in the thick stuff across the river. I think I'll rely on my M-79," Captain S said sarcastically.

"You're right. But, sitting on the riverbank, we can see, and if necessary, we can easily influence something well over a quarter mile away." Joe patted the sniper rifle affectionately.

"I see, I see, said, the blind man! We can see the sampan coming and leaving," Captain S said.

"I hope we can follow the sampan until it's secured by the VC." Butler appeared extremely concerned.

"It may entail following the boat for a distance," Armstrong suggested.

"There was no mention of following anything." Captain S looked at Armstrong in a questionable manner.

"Well, no. I didn't want to scare you off. I know how skittish you can be." Armstrong grinned.

"What else do we have in this goodie pack?" Joe changed the subject before Captain S could come back with a good retort.

Butler answered his question. "Nothing special. The bag is waterproof and made with floating material. We have ammo, red and green flashlights, first aid, a small vial of blood, and a couple of M-18 claymores for use if a problem arises. Joe, you and I will carry the sniper rifles. They'll carry. M-16's, and everybody carries pistols. You and I will take turns with the radio. The Lieutenant and Captain S will take turns with the pack. All our supplies will stay in the pack until needed."

"Like I said, I'll carry my M-79. You don't want me carrying a pistol," Captain S said. Armstrong grinned. "You'll be fine, Sandy. I take it; you're not comfortable with a handgun. We'll work out the details of who carries what."

"Comfortable with a pistol, no. More like dangerous to those around me." Captain S confessed.

"Hébert, come here." Lein called him from beside the office building.

They all turned and looked at Joe. "It looks like, I'm being paged. Anyway, we're about through here. You guys can find a bed, and I'll see you for dinner."

"If your woman calls, you better go." Butler teased Joe.

When Joe approach Lein, she asks with a big smile. "Armstrong, Butler here, we go to My Tho tonight?"

"No, no, Lein. They have work to do and need someone who can shoot. I can shoot exceptionally well. We'll go to My Tho soon." Joe watched her smile disappear.

"Not soon. You go, Hawaii soon to see American girl. I no like. I hear you talk to Captain S. Wheeler tell Baby San." Lein now frowned.

"Yes, I will go to Hawaii, Sunday. We'll go to My Tho when I come back. I'll be gone for seven days. Do you understand?"

"I know. I know you like see American girl." Lein said, now with tears in her eyes.

"I'm sorry. I make you unhappy."

"I be happy, you come back Vietnam." Lein looked up at Joe.

Putting his arms around her, Joe said, "Let's go talk to Sam. I'm going to miss the rascal."

*****

The sun had completely disappeared, leaving hardly enough light for the helicopter pilot to find the small clearance, thanks to a reflective marker which had been previously placed. They approached from the west. After five seconds over the marker, the chopper was on its way.

On the ground, only the sound of mosquitoes buzzing could be heard. After a moment, Armstrong said softly, "Okay, apparently we're not getting ambushed here. I'll take the point with the radio. Joe, you're second, Sandy, third, and then Butler. We go northwest at two hundred and seventy degrees for about a hundred fifty meters, or until we hit a waterway. We want to go slowly and quietly."

"I'll take the pack first," Captain S said, slightly above a whisper.

"Sounds good. After all, Sandy, this is why you're here." Armstrong replied, with slight laughter.

Fifteen minutes later, they had gone no more than fifty meters. All had fallen more than once.

"We want to sound like a leopard, but we sound like a herd of elephants." Joe said, loud enough for Captain S to hear him clearly fifteen feet ahead of him.

The noise they were making did not get any better. However, the closer they got to the natural waterway the deeper their feet sank into the soupy mud. The half-moon, now high enough to help them see, gave them more ambient light.

Tired and exhausted, they finally reached the open natural waterway, which had a slightly harder bottom and would quicken their pace. For the first time, they could use the Starlight scope to survey the area. They knew enough noise had been made to easily be heard by an alert VC guard at least a hundred meters away. A quick search using the Starlight scope revealed nothing threatening.

Butler attached three small thumbtacks with reflective heads to a low limb to mark where they entered the open water. Without close observation, someone would think the tacks were reflecting spider eyes.

They gathered and Armstrong softly said, "It was harder than I expected. I have never been through a mangrove thicket, but I can't imagine it being harder. I think we should stay in the water. It'll be faster and easier. Butler, you take the point, I'll take two. Sandy, you are third, and then Joe. Sandy, are you holding up, okay? Do you want to keep the pack? It floats so it'll be easier now. Or do you want the radio?"

"It's heavy, but I can manage. I'm fine with the pack." Captain S replied,

"Okay, Sandy, the radio is mine. We have enough time so, be careful and remember, when we reach the river, their rendezvous point will be about four hundred meters east, down the river. We need to work upriver three or four hundred meters to set up for our business."

They all agreed and moved out, staying close to the east side. The moon light reflected on the water, providing enough visibility where they could easily see each other. A near constant checking through the Starlight Scopes revealed no problems ahead or behind them. They reached the river in a remarkable brief time, but they dared not actually go all the way to the riverbank, for fear of being seen or heard. So, they stopped fifty meters shy of the river.

"We'll cross the waterway here," Armstrong commanded.

"Time to swim, Ke-Mo Sah-bee."

They moved to the near bank, slightly into the growth, and found a place to sit. Removing their boots was not easy, but necessary. After exchanging their boots for the flippers and placing the radio in the pack, they moved out into the natural waterway again. This close to the river, the waterway opened to over seventy-five meters wide. With Captain S and Joe hanging on and pushing the pack with the sniper rifles and the radio on top, and with Armstrong and Butler on each side, they crossed the open waterway with relative ease.

Now on the west bank, Armstrong said, "Sandy, you and Joe stay here. Butler and I will check the riverbank. We'll take one scope with us. You two use the other to keep an eye on our six. We shouldn't be more than fifteen minutes."

"Take your time. We'll be right here, unless some Mekong River monster gets us," Joe quipped.

"The only monster you have to worry about here speaks Vietnamese." Butler said and slowly eased away.

Using the Starlight Scope, Joe watched Armstrong and Butler's progress. "They've reached the river," he told Captain S. He then checked back down the natural waterway and saw no signs of trouble behind them. After another look toward the river, Joe reported, "They're on the way back. I'd bet everything is okay."

"At this point, the only thing I would bet on is, my face is going to look like one big mosquito bite. And I surely hope we aren't being sucked dry by leeches" Captain S sighed.

Joe replied, "Leeches shouldn't be a problem. This is flowing water. You can believe it or not."

When Armstrong returned, he said, "We didn't see anything moving. We'll head upstream, staying in the river. Let's go."

As they moved into the river, Captain S and Joe paused for a moment to look east. About four miles down the river, they could clearly see the luminescence from the lights of Dong Tam, and a large Navy ship sitting in the river. "It's probably the support ship. They often house the Riverine Force's personnel and communication equipment," Captain S whispered.

Checking his watch, Joe said, "2230 hours, it looks as if we missed the fireworks, the red flares signifying a mortar attack at Dong Tam by 10 o'clock Charlie."

"Let's keep moving. You'll have time for talking later." Butler admonished the two of them.

Upstream, Armstrong said, "This should do." He pointed to the bank. "Move to the edge of the brush. Remember, they may also have the capability to see at night."

They did as they were directed. Captain S spoke first. "Can I ask why here? I see nothing remarkable."

"This place meets our needs, one of which is being unremarkable." Butler softly explained.

"Now we wait. Butler, you get out there and watch. The sampan could be here in thirty to forty-five minutes. Joe, when it arrives, Butler and I will do our SEAL thing, and try to take the occupant alive. This is where you're needed. Remember, I told you we needed a shooter. If we do not get him in the water, or he manages to get a weapon, you take him out at once. Needless to say, be sure not to shoot me or Butler."

"I wouldn't be here if you had any concern about my accuracy. Do you have a preference in which eye I take out? "

"It doesn't matter but leave the ears. They're mine." Butler scoffed and moved with one of sniper rifles twenty feet beyond the edge of the water and squatted.

"Now, we fight the damn mosquitoes. I'm not taking my jacket off." Captain S said sarcastically.

Armstrong told him, "Damn, Sandy, all you have to do is rub mud on your exposed skin."

"Dumb ass, me! I'm seriously embarrassed." Captain S quietly laughed at himself.

"Before you do anything, Sandy, pull a couple of face masks and snorkels out of the pack. We're going to need them."

Sitting and waiting, they could hear nothing except the normal night sounds of frogs and insects. Occasionally, they could hear and see Butler moving and looking from east to west. Suddenly, Butler stood and moved toward them. "He's coming, Sir. He's between five and ten meters off the bank."

He handed Captain S his rifle in exchange for the mask and snorkel.

Armstrong said, "We'll move up fifteen to twenty yards. We don't want him to see our tracks."

"Okay, Partner. I'm ready to go. He should be here in no more than five, Butler replied.

Captain S and Joe had ringside seats only twenty-five yards from the action. With naked eyes they could barely get a glimpse of the two snorkels, with maybe four inches of head and mask above the water. With the Starlight Scope, they could clearly see them and the small sampan, with one man easing it slowly forward. As the sampan moved closer, Captain S heard the click of the safety on the sniper rifle in Joe's hand. A small splash of water on the bank side of the sampan caused its occupant to turn his head to the right. As he did, Armstrong lurched from the water surprisingly, quietly, and grabbed the man around his neck. When taken under water, he splashed, but not extensively. Captain S heard the safety again. This time, the click returned the weapon to safe.

Butler came out of the water towing the sampan and guided it to the bank directly in front of Captain S and Joe. Armstrong waded to the bank beside the sampan. He pulled a limp body behind him, which he secured on the river's edge.

Butler continued to hold the sampan as Armstrong approached. "Give me our mortar round and a green flashlight."

"Captain S searched the pack and gave him the items. Joe moved into the water's edge with his sniper rifle and began watching both east and west for anything moving.

Searching the sampan, using the green light, they found an empty, dirty rice bowl, an AK-47, and twenty-four, mortar rounds neatly stacked four deep and covered with a dirty canvas tarp.

"Put the round in the second row," Armstrong told Butler, who carefully removed the original mortar and replaced it with the China Lake mortar.

"Sandy, will you take the tarp and wipe some blood on it? The body has a hole in its chest. Holding the tarp down and mashing his chest should be sufficient."

Captain S did as he was requested and gave the tarp back to Armstrong. After examining it, he said, "Good, you can give it to Butler. He can replace it over the mortar rounds. To make sure, let's take the blood we brought and sprinkle around the sampan. Try to splatter it, so it looks as if Charlie fell out when shot."

After pouring the blood as directed, Butler said, "This should get it. How long of a firefight do we need?"

"Give me a short burst on automatic with the AK. Make sure part of the brass stays in the boat. And then a couple of shots with an M-16. Sandy, will you do the honors with the M-16 a second after the AK goes? Make sure some tracers fly low out over the river."

Captain S retrieved an M-16 and said, "You got it."

Butler, let go with the AK, and Captain S fired eight distinct shots, two at the time, with the M-16.

Any experienced VC within hearing distance would at once discern and name the two weapons.

"Butler, push the sampan back in the water. Sandy, you need to put weight on the body and sink it. I'll clean the bank of our tracks. If they come up here, they don't need to figure out, we were wearing flippers. They may draw a conclusion that we got our hands ahold of their sampan." Armstrong wanted to make sure each of the men understood everything.

Captain S responded, "The only thing we have that will permanently sink the body is our ammo and his mortar round."

"You can use the AK, too." Butler interjected, as he pulled the sampan back in the water.

"I don't care what you use. Use anything and everything. I don't want the body popping up in the next two or three days."

Ten minutes later, all of them were chest-deep in the Mekong River water, waiting and watching with the Starlight Scopes for the sampan to drift further down the river.

They hoped the sampan would stay close to the river's bank. If it should move too far out in the river, it may be missed by the waiting party. Hopefully, the fired rounds would alert them and would increase their awareness.

"I think our luck is holding. It's at the mouth of the natural waterway we used, and in good position. Let's hope the wind doesn't pick up," Joe said.

"Let's move a little closer. We'll follow it to the far side of the waterway and wait there until something happens or it's out of sight." Armstrong started moving.

Shortly before reaching the waterway, they had previously used, Joe, still had one of the Starlight Scopes whispered, "Holdup! Crap! We have movement, close by.

CHAPTER 36

Still chest deep in the Mekong River, Joe reported, "Two guys. Oh, crap! We have two on the east bank of the waterway in concealment. How, the hell, did they get there?"

"How they got there is not the question, Joe. How are we getting back to our pickup point is the problem?" Captain S expressed the real dilemma.

"Let me look." Armstrong took the sniper rifle from Captain S, who had been watching their six.

"I see them. They're hid well. I'd say no more than a hundred meters. I wonder if they were there when we passed, or moved in after they heard the rifle fire?

"Further down river, others are collecting the sampan closer than we expected."

Butler firmly said, "It doesn't matter. We're not going through there without taking them out."

"If there's more, they are well concealed." Joe continued looking through the scope.

"Or they may be further up the waterway where we can't see them." Butler offered another possibility.

"Okay, the sampan is in their hands. That was our objective. We accomplished it. Even if we wanted to fight, Sandy dumped all our ammo in the river." Armstrong chuckled. "Our mission now is to get out of here alive."

Butler bemoaned, "We aren't going back the way we came."

"I don't want to fight my way through the thicket again." Captain S stated his opinion.

"I don't either," Joe echoed.

"Then we have two alternatives. We go back upstream, or we swim." Armstrong summarized.

Captain S quickly asked, "Swim where?"

Armstrong said, "If we go back upstream and wait until daylight to be picked up, it's a long wait. Those guys might decide to move up the river to look for their comrade. There may be more

VC upstream. There's still the matter of us having no ammunition to speak of."

"Swim where" Captain S asked again. This time with a little more emphasis.

"To the big Navy ship sitting down there, off of Dong Tam." Butler pointed down the river.

"It's at least four miles, probably closer to five." Captain S hardly believed what Butler said.

"Sandy, three of us can do four or five miles in our sleep. We'll swim further out in the river and let the current do most of the work for us. All you must do is hold onto the pack. It'll carry you down there." Armstrong reassured him.

"Guys, in matters like this, I'm not as smart as you are. I'm a ground pounder. I haven't had all the fancy Navy SEAL training you have. I am, however, smart enough to know, if we get out in the middle of the river, there is a chance we'll be run over by a boat. Also, if by some stroke of luck, the boat misses us, I'm positive, there is a watch on the Navy ship who will not take lightly to four swimmers, with a pack, approaching his ship. I'm 100 percent sure; he'll blow our ass out of the water."

Armstrong said, "It's possible, but--"

"Let me interrupt." Joe held up his hand which they could barely see. "Lieutenant, you need to take a look down-river. One of the guys has taken the sampan. The other, now has company. Looks like four or five coming our way."

"I have them," Armstrong said. "This settles it. We swim. Now!"

They swam hard getting to the middle of the river, as fast and quietly as possible. They paused only to take a quick look over their shoulders. No one said it, but they all hoped Charlie did not have night vision.

"We can relax now. This should be far enough. The twinkle of lights you see on the far bank is the hamlet of Xa Kim Son. We don't want to get too close. Also, I don't see a speeding boat in sight." Armstrong now talked and laughed a little louder.

"All right, have all the fun you want at my expense, but there's still the possibility. And do you realize how dirty this water is?"

The other three laughed and Butler said, "Dirty? I see you've never swam in the Potomac around Indian Head, Maryland. Navy EOD students there say it's like swimming in a septic tank."

Captain S replied, "Guys, I like swimming in clean water like Crystal River, Florida, clean and clear."

"Feel around in the pack and get the flashlights out. When you see or hear a boat, start flashing the red and green light. They won't run over you. They may even stop and pick us up." Armstrong sounded surprisingly cheerful.

"Crap! Something big hit my leg." Joe tried to stay calm.

"Probably a shark checking you out," Butler said in matter-of-fact way."

Captain S mocked, "Come on guys. I'm not gullible enough to believe you. Sharks this far from salt water? You can do better."

Armstrong replied, "Actually, we are pretty close to brackish water. The South China Sea isn't far down the river. And sharks do, in fact, swim in freshwater. Bull Sharks have been caught in the Mississippi River as far north as Memphis, or maybe it was St. Louis."

"You make this BS sound true. No way sharks will be this far upstream," Captain S insisted.

"It's not BS, Sir." Joe supported Armstrong.

"They do indeed swim in freshwater. And they have also been known to fancy landlubbers." Butler teased Captain S.

"Man, I'm from Colorado! I know, I don't have to worry about sharks there. Let me guess, sharks are attracted to red and green lights, aren't they?" Captain S asked the question not genuinely wanting to know the answer.

"Yes, Sir. How did you know?" Butler continued the conversation.

"BS. On a serious note, Armstrong, why did you have to kill the man in the sampan," Sandy asks.

"Besides biting my hand, I knew as soon as I got my hands free, and his head got out of the water, he was going to start yelling. I couldn't let that happen."

"Damn it! I forgot to get my ears. Oh, well, there'll be others." Butler sounded dejected.

From the middle of the Mekong River, they could hear nothing except their own breathing and the occasional ripple of the water. With the moon, now in the western skies, and bright and plentiful stars, they could see each other. They continued to talk and joke, with Captain S taking the greatest number of the licks.

Finally, they could make out distinct features of the Navy ship which lay with its bow pointed west, upstream. Lights flooded the water outward for at least fifty meters. They could see big spotlights searching the darkness further out, two on the port side and one on the bow. They all knew more were working on the starboard side, and on the Stern.

Armstrong said, "Okay, time to do something. Does anybody know what frequency the 9th Division Tactical Operations Center, TOC, monitors?"

When no one answered, Joe spoke up, "Give me the mic., I'll wake Wheeler up." Joe changed the radio frequency and spoke into the Mic. "Course Jackal base, Course Jackal Base, this is Course Jackal Five, come in."

He repeated it four more times. Finally, Joe said, "Dammit, Wheeler! Quit dreaming about Baby San and answer the damn radio!"

After a short pause, they heard, "This is Course Jackal base, over."

"Base, this is important, so wake up. We need you to get in contact with TOC, the Tactical Operation Center. Can you, do it? Over."

"Five, you know I can. Over."

"Tell them to contact the big Navy ship sitting off Dong Tam, and let them know there are four, friendly swimmers in the water, with red and green lights approaching them from the west."

"Five, I copy four friendly swimmers in the water approaching the ship. Over."

"Roger."

"Five, are you drunk? Over."

"No, Six and I decided to go for a swim. We'll explain later. Contact the TOC, now, before we get too close, and they blow our ass off. Over."

"Five, I'll do it now. Over"

"Call me back when you get through to them. Five, out"

After a couple of minutes, the radio crackled, "Course Jackal Five, Base Over."

"This is Five. Give me good news. Over."

"Message relayed. They will manage it. Over."

"Thanks a lot Base. You can go back to sleep now. Five out"

"It looks as if your man came through for us." Butler sounded complementary.

"He's an outstanding young man, smart, honest, dedicated, and all the other accolades you can think of, and he will never receive appropriate credit, due him." Captain S sounded disgusted.

Noticing a tone of despair in Captain S's voice, Joe knew his thoughts were on Baby San, and he felt guilty. "Don't get sentimental. You--" Joe paused and decided to leave it there.

Armstrong filled in the silence. "When the message gets relayed to the Officer standing watch, we should see some activity on board."

They did not have to wait long. Now, no more than two hundred meters away from the ship, they were close enough to be looking up at it. The intensity of the lights seemed to quadruple. The ship flooded the water with visible light out near them. More spotlights flicked on and began to search the water. Within seconds, they were blinded by a big white beam of light and then another and another. They all waved, showing their arms.

"They heard a loudspeaker blare out, "Identify yourself!" Armstrong replied, "U.S. Navy SEAL's," knowing he could not be heard from this distance.

"Identify yourself!" Came another blare from the speaker.

With the knowledge of someone on the bridge watching them, with powerful enough lenses to see a pimple on their nose, Armstrong said, "Show your chest and dog tags. Show them our weapons." He repeated as loud as he could, "U.S. Navy SEAL. Team Two."

"Lieutenant, since EOD called this in, you better let them know we're here," Captain S' said.

"Identify yourself!" The speaker sounded again.

Still waving, Armstrong yelled, "SEAL Team Two and Army EOD." This time the speaker sounded, "Stand by!"

They were now close enough to the ship for the halo light to cover them. All the spotlights were now searching the water around them, as if looking for something.

Again, the speakers sounded, "Stand by!"

"Hold up, they don't want us any closer to the ship," Armstrong said.

After a couple minutes, they saw a John Boat dart around the stern of the ship headed their way.

Two armed men were pointing weapons directly at them and looking as if they were ready to shoot.

"Identify yourselves!" One of the armed men shouted, while shining bright handheld lights on their faces.

"Two Navy SEALS, two Army EOD!" Armstrong yelled.

One of the men yelled back, "What's in your bag?"

"Boots, radio and a few magazines of ammo. Take our weapons and I'll show you," Armstrong said, and nodded to Joe who started passing weapons to the John Boat.

After shining his light into the pack, one of the armed men laid his weapon down and said, "Come aboard, Lieutenant." He extended his hand to help Armstrong.

Once in the John Boat, Armstrong said, "Thank you Gunner." He helped Captain S aboard as another Gunner helped Butler and Joe.

A quick trip to the stern gave them the opportunity to put their boots on.

After climbing a ladder, they found themselves standing in front of, and saluting, a Navy Commander. "Permission to come aboard, Sir?" Armstrong asked for all of them.

"What are you dumb-asses doing approaching my ship like this?" The Commander growled at them after returning the salutes.

"Well, Sir, I can tell you we were out for a midnight swim. However, to be serious and honest, I decided I would rather negotiate with you than to fight Charlie with only three or four magazines of ammo." Armstrong remained standing at attention.

The Commander glanced at the Gunner, who nodded his head. "Come aboard men."

Looking at Armstrong and Captain S, he continued, "You two come with me. Gunner, take care of your guests."

After climbing more stairs following the Commander, Armstrong and Captain S were standing on the bridge. "You can wait here or find a seat. There's a small sitting room on the port side down the hall. It'll be more comfortable down there. I'll join you in a few minutes, after tying up a few things."

Recognizing the fact the Commander would prefer them to go to the waiting room, Armstrong and Captain S found it.

"I don't think we should sit on this leather furniture," Captain S told Armstrong.

"Our wet ass won't be the first or last on this faux leather Naugahyde vinyl." Armstrong sat down in an overstuffed chair.

Captain S found a glider and began to rock. "Nice."

"We'll have some coffee in here in a few minutes," The Commander said while walking into the waiting room.

"Thank you, Sir." Armstrong rose to his feet. Captain S followed suit.

"Sit down and relax." The Commander waved them down.

"This is a nice boat you have, Sir. I'm impressed." Captain S nodded and looked around.

The Commander glared at Captain S, "I'm glad you like it, Captain. Our Captain will be up soon, shortly after the sun rises. I'm sure he'll want to know, in detail, why you are here. Two Navy SEAL's and two Army EOD. The only connection I can see is alcohol."

Captain S asked, "Speaking of alcohol, is it too early for a scotch rather than coffee?"

Before the Commander could answer, Armstrong soke. "Sir, if possible, we'd like to catch a ride to Dong Tam with the first vessel going there. I need to get back to Bear Cat before noon."

"Lieutenant, you aren't going anywhere until the captain says you can. Unless you can convince me, you were in fact on a mission, rather than taking the midnight swim you spoke of."

After receiving coffee, Armstrong explained, into detail, what brought them to the commander's bridge.

"Your story sounds reasonable. As far as I can tell, neither of you, nor I suspect neither of your men, have been drinking. So, I guess I'll buy your story, and I'll relay it to the captain. You can take the first boat you wish into Dong Tam. Of course, I won't know for sure whether or not you have fed me a lot of BS, until I no longer see red flares over Dong Tam."

"Sir, it probably won't be tonight. If our rouse worked, certainly within three or four days, 10 o'clock Charlie will meet his fate."

Sipping on his coffee, Captain S said, "Sir, you didn't answer my question. Is it too early for a scotch?"

The Commander looked at Captain S and then at Armstrong. "Lieutenant, how well do you know this, Army Captain? First, he doesn't know the difference between a boat and a ship, and now he doesn't know it's way too early to have a scotch. He went to the Navy EOD school, so you aren't the only Navy personnel he's been around."

Turning back to Captain S, he said. "Yes, Captain, it's too early in the morning for Navy personnel to have a scotch. But it's not too late in the evening for Navy personnel to have a scotch. I'll fix you up with something good. Be back in a minute."

After the Commander left the room, Captain S said, "Wow, how about that?"

"Nice guy, and a good Officer, too." Armstrong commented.

The minute seemed short. The Commander returned with two glasses and a half full bottle with a blue label and set them on the coffee table.

"Wow, how nice? Two glasses? You're not joining us, Sir?"

"Lieutenant, I'm still on duty. You two men enjoy it. Finish the bottle if you wish. I have another. You've earned it, no matter if your mission was successful or not. Oh, yeah, if you need anything to eat, let me know." The Commander turned and walked out.

Captain S picked up the bottle and examined it. "I've never seen or heard of this. Johnnie Walker Blue Label! I've had my share of Johnnie Walker Red, and some Black Label. I know there's Green and Gold Labels. Does this fall between the Black and Gold?"

"Top-of-the-line, Buddy! Top-of-the-line! The only thing better stays on the farms in Scotland." Armstrong reached and poured two half-full glasses.

Captain S sipped on the scotch, leaned back, and rocked. "Self, take note. Leather chairs, exquisitely blended coffee, and the finest scotch money can buy. Hell, maybe I should have joined the Navy."

Captain S continued to sip and rock. "This surely beats eating SOS in the mess hall."

CHAPTER 37

Staff Sergeant Hébert's R&R to Hawaii began at Charlie Pad. Since he left incredibly early, Joe had told everyone goodbye the previous night. Dressed in his starched and pressed class B, khaki uniform, for the first time since he arrived in Vietnam, he boarded a Huey slick, a helicopter without weapons, on his way to Tan Son Nhut. There, at the R&R center, he attended a short briefing on do and don't do, while in Hawaii, and changed his MPC's into green US dollars. After two hours of waiting, he boarded a large aluminum freedom bird, a chartered World Airlines jetliner taking him to see the most beautiful woman on earth.

A minute later the flight attendant gave their safety lecture about the use of oxygen masks, flotation devices, and proper escape procedures. After reaching a cruising altitude, the captain welcomed the passengers aboard and told them there would be a layover in Guam.

Joe leaned as far back into the seat as he could. Trying to keep his mind off Ava, he tried to remember what he could about Guam, the largest and southernmost island of the Mariana Islands, and an US territory, whose people are non-voting citizens. The US had taken control of the islands in 1898, during the Spanish American war. However, Japan attacked and invaded the island on December 8, 1941, one day after Pearl Harbor. After they occupied the island, subjected the local population to incarcerations, slavery, rapes, and executions. The US forces returned in July 1944 and killed an estimated eighteen thousand Japanese soldiers. Less than five hundred soldiers surrendered to the allies. There were reports of Japanese soldiers still in hiding on the island. At one time in the past, only military personnel with security clearances could visit the island.

On the approach to Guam, Joe realized the smallness of the island, not small like Wake Island, but at ten thousand feet he estimated the island to be about thirty by thirteen miles.

The stopover took two hours as promised. This allowed a brief time to visit the terminal, where Joe thought he may be able to find a gift for Ava. However, the terminal appeared to be new and was not well stocked. Joe decided; Ava would have to settle for him.

Descending into Honolulu Joe could clearly see Diamond Head, Waikiki Beach, and Pearl Harbor.

The USS Arizona's crew members, who were killed in the attack on Pearl Harbor by Japanese planes on December 7, 1941, were entombed there.

Joe thought about the beauty of Hawaii and remembered he had been here a short seven months ago. There had been so many changes since then. Nixon was now in office and will soon reveal his secret plan for Vietnam. The antiwar movement had ballooned, and the war itself had gone nowhere. The more VC they killed, the more appeared.

When the wheels of the plane touched down, Joe suddenly became aware of his own body odor. Although he did not have a manly beard, it had been a long time since he showered and shaved.

As the passengers were primarily Officers and Senior NCOs visiting their wives, Joe concluded, incorrectly, the seats in the rear of the plane, where he sat, were assigned to lower ranked soldiers.

His anticipation of exiting the plane and seeing Ava waiting on him caused his adrenaline to flow. It seemed as if he had to wait for two hundred people to exit before him.

In the terminal, he saw dozens of men in the arms of their loved ones. He frantically searched the crowd and, finally, found Ava on his left. She had spotted him at the same instant. She was dressed in all white, with a sun hat and shades, and her hair down just below her shoulders. She held a lei in her hands. She quickly placed it around Joe's neck. "Aloha."

The long and tight embrace resulted in tears flowing from both of their eyes. "Aloha, Baby." He lifted her and spinning her around.

"Oh, God, thank you." She softly prayed, followed by a long enthusiastic kiss.

"Wow, you are well worth the long flight." Joe sighed with pleasure.

"No, hardly. Later, I will show you what a long flight is worth," Ava kissed him again.

"How long have you been waiting?"

Ava coyly said, "Since August. However, I flew in yesterday. I wanted to make sure I got here on time. We can grab your bags and get out of here."

"I don't have any bags other than this carry-on. It's a shaving kit and a couple pairs of underwear."

"I see you came prepared for a week in Hawaii!"

"It's all I have. I have no civilian clothes. As you remember, I left Fort Ben in a hurry and didn't think I would need civilian clothes in Vietnam. I guess, if necessary, I could pick up a pair of Bermuda shorts and a bathing suit." Joe winked at her.

"I cannot imagine you thinking, you do not need clothes for a week." Ava said coyly.

"Well, I've never been accused of being Einstein. Let's go. We can catch a bus over to the R&R hotel." Keeping an arm around her, they turned to leave.

"No, I have a rental car. You can help me with the road signs."

Wanting to get a good look at her, Joe suddenly stopped. "Wait a minute." He lifted her sun hat and her shades. "Oh, what is this?"

Ava slapped his hand away. "It is nothing. Remember, I told you I work out every night. I just caught an elbow."

"I thought it may be from last August. What aren't you telling me?"

"Nothing. Let's walk. I am taking judo lessons. I am learning how to fight. If you are not good to me, I will kick your ass."

"Are you serious? The eye looks bad." They continued to walk.

"I am serious. And it is not bad. I have had worse. After the beating I took, I decided, no man will ever do it again. I have been working out five nights a week for almost four months. My body is finally getting in shape for a real confrontation. I bet I can do more pushups than you can. I am in the best physical condition of my life. And remember, I was a rather good athlete for many years. Can you tell the difference in my muscle tone?"

"I, I don't know what to say, except congratulations. But how did you get the black eye?"

"I told you. I took an elbow during a fight." Ava shrugged and passed it off as no big deal.

"A fight!" Joe almost shouted.

"Yes, a fight. Not a street-brawl, but in training. You do not learn to fight without fighting. And I am getting pretty good, so my instructor tells me." Ava beamed with pride.

"Again, I don't know what to say, except it worries me. But even with a black eye and shorter hair, you're still extremely beautiful.

"What's going on with the hair. You should know the eleventh commandment states, 'Blonds shall not wear their hair short. "Joe put his arm around Ava and they continued to walk to the car.

During the drive to their hotel, they discussed everything they had been doing over the past seven months. In fear of giving her something to worry about his safety, he exercised extreme caution in what he told Ava. And of course, he never mentioned Lein. Ava, on the other hand, elaborated on everything, part of things she had written about earlier. She did have real news for Joe.

"It looks as if my divorce will be finalized by the middle of June. He is not contesting the divorce and is willing to pay me four hundred dollars per month. I do not need the money or want it, but I will take it for a while, spitefully to punish him."

"I guess, I agree. As a single woman, what will you do?" Joe squeezed her thigh in concern. He had placed his hand there as soon as they got in the car.

"We will see." Ava glanced at Joe and smiled.

Joe asks, "Do you know where we're going?"

"Do you mean right now or in the future?" Ava glanced over at Joe.

"Well, both." Joe's expression changed.

"We will worry about the future later. We do not have to think about it now. There will be time for thinking later. This trip is about you and me, this week, this moment of our life. As for as the directions to Fort DeRussy, I am trying to get there as fast as I can. Do you want me to drive slower?" Ava teased.

Joe quickly replied. "No, oh no! You are doing fine. Did you stay at our hotel, the Hale Koa, last night?"

"I stayed at the Royal Hawaiian. It is commonly known as the Pink Palace. Can you believe it is painted pink? It is absolutely a classic and charming hotel. Someone mentioned to me, Sheraton is in the process of purchasing it."

"The way you light up, talking about the Pink Palace, it almost sounds magical. I know nothing about the Hale Koa, except it's cheap when compared to other hotels on Waikiki Beach. I would bet it's nowhere near as enchanting as your Pink Palace. After all, the Hale Koa is part of Fort DeRussy, or in other words, parts of the Army. When the Army bought the seventy-two acres, which encompasses Fort DeRussy, from a wealthy chainman, it had been advertised as undesirable land. No matter, it'll beat my bunk and will give us clean sheets every day."

*****

Joe had stayed in better hotels. However, the Hale Koa could not be described a hell hole, but it looked run down, well used, and in need of a face lift. Of course, as they say in real estate, it had location, location, location. The hotel set right on Waikiki Beach, with its beautiful sand and the blue Pacific Ocean.

Their dim room provided almost no charm nor, of course, a view of the beach, as other rooms did. It did, however, provide two necessities, a bathtub, and a nice bed. They soon put both to use.

It had been about twenty-four hours since Joe climbed out of bed at Dong Tam. The over five-hour flight from Saigon, Tan Son Nhut, to Guam, and the nine-hour flight from Guam to Hawaii covered over seven thousand miles and one extremely short night. After their bath and having tender sex, both were overcome with restful sleep.

When Joe awoke, Ava still lay beside him, with her big blue eyes wide open. He compared her silky white skin to his dark, sun-dried skin. He looked much darker now than when they lay together the last time. And, yes, he could tell a difference in her muscle definition. The window, which had offered a view of buildings in Honolulu, now appeared dark, except for the night lights. "How long have I been out?"

"We have been here for almost five hours," Ava said without moving.

"I'm sorry, but you pleased me, and I fell asleep. You know, if I get any darker, people will think you are with a Mexican, or a light-colored Black man." Joe looked at his arm and sighed.

"It is all right. The color of your skin means nothing to me. It is the color of your heart and your brain, to which, I am particularly interested. This, my dear lover, is why I am laying in your arms. As you say, you may not be Einstein, but you are no dummy either. Also, you are honest and caring. Stay the same. But now it's time to get up and get something to eat. I worked up with an appetite."

"Yeah, finding something to eat sounds good to me. As long as we come up with something with a bone in it, I could care less what we eat."

"We can see if we can find a rib-eye with bone-in." Ava sounded considerate.

"Sounds great!" Joe jumping up quickly. He donned his wrinkled and stinking uniform. "I think I'd better find some more clothes before you trade me in for a Polynesian."

"Don't worry about it. Although, you do smell like some of those Big Boys."

Lifting his arms to expose the armpits of his khaki shirt, Joe said, "Spray some of your Chloe perfume on me. I'd rather smell like you than them."

They walked Kalakaua Street where Joe found two pairs of Bermuda shorts, a bathing suit, a pair of flip-flops, and a T-shirt with a Diamond Head logo. He changed into his new attire and carried his uniform and shoes in a bag provided by the store.

They found no suitable steakhouse but quickly decided on pizza which satisfied Joe. Pizza did not appear on the menu in Master Sergeant White's mess hall. After walking for approximately a half mile, they decided to return to their room where they spent the night in each other's arms. Joe enjoyed becoming acquainted with Ava's new muscle tone.

Joe woke up first. When Ava finally opened her eyes, he said, "I've been waiting for this moment for two years. And you are everything I thought you would be."

"What are you talking about?" Ava rubbed her eyes.

"This is the first time I've awakened next to you after a full night, and a satisfying one, in bed with you. In other words, it's the first time, we have ever spent the night together. I pray there will be a lifetime of them." Joe whispered the words.

"We will see, but now we have places to go, and things to do." Ava quickly got up.

By noon they were on the beach. Joe, unsuccessfully, tried to ride a surfboard on waves which he thought were no larger than those found on the beaches at Pensacola, Florida. He became sure the Hawaiian sand did not favorably compare with Florida's. After a couple of minutes, Ava decided she wanted no part of the sand and sun the beach offered. Her white skin preferred a recliner in the shade, provided by an umbrella. After reclining for a while, she finally, seductively, told Joe, "You look like a little boy playing in a big, salty pool. If you would like to play like a grown-up man, you could follow me upstairs."

Later in the day, after playing with Ava, Joe took his dirty uniform to the hotel cleaners to be washed and pressed. He and Ava then checked the tours and activities offered by the R&R center. Since Ava had a rental car, they decided they would forget the tours and do their own sightseeing. They did, however, sign up for the luau scheduled for the night before Joe leaves.

Ava wanted to show Joe the beauty of the Pink Palace. So, they walked through it, acting like they were guests, and strolled the beautiful garden, stopping to smell the flowering plumeria trees.

Afterwards, they again walked the streets around Waikiki Beach. Joe ate pint of ice cream and two hamburgers. He bought Ava a muumuu, which matched her sky-blue eyes, and an orchid for her hair. Ava bought Joe another pair of Bermuda shorts, with matching Hawaiian style shirts, and a puka shell necklace, one like the necklaces worn by virtually every male they had seen during their walk.

The next morning, they chose to visit Diamond Head. Upon arrival they learned it did not receive its new name until the early eighteen hundreds, when sailors mistook worthless crystals in the lava rocks for diamonds. The Diamond Head moniker had virtually unseated its original name, Mount Leah. They were surprised about its altitude, less than eight hundred feet. It looked taller from

Waikiki's shores. Since their shoes were not suitable for hiking, they decided not to walk one the adventure trails offered by the park. Perhaps, they had a subliminal agenda. They both wanted to get back to the hotel for a nap and a late evening swim in the pool.

The next day Joe and Ava drove out of Honolulu area on Route 72, Alanianaole Highway, the main route to drive around Oahu. With Diamond Head in the rear, they were looking for the He'eia Kea Blowhole, which had been recommended to them by personnel at the hotel. They found the sign to a small parking lot, which allowed for only four or five cars.

After walking to a handrail, with signs posted prohibiting going father, they were at once sprayed with salty water. Joe stood behind Ava with his arms wrapped around her and enjoyed every wave which washed ashore. The waves crashed into the lava rocks and flowed through tubes which were created thousands of years earlier when molten lava cooled, when it reached the ocean. Water sprayed like a geyser through the Blowhole, as high as ten yards. The ocean breeze pushed the spray into their faces. Joe pointed to a small sandy beach to their right and said, "They filmed Burt Lancaster and Deborah Carr making love in the movie, *From Here to Eternity'* over there.

"Am I supposed to know what you are talking about?" Ava glanced up at Joe.

"No, I guess not. The movie was about the start of World War II when the Japanese attacked Pearl Harbor. It was a big hit. Surely you know who Burt Lancaster is. Anyway, thinking about it--"

"Do not get any ideas. I am not making love with you on that beach." Ava interrupted Joe.

"Okay, our bed will be fine. Look on the horizon. Can you see another island?" Joe pointed to the horizon.

"Yes, barely. Why?"

"I bet it's Molokai, something like twenty to twenty-five miles away."

"If you say so, but I bet there is a nice beach over there as well." She smiled.

"I'm sure there is, but you can't swim over there. As I said, our bed will be fine. Let's go. We have a long drive." Joe nudged her toward their car.

They drove north and northwest keeping close to the beaches. The road turned into Highway 83. Shortly the road turned westerly. They drove slowly, looking at the beautiful scenery, stopping briefly for a pleasant view of the distinctly small, rocky, enchanted offshore islands. They continued southwest until they found a large gathering of people surfing. They decided to stop and watch. Joe imagined himself riding a surfboard. He thought with his athletic and agility abilities; he could conquer the big waves. "Come on, Ava, let's walk down to the water's edge."

Ava stopped well short of where the waves were ebbing and flowing, but Joe continued and chased the ebbing water out, until the waves rose to about eight feet and reversed direction. Joe would then retreat from the flow. After doing this a couple of minutes, he watched a wave rise above him. "Oh, hell!" He shouted and ran as quickly as he could to escape.

After reaching Ava, Joe excitedly and exhausted said, "Did you see the monstrous wave? It had to be at least fifteen feet, probably closer to eighteen feet. Hell, it looked like a large goliath!"

"I saw you and the expression on your face, and I could not keep from laughing! I never feared for your safety." She bent over still in laughter.

"The wave challenged my manhood, and I lost, badly!" Joe also laughed.

"Well, my brave darling, I'm proud of you. You did fine with those three-foot waves yesterday." Ava continued rubbing it in.

"Come on, we'll go to the Pool. I'll challenge the three-foot diving board," Joe proudly announced.

They turned south past North Shore and soon found Rout 99, which they followed back into Honolulu.

After a quick dip in the pool and watching the fading sunset from the recliners on the beach. They walked to a restaurant nearby, which had been recommended, and ate Mahimahi fish for dinner. Joe drank beer and Ava had, as she called it, a sorry Sonoma Valley, Chardonnay. Later, they retired to their room.

The next morning, after confirming Don Ho's impending appearance, they made reservation for Kane'ohe Honey's. Neither wanted to go anywhere but decided to visit the Dole pineapple plantation. Ava appeared more pleased with the outing than Joe. For the first time in her life, she saw banana and papaya trees. Joe appeared to be amazed by the prickly pineapple plants, and how they were harvested. He told Ava, "They should bring the local criminals from jail out here to cut the pineapples. I would rather live in New York City than go down a row of pineapple plants. I don't see how the Kamaainas do this. It has to be painful."

After sampling the fresh pineapple, they returned to their hotel by the middle of the afternoon, giving them enough time to rest, or not.

That evening Ava looked exceptionally beautiful in her new muumuu. It accented her magnificent figure and blue eyes. Every man at Kaneohe Honey's seemed to take a second look at her. Joe wore his new Hawaiian shirt and shorts with flip-flops. They both ordered bone in steaks, marinated in teriyaki.

Joe convinced Ava, who always drank wine, to try a Mai Tai. After completing their meal, Ava ordered her third Mai Tai, and the entertainment began. Everybody joined in singing Tiny Bubbles which was number eight on the charts. Later all service members and their wives were recognized, with special honor given to one couple who were at Pearl Harbor on December 7, 1941.

After a couple of sing-a-longs, Ava pleaded, "Joe, would you order me another drink, while I go to the ladies room?"

When she returned from the restroom, Joe asked, "Is this your fourth or fifth? You are already a little loquacious."

"I do not know how many. I like them, and this is drinking music. It makes me want to move my body. If I get drunk, I have a big brave and strong man to take care of me."

"And if I get drunk, will you take care of me?" Joe teased.

"Yes, I will. If someone touches you, I'll break their collarbone and claw their eyes out," Ava retorted and offered a toast to Joe.

They moved their chairs together so they could touch each other and rock with the melodies and laid-back style and the sounds of the strumming ukuleles, occasionally hugging and kissing.

Near the end of the performance, they sang "I'll Remember You". Joe and Ava were standing, like nearly all of the couples present, holding each other closely and singing. The words in the song, 'to your arms someday, I'll return to stay till then, I will remember you,' seemed to be heartwarming to every couple that were holding their loved one.

When Joe woke up the next morning, he knew, at once, he would pay, and pay dearly today, for the delightful and merriment time of the previous evening. His weak stomach and dizzy head screamed, Mai Tai's revenge. As he headed for the bathroom, he looked back at Ava who still lay motionless in the bed.

After a quick shower, which helped his feelings, he returned to the bedroom where Ava had begun moving. "Why did you let me get drunk?" Ava groaned.

"Me, why me?" Joe innocently asked Ava, even though he knew exactly what she meant.

"Oh, I feel terrible. You got me drunk." She moaned, as she rose up and wiped her eyes.

I got you drunk! I thought you got me drunk." Joe moved to her side and kissed her forehead.

"What time is it?" Ava whined.

"It's time for you to get out of bed, if you can. I'll find some coffee and tea while you shower. Do you want anything else to eat or drink?" Joe stood and began dressing.

"No. And, unless I start feeling better soon, we are not going to Pearl Harbor. I am staying here, in bed. Mark this down. I am never drinking again!"

With the way Ava looked, Joe knew they were not going to Pearl Harbor. He thought how pleasing it would be to lie in bed all day with her. However, Joe had looked forward to seeing Pearl Harbor and paying final respects to the resting place of the sailors of the USS Arizona who gave their lives for their country. He had heard the almost unbelievable story about the USS Arizonan's anchor, which weighed over nineteen thousand pounds, being tossed over one hundred yards away by the explosion ripping her apart. As someone who knew about explosives, this amazing incident perked his interest.

While getting coffee and fruit bowls, Joe picked up his clean uniform. He would need it tomorrow. The last day of his R&R, and the last day he would see Ava for five months. This day will be extremely hard on both.

After spending the afternoon under the umbrellas on the beach and taking short dips in the pool, Joe and Ava began to feel as if they were returning to the living. Their strength, heads, and stomachs were better. Both were finally able to smile and continue a conversation, albeit a somber tone.

"Tomorrow at this time, you'll be flying east at five hundred miles per hour. I'll be flying west at five hundred miles per hour. We'll be separating at one thousand miles per hour. Now, the thought of that is extremely depressing to me," Joe spoke to Ava, as they sat in adjacent recliners, holding hands and looking at the beautiful Waikiki Beach and Pacific Ocean.

"I know. How I know! You will be going back to war, and I will be going back to my apartment. Both of us will be waiting on our future, our destiny." Ava did not look at Joe. She simply kept looking at the ocean.

'Waiting on our future, you said? During the last few days, I have mentioned the future to you, on at least two occasions. You merely cast the thought aside and said, 'We will see'. So, can we now talk about the future?" Joe seemed lugubrious.

After a long pause, Ava replied. "You described our future as moving a thousand miles per hour in opposite directions. Joe, I love you, but after tomorrow, I will not allow myself to think about our future. I will think only one day at the time and pray every night, we have another day to look forward to." Ava looked and sounded mournful.

"I think I know what you mean."

"No, you do not! Joe, you are in a war zone. I watch TV and read everything I can find about the war. I have an appreciation of what you face, day in and day out. You write to me nearly every day. When I read your letters, I can see, you are not telling me anything. When you tell me nothing, you are telling me something. You do not want me to know what you are doing. The reason for the lack of information concerns me. I will not ask." Now, Ava stared hard at Joe.

"I don't--"

"No, let me finish. I know you are not sitting in a safe office somewhere. I know what your job in EOD entails. I cannot allow myself to think of a future with you, until you are back home safely in my arms. It will be in August. There is also the matter of my divorce. I will wait for you, and we will discuss our future at the right time."

Joe sincerely stated, "As usual, you read me like a book. You're correct. I don't tell you about my day-to-day activities. As you know, some of what I do is dangerous, and I don't want you to worry about me."

"My heart tells me one thing, and my brain tells me another. I do not know which to listen to." Ava shook her head and tried to fight the tears back.

"Ava, I believe our heart, brain, and our soul whisper different things to us. The soul whispers softly, while the heart and brain sometimes shout at us. These three voices, coming from within us, are influenced by our five senses. They guide us through life. My heart and soul want to be with you, but my brain is telling me, I had better be on the plane at 1000 hundred hours tomorrow morning. After August, I pray we shall never again have to worry about our future or destiny." Joe leaned over and kissed her on the cheek, while squeezing her hand tightly.

"I hate to think about tomorrow, but I am looking forward to August." Ava totally lost her fight with tears.

"I know our courtship has been formidable, but I take your comment as a positive, meaning, I shouldn't worry about you rolling around on a mat with your judo instructor? Let's take a nap and get ready for a luau." Joe tried to cheer her up.

*****

When they entered the luau, a crowd had already gathered. Like Joe and Ava, the men were wearing colorful shirts with leis around their necks, while the ladies were wearing muumuu's and had orchids in their hair.

The performers were warming up by twirling and tossing flaming batons. Two tables, about forty feet long, were set up parallel to each other. They were covered with white cloths, palm fronds, and diverse types of colorful flowers. After finding a seat, they enjoyed the festivities. "

I see you can't keep your eyes off the pretty hula dancer." Ava grinned.

"Guilty as charged. I'm blameworthy. The one on the end is beautiful, and she certainly can move her hips."

"It's okay. You can keep watching her. I like the muscular Polynesian men who are wearing nothing but colorful towels and doing their Haka war dance, while whirling flaming spears, and fire knives. Do you think you can do the Haka?" Ava teased Joe.

"Wear a colorful towel? Yes! Everything else? No! I wouldn't try, but you surely would look good in one of those grass skirts." Joe smiled and put his arms around her.

A pig, which had been wrapped in banana leaves, roasting in a hole in the ground on hot coals, lifted by two of the Polynesian men, and prepared for dinner, lay on one of the tables.

Other items on the menu were fresh pineapple and papaya, sweet potatoes, banana fritters, fried rice, and poi. Dessert consisted of coconut cake and haupia pudding. A pay-as-you-go bar, available for exotic drinks, stood on one side.

After sampling the menu, Joe asked, "What do you think about this kind of party, Baby?" He swept his arms around.

"Everything is beautiful, and the food is delicious. What do you think, and have you ever seen anything like this?"

"It's nice. Except for the poi, the food is good. Poi should be called pukey. And I've been to a hundred gatherings like this."

"How is that possible? You said you've never been to Hawaii before except for the short on your way to Vietnam." Ava looked perplexed at him.

"No, but this luau is nothing more than a Fais-do-do, or a Cochan De Lait Festival down on the Bayou. Things are different, yet essentially the same. We'd have a pit with a fire for a suckling pig on a rotisserie. We'd have a little Boudin, Andouille sausages, and whatever wild game is available. Of course, we'd have rice and some vegetable dishes. For dessert we'd have rice or bread pudding and maybe beignets. Now, the music will be zydeco, with a fiddle and accordion. And everybody would be dancing.

"When I get home, we'll go to the Bayou and find a Fais-do-do to attend. On top of this, I'll give my *jeune fille* a Magnolia blossom for your hair and take you for a ride in my old pirogue."

The next morning, the goodbyes were hard. Joe had to be at the gate by no later than 0900 hours. Ava had to return her rental car and be prepared for an 11 o'clock departure. With a long layover in San Francisco, her flight to Atlanta, and her drive to Fort Benning, it would be a longtime before she reached her apartment.

After a long embrace, with teary eyes Ava said, "You take care. I will see you in August, but I will be with you for every step you make until then. I will send you my phone number where you can call me, the instant you arrive in the States."

"I'll do it, and you take care of yourself. As we previously sang, remember always, I'll remember you, always. I love you and Dieu te Beni, God bless you." Joe said and walked away.

Glancing over his shoulder for one last look, Ava looked like a small, whipped child, as she blew him a kiss.

CHAPTER 38

The pouring rain did not resemble the typical wet seasonal day of drizzling rain.

Captain S and Joe stood at Charlie Pad, waiting on their chopper to take them close to Rach Gia, almost to the Gulf of Thailand, into the wide stretch of marshland zigzagging southwest of Can Tho to the notorious and legendary U Minh Forest. Bandits, Pirates, and smugglers had occupied this area for centuries. Of late hundreds, if not thousands, of VC controlled the area and used it as a sanctuary for training their personnel, for storage of giant quantities of food, medical supplies, ammunition, and other necessities of war. It spans a thousand square kilometers and held the largest mangrove forest in the world, outside of the Amazon basin. The Americans were still in a giant defoliation effort, using Agent Orange, to better gain visibility of the enemy.

During the 1968 Tet offensive, roughly thirteen months earlier, massive, and brazen guerrilla attacks occurred throughout the Delta. Part of the sixteen thousand VC and NVA who were killed, in World War ll type of street fighting in the Delta, were believed to have come from the U Minh Forest.

When the call came in a brief time after breakfast, it simply reported a down helicopter in a rice field. The kicker, it had been there overnight, and the rice paddy had little to no reliable security. This presented a scenario to which the 9th Division rarely applied its EOD assets.

Although they had a rather rough flight to Can Tho, the Huey plowed through the torrential rain like the warrior it was. Sitting totally drenched in the open helicopter with the wind blowing, Joe was freezing. He thought, this was the coldest he had been since leaving Germany. Specifically, the coldest he had been since the day he pushed Ava out of the helicopter. At least, then, he wore dry clothes which prepared him for the occasion.

Captain S and Joe were not told about the stop at Can Tho, but neither were surprised when they recognized the familiar airport where they were about to land. Once on the ground, a young

Specialist approached Captain S and said, "Captain, would you like to come inside for a few minutes? They're going to refuel, so it'll be a while."

"Sure, we will. A dry place might feel good." He and Joe followed the Specialist and were met by Major Cash, the 9th Aviation Battalion Executive Officer (XO). After the introductions and finding a seat in a small office and a cup of coffee, Major Cash said, "Let me brief you on the situation we find ourselves in."

Captain S said, "That sounds good to me. So, what's going on, Sir?"

"Yesterday, we were moving some troops into a staging area here." Major Cash pointed to a spot on a wall map west of Ca Mau, near the borders of An Gian and Ca Mau Providence, and only a few kilometers east of the gulf of Thailand. "On our way back, one of our choppers had some mechanical problems. The cowboy, the piolet, set her down here, about five kilometers from the staging area. The two gunners removed the M-60 machine guns, and we extracted the crew. Before you ask, the nearest US troops are five kilometers away. Some ARVN troops are in the area, but we don't know their exact locations."

"Sir, are there any other armament on board, such as rocket pods, that we should be looking for? Captain S politely asked.

No, none we know about." Cash shook his head.

"So, what do you want us to do, Sir?" Joe spoke up before Captain S could.

"We want to lift her out of there. Before we do, we'd like you to check her for booby-traps.

Once you clear her, we can hook up to a Chinook and bring her home. A couple of riggers with a radio will accompany you." Major cash explained the plan.

"Given an unguarded, nice shiny Huey, sitting in the middle of a rice paddy in VC country, I wonder, what are the odds that Charlie hasn't checked it out and left us some presents?" Joe scoffed.

"This is why you're here Staff Sergeant," Major Cash pointed out.

"Yes, Sir. That's why we make the big bucks, a dollar and eighty-three cents per day extra for hazardous duty pay. We clean up other people's messes." Captain S also sounded sarcastic about the situation.

"We're sending a Cobra to help with security. We'll drop you and the riggers as close to the Huey as possible. The Cobra and your Huey will patrol the tree line while you do your thing. You'll have two gunships above you. We'll hold the Chinook three or four minutes out. Any questions?" Major Cash looked at both.

"No, Sir. I Can't think of anything. How about you, Staff Sergeant Hébert? "Captain S asked.

"Sorry, Major, I can't leave here without knowing something. Are you related to Johnny?" Joe asked, with a straight face.

"I get it from everybody." Major Cash rolled his eyes and shook his head. "I do not know him, but I was always told; we share the same late great-grandfather. Like him, I can't carry a tune in a bucket. Although, I must admit, he makes nice music. Now, have another cup of coffee. Your pony will soon be ready."

Once in the air, they covered the roughly fifty miles southwest quickly. At first, neither Captain S nor Joe could see the downed chopper. They did, however, see the Cobra which had joined them.

On the second circle around the rice field, this time close over the tree line, the downed helicopter became obvious. As advertised, it set in the middle of a flooded field about three hundred meters from the closest line of trees. Their helicopter suddenly turned sharply, and within seconds they hovered two feet above the water and a hundred feet from the downed chopper. It took less than a minute for Captain S, Joe, and the two rigors, each carrying straps for the rigging, to be standing in water about ten inches deep in the paddy. The crippled helicopter sat, in the misty rain, about sixty away.

The departure of their ride caused a sudden silence. It became almost deafening. A quick look around the area revealed nothing, but the downed chopper and a green haze. The haze came from a heavy cloudlike mist, the green from the horizon, and the young rice protruding out of the water as far as they could see.

Talking to the riggers, Captain S said, "You two stay here and get as low as you can. There may be snipers in the tree line. Staff

Sergeant Hébert and I will search the chopper and the area around it. Later, you can move in and hook your slings to the chopper."

"The way I see it, the only thing we can do is feel for trip lines and hope we don't find anything, especially, a pressure plate on an explosive item. Anyway, we need to feel around to see if there has been any recent digging." Joe looked at Captain S for his thoughts.

"I guess so. We need to work all the way around the chopper ten feet out," Captain S added.

"I'll lead the way." Joe announced and rolled his sleeves up as far as possible. He bent over and began feeling his way toward the downed chopper. After a couple of minutes, he rose and spoke. "This is an Officer's plan. There's no way I can distinguish between rice and a trip line. Besides, we can see well enough to figure out if anybody has mashed the rice down, I see no evidence of footprints. What do you think?"

"I think you devised the plan. You are leading, and I'm at least ten feet behind you." Captain S smirked.

"I read you loud and clear, Sir. Let the fool take all the chances." Joe joked.

"You know I have never thought of you as a fool. But you also know there is such a thing as RHIP. You know, rank has its privileges. Also, you did volunteer to go first."

"Okay. So, you still let me take all the chances."

The sound of a spat, spat got their attention, and then came the delayed sound of two shots from the tree line. They knelt, and then they saw the two circular ripples forming about fifty feet away. The only thing to be seen of the two riggers, were their heads, weapons, and the radio. Then came the sound of more shots from the tree line, this time, apparently, not directed toward them. Of course, the Cobra and Huey were on the wrong side of the rice field.

"The dude can't shoot worth a crap!" Joe scoffed.

"Yeah, but he could get lucky." Captain S replied.

"I think we need to work faster. We don't need to be here too long. Charlie will soon be all over the tree line." Joe nodded toward the tree line.

"I agree, Tonto."

Before they reached the chopper, they noticed obvious disturbance in the rice. "That should be caused from the crew leaving the area, yesterday." Joe replayed the prior day's event per Major Cash in his head.

"Look, lying in the chopper. I see a belt of 7.62-ammunition. If the VC were here, they would've taken it," Captain S pointed out.

"However--" Joe knew there could be more to this picture.

Captain S cut in, "However, it may be bait. You check around the chopper, and I'll check inside."

More shots and an explosion, most likely a grenade, were heard from the tree line. This time they were further away from them. Joe worked around the chopper, looking for any signs showing Charlie had been there. He found nothing to worry about.

Captain S climbed into the chopper and reported. "I found more ammunition and a homemade knife lying in the pilot seat. What that says, I don't know."

More gunshots from the nearby tree line were heard. Captain S continued, "Tonto, I think we better get our ass out of here. I don't believe Charlie has touched her."

"I agree. This place is going to be like a target range before long."

Joe guessed about the situation.

"You two come over here and hook her up! Call whoever you need to and get the Chinook in here!" Captain S yelled at the riggers.

The riggers complied, and within minutes they had straps attached to the downed chopper.

The sound and sight of the Chinook were welcomed.

More shots came from the tree line, this time directed at them. Green tracers were seen headed upward toward the Huey. Within seconds, the Cobra's mini guns fired into the tree line. It resembled a water hose squirting fire.

When the Chinook hovered overhead, the prop wash seemed like a torrential storm. Captain S and the two riggers were standing on one side of the downed chopper, with Joe standing on the other side. The roaring Chinook lowered its cables with a hook, and the riggers connected their straps.

As the Chinook began to slowly rise, and the chopper's skids came out of the water, Joe saw it. Time seemed to almost freeze. A monofilament line was laying over the skid. Suddenly his body was bolted with a shot of adrenaline. Joe noticed his heart first. It pounded hard and then skipped a beat. His brain raced. *Damn, it's over! I made my one and only allotted mistake! There is probably a five-hundred-pound bomb under there. I screwed up, and it's going to cost some good people their lives. And what about Ava.* Joe couldn't move. He watched the skid rise, inches by torturous inch.

Regardless of the prop wash, joe could see water flowing off the skids, and large drops of water rolling down the monofilament line, a couple of inches apart. To Joe they looked as large as a baseball. As the skids rose to chest high on him, Joe stepped back expecting the flash at any moment. Rather than a flash, the end of the fishing line quickly flipped harmlessly over the skid, striking Joe's face.

Suddenly, Joe had no strength in his legs. They buckled and he hit the water, butt first.

The noise of the Chinook roared in his ears, and the prop continued to rake him with water. A sudden darkness beset him.

"Are you alright?" Captain S yelled, now standing over Joe. "Tonto! Hey, you! Okay, come on man. What's going on?"

With the defining roar of the Chinook gone, Joe looked up to find Captain S's face, and managed to say, "Woe, I thought I reached the end of the tunnel, but I found no light."

"What happened to you, man? Let me help you." Captain S offered Joe his hand.

Rather than standing, Joe leaned forward on his knees. He pushed gently on Captain S's leg to get him out of the way and began moving his hands back and forth in the water in front of him.

Captain S asked, "What are you looking for?"

Joe continued to search and finally found it. "This! This lay over the skid when it came out of the water. I thought--"

"Ooh, we dodged a bullet!" Captain S realized what had shaken Joe so badly.

"It was the closest to passing out that I've ever experienced. I was knocked out once in a high school football game. There's no comparison. I'll take being knocked out anytime over this weakness. I lost everything, but my brain. It kept working, exponentially. I'm surprised I haven't pissed or capped on myself," Joe babbled and patted his shoulder where his imaginary angle sat. *Thank you.*

"Are you all right, now?" Captain S saw color returning to Joe's face.

One of the riggers extended his hand and helped Joe to his feet. Once standing solidly on his feet, Joe nodded. "I'm okay, Sir."

"Good, here comes our pony. We should be back at the unit in a couple of hours, time enough for a couple of scotches." As a sign of support, Captain S patted Joe on the back.

The flight back to Dong Tam, included a short stop, to pick up two NCOs and another captain, did not appear to take a long time. At Charlie Pad, the sun, now bright and lay deep in the western skies. It seemed extremely hot and humid. Puddles of water were the only reminders of the morning downpour, only hours before.

Seeing an extra Jeep with EOD markings parked outside the office building, Joe sighed. "It looks as if Jackson and Redding are here."

"Yeah, I see. I hope nothing is wrong. They're seldom here this time of the week."

We'll soon find out," Joe quipped and stepped out of the Jeep.

Walking into the office, they found Jackson sitting behind Captain S's desk, and Redding behind Wheeler's talking with Scott. Captain S asked, "What's going on?"

"Nothing special, Sir," replied Jackson, who stood and moved to allow Captain S to occupy his desk. "We picked up three 120-mm mortars a short distance north of My Tho and decided to bring them down here and put them in our dud Conex container."

"Okay, you two going to stick around tonight?" Captain S looked at Jackson and Redding.

"We thought we would, but Master Sergeant Scott told us you were getting hit unusually hard every night. Maybe we should go back to Tan An."

Joe surmised, "It's part of Charlie's fizzled out Tet Offense for this year. Throwing a few extra mortars at us is the best they can do."

Scott jumped into the conversation. "A few mortars! Hell, I'd call it more than a few every night. They are falling everywhere, not only on Charlie Pad. They're trying to demoralize our troops. Besides this year's Tet has been over for weeks."

"I would guess it's the only thing they can do. They surely won't try to occupy any cities again, this year," Captain S responded assuredly and folded his hands behind his head.

"It's going on everywhere and will continue until the end of the month. We can lean back and relax, and make sure we're in a bunker every night when the mortars start hitting," Scott stated.

Captain S said, "Jackson, if you two aren't afraid of mortars, you can stick around and party. I'm sure; Banks will warm up his guitar tonight… Scott, speaking of Banks, where are he and O'Neil?"

"They're over at the trash dump again, on a report of two grenades. I think the 9th's finest are using trash cans to get rid of ammunition when they return from the bush. You know where Wheeler and the girls are. The little twerp is demanding more attention. He responds to Wheeler when he walks in. Sam seems to take the stress out of our situation, and it's nice to have him." Scott sounded pleased.

"I think you're getting soft in your old age! Anyway, if you have nothing else, I'm going to find me a couple of scotch on the rocks. After today, I think Hébert needs something a little stronger than a beer." Captain S dropped it and headed to the O-club.

Scott looked at Joe and asked, "Would you care to explain his comment?"

"Nope. But if you care to share, I'll take a couple shots of the Black Label Jack you have in your desk drawer. Then, I'll go write a couple of letters." Joe pointed to Scott's desk.

*****

When the last bit of sun set, the usual crowd had gathered, and two tables of poker had begun. Everyone fully knew the fact; alcohol consumption would be limited because of the impending mortar attack. This did not deter Banks from putting on his nightly performance, singing from his repertoire of songs. Tonight, he started with the Ray Charles's version of "Crying Times."

Captain S saw a friendly face, one which to his knowledge, had never visited the unit before. "First Sergeant Farmer, glad to see you again. It's nice of you to stop by the unit. This is your first time, isn't it?"

"Yes, Sir. This is my first time here. I talked with Buck a week ago. He asked me over for little poker." Farmers nodded as he looked around the area.

"Good. As I'm sure you are aware, I appreciated and enjoyed your beer cooler, when I last saw you. I hope we didn't abuse your generosity." Captain S winked at Farmer.

"Not at all, Sir!" Farmer shook his head in a negative manner.

"First Sergeant. If you haven't discussed our first meeting with any of my guys, please don't mention it. I'll consider it a personal favor."

"No, Sir! Not a word. I understand, and I would expect the same of you." Farmer nodded his head in an understanding manner.

"All right then, let me introduce you to someone who can help you out with a cold one." Captain S smiled and led Farmer to the bar.

"Specialist Wheeler, this is First Sergeant Farmer. He's the First Sergeant for the 9th Finance Company. He makes sure we get paid. All his drinks tonight, and the next time he's here, are on me."

Farmer nodded and said, "Thank you, Sir, but it's not necessary."

"Yes, it is, First Sergeant. Enjoy yourself. Someone will vacate a chair at one of the tables before long."

Captain S turned his attention to a dirty Navy guy sitting at the bar.

"How are you doing, LeBeau? Captain S asked. "By the way, what's your first name?"

"My first name is Hunter, Hunter LeBeau. Also, I have a cold beer, and thanks to you Sir, a safe place to sleep tonight. So, I guess, I'm doing fine. And you, Sir?" LeBeau raised his beer, in a toast.

"I have a cold beer, and a friend who's constantly reminding me how stupid I can be sometime. So, I guess, I'm doing fine, thank you, Hunter." Captain S grinned and patted LeBeau on his shoulder.

Joe broke into the conversation and addressed Jackson, who also sat at the bar with the captain and LeBeau. "It looks as if you're staying straight tonight."

"I'm trying to. Scott has been talking to me, reminding me he writes my report card and telling me to check my attitude."

"And?" Joe raised his eyebrow.

"And, you know what. You know what I mean. I have been here for a good eight hours, and I haven't pissed anybody off, yet." Jackson said and chuckled loudly.

"Yet is the operative word there, brother. Before you do, let's get another drink. Wheeler, another two please." Joe put his arm around Jackson.

The evening went well, no drunken fights or loud arguments. As the evening wore on, Master Sergeant Scott, stood and spoke over the conversations. "Gentleman, it's almost nine forty-five, you know what happens about this time every night lately. We can stop 10 O'clock Charlie for a couple of weeks, but another one pops up. We only have enough room in our bunker for our men. I suggest you take positive actions to protect your ass. Staff Sergeant Banks, give us one more."

"Roger! As usual, we'll close with our favorite, Detroit City. I think everybody wants to go home."

*****

The red flares popped, and Charlie's mortars rained in as expected, starting at 10 o'clock. The durations of the mortar attacks were normally short, no more than ten minutes. The attacks usually targeted the north side, or Charlie Pad. Targeting the south side, or Navy side, rarely occurred However, tonight, after twenty minutes of incoming mortars, explosions could still be heard all over Dong Tam. Outgoing 155-MM and eight-inch artillery, from DEVARTY, were still active.

The only light in the EOD bunker came from flashlights. The expression on the men's faces revealed, they all knew and understood this night would be different. How different, they did not know. The sudden sound of close small arms fire told the story. Charlie wanted to breach the perimeter a little over two hundred meters away.

No longer able to take sitting still in the bunker, one after the other, except for LeBeau, wondered outside only to find green tracers flying overhead. "Boys, you better arm yourselves!" Scott yelled.

They retrieved their M-16's and ammo from the lockers in the office building. Captain S armed himself with his M-79, 40mm. Redding helped himself to an AK-47 with ammo.

After a mortar exploded close by, they decided to retreat to the bunker.

After what felt like eternity, they moved outside again. As Charlie's green tracers were still flying overhead, they sought cover behind the bunker. Redding, with his AK-47, climbed on top of the bunker and began firing over the perimeter.

Scott reacted first by yelling, "Get back inside! Inside! Get in the bunker!"

No sooner than the words were spoken, red tracers, accompanied by the sounds of impacting bullets, hit all around the men. As they entered the bunker, Captain S made sure they were okay.

On top of the bunker, Redding reloaded and emptied another magazine. Master Sergeant Scott stuck his head out of the bunker and barked, "Redding, get your ass in here!"

When Redding entered the bunker, Scott grabbed his collar and lifted him off the ground. "You damn fool, what the hell were you doing?"

"What? I was simply shooting at Charlie! What else do you think I did?"

Scott cut him off. "You, dumb Son of a Bitch! You're shooting an AK. What are our guys on the perimeter going to think, when they see Chinese made green tracers flying over their heads coming from our direction? Don't you know, Charlie uses green tracers, and we shoot red tracers at Charlie? I should have run your ass off months ago!" Scott, still yelling, pushed Redding to the ground.

"Ooh crap, what are we going to do now? Hollow is going to have a field day with this shit." Captain S ran his hand through his hair while thinking, aloud.

"Let me think. Do any of you have a grenade?" Scott looked around.

When no one else answered, Joe spoke up. "You can use mine. I'll put the delay element back in it making it functional. I'll go get it. Be back in a minute."

Scott looked at Joe and said, "Good. I'm right behind you. There's something I must get. Be careful, they're still shooting at us."

Joe returned in no time, without a problem, followed shortly by Scott carrying his pet rooster.

"Scott, what are you thinking about?" Captain S asked'

"Watch, Sir. Pray it works. Give me the AK. Does anybody have a cup or something that will hold liquid?"

After what seemed like a long silence, LeBeau spoke up from the far corner of the bunker. "I have a canteen cup."

"Great, give it to me!" Scott stepped outside with the AK and discharged a half dozen rounds straight up and then threw the AK on top of the bunker. As expected, red tracers flew around the area, coming from the perimeter. Then, Scott threw the grenade on top of the bunker and ducked back inside while waiting for the explosion.

"Captain, can you hold this cup still for me?" Scott gave the cup to Captain S.

Captain S held the cup. "Is this good enough?"

"Yes, Sir. Hold it still." Scott yanked the rooster's head off and drained the stream of blood into the cup.

"What--"

"Hold on, Sir. We need to hide this guy." Scott nodded at the rooster. He then stepped outside and splattered a splatter part of the blood on top of the bunker. "All we need now is a hero."

"A hero?" Captain S, not sure he heard Scott correctly, questioned his motive.

"Yes, Sir. A hero." Banks caught onto what Scott's intentions were.

"Come on, Captain. Somebody must get a medal for wounding the VC who got through the fence," Banks elaborated.

"Even though nobody will be found, blood at the scene and a little blood trail leading toward the river should be enough. It might work." Captain S thought about it and looked at the remaining small amount of blood.

"I'll say it again, who's our hero? Who gets a medal?" Scott loudly asked.

"I will, Master Sergeant." Redding eagerly spoke up.

"The only thing your getting is my number eleven up your ass!" Scot growled at Redding.

Captain S made the decision, and said, "I'll tell you who the hero is, tonight. LeBeau, get your ass up here! I'm putting you in for a Bronze Star for Valor. Do you understand?"

"No, Sir, I--"

"You better understand, you threw a grenade at a VC, setting on the bunker, shooting up the area," Captain S said firmly after interrupting LeBeau.

"But Sir--."

"No buts, LeBeau. If you open your mouth otherwise, all our dicks will be hanging out. You'll never see the insides of this bunker again. Now, do you understand?" Scott growled at LeBeau.

Looking at Captain S, LeBeau said, "Uh. Uh. Can you make it a Silver Star, Sir?"

"Spoken like a true Cajun. Are you sure you weren't born on the Bayou?" Joe slapped him on his back.

CHAPTER 39

26 March 69

Dear Pam,

Thank you for your last letter, which arrived while I vacationed in Hawaii. What a great R&R? I cannot find words that express how nice the week with Ava turned out. I told her, you and I occasionally correspond. She wanted me to tell you hello, and congratulations, about your marriage. She is fine and will be divorced by the time I return to the States in August. Maybe we can all get together before the end of the year. It would be nice to meet Stephen, and of course to see you.

I hope you and Stephen are enjoying married life. I'm pleased he has accepted a job with the FBI, pending his graduation in May. With him in the D.C. area for at least two years, you will have time to complete your degree. I think you mentioned, you will finish next summer.

The big news over here is the expectation of our bombing in Cambodia. We expect the NVA, who have their safe sanctuary over there, will infiltrate our way. Right now, we don't need any more bad guys in our area. This year, their Tet Offensive fizzled out, and we saw only a couple of weeks where there was an increase in activity. However, since I returned from Hawaii, we have been mortared nearly every night. Also, the VC have made two attempts to breach our perimeters, one of which was close to us. They appeared to be more probing than a real assault. I don't know what they expect to achieve by doing it. They certainly do not have the strength to do anything but harass us. At least, I hope not. The 9th Division has been hitting them hard all day. So, we all are expecting a good night sleep tonight. After dark, we will watch the movie, *The Sand Pebble* with Steve McQueen and Candice Bergen, and turn in early.

The only war story I have for you this time is about money. While I was in Hawaii, we had a country wide exchange of Military Pay Certificates (MPC's), where everybody exchanges their funny looking money for different funny looking money. This was done to stick it to the local people, mostly criminals, who are not authorized to use MPC's. They tried to account for MPCs on a dollar scale of one MPC dollar to one green dollar.

Where the process hurt was, everybody had to account for any excessive amount of money they had. In other words, if a young, enlisted person showed up with five hundred dollars in MPC's, he had to explain where the money came from. The problem for us was not our individual's money, but the unit's money. We have almost five thousand dollars in the unit fund. It was profit from beer sales. To change that amount of funny money, Captain S had to get a letter signed by the DESCOM Commander for an exception to policy.

I have mentioned Col. Hollow to you before, about how he does not like us. Well, you guessed it, the SOB would not sign the letter, leaving us with almost five thousand dollars of worthless paper, good only for wallpaper.

With me in Hawaii when this went down, I had the opportunity to exchange my MPC's later. I had no MPC's to exchange, because. I exchanged mine to green money before going to Hawaii. Of course, they did not know that. So, I was able to exchange money owned by our two hooch housekeepers. As for as the unit's money, we have a good friend, a senior NCO, in the Finance Company who was tasked with the execution of the program. He is helping us, a hundred dollars at the time. We will soon have all our old MPC's converted into new ones. Of course, this is strictly prohibited!

As for other news, you know it better than I. All our news comes compliments of the Armed Forces Vietnam Network Radio, AFVN.

I was glad the Apollo 9 crew safely evaluated the lunar module. And how about an American citizen, a woman, Golda Meir, becoming Prime Minister of Israel? This is a big step in the right direction for the women's rights movement.

Well, loved one, thanks for taking the time to read this. Study hard and take care of Stephen and tell him hello from me. You can also remind him how lucky he is to have you. Write to me soon.

With love,

Joe, your forever friend.

CHAPTER 40

Sitting in the BOQ bunker, while mortar rounds exploded everywhere, Joe remembered the words he had written to Pam earlier in the day. "How wrong could I have been? Charlie is flexing his muscle tonight." He mumbled to himself, "What happened to the good old days, when we had one 10:00 Charlie, who only targeted Charlie Pad? The VC had replaced him with at least ten or more like him, targeting the whole base."

He heard small arms popping. They were not like the ones fired when Charlie tried to breach the perimeter, but more like a large pack of firecrackers popping.

Captain S had expected an uneventful night. So, after watching a movie, he had gone to his BOQ for a good night's sleep. He wondered what Charlie expected to gain with the constant mortar attack. When he peeped outside the BOQ bunker, he saw a glow in the south. A better look answered the question. Charlie had hit the small arms pad at the ammunition supply point (ASP).

He intuitively knew, his worst fears about Dong Tam were coming true. Charlie intended to get the ASP.

It took no more than ten minutes for Captain S to get to the unit. There he found all his personnel, and LeBeau, armed and wearing steel pots and flack-vests. All were sitting in the bunker with flashlights.

Scott met Captain S at the bunker entrance. "Master Sergeant Scott, where are most of the mortars landing?" Captain S asked when he entered the bunker.

"Everywhere! They're going to get her, Captain." They looked toward the bright light given off from the burning small arms pad, less than three hundred yards away. It now resembled a huge reddish-orange sparkler. They had enough light to see a Navy Seawolf Pilot running for his helicopter. One of the choppers was lifting off.

A large flash of white light, followed by an extremely loud explosion, and an accompanying shockwave nearly blanked out the sight of the destruction of the helicopters, one falling from the sky and crashing, another rolling over and over on the small Navy helicopter pad. Flying debris, caused by the shock wave, flew. Smaller secondary explosions were occurring, and burning objects were piercing the night sky.

"Not good. The Navy has lost at least two choppers and pilots." Captain S somberly reported.

"That blast wasn't the small arms pad. I would guess pallets of grenades," Scott replied.

"Small arms are in pad nine. That came from pad eight." Joe moved close to Scott.

"This is going to get worse. Charlie has zeroed in on the ASP's pads, and he'll walk mortars all the way to pads one and two, where the eight inch and 155mm projectiles are. If that happens, our ass is grass." Captain S said and shook his lowered head.

"You're right, Sir. If it happens, there go the front gate and security. Then, if Charlie is capable, he can walk through the front gate and the entire Navy area, what's left of it? With everyone in bunkers, he'll never be fired upon." Scott, also, shook his head.

While thinking aloud, Joe said, "I doubt Charlie will want to be anywhere near this thing. I certainly don't! However, if lucky, a dozen well-trained men could get in here and do of damage in a hurry. I'd bet there's no more than one armed man in each bunker. You know what a grenade in one of these bunkers will do!

"Well, we won't be here to worry about it. We're moving further away," Captain S announced.

Lieutenant Commander Davis walked up and asked, "Are all your guys safe and accounted for?"

"Sir, you better find some shelter. But to answer your question, we're okay for now. Unless the 9th Division can't shut those mortars down, I don't think it's going to be safe here any longer," Captain S pointed toward the river and ASP.

Davis replied, "Senior Petty Officer Willis and I were making rounds, trying to get an assessment. It's bad down by the helicopter pad."

"I saw at least two choppers were lost. I'm sure the pilots went with them," Captain S said, somberly.

"Yeah, they were trying to get the helicopters out to a safe place. We have people trying to figure out if the pilots are dead or alive. To my knowledge, we have no other casualties."

"Sir, I'm concerned. It'll get worse. I'm taking my guys over to sit with LTC Phillips and his MPs. If I were you, I'd tell any nonessential personnel to cross the fence and find a bunker as far away from here as they can get." Captain S looked worriedly at Davis.

"I don't think I'll have to tell them. I need to keep moving, and Sandy, it looks as if you were correct with your assessment about the ASP a few months ago." Davis nodded his head toward the burning pads.

"You don't need to be walking around here. You might be the Commander of this place, and it may burn, but it won't sink. You don't have to go down with it."

"We'll see." Davis, obviously, seemed dejected.

"We'll see you tomorrow morning, Sir." Captain S said as the Commander and his senior NCO walked away.

"Okay, you guys, if you have anything in the office buildings, or the tents, you can't live without, you better get it now! We're moving back!" Scott yelled over the noise from the south.

As the jeeps were pulling out of the unit area, the sky lit up again. This time the areal display made it easy to decide which pad the VC hit. Red and green flares were kicked out and were burning overhead as well as over the other pads. Only a couple of minutes later another explosion occurred, the largest one, yet.

A couple of minutes later the grenades, 81mm mortars, and rocker pads went.

At the 9th MP's, they were met by Sergeant Major App, who said, "I thought you guys might be pinned down over there."

"That's the reason we're here. Right now, you're our best friend on post, and we're looking for a safe spot," Scott told App.

"Come in. I'm monitoring the radio. The last one actually knocked out our land line to the front gate, but we still have radio contact."

Captain S asked, "Where's Lieutenant Colonel Phillips?"

"He's over at the Division Tactical Operations Center (TOC). They called all the big dogs over there for a meeting. Knowing him, though, he'll find some excuse to get out of there. You know him, he's going where the action is. There's room in the bunker if anybody wants to join us." In the dim light, App looked at everyone and nodded.

"You heard the man." Scott turned to Joe, Banks, Wheeler, O'Neil, and of course LeBeau.

"I'm with Captain S wherever he goes." Joe asserted firmly.

"I'm no hero. I'm going in, and so is O'Neil. Come on LeBeau, Wheeler." Banks motioned for them to come.

Captain S said, "I'll wait out here for Lieutenant Colonel Phillips. When the big one comes, we should have time to find shelter."

"What do you mean by the big one? The last one, wasn't it?" App questioned him.

"No, not by a long shot. You'll know the big one when it comes. I had the pleasure of experiencing this in Korea." Scott shook his head.

"If I'm correct the last one was probably the pad where the 81mm mortar are kept. If we don't get Charley's mortar crews in a hurry, they'll get the others. The next one will be the 4.2-inch mortar. Then in rapid succession the105's, the 155's, and then the pad with the eight-inch projectiles.

"Depending on what's in stock, will determine how bad it is. This is Wednesday or was Wednesday. It's Thursday now. Anyway, I know the ASP gets supplied with big projectiles on Wednesday. It's certainly not good for us. You better bet Charlie also knows what he's doing." Joe enlightened the group.

Captain S looked at Scott. "Master Sergeant Scott, why don't you go, sit, and close your eyes for a while? It's going to be a long night and a very long day tomorrow."

"Yes, Sir, but I don't foresee us getting any rest, anytime soon."

As Scott turned toward the bunker, another extremely loud explosion occurred. This one is larger than the last. Flaming projectiles were piercing the sky in all directions. One landed harmlessly in the road no more than fifty yards away.

Lieutenant Colonel Phillips drove up, and before his feet hit the ground he said, "I'm glad you're here. I'm going to the front gate to check on my men. I'd like for you to go with me."

"Uh, Sir. Going down there is not a clever idea. As I understand, your men were okay before the last blast. I'm sure App is checking on them now. If you want to, you can confirm that. To put it bluntly, Sir, if you go down there now, you are a damn fool! Someone will have to carry you out of there. This thing is not over by any means." Captain S stated his opinion in a strong manner.

LTC Phillips stood and looked at Captain S. In the dim light, Captain S could not read his face. Without a word, Phillips turned to go find App.

"Hey, Ke-mo Sah-bee, how many times have you called a Lieutenant Colonel a fool to his face? That habit can't be good for your career."

"I didn't call him a fool, and he knows it. He's far from a fool. He's as fine of an Officer as I've ever met. He's justifiably concerned about his men."

Phillips soon returned and asked, "Sandy, what do you think is happening out there? Oh, and you were right. We still have radio communication with the front gate."

"Good, Sir. I think we still have two more pads which can blow, the big boys. Both are probably larger than anything we've seen. You know better than I, but I don't think Dong Tam, or your men at the gate, should fear Charlie coming through the gate. If they were my men down there, I'd tell them, or better yet, give them the opportunity, to leave the guard post and find the deepest hole they can crawl into. They can do it and possibly still watch the entrance without being in the open."

"So, you do not think this thing isn't over?" Phillips hopefully asks.

"No, Sir. I'm positive it's not. Unless the counter mortar fire has killed their mortar crews on Thoi Son Island, they'll keep firing. They can count and know what they're doing. In fact, I'm so certain, I'll bet you, double or nothing, on your bar tab for the next three months." His face could not be seen, but Phillips knew Captain S's face wore a smile.

"Okay, I understand, but how long before we know for sure?"

"Sir, you probably know more about blown up ASP's than I do. At least you've been to a seminar on the subject. I haven't, however I know explosives and munitions, and I have an appreciation of Charlie's work. The pads have been going up unsystematically. However, Charlie shoots at us and hides We shoot at him and wait. Then Charlie sticks his head up and shoots and hides, and the dance continues. I would say Charlie will be firing in about five minutes unless we have influenced him in a crippling manner. The question is, can he hit the pads?" Captain S gave Phillips his best advice.

"I can understand what you're saying. Let me talk with App and check on some other things." Phillips walked away.

Captain S and Joe were standing in an accessible area fifteen feet from the bunker concealing them from the burning and popping ASP, over six hundred yards away. The bright light, similar, but exponentially greater than a camera's flash came from the next explosion. Their brain told them they needed to do something, but their bodies did not have time to react properly. The accompanying blast wave lifted Captain S and Joe off their feet and tossed them like a rag doll, twenty feet from where they were standing. Shrapnel and other debris could be heard falling on the tin roofs all around them.

Clamoring to his feet and adjusting his helmet, Joe spoke first. "Sir, are you alright?"

"Yeah, and you, Tonto?"

"Nothing broken, but my pride. I should've known to stay closer to the bunker." Joe shook his head in amazement.

"Me, too. What do you think of the explosion?" Captain S brushed himself off.

"Yeah, what and explosion! I surely hope it was the climax you hinted about," LTC Phillips shouted, now standing behind them, wanted answers.

"Hell, Sir. Where did you come from?" Captain S almost jumped out of his skin.

"I was standing in the door of the bunker when it went. I saw you two doing your best imitation of Superman. I hurried over to help clean up the greasy spot! I guess it's not necessary." Phillips, obviously, smiled, but it couldn't be seen.

"Thanks for your concern, Sir. But we're fine. We may be bruised, but it won't affect us until tomorrow. As for the explosion, it was bigger than I expected. What's your opinion, Tonto?"

"I agree with you about being larger than expected. However, if my eyes and ears didn't deceive me, I think it was two distinctly different explosions."

"I had the same feeling." Captain quickly snapped back.

"What are you talking about?" Phillips asked the two of them.

Joe explained, "Sir, I think both pads went, one sympathetically detonated because of the other."

"Do you agree, Sandy?" Phillips quickly ask.

"Yes, Sir, and if we're right, the major fireworks are over."

Phillips quickly said, "Therefore, we can go to the front gate and check on my men."

"Not so fast, Sir. Do you know what it's going to look like down there? There'll be burning projectiles and other items laying around which will pop off in due time. Let's give it at least thirty minutes. I'll go check and see if we have anything left of our place. Then, we'll see about clearing a path to the front gate."

"We still have them. They're still alive with no major injuries!" App yelled from the door of the operations center.

"Thank, God." Phillips let out a heavy sigh, like he had been holding his breath.

"I don't know how they made it. The guard shack couldn't have been more than seventy-five yards away from pad nine," Joe replied, and seemed bewildered.

Captain S chimed in. "Sir, we'll see if we can make it to our unit and get a read on the road condition to the front gate. I have a safe down there with ten linear feet of classified documents, about half of which carries the Restricted Data label. You know how the Army is, or it's my philosophy. One can get away with almost anything in the Army, but don't screw with Uncle Sam's money or security. If you mess with either of them, they find quarters for you in Fort Leavenworth.

"Joe, go tell Scott, we're going to the unit, and we'll be back in thirty minutes. Sir, if you can find some strong lights, it'll be helpful. We'll need them when we clear the path to the front gate."

"Okay, Sandy. Get back here in thirty minutes, or I'm going without you." Phillips sounded adamant about the situation.

After dodging burning projectiles and other debris on their way to the unit, Captain S and Joe were surprised to see their office building still standing, although, severely damaged and bowed like a banana. Somehow the two tents miraculously survived with only holes in them. The lean-to over the bar did not make it and now lay on the patio. Fires still raged in all nine pads provided sufficient light, along with the moon, for them to see the Navy's new multimillion dollar buildings were now piles of rubbish. Other buildings in the Navy area were as well. No one moved around. They were still locked down in their bunkers.

"With due consideration, I think we came out okay." Joe looked around and compared their building with the Navy's.

"Yeah, if the office building is safe enough to work in, I'll leave it to my replacement to worry about. four us could be out of here in less than three months. We have three or four weeks of work cleaning Charlie's mess." Captain S put everything into content rather successfully.

After a quick walk around the area, Joe said. "If you've seen enough, let's get out of here. There are too many rounds cooking off for me to feel warm and fuzzy. The frag is going somewhere, and I don't want my name attached to any of it."

Back at the 9th MP Battalion Headquarters, LTC Phillips waiting patiently. "Sir, if we're careful, we can drive as far as my unit, but the roads beyond there are too cluttered with litter for our Jeeps. There're at least one hundred burning items, mostly projectiles, laying on the road between my unit and the front gate. Staff Sergeant Hébert and I will lead the way and point out anything to be of concern. Please be informed, every one of the burning projectiles can pop off at any time, especially if there is a fuze attached like rockets and the 40mm.

"What you hear now are low order detonations. Most of the projectiles will simply burn completely out because they didn't contain a fuze, but they can go high order. Most offers little to no danger. What you must watch out for are the small items, like a fuze which has been subjected to inertia or centrifugal force. They are extremely sensitive. Bumping one with your foot may cause it to pop off, which means you lose the foot or leg." Captain S explained the situation to Lieutenant Colonel Phillips, making sure he had a clear understanding of what to expect.

"I hear you, Sandy, and thanks. Are you ready to go? I have to check on my men." Phillips appeared anxious.

Captain S replied, "I would rather wait another hour, but I know you won't. So, let's be heroes."

After parking their Jeeps, LTC Phillips and Sergeant Major App followed closely behind Captain S and Joe. With the lights App provided, one could see a toothpick lying on the ground, ten yards away. But more important, they could see clearly, thirty meters ahead of them. Every square meter holds a piece of hot frag. Every nine square meter have something burning, mostly projectiles which had been kicked out of the stacked ammo in the pads.

"Captain!" Joe yelled, shining his light on a burning projectile approximate thirty meters ahead of their location.

"I see it. Get down!" Captain S shouted.

It took the projectile less than ten seconds to explode. "How did you know it would explode?" Phillips looked wide eyed at Captain S.

"When the fire changes from a normal flame to a pulsating flame, it's ready to blow. In this case, it was a low order, meaning not as powerful as a high order like it was designed to function. Low orders can cause the rounds to simply pop open, like what you saw there. Or it could throw deadly frag for hundreds of yards. Every explosion is different. It depends on the type, and the amount of explosive material, and whether or not the fuze is involved." Captain S explained.

"Okay, this is why we waited for you." Phillips patted Captain S on his back.

Moving slowly and carefully, they could see no buildings still standing near the ASP. Mr. Crawford's, the ASP Commander, office had literally disappeared. At the guard post, the only thing to be seen above ground level were sandbags and a huge forklift, with six-foot tall wheels, giving it the capable of lifting nearly a ton of ammo.

They found four soldiers near the place the guard post once stood at the entrance of Dong Tam.

Three MP's who were still staffing their post and one of Mr. Crawford's Specialists who was on duty at the ASP. They reported no major injuries, but the Specialist from the ASP had lost his hearing, likely due to a ruptured ear drum.

After communicating with him the best they could, Captain S told LTC Phillips, "He said he was laying under the forklift when it went, and there were twenty-six tons of eight-inch-high explosive projectiles in pad nine alone. He doesn't know how many 155mm rounds were in pad eight. And yes, they went simultaneously."

The three MP's, who had survived by laying behind the sandbags, insisted they could finish their watch and remain on duty at the front gate until relieved by the normal rotation.

While returning to their Jeeps with the Specialist from the ASP in tow, Phillips said, "Sandy, it looks as if you and your men will be busy for a while. I don't know what I can do for you, but if there's anything, don't hesitate to speak up."

"Right now, Sir, I don't know whether to pick my nose or scratch my butt. We'll sit down between now and daylight and give some thought as to where to start. Well, we know where to start. The first thing we'll do in the morning is open this road. But what comes next is the question.

"Where are we going to put the scrap? Where are we going to detonate the thousands upon thousands of pounds of stuff which didn't explode or burn? Of course, the logistics involved are some of the questions which need answers." Captain S, already tired, simply spoke his burdensome thoughts aloud.

"Like I said, you'll be busy for a while. You're lucky you have some good soldiers working for you." Phillips said.

"Yes, Sir, I do. And speaking of good soldiers, do you think your three men back there were simply trying to impress you by staying there?"

"It doesn't matter if they were or not. By 0900 hours, I'll be writing a recommendation for an Army Achievement Medal for valor for each of them," App stated and ended the conversation.

At the unit, Captain S and Joe found everyone, to include LeBeau, sitting or standing in the office building sipping coffee. Banks, standing closest to the coffee pot, quickly poured two cups and handed them to Captain S and Joe. He said, "I think you might need this."

Joe looked at the offered coffee, and said, "I'm surprised we have electricity. I didn't think about checking it when we were here before. I think; we all need a swig of Scott's private stock." He paused before asking. "Does everybody believe the building will hold up and not fall on us?" He gradually sipped the coffee and looked around at the sagging ceiling and the bent walls.

"It'll provide a roof over our heads, unless we get another explosion." Banks replied.

"From what I saw down there, we won't get any more big ones. I believe every pad has a fire in it. It looks as if the integrity of the pad walls held up and did what they were supposed to do by deflecting most of the blast wave upward," Captain S gave his assessment of the situation.

"Tell that to Commander Davis," Banks quipped.

Wheeler chimed in, "He will, but Davis won't listen."

Captain S chuckled, and said, "He might now. When I talked with him earlier, I believe, if I told him crap has a honey taste, he'd believe me."

"Before we forget our situation, Sir, I called Control and gave them a heads up and asked them to send a couple of people to Tan An as replacement for Jackson and Redding. I think we'll need them here for a while. They'll head this way bright and early." Scott informed Captain S.

"I'll be in the bunker. Maybe I can get three hours of sleep." LeBeau waived and walked out.

"Wheeler, I'll man the radio. You find a bunk. You'll be in here all day, tomorrow." Scott motioned for Wheeler to leave.

"We'll start clearing the road as soon as there is enough light. As far as I can tell, there's nothing there which will do significant damage to the road. There's about three-hundred yards of road which is completely contaminated. We'll take care of everything as quickly and efficiently as possible. We'll shoot to have it done in three or four hours. Does this sound reasonable to everybody?" Captain S looked around the room for any help he could get.

Nobody spoke up but merely nodded their heads.

"After the road, we'll let DESOPS, or I guess DESCOM, tell us what to do next. I think they'd want pad nine cleared quickly where they can use the area for storage. Somebody, give me help. I'm winging it here." Captain S ran a hand across his face.

Scott helped his Captain out. "Because of safety reasons, I don't think, we need over two teams working in the ASP at any given time during the entire operation. There'll be calls coming in from all over post tomorrow. You can work on the road, and I'll check out the calls. Before you say anything, Sir, if it's necessary, I'll wait on a second man. I don't think there'll be anything urgent on the Army side. Besides, Jackson and Redding should be here by 0900 hours."

"Okay, this sounds like a plan of action. Anybody else have comments? If not, let's get a couple hours of rest. Master Sergeant Scott, don't hesitate to call me if anything important comes in," Captain S said.

There may have been rest, but no sleep, for them. Their thoughts raced during the three hours before the first sign of light. When Captain S reappeared in the office building, he found Scott making a new pot of coffee.

After the customary good mornings, Captain S asked, "Is there any news that I should know?"

Scott replied, "Nothing, except, I talked to Control again. As soon as Major Sparks comes in, they'll try to find someone who has experience with ASP cleanups to head this direction."

Within the next fifteen minutes, the entire unit's personnel, except for Jackson and Redding, were standing in the office ready to go to work. Banks asked O'Neil, "Are you ready to start picking up scrap metal?"

"He should be ready. We have loads of crap, some presenting explosive dangers, to move and other stuff which don't drop on toes, DDOT, is the only danger and to be concerned about. Let's not get in a hurry and forget, there are a thousand things scattered about that will kill you if you aren't careful." Captain S hit everyone in the face with a large dose of reality.

"Hell, let's go! What was it a Chinese man once said? Something like, 'The first step is the beginning of a thousand-mile journey?'" Joe tried to add philosophical insight to their laborious task. However, no one else seemed to appreciate it. They simply shrugged.

As they were walking out the door, the phone rang. "Sir, its Major Sparks!" Scott called out.

"Good morning, Sir. Isn't it early for you to be in the office?"

"If the 9th Division could take care of their business, I'd still be sleeping. What's going on down there?"

"Sir, I'm sure you know, but we lost the ASP. We're all fine. We've already requested our on-site team to return to Dong Tam. We were about to start cleaning the road to the front gate. There's nothing else for us to do, but to go to work."

"I understand. We'll try to get you some help later. The reason for the call is, I wanted to give you a heads up. Lieutenant General Pickett, Commander, First Logistics Command, is in the air headed your direction. He'll want to talk with you."

"Sir, I don't know what I can tell him, or do, except show him around."

"You'll be fine. Be yourself and answer his questions. Don't let his three stars intimidate you. I talk with him quite often. He knows what your job is. He came up through the ranks, so don't try to BS him."

"Okay, Sir. I'll let you know how it goes."

"You don't have to call me, unless some kind of crap occurs. He or someone from his office will be calling me as soon as he returns to Long Binh."

"Okay, Sir. I'll go to work and watch for him."

"Captain, if you need anything, call me."

"Will do, Sir. Have a good day." Captain S hung up the phone.

*****

They went to work, moving scrap metal and other debris to the side of the road, while marking and leaving suspected dangerous material laying in place.

Seventy-five meters and forty-five minutes later, two Jeeps drove up and four occupants dismounted. They moved in the direction of the EOD team.

From a distance, Captain S only recognized Colonel Hollow and Mr. Crawford, but he knew who the others were the General and his Aide.

As he approached them, "Captain Summerville report, and saluted. The three-star General was dressed in jungle fatigues. Joe, who stood beside Captain S, saluted as well.

"You're the EOD Officer in charge, I assume." Lieutenant General Pickett asked.

"Yes, Sir. I mean, yes, General." Captain S stammered.

"Let's walk. I want to see how serious the situation truly is," Lieutenant General Pickett stepped out.

"Yes, General. But I don't recommend--"

"Forget it, Captain. I see the burning rounds. I'm going in there to see firsthand. It's your job to keep me safe." Pickett smiled and continued walking.

"General, be careful where you step," Captain S managed to say.

"General, I want to say, my EOD unit has done a fine job, and we all have faith in them." Colonel Hollow interrupted.

"I'm sure you do. You wait here! Mr. Crawford, walk with us," Pickett commanded.

As Pickett, his Aide, Captain S, Mr. Crawford, and Staff Sergeant Hébert walked toward the main gate, and the remains of pad nine, the deflation of Colonel Hollow's ego popped like a balloon.

Crawford said, "This was my office." He nodded to a pile of rubbish close to pad nine.

"I assume you have a current inventory of your stock." Pickett looked at Crawford and the remnants of the ASP office.

"Yes, General, I do. Or I did as of midnight last night when I left the office. I'm sure, if you would like to check, we can find the paperwork here somewhere over this forty acres," Crawford said with a smile and waved at the general area.

"I thought you would say something smart. Get me a report on your exact losses and needs by 1800 hours this afternoon," Pickett ordered, and returned the smile.

Watching a white phosphorus round burning close by which began pulsating, Joe shouted, "Down!" He grabbed the General's Aide, a Major, and pushed him to the ground. Captain S hit the General like a linebacker tackling a running back; so hard, the general's glasses flew off his head To Joe, the glasses looked as if they were suspended in the air, like action in a Road Runner cartoon.

Laying on the ground atop the General for a couple of seconds, which seemed like minutes to Captain S, his brain raced, what did I do? The loud explosion and the flying frag all around them answered his question.

After getting to their feet and brushing themselves off, Pickett asked, "Summerville, do you have a habit of manhandling General Officers?"

"No, Sir, I mean General. I knew the round was going to go, and I thought, at your age, you might be a little slow. I mean--." Captain S stopped himself and gave the General his glasses.

"Captain, what do you mean by my age and a little slow? I'll hear no more on this subject, but it was astute of you to know the impending danger," Pickett spoke, with a momentous smile.

"Yes, General. Not a word of this incident will pass my lips. As you can see, there's nothing, except for burning projectiles everywhere. May I suggest we get our ass out of here!" Captain S pleaded with the General.

"Mr. Crawford, I've seen enough of your ASP. I'll start supplying you tomorrow with trucks, planes, and boats. It's up to you and the 9th Division to determine what you need, and where you'll put it. You know the logistical system, so make sure the 9th Division understands the importance of prioritizing their requisitions. We can only push a fixed amount in a brief time. I'll speak to the Division Commanding General before leaving."

"Yes, General." Crawford nodded in an understandingly way.

Once back where they began, Colonel Hollow said, "I want to assure you, my EOD team will have the ASP operational in no time. I'll make sure they have all the support they need to get the job accomplished in a timely manner."

"Yes, Colonel, I know my EOD unit is capable of completing this project in a timely manner. And I'm sure you'll provide them with all the assistance they need. Now, will you escort me over to the 9th Division Headquarters to see your Commander General?" Pickett emphasized the word, 'my'.

"Yes, General. We'll go over to see him now." Hollow nodded like an obedient puppy.

As Lieutenant General Pickett stepped into the Jeep, he turned, looked at Captain S, and said, "Summerville, you have a lot of work to do. If there is anything you need, regarding this project, or anything else you have a problem with, call me directly. Trust me, I'll remember your name!"

"Yes, General." Captain S replied.

"Do it, and don't hesitate, Captain.

"Major, give the captain information, so he can contact us directly, anytime about anything." Pickett said and took a seat in the Jeep. The look on Hollow's face told the priceless story.

When Captain S and his three underlings walked into the office, Scott announced, "I talked with Jackson, they'll be here in about an hour. I also talked with Control again. They are sending a team to Tan An, today, and a team here to respond to incidents, as quickly as possible, while we work on the cleanup."

O'Neil smiled. "Good, maybe I can get a strong back to help with the scrap metal. I don't expect to get a lot of help from Redding, leaving only me. I know you will detail the duty to me."

"Scott, thanks for managing the call. Check on transportation. We'll have to haul the explosive stuff somewhere for safe disposal, and there's probably close a hundred tons of this type of material to be moved. If anybody would like to pitch in with a suggestion along these lines, please speak up." Captain S opened the floor for suggestions.

Joe spoke up. "Uh, I think I know a place which will provide us with easy transportation, and an unlimited explosion limit. Captain, we were there about six weeks ago."

After a second, Captain S said, "The other side of the river, but you said something about easy transportation." Captain S looked at Joe waiting for him to elaborate.

"Yes, Sir. The Second Brigade and the Navy have Mike Eight boats sitting around. All we must do is transport our goods to the boat launch ramp, which is less than a half mile, and load it into the boats. On the other side, we drop the ramp and unload everything on the shore." Joe extended his arms wide as if to say, voila!

"I'm sure Lieutenant Commander Davis will help if necessary. He had more pressing issues than for me to bring this up today. When the time comes, he'll be there for us. The only problem I see is our security on the other side of the river. I don't want to drop the ramp and have an RPG waiting to welcome us." Captain S pointed out the small flaw in Joe's plan.

"We can get them to pitch in a Swift boat, or two, to prep the beach and stand by for any emergency, if necessary," Joe quickly answered.

Captain S asked, "Scott, Banks,, what do you think?"

"I can get the vehicles, and I can talk to Donaldson about some people to help move the scrap metal. I see no reason we can't dig a hole for the metal and bury it in the dump. We better get permission from you know who before dumping anything at his garbage dump. Otherwise, everything we do is wrong. I'll also talk to Donaldson about it," Scott said.

"Okay. Banks." Captain S looked at him for a comment.

"Sir, I'm in." Banks replied.

"O'Neil? Captain S looked at him.

"Why ask me? I'm the go-fer around here. Ask Wheeler or the girls. They're higher on the power scale than I am." O'Neil playfully declared.

"I hear you. I'm glad you brought up the girls. I'm sure they won't be allowed on post, today, maybe not for a few days, so do what you must do to keep this place presentable. We'll have people dropping by," Scott ordered.

"Okay, if there's nothing else, let's see what Master Sergeant White has managed to disguise as food this morning. Then, we'll go back to work." Captain S smacked his head down on his desk.

CHAPTER 41

They did work, ten to twelve hours a day for twenty-seven days. They separated scrap material, whose only hazards were from cuts or toe injuries if dropped, from other material which presented various explosive hazards. The explosive hazards materials were transported to the south bank of the Mekong River, in loads of ten thousand to twenty thousand pounds at a time.

Movement presented a significant hazard because one of a hundred things could go drastically wrong. After all, every single explosive item presents an inherent danger by itself, and there were thousands of them.

As promised, Control had sent two EOD personnel to help, but they were gone after the first week. The girls missed only two days of work. Jackson and Redding worked extremely hard and presented a cheerful outlook, except for a couple of occasions where Redding showed his, better than thou, personality. The unit bar and evening activities had been closed for only two nights, long enough to remove the debris covering the bar and patio.

On the eve of the twenty-seventh day after the ASP explosion, the unit's bar seemed rather active. A total of four tables, for poker or simply sitting room, were available. While sitting at one of the tables, Captain S said, "Tomorrow, we'll have our last load, the last of the cleanup. Once it's accomplished, things will be a lot easier."

Banks proudly announced his departure. "Things are going to get really easy for me after tomorrow. I'm so short, I can barely see over my boots. My freedom bird lands on the second of May.

"I'm sorry, I haven't been able to let you have the customary kickback time before leaving, but you know why. After we load the Mike Eight boats tomorrow, you can consider yourself through. I'll help make the shot across the river.

"O'Neil has about a month but still has no orders for the date estimated to return from overseas, or DEROS date," Captain S looked at O'Neil.

"Yeah, I'm getting short. Actually, all of us are, except for Staff Sergeant Hébert." O'Neil smirked.

"All of us will be out of here by the middle of August, unless somebody extends," Captain S said with a smile.

"Two of us will really be out before the end of the year. Redding and I will be civilians. You lifers can stay in and rotate back over here in a couple of years. This war isn't going to be over anytime soon." Jackson raised his beer in a mock toast.

Joe replied, "Unfortunately, he's right. Jackson, what are you going to do once you're out?"

Jackson grinned and raised his eyebrows. "I've thought about going to college and let Uncle Sam pay for it. I'll find me some fine co-ed ass."

Banks chimed in, "If you're going to school, you better read a book or two first."

Captain S said, "Banks, I know you're going to the 71st EOD unit in Ohio, but have you considered contacting an agent and try to cut a record?"

"Of course, he has. But before he does, he'd better decide what types of gigs he wants to do." Joe cocked his head and looked at Banks.

"What do you mean? He can sing anything," said O'Neil.

"Joe's right. The first thing I need to do is decide if I'm going to sing country or rock. Right now, I'm leaning to country. I'm afraid rock and roll is trending down. Anyway, I need to get an agent and a couple pieces of contemporary music to sing before I can cut a record. Consequently, an extremely popular singer is a childhood acquaintance from Sevierville, Tennessee. If I can get in contact with her, I think she'll remember me and give me some pointers. She's really nice, or she was in grammar school."

"Redding, Jackson said you were getting out of the Army by the end of the year. What kind of plans do you have?" Captain S appeared sincere in his question.

"I don't know, Sir. I may try to go back to college, but as you know, it didn't work out too well the first time I tried it."

"Boy, you still have some growing up to do. Your father doesn't have a business for you to walk into. College isn't a bad place to do some maturing. You're certainly not going to use your Army trade, unless you're going to become an anarchist." Joe said, but it sounded like Scott's words.

"Yeah, I know, but you've been around Scott too long." Redding nodded.

"Jackson, you didn't answer Joe's question, have you given thought to re-upping?" Captain S looked at him.

"Sir, I'm due to reenlist in February. It's going to be hard to turn down the ten-thousand-dollar re-up bonus for my rank, but I'm going to look around Chicago, while I'm on leave, and see what's available.

If I don't go to school, I may try to open a bar."

"Running a bar sounds like a good idea. If you need a partner, let me know." Redding looked at Jackson.

"Sir, you'll probably be going to the Advanced Officer Career Course from here. Are you going to become a lifer?" The sincereness in Bank's question sounded obviously.

"I don't know, Banks. I still have two more months with Hollow trying to kill any career that I might want to pursue. If I can escape him, I'm sure I'll stay around for a while. If not, I'll find a government job somewhere. I can easily qualify for a safety officer position as a GS-9. Maybe with luck a GS-12. There are plenty of them in the D.C. and Hampton Roads area."

"Nobody asked, but I'm going to marry the most beautiful woman in the world, the one I'll always love. From then on, nothing else matters." Joe announced and beamed.

"I guess that's my cue to get up and sing something I've been thinking about," Banks picked up his guitar.

After bellowing out a couple of popular songs, he lowered his voice and softly said in a prayerful manner, "Take me home Lord, take me home.

Banks bowed in an exaggerated manner. "Thank you, and again my appreciation to you.

CHAPTER 42

The late-April showers were welcomed, especially when one had to load hazardous ammo all morning. With Scott in the office, the other six EOD guys had transported the final remnants from the ASP clean up, mostly eight-inch projectiles which had experienced shock during the explosion, to the loading ramp in the river basin. They were loading the last truck full onto the Mike Eight boat. They were using a bucket line procedure to move the projectiles from the truck down an incline to the boat. They were hot, sweaty, and shirtless. The shower helped cool the late morning heat, but it was still hot and humid.

When Colonel Hollow showed up at the top of the ramp, no one thought anything of his presence. They said nothing to him while continuing their work. After approximately five minutes of watching the EOD teamwork, Colonel Hollow yelled, "Captain Summerville, I want to talk with you!"

"Yes, Sir. Give me a second." Captain S replied. He wanted to finished loading the next projectile in the line.

"Now, Captain!" Hollow yelled.

Captain S took his time walking to the stern of the Mike Eight boat to place the projectile he carried and then walked up the ramp to Colonel Hollow. Waving his hand in a half-hearted salute, Captain S said, "Good morning, Sir."

"Don't you know what 'now' means, Captain?" Colonel Hollow barked. "Why are you out of uniform?"

"Yes, Sir. I do. I also know what EOD work is."

"Not an answer, Captain. I want to see you in my office. Get your clothes on and follow me."

"Sir, I have work to do. If what you have to say to me is not more important than my work, may I suggest later this afternoon, when we have completed this load?" Captain S respectfully replied.

"Your questions are part of the problem, Captain. You have no respect for rank. If you are not in my office in ten minutes, I'll have the MPs to escort you there." Colonel Hollow turned and walked away.

As Captain S put his shirt on, Banks and Joe came to his side. Joe asked, "What did we do this time?"

"Nothing, I know of, but after this, I'm asking Control's permission to try to talk to his boss, the Chief of Staff, 9th Division. I'm not taking this crap any longer."

Joe said, "We'll be through here in a few minutes. If you're not back by then, we'll go without you,"

"No. Hébert, you stay with me. I'm sorry, Staff Sergeant Banks." Captain S looked at Banks.

"No problem, Sir. We'll handle this. You better get out of here before the MP's show up." Banks nodded toward where Hollow had been standing.

"Hébert, get your shirt, and let's go see the Man. I may need a friendly witness. I have one of my strange feelings about this one...Joe, you may have to lie under oath for me, swearing he threw the first punch. Captain sounded serious.

He arrived two minutes late at Colonel Hollow's office. Sergeant Major Donaldson met them and shook his head in disbelief. He said, "I'll tell him you're here."

Donaldson returned shortly. "He said for you to have a seat. He will be with you in a few minutes."

"Do you know what this is about?" Captain S whispered to Donaldson.

"No, Sir. None whatsoever."

Thirty minutes later, Captain S told Joe. "They should be through loading the boat by now. I don't like this at all. It's--"

Joe interrupted, "Yes, Sir. Don't you think I should go with them?"

"No, Joe. Something inside says you're needed here. Like I said, this is it with the SOB. When he starts his crap, I may walk out on him. You stand by Donaldson where you can hear what he says. A friendly witness is what I need from you."

They waited another eight minutes before Hollow called for Sergeant Major Donaldson.

A minute later Donaldson told Captain S, "He'll see you now."

After Captain S reported, Colonel Hollow said, "Captain, I've had enough of your antics. I'm writing a letter through the chain of command to request you be relieved of your command."

"Fine, Sir, but let's not wait on a paper trail. Your letter must go through your boss, the Chief of Staff. I recommend we do this in person, right now! Let's see if we can get in to see him. The paper trail would look more impressive with him originating it. If it takes a while to see him, maybe you can explain to me what antics you are referring to." Captain S called his bluff.

"I don't have to explain a damn thing to you! Do you hear me, Captain? You have disrespected me for the last time. You should have been through with the ASP cleanup two weeks ago. This morning, you left me standing out there for ten minutes without showing me any kind of recognition. You were out of uniform, looking like an enlistee. You don't conduct yourself like an Officer!" Hollow bellowed.

"Sir, would you like for me to contact the Chief of Staff's office for an appointment?" Captain S remained calm.

"Captain, I'll tell you what I would like! I would like you, and your men, to get the hell out of my sight and off my post. All of you are a disgrace to the Army!"

"It's my understanding, my unit is off your post. I'm sorry you can see us on the Navy side. Perhaps you should build another fence separating the two sides or take it up with God." Captain S sarcastically offered a solution.

Hollow growled, "There you go again getting smart and obstinate."

"I don't know why you feel the way you do. I'm simply offering a couple of solutions to your problem. However, for now, can we get to the point as to why you so urgently needed to speak to me, and why you pulled me away from my dangerous work?" Captain S pointedly inquired.

"It didn't look too dangerous to me. It didn't look like you were needed." Hollow huffed.

"That's not your call. It's mine. As we have discussed before, we need to get this settled by our higher headquarters."

"As long as it occurs on my post, I'll make the decisions. You have shown no respect for me or my office for the last time. You showed me no respect when General Pickett visited here. You showed me no respect at the loading ramp today. Every time you are in here, you show me no respect. I'm going to write a letter of reprimand and put it in your official military records. And don't tell me, I can't! I command the personnel unit which controls your records!"

"Sir, you do what you want to do. I'll tell you what I am going to do. I am going to my office and call my boss. He authors my report card, and he decides whether I'm fit for duty or not. I'll tell him to expect a call from your boss. Because unless he gives me a direct order not to, I'm going to the Chief of Staff's office and sit until he sees me."

"You're going over my head, are you?" Hollow yelled.

"Yes, Sir, I am. I'm going to get this crap settled one way or the other. You write all the letters you want to, and you know what you can do with them. You can shove--"

The concussion wave, from an extremely loud explosion. suddenly shook the building. Captain S at once headed for the door.

"What the hell are your men doing now! " Hollow yelled.

As Captain S reached the office door, he placed his hand on the facing, turned, and said, "Dying, you Son of a Bitch!"

When he exited the building, Captain S could see Joe thirty yards ahead of him racing to the boat ramp. Other people were standing around looking south, toward the river where a black plume of smoke rose at least six-hundred feet high.

When they heard the explosion at the unit, Scott said, "Oh God," and ran for the Jeep, knocking Baby San down on his way, and telling Wheeler, "Stay by the radio. Call DESOPS and see what happened!"

When he reached the ramp, a crowd of twenty or more had gathered, looking, and searching for any answers from the river. Two MP Jeeps arrived at the same time. Relieved to see Captain S standing on the highest ground, Scott headed for him. Then, he saw Joe, who he reached first and grabbed by his shoulders, he asked, "What the hell happened?"

"I don't know! I don't know if it's our boat or not, but it doesn't look good." Joe ran his hand over his head.

"I knew it! Damn, I knew something was going to happen! Crap! I should have stopped them! Damn that SOB!" Captain S screamed with a shaky voice.

"Wait a minute, Captain." Scott said and grabbed him in a bear hug. "Whatever happened is not your fault. Besides, we don't know yet."

"Yes, I know! I knew something was wrong, and I did nothing. Our boat is the only thing that could make an explosion that large. It had well over seven tons of explosives items on it. You can't tell me that black- smoke cloud isn't carrying the ashes of our men. God, I hope I'm wrong, but I know; I'm not!" Captain S became bedeviled by the situation as tears streaming down his face.

"You can't see the river, so you don't know. It may take thirty minutes to know anything. The next boat in will have some information." Scott tried to calm Captain S.

After about ten minutes, the crowd had gathered to over forty people, all looking toward the river, watching, and waiting. Suddenly, Joe felt a familiar arm move around his waist squeezing tightly. "Lein, what are you doing, here?"

"Wheeler said run. Give this to Scott. I see you. I give to you. I, I scared." Lein gave him a note which Joe at once opened and read.

"DESOPS report, information from Navy. Mike Eight boats exploded. Suspect no survivors. Minor, frag damage to two other Navy vessels."

Joe's heart sank, and tears flowed from his eyes. After showing the note to Scott, Joe insisted that he needed to give the note to Captain S.

Captain S read the note and sank to his knees. With the help of Scott, Joe raised him to his feet and supported him.

After a couple minutes, Baby San appeared at Captain S's side with a new note from Wheeler, which read, "No signs of survivors and little signs of wreckage from the Mike Eight boats."

Tears were in the girl's eyes as well as Joe and Captain S's. They were holding each other tight when Scott said, "You guys have to keep it together. I know how hard this is. Trust me, I know. I've been here before. Get your poker faces on and get it together!

"I'm sorry, Master Sergeant Scott, I had to come. I must know if it's our boat or not," Wheeler said as he approached.

"It's all right, Son, you've done all you can do."

Taking a survey of the crowd, Wheeler knew who occupied the boat when it exploded. For him, seeing Baby San in the arms of Captain S seemed almost as painful as losing his friends. The pain overwhelmed him, but finally, he knew why he had not heard her proclaim, "I am a cherry girl," for a few months.

Shortly after they returned to the office building, the official word came down from the Division: five MIA, presumed dead, consisting of four EOD personnel, and one Navy River Pilot.

Only one phone call went out. Captain S called Major Sparks at Control to inform him of their losses. A half dozen inquisitive and well-wishing calls were received. But other regular evening patriots stopped by for first-hand information, and to pass on their regrets.

At one point when no visitors were present, Master Sergeant Scott said, "This place feels like a damn funeral home. Girls, get Sam and your stuff, and find a ride home. We'll see you tomorrow. Captain S, Staff Sergeant Hébert, get your ass out of here and write a quick note home. Someone there will want to hear from you. Hurry, and Wheeler can get it out today. When you finish with them, we'll sit down and have a stiff one, or two."

After Captain S, Joe, and the girls left the office, Scott called Master Petty Officer Willis and asked him to have someone bring him a bottle each of Black Label Johnnie Walker and Jack Daniels.

The small amount of scotch Captain S consumed did not help or deter his sleepless night. He rose early, showered, and went to breakfast. When he arrived at the office building, he found Major Sparks sitting behind his desk.

Captain S said, "Good morning, Sir. I wasn't expecting you."

"I flew in early. I wanted to talk with you folks, person-to-person, and assure you, we'll do everything within our power to help. I have a surprisingly good relationship with a couple powerful people like General Pickett. As I've told you, we talk at least every two weeks, and he doesn't call simply to say, hello. How are you managing the situation?"

"I could use some better sleep and some answers, but there's only One who can answer them, and He has never spoken to me. First, are you here to fire me, relieve me of my job?" Captain S let out a deep breath of regret and loss, not to mention his emotional exhaustion.

"Hardly! You must be referring to yesterday's conversation with Hollow. Staff Sergeant Hébert told me what he knew of the accident, how Hollow kept you cooling your heels in his office, and his threat to get you relieved. He wouldn't say anything more, other than you would fill me in."

"Well basically you have the story, except I requested that we talk to the Chief of Staff about the situation. Also, after the explosion, I called him a SOB." Captain S shrugged his shoulders. "It may not have been professional, Sir, but it was appropriate at the time. In all honesty, it felt good. The man is a Son of a Bitch, and he got my men killed!"

"Captain, if anybody loses their job over this incident, it'll be Hollow. There'll be a safety investigation, and he'll be asked why he interfered and pulled the Officer from the job. I'm sure General Pickett will be talking with the Ninth Division Commander General on the subject as well."

"Sir, no matter how true, or how good it felt, I shouldn't have called him a SOB, however at the time, it was better than punching him."

"Yes, but I would have done the same thing in your situation. You should never worry about him. I assure you; we have your back.

Do not give any more thought. As you know, EOD commanders have the unique authority to write General Orders. I think it's time to have an EOD conference in Vung Tau for four or five days. However long you want, I'll back you up. Take your partner, Staff Sergeant Hébert, with you. Go have a good time on Uncle Sam's TDY money. This unit is, as of now, I signed the orders late yesterday, officially non-operational. That should get the 9th Division's attention.

"Now, I need to go find something to eat. Scott can take care of me. Captain, you and Staff Sergeant Hébert, grab your ditty bag and bathing suit, go to Charlie Pad and catch the first chopper headed north. If I have to, I'll make it in order."

"Before I do anything, I have four letters to write." Captain S drooped lower if possible.

Scott informed his Captain, "You have four letters to sign. They'll be ready for your signature before you leave."

The war had practically eluded Vung Tau, the beautiful and secure beach city east of Saigon, and the location of the Army's in-country R&R site. There were loads of available women which neither Captain S nor Joe considered, and a beautiful beach where they stayed for two days. After the two days, they decided they would rather be in My Tho, at Colonel Neueng's hotel with Lein and Baby San.

CHAPTER 43

"Major Sparks, this is Captain Summerville. Staff Sergeant Hébert and I are in Dong Tam, and if you need us, we're ready to go to work, any time." Captain S spoke into his office phone.

The Major asked. "How was your time in Vung Tau?"

"Fine, Sir, but we could only take the beach so long."

"Do you have your head on straight?"

"Yes, Sir. We're ready to do some work."

"Okay, Captain. Good. Your unit it still down, but we need warm bodies. We had a call from MACV, informing us of a five-hundred-pound bomb over in the Seven Mountains area, Cam Mountain to be exact. This is part of the IV Corps area of operation, which means it is yours. Your contact there will be a U S Army advisor from the 44 STZ, an ARVN signal unit, I think. We'll have them call you.

"There's a couple of other things. First, we'll try to get you some help down there later in the week. Secondly, you should not have any more trouble with Colonel Hollow, and before you ask, I'll not get into the matter."

While waiting for their chopper at Charlie Pad, Joe said, "So, Ke-mo Sah-bee, you are taking me to the Forbidden Mountain!"

"Yelp, Cam Mountain. Legends say it is rugged with many frightening beasts. This is the reason it's called the Forbidden Mountain." Captain S tried to hide his excitement.

"Maybe we'll see a man-eating Manussiha, or a Vetala who has knowledge of the past, present, and future." Joe broadly smiled. He commented, "With rugged and frightening beasts sightings, are you sure we're not going to D.C.?"

"Yeah, you're right, Tonto. D.C. is more frightening!" Captain S admitted the truth.

"A Forbidden Mountain with beasts, over close to the Cambodian border. I can hardly wait. This sounds as if it could be fun." Joe bounced on his toes like a little boy.

"Yeah, the Seven Mountains are part of the western edge of the Plane of Reeds, or as the French say, the Plaine Des Jonce, which sounds more friendly. It's in An Giang Provence which some scholars, back in D.C., think is the most pacified region in South Vietnam. The only reason they think this is, there are few US troops engaged there, only ARVN soldiers. Their brilliance astounds me." Captain S enlightened Joe.

"With the end of the Ho Chi Minh trail so near, I'm sure it's pacified." Joe smirked. "I mean, scholars can't be wrong, right?"

After a long uneventful flight, they could see Cam Mountain on the horizon. They knew, the Mountain, at over 2300 feet, is the tallest of the mountains, and they are landing on its peak.

When Captain S and Joe ran from the prop wash of the chopper as it lifted off, they met SEC Raymond, who reported to Captain S. He stood and weighed about the same as Joe and spoke with a southern accent.

"Good morning, Captain Summerville, or is it afternoon?" Raymond asked.

"Good afternoon, Sergeant First Class Raymond. This is Staff Sergeant Hébert. He will not mind if you call him called Joe. What do you have for us, other than this fine, cool weather?"

"I think, we have a five-hundred-pound bomb about forty yards over the crest of the hill. It's not much over a hundred yards from here. You can see we have signal equipment up here. We use it to listen to the NVA who are a little over twenty miles west of us. We think, there are at least forty-five hundreds of them encamped there, waiting on orders to move in any direction. However, we feel this area is safe, so we do not have many people for security. The VC and NVA over there can take the mountain anytime they want it, but it would cost them dearly and they couldn't hold it." Raymond pointed toward the Cambodia border.

Joe asked, "Why didn't you blow the bomb and get it over with?"

"Well, if it was a projectile, we would have taken care of it. However, we were not sure what kind of damage a large bomb like this one would do. As I said, we have communication equipment close, and it is sensitive. Also, there is a Buddhist temple with a large statue close to here. We thought we should call someone with more experience with bombs." Raymond explained their thought process.

"All right then, let's go see what we have. We do have security, don't we?" Captain S asked.

"Yes, Sir. We have a squad size unit of ARVNs in the immediate area," Raymond said, as he walked toward the crest of the mountain. Their vantage point of almost a half a mile high offered them and unobstructed southwestern view of the vast plains of the Mekong River as far as the eye could see. Being this high, they noticed a distinct coolness of the air, caused by the altitude.

As Raymond had told them, the bomb lay over the crest of the mountain, no more than one-hundred and fifty yards from where the helicopter had dropped them. Raymond pointed out what he called a five-hundred-pound bomb. Joe knelt on all fours and brushed dirt off the item, which was 98 percent buried in the ground. He searched for any kind of markings, and said, "It looks like a bomb, but how large and its nomenclature, I can't tell you, Sir."

Captain S looked at Raymond and asked, "You found this thing yesterday?"

"Yes, Sir. We walked around here at least three times a week for the past year and didn't notice it. It was likely covered with dried foliage." Raymond nodded his head.

Joe said, "I can understand how you missed it. It's laying right at the base of this humongous boulder, but is covered with dirt, leaves, and rocks. Plus, there's a steep slope leading down to and from it."

Captain S replied, "Look at this monster of a rock. Geologically, I wonder how it got here. It looks like a huge river rock. Flying in, I saw them on the northwest face of the mountain, but no other on this end or side, the south side. I have seen boulders like this outside of Tucson, Arizona, although they weren't nearly as large. Someone told me; the ones in Arizona were deposited there by a glacier, thousands of years ago."

"I don't know about old boulders, Sir, but I bet this is an old French bomb, which means it's not a five-hundred pounder, but probably two-hundred, fifty kilos. We can look it up when we get back to the office." Joe directed the conversation back to the task at hand.

"French bomb!" Raymond softly said.

"Yeah, it's been here for a long time. The dirt around it is as hard as a rock. Sir, I'm not digging this thing out, unless you tell me to."

"Well, Tonto, it looks like a five-hundred pounder. So, we'll call it five-hundred pounds. Taking care of it won't move the boulder more than a couple of feet. If somehow it moves, it may cause it to tumble down the ridge, but that shouldn't be a problem. Sergeant First Class Raymond, I don't think it'll touch a thing over the ridge up top, and it certainly won't cause a seismic shock wave sufficient to hurt a statue some distance away. If you'll get your men up the hill, we'll solve your problem in fifteen minutes."

"I'm out of here!" Raymond quickly turned to leave.

"Give us ten minutes on the time fuse, Tonto."

"I'll make it twelve, and we don't have to rush. It's pretty steep going back up the hill." After Joe set the shot and yelled 'Fire in the Hole" three times, he pulled the ring on the firing device. They scampered back uphill.

Minutes later, when the explosion occurred, no in line frag reached the communication area, but a little harmless debris did fall on them. Joe asked, "Raymond, how long will it take to get the helicopter back here to pick us up?"

"I don't know for sure. He probably went down to Cao Lanh. It shouldn't take over thirty minutes." Raymond shrugged.

Captain S spoke up, "Hold on. I want to get back in time for a couple of scotches before dinner, but we still must check the shot before we leave. I don't think we need any security going back down there, so we can get this over with quickly."

Joe knew the captain wanted to do it by the book. "Okay, Sir. I agree. I want to see what we did to the boulder." On the approach downhill to the blast site, they could tell the boulder had not moved an inch. "Damn this thing must be a heavy as a rock!"

"Tonto, sometimes your brilliance amazes me. You smell the air; the stench is not from an American made explosive. I've never smelled anything like it. Therefore, it certainly was French or some other country, definitely not a modern American-made."

"How about this crater, chest deep on me." Joe jumped into the hole.

Captain S ask, "What are you doing down there?"

"Looking for some frag. I thought it might tell us something about the bomb." Joe began digging into the sides of the crater and under the boulder. "Uh-oh, uh-oh!"

"What? What have you found?" Captain S tried to see into the crater past Joe.

"Crap! I have a small hole." After a couple of minutes digging, Joe continued. "It looks like we found a VC tunnel under here." Joe looked up.

"Well, get your ass out of there. You idiot! Get away from it! The two of us are not prepared to face a snake hiding in the tunnel, certainly not Charlie." Captain S wanted to strangle Joe.

"There's no danger from Charlie if he was in this hole. If there, he was hurt badly." Joe stripped his backpack off and looked for a flashlight.

Finding the light and shining it into the hole, Joe reported, "It opens up inside."

"Don't get any ideas of becoming a tunnel rat." Captain S sounded authoritatively.

Joe opened the hole larger and told Captain S, "I believe it's a cave. It's not a tunnel. Ke-mo Sah-bee, you know there's no damn way we leave here without checking it out. I'll do it, you stand guard."

"You're right, Tonto, but dammit, be careful!" Captain S turned and surveyed his surroundings.

Holding his M-16 in one hand and a flashlight in the other, Joe squeezed under the boulder through a hole slightly big enough for his shoulders. "I'm through! I can stand up!" Joe yelled out of the hole.

After a while, Captain S jumped into the bomb crater and yelled into the hole Joe had crawled through. "Are you okay in there?"

When no reply came, Captain S yelled again. "Tonto, answer me! Are you okay?"

"Yes, Sir. I'm okay! Give me a couple minutes!" Joe weakly called back.

Joe pushed his weapon out and crawled back through the hole. Captain S noticed Joe looked a little chalky and breathed heavily.

"Are you okay? The last time I saw you look like this; you had missed a monofilament line under a downed helicopter." Captain S watched Joe carefully.

"Let me catch my breath a minute." Joe sat down in the crater and said nothing.

"I assume you didn't find Charlie, so what did you find?" Captain S noticed Joe seemed to be more relaxed.

After a short pause Joe said, "I would rather you see for yourself. You don't need your weapon. But Captain, you're not going to get those two scotches this afternoon.

CHAPTER 44

Captain S knew something had upset Joe, and he also knew this seldom occurred. He jumped to his feet, deposited his hardware, took Joe's light, and quickly disappeared into the hole under the boulder. He did not reappear for a good five minutes. When he did, he initially said nothing, seemingly happy to simply sit quietly beside Joe.

"Tonto, you've had a few more minutes to think about this than I have."

"Think! Hell, Sir. I can't tell you, my name! I never ever dreamed I would see anything like that. I haven't the slightest idea as what comes next. I hope you have some answers." Joe blew out a big breath. "This is a time when I'm glad you're the captain and I'm a meager sergeant."

"I don't know who we should call? Certainly no one in the 9th Division." Captain S went through every possibility he could think of in his head.

"We could cover the hole and come back after the war. Of course, as sure as we did, Charlie would show up and claim it. We have no choice. We have to tell someone up the chain, but this means, it belongs to Uncle Sam and not us." Joe espoused the possibilities as he saw them.

"What do you estimate is in there? Captain S couldn't begin to speculate.

"A lot! I would guess, when the containers are put together, there'll be somewhere near one and a half, fifty-five-gallon barrels of jewels, and about ten tons of gold." Joe tried not to giggle.

"I think there's more gold. Remember, we recently made a bunch of hazardous material shots over ten tons. Each shot was about the same size in volume size, as we have here. Gold weighs a lot more than steel and explosives." Captain S contrasted the two.

"Hello down there, are you guys still here?" Raymond yelled from somewhere above them.

"Yeah, we have a problem! We'll be up there in a few minutes. Don't come down here! It could be dangerous! Raymond, you better get your security back downhill, but don't let them come near this place! We have a situation which was caused by the explosion. It must be secured until, we can get someone in here to remove it!" Joe yelled up to Raymond, trying to quell any curiosity.

"Ok, I'll get the security moving!" Raymond replied.

"You're right about moving it, but who does the job is the question. Let's go up there and contact someone and get the ball rolling." Captain S stood slowly.

Once back on top of the mountain, Captain S told Raymond, "I need to report this as far up the chain as possible. There's a signal unit up here. Can you get me a secure line to the Commanding General, First Logistical Command?"

"I can't answer your question, but I know somebody in the 52nd Signal who can. Follow me." Raymond led him to a small, cubed, cinderblock building behind roles of barb-wire fence.

"Sir, I can talk to anybody in the world. I volunteered to come up here so I can call home." The signal Specialist staffing the communication equipment told Captain S.

"Good, get me a line to the Commanding General, 1st Log, and tell them Captain Summerville wants to speak with Lieutenant General Pickett."

"The CG, 1st Log! I, I, I." The Specialist stuttered.

"I didn't miss speak. Let's get started, and how secure is this line?"

"It's going over the air. You know what that means." The Specialist started working to get the call through.

"When we get an answer, can you leave me for a few minutes? It's classified." Captain S essentially ordered the Specialist out of the communication room.

After a minute of popping and static, a female voice answered. "1st Log, how may I direct your call?"

The Specialist handed the headset to Captain S and left the cube. "Yes, please connect me with General Pickett's office," Captain S said.

"One moment, please." The female voice replied.

"General Pickett's office." Another female voice answered.

"This is Captain Summerville. I need to speak with General Pickett. He told me to call him if I had a problem, so I'm calling."

"I'll connect you with Colonel West."

"This is Colonel West, what can I do for you, Summerville." The Colonel came on the line almost at once.

"Colonel, I need to speak directly with the General. I am the EOD officer from Dong Tam, and I have a problem. He told me to call him if I needed him. And I need him now! Not tomorrow." Captain S presented a respectful but blunt voice.

Colonel West replied, "I'm familiar with your problems at Dong Tam. Can I help you?"

"This call is not regarding Dong Tam. It's bigger and more parlous, and Colonel, not to be disrespectful, but the problem is over your head. Please, ask the General if he'll speak with me. I believe his words to me were, 'Don't hesitate to call me if you need me about anything', and I need him badly, now!" Captain S repeated the General's words.

"Okay, Captain. Give me a minute."

"Captain Summerville, let me first pass on my condolence about your personnel. It's part of war. Now, since you have a problem larger than my 0-6, I think you need to explain why you called me," Pickett said, after he picked up his phone.

"Thank you for thinking of my men, General. I did tell the Colonel it was over his head. To be honest, General, with no disrespect to you, it's probably over your head, too, and it's not your problem. In fact, I feel this may not be an Army problem at all. However, you're the biggest fish in the ocean that I know, and I'm asking for your help."

"Well Captain, you sound grandiose, so you better get it off your chest."

"General, I found something, but this is not a secure line, and I expect Hanoi is listening to every word. Before you ask me, I can't say where or what."

"Let me get this straight, Captain. You call me with a problem. You can't tell me what or where the problem is!" General Pickett snapped.

"You summed it up about right. You know who my boss is. He assigned me the mission this morning. It should take one of your men no more than two minutes to contact him on a secure line and find out where I am." Captain S schemed.

After a short pause, the General said, "Go ahead, Captain. This is getting interesting. First, be specific, what do you want me to do?"

"General, I want you to come here to see what we have found, and tell me what to do, or who to contact." Captain S pleaded.

"Who is this we?" They General quickly responded.

"My NCO, Staff Sergeant Hébert. Nobody else knows about this.

"He is the Sergeant who tackled my Aide, when you tackled me. At the time, I thought you might have a future in the Army. I hope this incident doesn't change my mind."

"Yes, General. He's the one, I'm talking about. I'll bet my bars on this incident, because this is bigger than the ASP explosion."

"I won't take your bars. I'll take your dreams. Okay, Captain, I know where you're located. I'll send Colonel West out to see what you've found."

"I don't like telling a Three-Star General he's making a mistake, but the fewer people with knowledge of this, the better. When he comes back to the office, he'll have to tell you, and who knows who else." Captain S assured him and did not back down.

"To get me on a helicopter, you're going to have to give me something. If you have nothing more, West will be headed your direction in fourth-five minutes."

"Well, General, the only thing I can say over the air is, Ke-mo Sah-bee and Tonto were looking for it. I can't remember if they found it, but Staff Sergeant Hébert and I did. Also, I reiterate, if I knew a bigger fish to call, I would have."

"Give me a minute." After a long minute, Pickett said, "Captain, I'll be at your location in an hour."

"See you then, General!"

Captain S first briefed Joe on his discussion with Pickett. He then told SEC Raymond, "Some high-ranking people will be coming in. Is your security tight?"

"It's as tight as I can get it with what I have."

When the helicopter arrived, Captain S looked surprised to see Colonel West with General Pickett. When they stepped down, and after the traditional introductions and the departure of the helicopter, General Pickett asked Raymond, "How secure are we here?"

"I'm betting my life, we're secure. However, those three stars offer a tempting target." Raymond said with a big smile.

"You're so reassuring!" Pickett replied condescendingly.

Captain S stepped in. "General, you're safe. No one knew you were coming except Staff Sergeant Hébert and me. I only told Sergeant First Class Raymond; some high-ranking officers were coming."

"Yeah, I expected a Major or LTC." Raymond stared wide-eyed at the General.

"Okay, let's go see what has your dander up. West, you wait here with Sergeant First Class Raymond. We shouldn't be long."

Captain S lead the way over the crest of the hill to the bomb crater where they found Joe sitting in the crater to assure no one approached.

"Staff Sergeant Hébert, good to see you again… Now, Captain, are you ever going to tell me why I am here?" The General asked.

"I'm going to show you, General. You'll get dirty, and you'll need this light. It's not too bad. Follow me." Captain S handed him a light and crawled through the hole under the boulder.

Ten minutes later, Captain S yelled from inside the hole, "Coming out, Tonto." When they reappeared, the three of them sat silently in the crater for a couple of minutes. Finally, the General sarcastically spoke. "We have four-hundred-thousand troops in country. And who finds this mess: a captain, whom two weeks earlier, I told to call me if he had a problem! Thank you, Lord!" He shook his head and rubbed his forehead.

Captain Summerville, I have been in the Army for almost thirty years, and thought, I'd seen everything." He continued shaking his head.

"General, I'll go so far as saying, we three are the only living humans who have seen anything like this. It's likely been hundreds of years. The question is, what are we going to do with it?" Captain S restated the question of the day.

"I'll have to give it some thought." General Pickett pondered the situation.

"I tried to convince the captain to cover this hole and come back after the war and get it for ourselves." Joe spoke with a big grin.

"Spoken like a good Sergeant. Although, what you suggested is still an option." General Pickett chuckled for the first time.

"We all know it's not an option, and this is why I called you." Captain S tried to bring the subject back to reality.

"Well, I'd like to thank you for laying this in my lap, as if I don't have enough to worry about." General Pickett hung his head in thought.

"Sorry, General, but like I said, you're the biggest fish that I could reach out to. If you wouldn't have taken my call, I would've probably been an extremely wealthy man in my old age."

"Don't be sorry, it's why I'm paid the big bucks. I heard you call Hébert, Tonto. What's going on there?"

"It slipped. I never call him Tonto in public, only when we're working. He calls me Ke-mo Sah-bee. It started months ago. I would say it's more of a respect thing to ease tension when working together." Captain S shrugged.

"I find it ironic, almost foretelling. I must let you know. I wasn't coming out here until you gave me the clue. I didn't have the slightest idea what you were talking about. My secretary, who is much younger than I, right off the tip of her tongue, told me the Lone Ranger and Tonto were looking for the City of Gold in a movie. I thought you may have found a gold mine or perhaps an old Buddhist temple with gold relics. What we have here never crossed my mind." The General shook his head again.

"I didn't think, I could tell you what we found on an open line."

"You were smart to do so. However, for your information, you didn't have to worry Hanoi listening to us. It's Moscow, we have to worry about."

"Hello down there! I'm only checking on you!" SFC Raymond yelled.

"We're fine! Stay up there!" Joe quickly responded.

General Pickett yelled, "West, are you there?"

"Yes, General!" He replied.

"I've seen enough! Get the chopper back in!"

"General, we'll be here all night. Can you have someone call my boss and let him know? He can call my unit, my senior NCO. After our recent troubles, I don't want him to worry."

"I understand, Captain. I'll make sure he's aware of your situation. Is there anything else I can do for you?"

Joe spoke up, "Well, since you asked, the last time we ate was breakfast, and our canteens are getting low. Also, Raymond and his men, I don't know how long they've been up here."

"Spoken like a good NCO, thinking about the stomach, but I hear you. I think we should find more security. Anything else?"

"No, General. We'll sit here until you tell us to move," Captain S replied.

"I'll have to run this by my boss, The Commanding General. When I leave here, I'm going there. As far as I can see, and as you suggested earlier, this is not an Army problem. However, we're currently controlling the situation. My boss will tell me what to do or take it out of my hands. One way or the other, I'll be back, early tomorrow morning with a solution. In the meantime, you might get a rough estimate of the inventory. Also, I want one of you to always stay in this crater. No one comes close. Hébert, shoot anybody who sticks their head in this crater. And I mean anybody." The General was not kidding.

Joe spoke. "General, we told Sergeant First Class Raymond, we found a heavily booby-trapped cache. Curiosity will mount. With your appearance, may I suggest our story include first seen items with possible chemicals. I don't like lying, but the explosion and the cave had a foul odor." Joe suggested a cover story.

"I think we could make the story about first seen items hold up. How about you, Summerville?"

"I see no problems with the story. So, it sounds good to me." Captain S nodded in approval.

"Let's get out of here before they come back. I don't want Staff Sergeant Hébert shooting West. I saw what he did to my Aide. Good luck Staff Sergeant. See you tomorrow morning." Pickett smiled and offered Joe a handshake.

While waiting on the chopper, Pickett told Raymond, "You can expect reinforcements, and there is a possibility you'll be here all night."

Colonel West did not ask about the situation.

As General Pickett's helicopter lifted off headed east, Captain S turned to Raymond and said, "It looks like we have it!"

"Yeah, but what do we have, Captain?" Raymond's curiosity peaked.

"I'm not supposed to say anything, so don't repeat what I'm about to tell you. We opened a tunnel under the boulder. There were things there which neither Staff Sergeant Hébert nor I have never seen. I expect the General will get someone in here tomorrow to take it somewhere for safe evaluation." Captain S looked Raymond straight in the eye.

"Do you guys run across many situations like this?" Raymond showed his curiosity.

"No, and this stuff has a foul smell to it. "Captain S laid it on thick.

"Okay, now I see. Now, I understand. You think you have found some unknown chemical ammunition." Raymond nodded his head, while putting make-believe puzzle pieces together.

"I didn't tell you that, and don't pass it on to anybody. I can, however, tell you the man leaving here has by now made a call to MACV. I don't know your chain of command, but I bet somebody you know will soon be calling you wanting some answers. When they do, tell them there is an EOD Officer here, and he won't tell you anything."

"Yes, Sir," Raymond said.

"It's about an hour until sunset. I suspect we'll see a couple of helicopters in here with reinforcements and something to eat. Make sure no one goes close to where the bomb was. Staff Sergeant Hébert and I will be there. We get hazardous duty pay every month to take chances with hazardous material." Captain S managed to keep a straight face.

Fine with me, Sir. I'll tell them. I'm sure we'll establish some listening post beyond you, but I'll tell them to stay clear of the site."

"Okay, Raymond. I'll go back down there. If you have any problems, come get me. When they send food, I presume C-rations, bring them down to the top of the boulder."

"Yes, Sir," Raymond said, as Captain S headed back down the mountain.

When there Joe said, "It's going to get dark soon, Ke-mo Sah-bee."

"Yes, and I know what you want to do, the same thing as I do. You've been sitting here the longest, so go ahead, go back in, and take a good look. I'll stay here."

Before Captain S finished the sentence, Joe jumped to his feet and started preparing to enter the hole. In the cave, he began by looking and running his hands through the jewel laden, leather-covered baskets-like containers. Each of which he estimated to hold approximately five to seven gallons of various colored jewels. With his light, he could see jewels of every color of the rainbow. Most were small, but he pulled a few almost as large as a ping pong ball to the top. He wished he knew what to look for. He counted seventeen containers.

There were two stacks of gold, each stack would easily fill the bed of his 1955 Ford truck two times. One stack consisted of gold blocks slightly smaller than a standard brick. The other stack consisted of smaller blocks, a little larger than two decks of cards. The gold stacks and jewels were symmetrically placed equal distance from each other and from the walls of the cave.

His thinking turned to the possible history of such a trove. Genghis Kahn kept flashing in his mind as the only person with this capability. Yes, he would have had such wealth, but he never ventured this far south, or so he thought.

As for its future, it will be turned over to the corrupt Vietnamese government and used to buy power. Or perhaps, it will be transported to the States, where it will go into a hole at Fort Knox, or more probable, meet the same fate as giving it to the Vietnamese government. No matter what its future, it'll have no effect on Captain S or me. Unless I can find a way.

Crawling out of the hole, Joe's heart suddenly pounded irregularly. Captain S could not be seen, but the weapons were still there. Grabbing his M-16 he yelled, "Captain!"

"Yoe, up here." Captain S replied from above him.

"Sir, you scared the crap out of me." Joe let out a breath which he did not realize he had been holding.

"I had to come up here to meet Raymond. He brought us C-rats and water. Come on up, we have a better view from here." Captain S waived Joe up.

Joe, carrying his M-16, climbed up the ridge about forty feet and stepped out on the boulder. "Wow, we do get a nicer view from here. I'm sure we can see into Cambodia, but I wonder how far it is?"

"I don't know, but we're going to see a beautiful sunset, and later, the stars in the Southern Hemisphere will pop. With this cool air, we can enjoy it." Captain S pointed to the horizon where the sun had begun setting.

"I was thinking about this treasure. Was there anywhere in the expensive, Duke education of yours, they taught you anything about a dynasty who could have parked this stuff here?"

"You were thinking, Tonto? Impressive!" Captain S grinned at Joe. "But to answer your question, I was never taught anything which could explain this. I think it originated in China or India. What I find interesting is whoever put it here, probably moved this boulder to cover the cave, which I bet was dug by hand. Moving the stone would have taken at least five hundred people. Nobody in their right mind would let five hundred people know where they were hiding the treasure. Their fate was probably sealed."

"Maybe some elephants from India were used. I'm not giving it any further thought. I don't think it's relevant to our situation. I'm thinking about, how we can carry some of the gold out of here." Joe wanted to see how Captain S responded.

"We can't. Hell, whoever comes and gets it will tell us thanks, and pat us on the back. It's not ours. We found it, and there is no more to the story. It belongs to the people of Vietnam. I did a little quick estimation on the gold. At forty dollars per troy ounce, I bet the gold is worth more than a million dollars. After the war, Vietnam can use it to help rebuild." Captain S broke the sad news to Joe.

An hour after dark they were still sitting on the boulder, watching the skies southwest of them. They saw what they thought were artillery firing south of them. They also saw larger flashes of light west of them, one after the other, maybe seventy-five flashes would occur, the ground quivered, and then it would begin again.

"B-52's at work in Cambodia." Captain S pointed out.

Joe suddenly realized; he had seen these flashes seven months before, during his arrival into Vietnam. "I wonder if the timing of the bombing is a consequence, or if it's related to our find."

"The B-52's would have likely been in the air before anyone could change this bombing run. However, a Three Star General can change targets." Captain S thought aloud.

"Damn, I wish Ava was here to see this. We've never been out at night laying on a blanket, watching the stars, and listening to the night noise." Joe sighed.

"That sounds good, but Baby San and Lein wouldn't be bad right now." Captain S stretched out.

"Ke-mo Sah-bee, I've said it before, but I like the way you think. It didn't take long for our conversation to turn to a meaningful subject."

"Do you know her name?" The captain folded his arms under his head.

"Who? Whose name?" Joe's questioned, Captain S.

"Baby San's, who else?" Captain S looked at Joe.

"Do I know Baby San's name? It's Baby San! No, that won't be her real name. I guess, I don't." Joe admitted shaking his head in disbelief.

"It's Mai Ly. I think it means apple blossom. It's a crime against nature for this world to have people as nice and as smart as she is, and the world craps on them. There's probably millions like her. Think about it. If we could pluck them out of their environment and put them in one country somewhere, what would that country become?" Captain S honestly asked Joe.

"Your voice sounds full of reverence when speaking of Baby San. I believe you care more about her than you have admitted. However, I don't have to worry about being moved to your fantasy country. I'm not smart enough to be selected. Did you notice when we're out under the stars, we always end up talking about women?"

"Yeah, and I guess, I do have strong feelings for her. I really like holding he. She so small. Heck one of her breasts will hardly fill a coffee cup. Hell, I never thought that I would fall for her. But I catch myself waiting to see her every morning. Thin I catch myself glancing at Wheeler. He's watching for her to walk through the door. I must remind myself she belongs to him. However, I'll hold on to her as long as I can. Then, she'll turn to Wheeler." Captain S slapped his hand on his thigh.

"We better get down in our hole. Maybe we can get some sleep. At least there are no mosquitoes on the Forbidden Mountain. Tonto, I want one of us awake in the crater, and one in the cave, sleeping. I'm sure you have more experience standing watch than I do. So, I'll take the crater first and will wake you at 0100."

"Sounds good to me, Sir. I'd recommend putting our packs in the cave so if crap happens outside, we can crawl into the cave and act like the 300 Spartans. It would be the battle of the Forbidden Mountain and would replace the battle of Thermopylae in the history books." Joe pounded on his chest.

Captain S mockingly looked at Joe. "You do know how the battle ended, right? However, it's a sound idea for a Cajun. We'll do what you said about the packs, but you make sure to get some sleep."

*****

With the sun not completely up, Joe heard the first helicopter coming in. He stuck his head in the hole and yelled to Captain S. "It's time to get up. Somebody's coming!"

The somebody was Lieutenant General Pickett. By the time Captain S scrambled up the hill, the helicopter had disappeared. SFC Raymond stood briefing the General, "We had no problems. It was as quiet as a mouse all night."

"Summerville, did you get any sleep?" The General asked as he approached.

"Probably more than you, General."

"Sergeant First Class Raymond, have your people maintain the perimeter. We don't need any unwelcome visitors. There's a chopper about thirty minutes out. If I'm not back when they arrive, bring the crew down to the top of the boulder. Summerville and I will meet you there." Pickett ordered and headed downhill toward the crater.

Captain S asked, "Who's coming in?"

"Would you believe, I don't know? As you implied yesterday, it's over my paygrade. I do know we have to find space enough to place a Conex as close to the crater as possible. You're going to be here for a couple of days, or more. I gave my boss the estimate of cubic feet of gold we have. He called back late and told me it may take fifteen loads per stack. Obviously, it's not the volume. It's the weight. I want to know how long it'll take you to load all that gold?" Pickett smiled broadly.

"I don't know how long, but it'll be done one bar, or block, at the time." Captain S rubbed his face while thinking about it.

They decided on a spot, next to the crater at the bottom of the boulder, for the Conex. "The only problem is, it's covered with brush." Captain S expressed his concern.

"Captain, the brush is not your problem. Whoever is in the chopper, on its way in, will manage it. This mountain belongs to them now. You'll take your orders from them."

"Okay, General."

"One other thing, Captain. In case it crossed your mind, neither you nor Staff Sergeant Hébert will receive any kind of recognition or award for what you have done, here. There are only four people in the Army who knows what is going on here. Three of us are here. After you leave Vietnam, I'll put a letter in both of your official records. It may be indorsed by my boss. This will give you some fine visibility, and you'll be watched and nurtured. Right now, I want to see it again. Then I'll get out of your hair."

They had returned to the top, and the General had left when the next chopper arrived. The first man out said, "Captain Summerville, I'm James Smith. As of midnight, last night you work for me. You'll answer to only me, until further notified. When we finish here, you'll have the opportunity to retrieve your personal items from Dong Tam. Afterwards, you'll go wherever this material goes. Now, show me what we are working with. We have a Conex scheduled to arrive in less than an hour." The man wore jungle fatigues with no rank or markings, except for the J Smith name tag.

Captain S wondered if he had heard wrong or misinterpreted his meaning but now was not the time for questioning. He noticed the four men with James Smith were dressed the same, including the same name tags. They were carrying shovels and a chainsaw.

"We'll have time for further introductions later." James Smith did not even blink.

Without saying a word, Captain S took the five Smiths to the crater. He couldn't help but notice James Smith looked about his size, but more muscular. He had graying hair on his temples. Captain S guessed his age at late thirties.

When they arrived at the crater, Joe stood, but seeing no rank he merely said, "Good morning."

"Staff Sergeant Hébert, I understand you were a cold night away from becoming a SEAL." Smith looked Joe up and down presumably sizing him up.

"I guess you could say that. You probably know what high school I graduated from, too."

"You're from Lockport, Louisiana, class of 1960, finished twenty-first out of a class of sixty-two, played tackle in football, your father died in an accident, your brother died from a snake bite." Smith rattled off.

"I didn't know I finished twenty-first in my class! So, I'd say you did your homework, and you slept about the same amount of time as we did last night." Joe smirked.

"Sleep, what's that? I have four guys with me, all of them are named, Smith. From now forward, shoot anybody not named Smith coming down the slope. Well, you better not shoot Summerville. Now, show me the goods." Smith flashed an insightful smile.

After Captain S and Smith disappeared into the hole, the four Smiths showed up with two shovels, a chainsaw, and two coolers. Also, each carried an AR-15.

"Joe, I'm Joe Smith, this is Jerry, Josh, and John. If this is where we're setting the Conex. I assume we are looking at the cave entrance."

Joe Smith then turned to John Smith, who held the chainsaw, and said, "When you're finished here, go to work on the stuff up the hill. We do not want a prop to get into it. The chopper will need to get as low as possible. Jerry, help him." He then turned to Josh and said, "We'll use the shovels to enlarge the entrance to the cave."

Inside the crater, James Smith said nothing as he carefully evaluated the situation. Standing over one of the gold stacks, Captain S broke the silence. "It may be gold but is a terrible bed."

"You're complaining? After all, it was a bed! I'm shocked there's no silver. It means something and may be a clue to its origin. I've seen enough for now." Smith appeared dismissive.

Outside, Captain S said, "The area is opening up nicely and the hole can be made even larger."

"John, get the Conex in here. I want to be moving gold bricks within an hour," James ordered.

"In an hour? Where's the Conex coming from?" Captain S could not believe everything happened so quickly.

"It's about thirty miles right over there. We moved it in last night." James pointed northwest.

"I'm impressed. Is there anything I can do?"

"Rest, if you can, Summerville. However, Staff Sergeant Hébert, would you go up top and tell the NCO in charge, we should have a Conex coming in soon, and the prop wash will be significant? He should take the necessary cautions for the safety of his troops," James spoke bluntly.

"When the Sikorsky CH-54 sky crane dropped the Conex container in the cleared area and departed, Joe, Captain S, and the five Smiths, were safely huddled inside the cave. Through the enlarged hole, they could see the Conex hit the ground in the clearing about ten feet from the cave entrance.

Captain S and Joe found a seat on the perch atop the boulder and watched the five Smiths work. They pulled a generator out of the Conex first, followed by three boxes, and a long, narrow, sectionalized conveyor-belt. "Damn, they know how to plan and get things together. I bet there aren't a dozen conveyors like that one in all of Vietnam. Who are these guys?" Joe asked in a truly perplexed manner.

"They didn't tell me. It's above my pay grade. They could be State Department, CIA, Department of Treasury, or some acronym we've never heard about. But look at James, he's a pro. He did tell me something, I should tell you. He didn't direct me to keep it secret." Captain S started thinking throughs about everything he had recently seen and heard.

"What are you talking about, Ke-mo Sah-bee?"

Captain S told Joe what James had said earlier. "He surely sounded convincing, and it looks as if I'm leaving. I don't know where, but I'm going somewhere. He didn't mention you, and I didn't get a chance to ask." Captain S looked at Joe.

Joe surmised, "It sounds like you're going to Fort Knox."

"I could be going anywhere in Vietnam, CONUS, or even to another country. As you always say, I guess we'll find out." Captain S shrugged. "You know this is a government operation, hurry up and wait. They'll tell us what we need to know, when we need to know it."

The five Smiths assembled the conveyor in a professional manner. The generator powered an electrical motor, which drove the conveyer, and powered floodlights inside the cave. The conveyor ran from the Conex to the second stack of gold.

James Smith looked up and said, "Captain S, Staff Sergeant Hébert, we could use your help. We want to put approximately three-hundred and eighty-five blocks in the Conex and move it out. It doesn't sound like a lot, but it's a lot of weight."

"It looks like we'll be here all day." Joe exhaled loudly.

"Do your math, Sergeant." Smith smiled.

After loaded, at 0855 hours, a sky crane lifted the Conex, and wrenched it tightly to its center spine, which lessen its drag and helped to prevent the pendulum effect. This stabilized the flight.

Another empty Conex appeared within ten minutes. Fifty minutes later, the second Conex departure, and the third bird arrived five minutes later, with instructions to increase the load to four hundred bricks. With three men loading the conveyor, and four men placing the bricks in the Conex container, the operation went smoothly. To everyone's surprise, when the fifth Conex arrived, it held a cooler with hot lunches.

By sunset, they had moved nearly four thousand of the over seven thousand large gold bricks, which weighed approximately forty-eight pounds each. The eleventh Conex held more hot meals, cots, bed rolls, clean clothes to include underwear, personal hygiene kits, and seven, five-gallon water cans, enough for each of them to have a nice bath.

As they unloaded their supplies, Captain S said, "Tonto, I don't know where this came from, but I'm absolutely sure the Army had nothing to do with this operation."

"You're right. The Army would have sent us some water to drink and C-rats, period." Joe sarcastically agreed.

The operation continued for three more days. The small bricks were physically easier to move, but because of the sheer quantity, a little over eighty thousand blocks, at over four pounds each, consumed more time. Moving all the jewels presented no problems. They were simply scooped up and put into ammo cans.

The last Conex leaving also held all the used equipment, including the conveyor. It lifted off about ten minutes before dark on the fourth day.

On top of the Forbidden Mountain, while waiting on their helicopters, James Smith told Joe, "Staff Sergeant Hébert, the first chopper in is yours. You'll go back to Dong Tam. You'll have a stopover in Can Tho. I must remind you to never whisper a word of this operation. Thank you for your help and cooperation. You'll need to carry Captain S's pack and weapon with you. He won't need them. I should have checked your packs before now. Did you fill them full of jewels and gold?" Smith looked Joe directly in the eye to see if he squirmed.

"You can check my pack. I don't think you'll find anything in them, except C-4, det cord, of interest." Joe presented a large smile.

Smith took a quick glance into each pack. After seeing nothing suspicious, he said, "Okay, Joe, thanks again, and keep your head down."

CHAPTER 45

"Well, you decided to come home. You took some more days off and didn't let me know where you were." Scott had acid in his voice as Joe walked into the office the next morning.

"Good morning to you, too. Everybody can use an extra four days. Right now, I need coffee. I didn't get in until midnight. While walking from Charlie Pad, an MP picked me up and brought me in. Wheeler, you didn't even know when I arrived. You were sound asleep."

Wheeler replied, "It's been quiet around here with only Master Sergeant Scott and me. We've been turning in early. The girls have had little to do, so the four of us simply sit around all day."

"I thought Control was going to send us another team?" Joe slipped into Captain S's chair with his cup of coffee.

"They were, but they changed their mind. There's a team at Tan An, but we're still non-operational. Does Control know you two came home?"

"No, Master Sergeant. I guess, you should call and let them know, I'm back at Dong Tam." Joe looked at the floor.

"I'm back!" Scott snapped. "What do you mean by, 'I'm back'? Where's Captain S?"

"I came in by myself. I don't know when the captain will be back." Joe looked directly at Scott.

"What's going on, Staff Sergeant?" Scott pinned Joe down with a look.

"Maybe a call to Control can answer the question, better than I can." Joe broke eye contact.

"Wheeler, get Sergeant Major Hicks for me." Scott turned to Wheeler.

"Good morning. How are things down there?" Sergeant Major Hicks answered the phone.

"Why do you think I'm calling? I sent a team out five days ago and nobody will keep me up to date on their activities, except to say, they're working. Half of the team shows up this morning, and he doesn't know when his Commander will be coming back. I think I deserve some answers." Scott tried hard to remain calm.

"I don't know where they've been or what they've been doing. I also don't know where Captain Summerville is. I'll let you talk with Major Sparks." Hicks seemed as confused as Scott.

"I don't have any answers for you, Master Sergeant Scott," Sparks said, when he answered the phone. "Am I to understand Staff Sergeant Hébert is back at Dong Tam? If he is, it's news to me."

"Yes, Sir. He came in late last night."

"Good. At least we now have a team down there, even though you're still considered non-operational. However, if some powder-puff incident comes up, I may have to call on you two." Sparks informed Scott.

"Okay, Sir. Can I expect another team anytime soon?"

"Not yet. Have a good day, Master Sergeant." Sparks hung up.

"They were informative! There's something in the air, and I don't like being left out of the loop. What, the hell, have you been doing for the last week?" Scott rocked in his chair and demanded an answer from Joe.

"Well--" The girls coming through the door interrupted Joe.

"Hébert, you come home." Lein said loudly. After handing Sam to Wheeler, she went to hug Joe, who had stood.

"Are you and Sam, okay?" Joe hugged Lein back, without any pretensions.

"Yes, but still sad." Lein retorted.

"Good. I want to see the boy. And how are you, Baby, I mean Mai Ly?" Remembering his prior conversation with Captain S, Joe corrected himself.

"I am fine, Hébert." Baby San rose on her toes and wrapped her arms around his neck and kissed him on his cheek.

"Wow, maybe I should leave more often and come back. Or maybe I should have called you Mai Ly sooner. Now, let me see the boy." Joe took Sam from Wheeler.

"Take the rascal out of the office. Wheeler and I need to get some work done." Scott growled.

"I have to go to the exchange. Later, I'm going back to bed, and don't disturbed me until after lunch. Do any of you need anything from the PX?" Joe looked at them for an answer.

When Joe returned from the exchange, knowing Lein or Baby San would be the only one who would come into the big tent, he reminded them not to disturb him because he needed sleep.

He had originally thought, two shaving kits would be a sufficient size for his project, but now, with the addition of Captain S's pack, he needed a larger bag.

At the exchange, Joe bought a standard size gym bags and two large bottles of Elmer's glue.

Now sitting on his bunk with his and Captain S's pack, he surgically removed the inner bottom of the new gym bags and evaluated it.

Satisfied that it would nicely fit back in the bag, he took one of the blocks of C-4 from his pack and carefully removed the sheet of wrapping paper from around it. For the first time, he noticed the block of C-4 looked larger than it should. He began flattening the C-4 like a pancake, exposing several large lumps, almost the size of ping pong balls, and more than two cups of smaller marble sized lumps. Using a towel, he wiped the sticky C-4 from each of the stones.

Rubies are red, diamonds are clear, and big is better than small amounted to his total knowledge of gemstones. However, the people who stored the trove appeared to not value one stone over the next, and they surely knew their value. When selecting his prize, he simply took a sample of all, with a heavy priority to red. He knew the Queen of England had an unusually large ruby collection, and he thought it would be profitable for him to have large rubies.

After he removed the stones from all the blocks of C-4, he and Captain S were carrying, he had about one and a half gallons of mostly marble size jewels and sixty-six larger size jewels. He placed all but two of the marble size, red jewels into the bottom of the new gym bags. By adding glue and paper filler to the bottom and covering it with the bottom of the bag, likely no difference was noticed when looking down into the bag. Someone would have to be good to notice his finished work, but the weight and the depth of the bottom could be a problem. He would have to risk it.

His work began the first night in the cave when Captain S guarded from the crater. Inside the cave, Joe removed everything except for the C-4 blocks from their two packs. He hid the contents. He hoped Captain S would be sleeping too soundly to notice him when he returned inside the cave to recover the packs. He filled the two packs with jewels, taking equal amounts from each basket or chest. When he assumed the guard position, and after he knew Captain S slept, he retrieved the packs holding the jewels from inside the cave. He placed about three gallons of the jewels under a large, flat stone, which weighed about a hundred pounds, twenty feet west of the top of the large boulder. He thought they would be safe there until the war was over. He kept about a gallon.

After burying the jewels, he carefully removed the wrappings from the C-4. He split the blocks into halves, and hollowed out each side, where he placed the remaining gallon of stones and re-assembled the blocks of C-4. He burned the residual explosive, returned the blocks of C-4, and other supplies to their original packs. Then he placed the packs in their original position in the cave.

Now, satisfied with his work on the gym bags, Joe lay in his bed smiling and examining his two-marble size, red jewels which he thought were rubies.

Later, at lunch, Master Sergeant Scott told Joe, "Captain S called, and said he would be back late this afternoon.

"Good." Joe gladly replied.

Scott added, "Major Sparks also called. He said, he and somebody from Headquarters, 1st Log will be here tomorrow for an award presentation at 1330 hours. He asked me to set up a place and tell anybody who wanted to attend. Do you know anything about this?"

"No, nothing." Joe shook his head.

"Well, I know they aren't giving Wheeler, or I awards for timely getting the morning report in. Therefore, it has to be for Captain S for cleaning up the ASP."

"That sounds like the Army. Hollow wants to relieve Captain S, and First Log wants to give him an award, because of the same action." Joe couldn't believe it.

"This, my friend, describes the situation perfectly. Now, I'm pulling a Captain S. I'm going to see Donaldson, and then, I'm going to the Chiefs Club. Don't bother me unless the place is on fire." Scott stood to leave.

"What are you cooking up?" Joe knew Scott leaving his office meant something.

"Nothing for you to worry about." Scott's eyebrows nearly reached his hairline, daring Joe to ask any more questions.

With Wheeler and Baby San in the office, Joe and Lein were in the small tent having a conversation with Sam. After Sam became bossy, Joe told Lein, "He can go with me, and we can take a nap. If you have nothing to do, you can come with us."

After Sam fell asleep on one bed, Joe and Lein lay in another bed, covered with a sheet, holding each other, and letting nature take its course, something neither would have thought about doing a month earlier.

When Captain S arrived, shortly before sunset, Joe noticeable his clean uniform. However, his eyes and shoulders said he had not slept in forever.

Hey guys, you're doing, okay?" Captain S spoke to the remaining members of his unit.

Yes, Sir." The three of them said in unison.

Scott replied, "And you, Sir?"

"I could use some sleep but more important, are we good to go?" Captain S looked at Scott.

"We're good." Scott nodded his head.

"You look like those call girls in Saigon didn't let you sleep at all last night." Joe laughed and waved his hand at Captain S's uniform.

"Not a lot. What little I got seemed like a hard bed in a Conex." Captain S gave Joe a look which told him to drop it.

"Maybe you'll get some sleep tonight." Joe grinned and did as Captain S implied.

"Joe, I have some things to do tonight, and I'll turn in early. It'll likely be an early morning. I might as well tell you now. Tonight is my last night here. I'll be leaving tomorrow afternoon."

This did not surprised Joe, so he watched Wheeler's reaction. *The man should be a gambler.* Nothing revealed what his thoughts were whether losing a good Commander or losing a competitor for someone he dearly loved. *You are a good man, Mr. Wheeler.*

Scott found the bright spot. "I'm surprised and disappointed, Sir, but under the circumstances this is probably a good thing. If you stay here, Hollow will find a way to get you."

"Yeah, timing wise, this couldn't be better. Right now, I'm going to find Commander Davis. He may still be eating."

Early the next morning found Captain S, Scott, Joe, and Wheeler sitting in the office drinking coffee. "There's nothing in the office I need except for my nameplate. I still have a little packing to do at my BOQ. I'd like for the girls to come over and clean my room. Later, I'll pick up my medical and personnel files, and I'm out of here." Captain S looked at his coffee cup.

"It's strange, Control couldn't tell you where you were going." Scott sat in disbelief.

Wheeler surmised, "Since you only have a month before you're supposed to return home, maybe you'll get a drop and go home early. DA's involvement would explain everything."

"I'll find out soon--" The phone interrupted Captain S.

"The call came from DESCOM, or to be more precise, Col. Hollow's office. There's a bomb in his office. He wants someone there, now!" Wheeler announced the news to everyone.

"A bomb?" Joe jumped up.

"I think we should have another cup of coffee. After all, we're non-operational because of him." Captain S calmly remained in his chair.

"Yeah, we should. But you know we have to check it out." Joe looked at Captain S.

"No, Tonto, we don't. You stay here. Master Sergeant Scott, you come with me. It's time you earn your hazardous duty pay," Captain S announced and pushed his chair back.

"You want me to go with you?" Scott showed concern and disbelief in what he heard.

"You heard me, Master Sergeant. I'm still the boss, until I leave. Get your gear on." Captain S stood and went to get his own gear, one last time.

Captain S and Scott walked hastily and jogged intermittently to DESCOM headquarters, where they found people standing outside the building. Colonel Hollow and Donaldson met them.

"What took you so long, Captain? I should have known you would take your time getting here!" Hollow scowled.

"Sir, tell me what the situation is." Captain S sounded blunt.

"There's a bomb--".

"Be more specific, Sir." Captain S said, cutting him off.

"I opened my desk drawer and found a clock, some wires, and some C-4 explosives. Am I specific enough for you, Captain?" Hollow said sarcastically.

"Did you see a power source?"

"Captain, I told you what I saw. Get in there and do your job!" Hollow shouted.

Scott told Donaldson, "Sergeant Major, I recommend you get all these people back at least a hundred yards, and behind some kind of cover."

Captain S and Scott did a quick check of the building to ensure no one remained inside. Finding the building vacant, they entered Colonel Hollow's office and closed the door behind them.

Captain S sat in the Colonel's leather, high-back chair. Scott sat down in an intricately carved teak chair. They both leaned back and propped their feet on the massive desk and smiled at each other.

"This feels like a cigar moment." Scott looked around the office, perfectly relaxed.

"Damn, I didn't think of that! But everything seems to have gone as planned. Donaldson came through as you said he would." Captain S put his arms behind his head.

"Yeah, but now is the critical part. Are you sure you want to go through with this? I'm fine with it." Scott stayed as cool as a cucumber.

"You're damn right, I am! Nobody else will ever get an ass chewing in this office for BS."

Captain S removed the fake bomb from the desk drawer, and replaced it with a real one and said, "We have three minutes."

Approximately a minute and a half later, Captain S and Scott were standing in front of Hollow, who shouted. "What do you mean it's not safe to go inside?"

"Sir, we were unable to render the item safe. We need more tools. We were on our way back to our unit to get the tools when you stopped us." Captain S explained the situation.

"You get back in there and do something, now! It's an order!" Hollow growled.

"Do you want to kill us, the same way your actions killed four of my men? If it hadn't been for your pompous ass interrupting, they may be alive today. Now, if you would like to go back inside with me, I'll certainly go back with you. I don't recommend it. You are the man here. You lead. I will follow. Otherwise, I'm going to get some more tools where I can do my job correctly!" Captain S spoke loudly. He took a couple of steps before the explosion ripped through the office.

Joe and Wheeler were running as fast as they could toward the sound of the explosion when they saw Captain S and Scott calmly walking toward the unit. The girls followed. When Joe saw the big smiles on their faces, he said. "You bastards. You scared the crap out of me. Besides, you should have let me in on this."

"In on what?" Scott smiled and tried not to laugh too loudly.

"Even I know you two did it, or at least, didn't prevent it." Wheeler smiled and shook his head. He felt like a faithful member of the unit.

"What did we do? We were lucky. We could've been killed." Captain S winked his eye and put on his best schoolchild look.

"BS and you know it, but it's okay. Congratulations, anyway! You make me proud to be on your team." Joe patted Captain S on the back repeatedly. "Damn, Buck, it's great to have you as a working member of the team. I couldn't be prouder."

"Think what you want. There is nothing, I can do to change your mind. However, since the girls are here, you and the girls can come over to my BOQ and help me finish up." Captain S looked at Joe.

When Captain S, Joe, and the two girls drove up to the BOQ, Joe said, "Lein, you stay out here with me."

Knowing there would be no cleaning needed, Lein and Baby San smiled at each other. After the door to the BOQ room closed, Lein said, "This is good."

"No, no Lein. This is not good." Joe then explained the situation.

After Captain S and Baby San made love and were lying in bed, Baby San asked, "Why us no, why have we not come here more often?"

"I told you when we were here before, it isn't safe. I'll get in a lot of trouble if we're caught."

"It is safe today?"

"No, but I need to talk with you about something." Captain S took a deep breath.

"Is something wrong?"

"Yes. This will be our last time together. I am leaving Dong Tam." Captain S sighed heavily.

"When, where you go? You go to States?" Baby San's mouth gaped. Her eyes showed dejection.

"I don't know where, but I leave today."

She did not react as he expected she would. Only a single tear rolled down her face. "I am sad."

"I am also sad. I like you a lot and always will and I'll always care profoundly for you. There will always be a place in my heart for you, but you'll be okay. I'll give you some money, and Wheeler will give you some more money. You know he loves you, and he'll take care of you." With a heavy heart, Captain S tried to make things right and make himself feel better at the same time.

"I know. I like Wheeler. He is good to me and do what I say."

"Mai Ly, you are a pretty and a smart woman. You have come a long way since I first saw you. Then, you were a scared girl. Now, you are a confident woman who speaks English well enough and knows math. A smart and beautiful woman can accomplish a lot in this world. I don't know mine or your future, but I do know, our destiny is directly related to our achievements and efforts. You keep trying hard and learn everything you can, and things will work out well for you." Captain S hugged her closely.

"I work hard. I study hard." She nodded in agreement.

After round two of lovemaking, Captain S loaded his duffel bag in the Jeep, and they returned to the unit. A little after 1300 hours, a crowd of about thirty people began to gather. Nearly everybody, who once attended the nightly activities, were in attendance, to include LeBeau, and wished Captain S the best of luck. Everyone seemed surprised to see Hollow with Donaldson. Major Sparks and Colonel West were the last to arrive.

After a couple minutes of introductions and chatting, Master Sergeant Scott yelled, "Can we get quiet, please? The sun is hot, and we want to take a moment to recognize two outstanding soldiers!"

"Two!" Joe whispered quietly to Scott.

"Yes. Boy. You're about to get some jewelry." Scott smiled at Joe as

Colonel West began speaking.

"Thank you for coming, I'm here representing Lieutenant General Pickett, the Commanding General, First Logistical Command. I have come to recognize two of our finest soldiers, who have performed in an exceptional manner. I must add a personal note. I have had the opportunity to meet both in the past. I couldn't ask for better soldiers than the two of them. By the size of this gathering, I believe you share my opinion about them. As Master Sergeant Scott said, it is hot out here, so will Captain Summerville and Staff Sergeant Hébert come forward and stand beside me. Please come to attention. Master Sergeant Scott, will you read the citations? I will pin the awards."

Scott began reading. "By the direction of the President, the Bronze Star Medal is presented to Captain Sandy E. Summerville for distinguishing himself by exceptionally meritorious achievement in connection with ground operations against an overwhelming hostile force in the Ben Tre area of South Vietnam during the period of 28 and 29 January 1969. While on a routine mission with forces of the Second Brigade of the 9th Division, he assumed command of an infantry unit, after taking heavy casualties, including the unit's commander, while engaged with a larger enemy force.

Through his highly professional and efficient command, he was able to outwit and outmaneuver an enemy force estimated at five times his size. Through his outstanding intuition and sound judgment, he led the unit to safety without further casualties, while exacting heavy casualties on the enemy force. His outstanding achievement during this cited time, reflect great credit upon himself, his unit, and the United States Army."

Scott continued reading. "By direction of the President, the Bronze Star Medal is presented to Staff Sergeant Joseph A. Hébert for distinguishing himself by exceptionally meritorious achievement in connection with ground operations against an overwhelming hostile force in the Ben Tre area of South Vietnam, during the period of 28 and 29 January 1969. During his unit's engagement with a larger hostile force, he volunteered to stay behind to confuse the enemy and allowed the main force of his unit to disengage the enemy, by using a silent nighttime maneuver. He was able to convince the enemy force, he was a significantly larger force, thus causing them to hold their position, while the main force of his unit maneuvered to a safe distance. He later led his men on a three-kilometer night march without lights, through hostile territory. His outstanding achievement, during the cited time reflect great credit upon himself and the United States Army."

"By direction of the President, the Bronze Star Medal with the "V" device and first oakleaf cluster, is awarded to Captain Sandy E. Summerville (and to staff Sergeant Hébert) for heroism, not involving or participating in aerial flight, in connection with military operations against hostile forces. Captain Summerville (and Staff Sergeant Hébert) distinguished himself by exceptional valorous actions on 26 March 1969 by serving with the 269th Ordnance Detachment Explosive Ordnance Disposal) in the Republic of South Vietnam. During the early morning hours, the Dong Tam ammunition supply point was hit by enemy mortar fire. One after the other ammunition bays caught fire and exploded, showering hazardous projectiles over the area. During this action, Captain Summerville (and Staff Sergeant Hébert) volunteered to escort the Provost Marshal through an area near the exploding pads to assist with damage control and casualty assessment. For approximately two hours he cleared a route which was literally covered with highly dangerous, still smoldering ammunition which had to be cleared to gain access to the main gate. His personal bravery and devotion to duty were in the highest tradition of military service and reflect great credit upon himself, his unit, and the United States Army."

Scott continued. "By direction of the President, the Bronze Star Metal, with second oakleaf cluster, is presented to Captain Sandy E. Summerville (and Staff Sergeant Hébert) for distinguishing himself for exceptional meritorious achievement in connection with ground operations against a hostile force in the Republic of Vietnam, during the period 26 March 1969 to 27 April 1969 while serving with the 269th Ordnance Detachment, First Logistical Command. His outstanding performance during the cited period was instrumental in clearing approximately one hundred tons of scrap and hazardous material from the Dong Tam ammunition supply point, which had been destroyed by enemy mortar fire. Through his highly professional and effective actions, the ASP was able to remain functional during this time. His outstanding loyalty and will to succeed has been in the highest tradition of the military service during the cited period, reflecting great credit upon himself, his unit, and the United States Army."

"At ease!" Scott ordered. "Captain Summerville, would you like to say a word?"

"Gentlemen, if you don't mind, I would like to make a short comment. As I am sure all of you are aware, today is my last day with you. Fist Log has decided, I'm needed elsewhere. Speaking for all the members of my unit, I would like to thank you for understanding our unique mission, and for providing us aid in too many ways to mention. Primarily, we thank you sincerely for your friendship. Without you, this moment would not exist. I can't leave Dong Tam without mentioning our losses. We lost four outstanding soldiers and friends, which I think could have been prevented. The Army will reward them for their service, posthumously. You will remember their names for a while. I assure you; I'll remember them for a lifetime. Again, thanks and keep your heads down."

As everyone formed a line to personally congratulate Captain S and Joe, Captain S kept his eyes on Hollow, who had not cracked a smile during the entire proceedings. He looked as if he had been forced to eat green persimmons and did not enter the line to congratulate the two.

When the crowd dispersed, and they were in the office building, Captain S could hardly wait to talk with Scott. "What did you get from Donaldson?"

"First, Hollow was forced to attend the ceremony. It seems as if somebody at 1st Log called the Chief of Staff's office and said it would be proper if someone who represents the headquarters, is present. So, the Chief of Staff told him to come,"

"God, I love watching him squirm. What else did Donaldson tell you?" Captain S acted like a schoolchild waiting for gossip.

"As for the office, we, uh--" Scott cleared his throat. "All his fine furniture was destroyed. A small fire occurred but was quickly extinguished. Donaldson was extremely satisfied. He said Hollow, 100 percent, blamed you and was absolutely sure, you were responsible for the entire thing."

"Oh, I love it!" Captain S practically bounced.

"You love what" Joe asked as he walked into the office building.

"I love, the beer you have. I assume one is mine, and the third is Scott's. Wheeler, I know you don't drink a lot. But hell, you went to college, so you had to drink in the past. It's a law of higher learning! I would consider it an honor if you would have a drink with us and get two for the girls and have Mai Ly join us. Lein, would you get the little man for me to hold? I have a little over thirty minutes before my ride shows up."

They talked and laughed and reminisced about the good times. Captain S gave Lein and Baby San two-hundred dollars each. This brought tears to their eyes. He told Wheeler, Take care of the two girls, and Sam, with my share of the unit's money. What is my share?" Captain S honestly did not know.

"Since there is now only three of us, It's only a little over eight-hundred dollars, Sir." Wheeler calmly told Captain S.

"What! Did I hear you right? Ladies, can I have my money back?" Captain S laughed.

Joe said, "Dang, we've done well!"

"What do you mean, 'We'? I believe the ladies have done well, thanks to Chubby." Scott raised his beer to Lein and Baby San.

"I think with friends like this, we all did well. I need to get out of here. I'd like to offer a toast to our four friends who aren't here. Here's to Banks, O'Neil, Jackson, and Redding." Captain S raised his beer.

"Here, here!" The others raised their cans in unison.

After shaking hands and exchanging well wishes with Scott and Wheeler, giving and getting a long full-bodied hug from Lein, and a giggle from Sam, Captain S hugged Mai Ly and whispered in her ear, "I love you." He turned and said, "Tonto, let's ride!"

As they walked out the door, Scott stood, saluted, and called, "Captain Summerville, it's been a pleasure, Sir!"

The chopper arrived early, so they had no time to talk. A big manly hung would have to do. "Ke-mo Sha-bee, take care of yourself. Our paths will cross again," Joe said with certainty in his voice.

"My friend, you can bet they will. I'll be looking for you when you get back to the States."

Captain S headed for the chopper without looking back.

CHAPTER 46

The next morning Joe set down at the table in the mess hall, and said, "Good morning, Master Sergeant Scott. Phillip, I see nobody is manning the radio."

"We're still non-operational, remember." Wheeler reminded him.

"Yeah, we are non-operational. And they're not sending anybody down here. There's more to this story than we know. There's something going on. It's probably a power struggle at higher, higher headquarters." Scott moved his coffee cup around while in thought.

Joe surmised, "It sounds like we're pawns."

"We're more like a grain of sand which the pawn is sitting on. With this wisdom, I'll go start my paperwork. Operational or not, the Army's paperwork continues." Scott sighed and left the mess hall.

When Joe and Wheeler returned to the office, they found Scott with his pack and his M-16 laying on his desk. "Going somewhere, Master Sergeant." Joe raised his eyebrow.

"Yes, we are, Staff Sergeant."

"I thought we were completely down." Wheeler tried to figure out what Scott intentions were.

"We are down. Nevertheless, Control called and wanted us to go on a VIP mission."

"A VIP mission? What VIP is coming to Vietnam?" Joe couldn't believe it.

"Some Air Force General who wants to see the Pacification program up close and personal. Have you ever been on a VIP mission?" Scott looked at Joe.

"Once, in Germany, for the State Department," Joe replied. "I volunteered because the Army would buy me two civilian suits. There's nothing to it, simply search an area, where the VIP is going, for explosive devices. We don't have to worry about the VIP getting shot. We're only concerned with explosives." Joe summed up his knowledge on VIP missions in about ten seconds."

"Before the second Kennedy assassination, we only provided assistance to the Secret Service for the protection of POTUS and the VP. As for the State Department, we only provided help for foreign Heads-of-State. After the assassination of the second Kennedy, the Secret Service began coverage of Presidential Candidates and the VIP's families. The Secret Service was scrambling for warm bodies to include EOD people last year during the election. Before coming over here, I was involved with several of the missions." Scott expounded upon Joe's brief explanation.

Joe replied, "Okay, who, where, and when?"

"An Air Force General Robert Manning, at Go Cong. He's showing up around noon. Our chopper will be here in about thirty minutes."

"Do you think Go Cong is safe enough for a VIP?" Joe sounded concerned.

"The short answer is, hell no! However, as you know, the Pacification Program is all about the battle for the hearts and minds of the local people. The VC uses the population as a source of intelligence, food, and other supplies, as well as warm bodies to fight. If the population doesn't provide the VC their necessities, the VC will punish them. To counter this, the government must secure the people by providing a safe environment from fear of retaliation. I'm not sure the area around Go Cong meets those criteria." Scott shook his head.

"There should be plenty of security there, albeit provided by MACV soldiers. "Joe did not sound reassuring.

Go Cong, a small town only thirty kilometers east of My Tho and forty-two kilometers south of Saigon could not be called pacified. VC veterans from the battle of Ap Bac in 1963 settled there. Ap Bac was the first major battle a VC force defeated a larger government force. They also took part in a large battle in Go Cong. Here the VC forces were convincingly defeated, while suffering heavy casualties. Nevertheless, the area has still been a haven for VC forces.

When Joe and Scott flew to Go Cong, it had recently been proclaimed as a model for the Pacification Program. They were met by an American Captain, who served as the MACV advisor for the area.

When he briefed Scott and Joe, the Captain explained, "The General will land where you did, on Highway 50. He'll ride or walk to the Royal Mausoleum, where he'll meet the mayor, and then return to the highway for departure. We have a full company of men scattered in key positions around the area."

"Captain, as we walk, can you tell me about the Mausoleum?" Scott looked around their Immediate area.

"It's a place where a leader of a Mandarin clan was entombed sometime during the eighteenth century. The complex is about thirty yards square. It is surrounded by a stone wall about three feet tall. The tomb sets in the middle of the place. It is only about twelve by thirty feet square. It's located about three hundred yards from here, toward the center of town."

"All we need to do is check the Jeep, which he may ride in, the sides of the route he'll be taking, and the Mausoleum where he'll go." Joe confirmed this with Scott.

"Yeah, but the side of the road is a problem. We can only check them two or three yards out into the rough bushes. A claymore could easily be sitting five to ten yards away, and we couldn't find it in a week. We have about forty-five minutes to do our thing. I suggest we start at the Mausoleum and work our way back, and be here when the General arrives," Scott said as he surveyed the area.

The captain led the way to the small, cut stone Mausoleum. They found the inside simple to search. It consisted of only walls, columns, roof, and floors. Except for six chairs in a semicircle, the grounds were clean and well defined by the stone wall. Outside the wall, shrubbery, and trees stood at its base. They could find nothing suspicious that looked like an explosive hazard. There were MACV soldiers at the main entrance and at each corner of the wall.

"I presume the businesses and homes across the street are secure, Captain?" Scott nodded his head in the direction of the structures in question.

"Our troops have talked with everybody along the route. That's the only thing I can guarantee. We have troops intermingled with the property owners." The captain shook his head.

"Okay, let's walk the route back to the landing site. Joe, you take the left side, I'll take the right. You know what to look for."

As expected, they found nothing vaguely resembled an explosive hazard. A small crowd had gathered on the roadside. Scott and Joe suspected one to be the mayor of civilian clad and the others his staff. Others were in ARVN Officer's dress uniforms. As the helicopter landed, Scott and Joe watched the crowd of onlookers in the immediate area for any suspicious movement.

Two men in civilian clothes, an US Air Force full Colonel, and the Air Force General stepped out of the chopper, which quickly became airborne.

The captain reported to the Colonel, who motioned for Scott and Joe to come over. The men in civilian clothes were speaking Vietnamese and probably were introducing the General to the local government. Scott and Joe saluted the Colonel and said, "Sir, we're your EOD support team."

The Colonel quickly dropped his salute, and said, "Good, it's always nice to see US uniforms in a situation like this. I hope you toured our route."

"Yes, Sir. Nothing, about explosive hazards, looks suspicious to us. But things get rather close in a couple of places." Scott explained the situation.

"Okay, let me introduce you to the General," the Colonel spoke loud enough to get the General's attention.

"General Manning, I'd like for you to meet our two Army EOD NC0s, Master Sergeant Scott and Staff Sergeant Hébert."

"It's a pleasure to meet you two." General Manning said and offered his hand.

"Bob Manning!" Joe blurted out and at once covered his mouth with his hand. "I'm sorry, General. I didn't recognize you, until I heard your voice and noticed your red hair." Joe recognized the General as one of Hollywood's most famous actors. He stood about five foot ten inches tall.

I get it all the time, young man. Your next statement is going to be, what, the hell, are you doing in Vietnam. I'll answer it before you ask. I simply wanted to see firsthand what's going on over here before I retire. In the future, when I speak about the war, I want to be able to reference first-hand experience,"

"The Delta is a good place to get an idea of what's going on, General." Scott kept his decorum, unlike Joe's first response.

"General, would you like to walk or ride? The Mausoleum is approximately three hundred yards." The Colonel gave him the options.

"It's a nice day, we'll walk." Manning stepped out like he was in the middle of Any Town, USA.

"I'll stay in the back," Joe told Scott, and waited for the entire group to get ahead of him. However, he was followed by two Jeeps, one, an ARVN gun Jeep, and the other had no passengers.

The narrow, side streets had been blocked off, which allowed the group to walk in the middle of the road. Locals, mostly women and children, gathered on the sides of the roads chatting and pointing. The contingent walked slowly. Apparently, judging by all the vociferous conversation, the local government people had something to talk about. From Joe's view from the back of the crowd, he thought, *there's nothing to worry about here.*

At the Mausoleum, Joe remained at the entrance of the wall. As a couple of the locals and General Manning entered. Scott remained at the door of the Mausoleum. When they came out, the delegation sat in the chairs forming a semicircle and talked for about five minutes, after which they started leaving.

At the entrance of the wall, where Joe stood, the Colonel's head suddenly exploded, accompanied by the sound of a shot not too far away. ARVN troops, to include the M-60 on the accompanying gun Jeep, fired in all directions.

Joe initially thought, *sniper.* But the spray of impacting bullets around him, which he saw hit members of the delegation, to include one of the American men in civilian clothes and the captain, erased the thought.

Joe lunged at General Manning, knocking him down and pushing him to the wall and shielded him. He saw Master Sergeant

Scott had already moved to the wall. He changed magazines in his M-16. The ARVN soldier at the front of the Royal Mausoleum went down, as well as the one staffing one corner of the wall. The ARVN soldier manning the other corner pulled a grenade and tossed it in the direction of Manning.

Without thinking, Joe caught it in flight and fell on it. As he had done hundreds, if not thousands of times laying in his bed, in less than four seconds after leaving the soldier's fingertips, he quickly twisted the head of the grenade off. Rather than an explosion, a pop, which sounded like a firecracker, occurred. With blurred vision, Joe saw Scott shoot the ARVN who had thrown the grenade and then move to occupy his tactical position. The machine gunner on the Jeep no longer fired and could not be seen. An RPG exploded near them. Through blurred vision, Joe saw movement in a window across the street. He emptied his M-16's magazine in the direction and quickly replaced another.

Almost as sudden as the firing began, it ended, except for some distance shots. Scott limped back to where Joe and the General were lying, and shouted, "We have to get out of here!"

They could see one of the men in civilian clothes on the radio. The captain and the other civilian clad man laid in a pile with a half dozen other people who were wounded or dead.

"The chopper is coming; we have to get to the landing area!" The civilian clad man shouted.

"Get our wounded people in the Jeeps! I'll man the machine gun," Scott yelled, and headed for the gun Jeep.

Joe lifted the captain and pulled him into the Jeep. The man in civilian clothing and General Manning dragged the dead Colonel and civilian to the Jeep. Scott fired a couple of bursts from the M-60.

After the two bodies and the wounded Captain were secured in the Jeep, Joe, leading the way, drove the Jeep with the dead and wounded, while Manning drove the gun Jeep close behind. While expecting to be ambushed, they drove fast.

At the landing site, they found a half dozen ARVN soldiers in a defensive position, one waved them forward. They did not have to wait long for the chopper. When it touched down, the ARVN soldiers helped with the two bodies and the wounded captain. Maning, Scott and Joe climbed aboard.

They were off, headed north. For the first time, Joe noticed the back of his hand, his left thumb, and the sting in his left eye, accompanied by blurred vision and blinking. He had paid little attention to the bloody hand and a dozen, or so, small bloody spots on his left arm and right hand. *Thank God,* he thought about having less than four seconds to remove the grenade's head before the detonator functioned as designed inside the grenade. Looking at Scott, he noticed blood on his trousers. He yelled over the roar of the engine, "Is that your blood?"

Scott yelled back, "I got shot in the butt! Nothing bad! No bone!" Scott tried to muster a smile.

The chopper landed at the 3rd General Hospital at Tan Son Nhut, where personnel, to include Round Eyes, were waiting with stretchers, to take the captain to surgery. General Manning walked with him trying to give him encouragement. The man in civilian clothes remained with the two bodies. Scott found walking troublesome, worse now than when the adrenaline was pumping, so he accepted the offer of a wheelchair.

Joe had clinched his left hand sometime during the flight. It, now, looked like a ball of dried blood. His left eye looked completely closed, with dried blood. Nevertheless, he decided to walk, even though, the weight, of his pack and weapon seemed heavy. He was soon relieved of it.

Joe did not know where Scott had gone, but he thought he would be okay.

The shot of a pain killer in the left-hand and the left cheek eased the throbbing. Medics put a patch over his eye while working on his hand. Doctors and round eyes went in and out of his room. One of the doctors, finally said, "Your hand will be fine. There appears to be no ligament damage. It'll probably take three or four stitches. It's going to be painful for you for a while because, you lost a lot of skin. Also, we have scraped at least ten pieces of small frag out of your hand and arms. We'll see about an x-ray of your eye after we get you stitched up."

"Okay, how's my partner? Is he next door?" Joe leaned his head toward the room next door.

"He'll be fine, only a flesh wound. Now relax the hand and arm." The doctor went to work on his left hand, which presented no pain whatsoever. After the doctor completed stitching the hand, he examined the small scrapes and cuts in his arms and right hand. Finally, they bandaged his hand. The doctor removed the eyepatch and swabbed the dry blood away. Five minutes later, another doctor examined his eye, this time with a bright light. "Staff Sergeant, we are going to take you down to the x-ray room and check you out for frag."

In the x-ray room, they not only X-rayed his hands and arms, but also his head, each from four or five different angles. When Joe returned to his room, the medic said, "Staff Sergeant, the doctor would like for you to lie on your stomach until he gets here." Joe thought, how strange, but he complied.

"How are you making out, Staff Sergeant Hébert?" Manning appeared at the foot of his bed.

"Not bad, General. The pain killer has worked. No pain at all." Joe tried to see the General.

"You think not. Wait until tomorrow! I know first-hand what frag can do to you." Manning moved to where Joe could see him and sat down.

"I can take it." Joe assured him.

"For some reason, I'm not surprised. Is this your first Purple Heart?" Manning asked.

"Well, I guess so. But I refused to accept two of them for minor crap."

"You turned down two Purple Hearts, because you didn't think your injuries were sufficient to accept them? "Manning couldn't believe his ears.

"Yes, Sir. I mean, General." Joe corrected himself.

"That's okay, Staff Sergeant. You can call me whatever you please. You saved my life this afternoon while displaying a heck of a lot of bravura."

"I don't think it took valor, and between you and me, it wasn't your life I tried to save." Joe chuckled but couldn't manage a smile.

"It surely looked heroic to me. In fact, I can't think of anything more heroic than jumping on a grenade. I would pay good money for a writer to script something similar for my next movie."

Joe asked, "How is the captain doing?"

"The doctors say he'll make it. He's in surgery and may lose a kidney. He'll be heading home soon. Master Sergeant Scott is laughing and bragging about being among only a handful of people who has been shot in three different wars. I'm going to check on his background. He acted like a real warrior today." Manning seemed amazed at Scott's performance. Joe replied, "I'm surprised he's bragging about anything. It's something I've never heard him do."

"Excuse me, General. We need to move the patient to ophthalmology," the orderly said coming through the door.

"It's all right, take good care of him. Staff Sergeant Hébert, good luck to you. I'll follow your movement and contact you shortly after you return to the States to make sure you're doing fine. And again, thank you for saving my life." The General patted Joe on his shoulder.

After the ophthalmologist examined his eye, Joe asked, "What's the problem, Doc?"

"You have a piece of frag inside your eyeball. It's close to the retina which is not good. There's also, something behind your eyeball close to your optic nerve. We don't know how it got there which is also not good. We must talk with other doctors before we decide what to do with you. In the meantime, I want you to hold your head down, no jerking movement, no lifting over fifteen pounds, and keep the patch we're placing over your eye clean and dry. Your eye will require surgery and a long healing process. The question is, where will the surgery be performed. We'll let you know when we know. Right now, go back to your room and do the Army shuffle, wait." The Doctor did not pull any punches.

Joe asked, "Why did they tell me to lie on my belly?"

"One of the MD's thought the frag in your eye would be less likely to move and disturb your retina. If you had steel in your eye, it might be true, but since it's aluminum, I'm not as concerned. You can get up. However, keep your head down and try not to lie on your back. Your right side is fine. Remember, no sudden moves.

Don't do anything stupid! There's no need to take extra risk. Anything else?"

"What are you going to do with me?" Joe sounded concerned.

You ask a good question. The simple answer is, I don't know. You're going somewhere for surgery. It will not be here. I'll make a recommendation, but people in Saigon, Japan, and Clark Air Force Base will then try to decide. I expect D.C. will make the final decision on your destination hospital. They don't do Neural-Ophthalmology surgery like this at military hospitals over here. Dozens of factors will be considered and influences where you're going. It'll take until tomorrow morning. This thing is not going to kill you unless it gets a bad infection. However, your eyesight is at significant risk. You are ambulatory, so I'm recommending you as a low priority for surgery."

"Doc, are you telling me I'm going to leave Vietnam to have the surgery?"

"Oh, yes! And since recovery from the surgery will be over sixty days, I'm telling you, your days in Vietnam are likely over. It's D.C.'s decision, though. I'm going to release you to return to Dong Tam to get your affairs in order, but you are to be back here by 1300 tomorrow." The doctor left Joe to think about his situation.

When Joe returned to his room, he found Major Sparks and Scott waiting on him. "Sir, what are you doing here? I've seen more of you in the last couple of weeks than in almost a year." Joe, unsuccessfully tried to smile. The big bandage and narcotics kept his facial muscles from working.

"I sent you out on a cupcake mission, to the most secure place in Vietnam, and you two go and create a disturbance by picking a fight. What were y'all thinking?" Sparks responded with a big smile.

"Well, you know, Sir, one does whatever it takes to get out of country. How's your big, black ass, Master Sergeant Scott?"

"It'll be in working order, when I get home to my fine Black woman with her big, black ass." Scott chuckled. "Although, I'll be using crutches for a while. So, what is your status, Popeye?"

Major Sparks interrupted. "Wait a minute. Where's the comment about out of country coming from?"

"The Doctor told me to go back to Dong Tam tonight and get my stuff together and be back here tomorrow to go somewhere for eye surgery."

Sparks replied, "It sounds rather ominous to me."

"Damn, Joe, I don't know if it's good or bad!" Scott shook his head.

Major Sparks assured them, "I know. If the attending physician says you go out of country to have surgery, without question, you go. I'll go back to the office and see what I can learn and see if I can find a chopper going to Dong Tam.

Joe knew telling Lein about his leaving would be hard, but it became harder than he expected. The instant she and Baby San walked into the office building the next morning his heart sank. Not because of his loss, but because he knew he would destroy a beautiful and loving lady, somebody who had seen enough pain for a lifetime.

"Hébert, what you do! Your eye!" Lein yelled as she came rushing toward Joe, who sat in the captain chair.

"One of your VC buddies decided I could see without it." Joe tried to put a smile on his face, one he did not feel.

"It hurt? What happened? Oh, your hand!" Lein now placed her hand on his cheek.

Looking at the crutches behind Scott's desk, Baby San, asked Scott, "For you?"

"Yes, Mai Ly, they are." Scott nodded.

After explaining what led to their injuries in more detail than perhaps, they should, Joe asked Lein to walk with him. He took her hand and led her to the big tent. She at once recognized his full bags sitting on his footlocker, and the absence of his other usually visible possessions. She stopped. "You go home to States." Lein said softly and looked up at him. Tears began flooding her face.

"Come sit with me for a minute." Joe pulled her to his bunk and sat close to her with his arms around her.

"It's time. We both knew it would come someday. We didn't know it would come this soon. Lein, I don't know where I'm going. Maybe to the States, but maybe to Japan or the Philippines. I may or may not return to Vietnam. If I do return, I will likely go somewhere else."

"You hurt. Why you go now?"

"I hurt my eye badly. I must have surgery on it. Do you know surgery?"

"Yes, I know. I hope you come back to Vietnam."

"You know, I have no say in this. I am a soldier. I do as I'm told. I do want you to know, I'll never forget you, because you are a strong and beautiful woman who cares for me, as I care for you. You'll be fine without me. You'll probably forget and replace me next week." Joe tried to get her to smile.

"I no forget you. My heart always hurt for you." She looked into Joe's eyes.

"You'll be fine. The war won't last forever. You, like Vietnam, will grow and become strong and influential. I'll leave you my share of the unit fund. You can take care of Sam for a while with it." Joe tried to make it as easy as possible for her.

"You give me eight-hundred dollars!" Lein said surprisingly and blared.

"Yes, for you and Sam. I also have a gift for you." Joe stood and removed two red marbles sized, stones from his pocket and sat on the footlockers facing her.

"Lein, I want you to have these. I don't know for sure, but they may be valuable. If they're rubies, like I think they are, you can probably buy a house or start some kind of business, but I must insist that you never tell anybody where they came from. It is extremely important." Joe watched Lein's face as he spoke.

Lein looked at the jewels Joe held in his open palm and gasped for a breath. She covered her face. After a long pause, she asked, "Why you give to me?"

"Because I love you, and you are a good person."

"You no love me. You love American girl." Lein shook her head.

"Yes, I love my American girl. It doesn't keep me from loving you, too. I also love Sam, and Baby San. There are other people I love. There are various kinds of love. However, before I give these to you, you must promise me, you'll never tell anybody where they came from." Joe watched Lein closely.

"What I tell?"

"You told me your family once had money. If you must tell someone, tell them your father and mother gave them to you when you were young. Lein, you must promise me, no one, not even Baby San, or I can't give them to you." Joe sounded adamant.

"I no understand, but I promise." Lein nodded.

"If and when you sell them, get at least three or four bids. Do not take the first offer. Do you understand?" Joe handed her the jewels.

"I understand. I know how to sell." Lein stared at the jewels.

Joe stood and handed her a handkerchief and spoke. "Wrap them in this and remember, show and tell no one."

Lein did as Joe said. She wrapped the jewels and tucked them away in her bra. Her tears had stopped, and her face now showed no sadness, rather it looked expressionless, a face in shock. She moved close to Joe, wrapped both her arms around his neck, held him tight, and said nothing.

After arriving back at the military hospital at Tan Son Nhut, Joe received an assignment to a room and given pajamas. He saw a doctor who examined his eye and cleared Joe for the flight. He explained to Joe, "Flying can present a possible hazard. Air can expand in your body cavities in proportion to altitude. If you feel any pain sensations alert the flight surgeon or one of the flight nurses."

After giving up his bags for identification and loading, members of the casualty staging unit explained to Joe where his destination would be, Brooks Army Hospital, San Antiona, Texas. He had schedule stops in Guam, Hawaii, and Travis Air force Base, California, where part of the patients would deplane and go to their designated hostilities. Since there were serious burned patients onboard, his plane would continue from Travis to Brooks because of the burn center there. They also had an outstanding ophthalmology surgery center. He would be flying at five hundred miles pe hour, on a C-141 Starlifter, flown by the Military Airlift Command.

Although ambulatory, they assigned him one of the eighty litters which were onboard the plane and offered him tranquilizers or pain killfiling drugs if needed. Because the more serious wounded soldiers were placed as far forward as possible, near the nursing station, and in the lower litters, Joe boarded last. He accepted a tranquilizer, reclined in his litter. He first thought about his months in Vietnam. *I made decisions with meaningful consequences, often life or death decisions. I have suffered pain and hurt and felt joy and love; all of which are curves in the road called life.*

I could be like my fellow passengers, returning home with badly broken bodies. Along with their lifelong pain, all will likely suffer from PTSD. A certain percent will experience the effects of agent orange. I could be crippled or killed, shot, blown to pieces, or even snake bitten. But, no, I wasn't. Except for the eye injury, the angles riding on my shoulders took care of me. Thank you, Lord.

Now I will return home to a country in turmoil where the people shout, 'Hell no I won't go' and 'make love not war' and have no respect for what sacrifices my fellow passengers, and I have made in the name of God, Country, and Family.

That's alright. I'll soon be in Ava arms. It will be my time to make love.

Soon, his thoughts became dreams about the rest of this BAYOU BOY's life with Ava and his FRIENDS AND FAMILY.

Author's Note

THE LAGNIAPPE SAGA CONTINUES

432

In the second book of the Lagniappe Saga, FRIENDS AND FAMILY, Joe heals from his war wounds and begins to settle into a new life with Ava. The couple experiences fantastic and unexpected surprises as they begin working on their individual businesses. However, both soon find themselves confronting a devastating event that delays all of their progress.

ALSO BY T.L. STARK (Coming soon…)

THE LAGNIAPPE SAGA

BOOK TWO: Friends And Family
BOOK THREE: Cash
BOOK FOUR: Filthy Rich
BOOK FIVE: The First Shot